LOVE IN REWIND

a novel by
TALI ALEXANDER

Copyright © 2013 Tali Alexander
Formatting and interior design by JT Formatting
Cover design © Sarah Hansen of Okay Creations

Tali Alexander Books Inc.
For information email Tali Alexander at:
TaliAlexanderBooks@aol.com

Printed in the United States of America
Library of Congress Cataloging-in-Publication Data

First Edition: May 2014
Alexander, Tali
    ISBN-13: 978-0-9960529-1-7
    1. Love in Rewind—Fiction   2. Fiction—Romance
    3. Fiction—Contemporary Romance

A Note from the Author

To help you, the reader, have a more complete experience of **Love In Rewind©**, there are words/songs within the novel that will include a superscript number. This number will reference a web-link within the LINKS page located within the back of the book. Please feel free to browse to the referenced link of any of the song titles mentioned within this novel while reading to be directed to: **www.TaliAlexander.com** where you'll have the opportunity to read the lyrics and hear the songs mentioned inside **Love In Rewind©**.

I could not unlove him now, merely because I found that he had ceased to notice me

– Charlotte Brontë, Jane Eyre[1]

Love doesn't live here anymore...

"Louis, are you up? Baby, please you gotta wake up," I cried out as I woke up covered in cold sweat, trying to pull awake my sleeping husband beside me.

"What is it, Em?" he mumbled groggily in a disoriented state. "Are the kids calling? Are they okay? Em, are you all right? Shit, what's wrong?" he asked in a now worried tone as he sat up. The bed dipped. I could feel him turning to face me in the darkness.

"Louis, the kids are fine. It's me. I just had a horrible dream about us. It didn't even feel like a dream; it felt so real." I took another deep breath to try and shake away the images still flickering in my mind. "We were making love ... No! Not love; we were fucking, but not each other. I was watching you having sex with another woman. You were happy. I was crying, begging you to stop. It was so painful to watch. The sick part was that you were watching someone else fuck me and you were smiling and nodding. You had this expression on your face as if watching me with another man turned you on. It was so perverse. I can't get these images out of my head."

I looked at my husband, hoping he felt how vulnerable I was at that moment. He needed to take me in his arms and obliterate my nightmare with his soft lips, his gentle hands and soothing words. He was supposed to tell me how much he loved me, only me, and no one else. Hearing me say that in my sick dream he enjoyed watching someone else have sex with me should've made him enraged and outraged simultaneously. The man I married would've gone on an imaginary crusade into my subconscious to annihilate any man looking at me, let alone fucking me. But tonight there was no war, just silence.

"Baby, I need you to touch me," I begged him in the dark. Even I could hear how desperate I sounded. "Louis, you have to make love to me. It's been too long," I commanded while trying to pull him close to me. I couldn't see his eyes in the dimness of the night. All I saw was his face, cast in dark shadows, looking away from me. He was moving his head from side to side and irritably sneering. He had to know how much I needed him to reassure me that he would never ever be intimate like that with another woman.

"Say something. I'm falling to pieces in front of you and you won't even make a move to touch me!" I yelled at him, trying to get close to him. He moved farther away from me on our big bed while tears silently rolled down my face at his lack of emotion and coldness. How could he not even attempt to console me after my heartfelt plea? He turned to look at his watch laying on the nightstand.

"What time is it? Fuck, are you crazy? It's five o'clock. It's still dark outside. I have a meeting in less than three hours. Let me sleep, for God's sake. Em, forget about that stupid dream and calm down. You need to just go back to sleep. Don't get yourself all worked up over nothing."

With that, Louis turned his back on me and my tears. To add insult to injury, he murmured to himself, "I can't believe you woke me up for this shit." Then he went back to sleep as if nothing had happened. There was no hug, no kiss, and no contact whatsoever. I was hoping this was still part of my nightmare ... I wasn't that lucky.

With tear-stained cheeks, I lay on my side of the bed shaking and screaming on the inside, yet strangely still and quiet on the outside. Was the man sleeping beside me really my Louis? I looked down at my now blissfully sleeping husband. I didn't quite believe what I was hearing, or not hearing, from this man who once upon a time couldn't get enough of me. Where was the man who promised to move heaven and earth to make sure I was his and no one else's?

I took small shallow breaths to try to calm the tremor inside. I kept counting down from a hundred to stop myself from screaming out loud and frightening the kids. *He doesn't want me!* kept repeating in my head. *He doesn't need me! He doesn't love me!* What did I do wrong? How did I let us get to this fucked up point in our love story? I realized sadly that even in my dreams I couldn't have Louis the way I once did.

I woke up a few hours later numb, cold, and broken. I was all alone, both physically and emotionally. That was when I knew that our happily ever after had gone terribly wrong.

Ninety-five days.

That's how long it's been since I last had sex with my husband. I shouldn't be sad or pity myself, right? I live the life! I have a great man who adores and loves me—or did once. Louis works incredibly hard. He has built up his New York-based real estate development firm from nothing to a billion dollar company in less than fifteen years.

We have two beautiful kids: Rose, who just turned eight two weeks ago; and Eric, who's almost four. I gave up running an event planning company with my sister to stay home and be there for the kids and Louis. My husband wanted me to always be available for him.

We live in New York City the majority of the year. Our Upper East Side townhouse was once an embassy and takes up a good half of a city block. If I walk a few feet to the right, I'd be in Central Park, and if I take a few steps to the left, I'd be on Madison Avenue, the shopping mecca for the rich and famous. I have need for nothing. I have a live-in nanny, a housekeeper, a cook, a driver, a masseuse, and a trainer. However, I would give it all up to have my husband want me like he once did. I'm twenty-nine years old but I feel like I'm eighty. You couldn't tell I suffer from depression and self-loathing by looking at me. On the outside, I'm glowing and happy. I'm skinny thanks to André, my personal trainer. I look twenty-one thanks to Botox and my mom, who's a dermatologist and keeps my skin looking young and flawless. Bergdorf Goodman keeps me dressed like a movie star and yet neither Hermès nor Van Cleef can put a genuine smile on my face these days.

Some who don't know me would say Emily Bruel is just another spoiled little rich bitch. Well, that's why I keep my mouth shut. I don't complain. I take it as it comes and yes, I thank my lucky stars. But I'm starting to think that if I keep going at this pace, I'll lose the love of my life.

My husband is the one and only Louis Bruel. He was once deemed New York's most eligible bachelor; now they call him "The Baron of New York Real Estate." He, like the rest of the world, seems to be oblivious to my dissatisfaction with our love life. He works fourteen-hour days and comes home to the picture perfect family he created. He has provided lavishly for us, and as I already mentioned, we need and want for nothing. Except, of course, the need I have for him to stop ignoring my existence.

When we first met, I was an eighteen-year-old nobody. He was almost thirty years old and very much a somebody. How could I not fall madly in love with the wonderful Louis Bruel all those years ago? Lord knows, every woman who sets eyes upon him still does! Why should I be any different? Besides his obvious sexy good looks, he has this animal magnetism, a kind of swagger that attracts anything in its path. I will never forget that magical night eleven years ago when I first laid eyes on Mr. Louis Bruel. I can see it all play out from the very start. If I close my eyes and rewind, it seems like yesterday.

Meet my dream boyfriend...

If one were to observe that party eleven years ago, I wouldn't need to point out who Louis Bruel was. He would stand out in a mosh pit. He was the tallest male in attendance, well over six feet. I, on the other hand, think I could've blended into any background unnoticed. I was working that evening as a waitress. He seemed very charming from afar. I couldn't tear my eyes from him all night—well, me and every other red-blooded female in the room.

I could hear his sexy baritone voice and laughter resonating above the piano playing in the background. When I would get momentary sprouts of courage that night and lift my gaze to meet his dark sensual eyes, I'd look away almost immediately. I was too afraid to let my stare linger and look foolish. I think I felt his eyes on me from time to time, but there was no way he could've noticed me with all those beautiful women bobbing for his attention. It was nothing more than wishful thinking.

A few times during the party, I was able to catch a side view of Mr. Incredible. He had the most beautiful long, dark lashes I had ever seen on a man—or a woman, for that matter. The lashes framed and outlined his big caramel colored eyes like eyeliner.

His straight Roman nose, combined with his defined angular jaw and full lips, looked almost as if he was conceived out of my latest fantasy; which still sadly consisted of John F. Kennedy Jr.[1] in the prominent role of my boyfriend. Even after JFK Jr.'s sudden tragic death, I hadn't been able to find another living, breathing man, to take his position as my imaginary lover until that very moment. At that moment, all I wanted and desired was for that magnificent stranger to just look at me. I wanted him to stop talking to the girl with fake boobs who forgot to put her skirt on before she came to the party. I needed him to stop smiling at her and showing her his dimple; the dimple that somehow I felt belonged to me. *Mr. Perfect, why can't you see me?*

I had this indescribable need to walk over to him and run my fingers over his chiseled features, up that high forehead and into his thick mane. I had to prove to myself he really was a human and not some figment of my overactive imagination. At the time, he wore his dark brown hair slicked back, very *Wall Street*[2] young Michael Douglas[3] style. His hair was so thick and wavy that no amount of gel could've kept it flat. I wanted—no, I needed—to run my fingers through his hair and pull it from the moment I first saw him.

His tanned face was clean-shaven and kissably smooth. That small dimple on his right cheek I noticed was visible only when he fully laughed. That dimple made him seem sweet. I wondered if he was just another guest or a hired model for the event.

As much as I couldn't stop admiring him that night, in my head it wasn't all one sided. I sometimes felt his dark eyes following me when I wasn't directly looking at him. Could he actually have seen me while encompassed by the constant swarm of women all around him? It appeared that every female in the room that night had her eye on him. His magnetism was palpable. He, however, kept turning his body to keep me in his line of vision all night. Or maybe it was all in my head. He was probably just moving around to talk to the people in the room and I just happened to be in the same direction he was facing.

I was at the party helping out my older sister, Jenna. Her event planning company was hosting this gathering for a well-known real estate firm. Jenna had a last minute scheduling nightmare when two of her servers called in sick. My sis called me thirty minutes before the event was scheduled to start, frantically begging me for help.

"Emmy, how would you like to make a few extra bucks and save your loving older sister from a disaster of epic proportions?"

I loved Jenna when she was desperate.

"Okay JenJen, I'll bite. What did you have in mind for me?"

It was the summer before I started my first year of college. I was fresh out of high school with no real excitement in my life, especially in the boy department. I was not one of those forward or overly expressive girls. I would even go so far as to say that I was shy and guarded. I would never openly ogle a boy or, in this case, a man. That was more my best friend, Sara's, department. If it wasn't for Sara and her big mouth, my first kiss would still be with my Johnny Depp[4] poster. She practically forced me to kiss Steven Owens at our junior prom. During a slow dance, she pushed me into that poor boy and mouthed, *"Kiss him now!"* I still feel like such a moron every time I think about that kiss; it was hands down the driest peck ever. Johnny on my wall got more tongue action than Steven.

That night, however, I was completely enchanted by this very sexy older male specimen that I kept a watchful eye on. Very uncharacteristically, I kept trying to be in his way. I was offering him and his colleagues champagnes and canapés. He had yet to say a single word to me. I was starved for any kind of verbal acknowledgement from him. In my head, A-Ha was on loop singing "Take On Me"[5]. But all I got from him was a nod and a dimple-less smile. It seemed my eyes were having a silent one way tète-à-tète, scanning and admiring him sans words. My delusions of grandeur finally came to a screeching halt a few hours later. He (the most beautiful man in the world) abruptly left with two attractive women a few minutes before the party officially ended.

All I got was one last glance and a knowing smile from him before he slipped away and out of my life. His sudden absence left me shocked and hurt. In my utopian paradise, he was head over heels for me and waited by the door until I finished serving him and his friends to profess his love. I was a silly little eighteen-year-old. I must've watched *Love Story*[6] one too many times. Jenna always told me that most boys were jerks. If you give them what they want too quickly, they take it and move on to their next conquest.

That night when I was in bed trying to sleep, I remember childishly crying at his rejection. I was heartbroken and mad at myself and at him. I had so much bottled up sexual tension from the whole frustrating evening that I had to touch myself. I visualized him kissing me, while I touched my sensitive breasts, imagining it was him rolling my aching nipples between his long, tanned fingers. I fantasized about that gorgeous man for hours until I finally made myself climax for the first time in my life. I didn't know what I was feeling, but it felt liberating to let go and surrender to my needs. My body was wound up so tight that when that first spasm ripped through my body, I almost launched off the bed. I tried touching myself and making myself orgasm before that night, but nothing had ever come close to what I'd just felt. Sara told me about her first orgasm but until then, I had no idea what she was really talking about.

I wasn't able to stop myself from thinking about him all the time. I kept wishing I were prettier, taller, older, and sexier so he would've wanted to talk to me that night. I imagined X-rated scenarios in my head of him with those two women. He probably sat in a chair facing a big bed with his long, muscular legs parted and watched the two women take off all their clothes for him. I pictured him telling them in his sexy deep voice to make out with each other in front of him, like in that movie *Wild Things*[7] that I had just watched a few weeks before. Then they would eventually all have sex together. *Lucky women,* I thought.

The next day I had it all worked out in my head. My dream man must have thought I was just a silly little waitress at that gathering. I was probably too short for him. He must've liked his women tall and model material, not girls like me, right out of high school. I'd always considered myself *cute* but nothing that would make someone say *Oh my God; she's drop dead gorgeous.* Well, my parents say I am, but they're biased. My full boobs always make me look heavier than I really am. I was only one hundred and ten pounds back then, and at five-foot-three, my 32C gave the illusion of a much plumper girl. I always wished I were tall and flat like the girls on the covers of *Seventeen* magazine, but my sister always said that men loved girls with my kind of body. *Maybe some men, but definitely not this particular man,* I thought sadly.

I told Sara, my promiscuous alter ego, through whom I've always lived vicariously, all about him. But she just laughed and told me to practice on boys before I go after men. She was so right. A week later, however, I was still masturbating to the image of him any chance I got. I even went out to Greenwich Village with her to buy a vibrator in one of those shady sex stores. I was starting to get carpal tunnel syndrome in my wrists from my new favorite pastime of stimulating my genitals to thoughts of the hottest man I'd ever laid eyes on.

"Start with this one," Sara said picking up a pink colored gigantic appendage off the shelf. I noticed the pimply-faced guy at the counter tear his eyes away from the lewd porno playing on the big screen TV and raise an eyebrow at us and smile.

"Put that down, Sara, that's huge!" I protested, trying to hide the embarrassing silicone toy unsuccessfully.

"Emily, you're dreaming of a man and you can't even look at a dildo? What happens when some guy whips out his dick and says 'touch it'? We're buying this vibrating dick and you're going to pretend it's your new best friend. This pink penis will know you better than you know yourself," she said, as we made our way to pimply-faced guy at the counter. We still had to pay and take home my new handheld best friend without me fainting of embarrassment.

I remember one morning when my house was weirdly quiet. Both parents were at work and the housekeeper was running errands. I quickly ran upstairs as if I were being chased. I locked the door to my room and leaped toward my bed. My brain was way ahead of my actions. I removed my pajamas and panties and before I lay down on my fluffy bed, I put one of my favorite songs on. The song I always imagined would play in the background while I was making love for the first time. Berlin filled my room with their song, "Take My Breath Away."[8]

Once I closed my eyes I didn't need to imagine Maverick— a.k.a. Tom Cruise[9]—in my bed. I had a much better stand-in in mind. It was him touching me and not my own hands. He was the one slowly running his fingers down the valley between my aching breasts. He was the one slipping his fingers into my wet core. Since no one was home, I moaned as loudly as I wanted. "Oh, yes, please don't stop. God, I want you so much." A delicious feeling spread through my body. I didn't need a vibrator that morning. I just needed me, him, and Berlin. I harshly pumped my fingers in and out of my clenching hole at a frantic pace. All I could feel was him. All I could taste was him. It was all him, him, HIM. "God, I'm coming ... oh God, I'm coming!" The song wasn't even halfway through and I was already a wet limbless mess thanks to HIM. I was begging my gorgeous apparition to stay with me and cuddle me forever. But my phantom always left me silently...

I had to find him, just so I could sharpen the fuzzy image I had of him and improve my erotic fantasies. I started doing research into finding and getting another glance at my dream boyfriend. I knew his first and last name because I'd overheard my sister talking to him that night before he vanished. Jenna referred to him as *Louis* so my guess was that they must be acquaintances of some kind.

I also remembered when Louis headed toward the door for his grand escape. He was holding the door open for his chosen tarts, and while glancing my way for a silent farewell, someone stopped him by the door and shook his hand saying loud enough for me to hear, "Great party, Mr. Bruel."

With a first and last name, I was able to figure out that he must be one of the owners of Bruel Industries, the company hosting the event Jenna planned. With a little more investigating, I located the main offices of Bruel Industries, which just happened to be on the Upper East Side, within walking distance of my house. I also found some pictures of him online with a different girl in every shot. It was safe to say that Louis Bruel definitely got around.

I had to take a stroll and see where he worked. I was like a groupie hoping to catch a glimpse of him. I passed his building at least twice a day with no reward. I just couldn't stop thinking about him. I was becoming pathetic and totally obsessed. I called Sara; I had to talk to somebody.

"'Every Breath You Take[10]' by The Police," I said as soon as she picked up the phone.

"Are you fucking kidding me? Have you been stalking him, you idiot? He could be married or gay or both."

Sara and I had this thing since we were twelve, where we expressed our feelings through '80s song titles. Since we knew the lyrics to almost every song that came out of the '80s, naming the title and artist of a song would eliminate us having to spell things out. It was our little secret language. It was great. We could be anywhere, around anybody and all we had to do was say the title of a song and we instantly knew exactly what was up. We both believed that every human emotion has been expressed in a song written in the '80s. Basically, '80s songs made up the playlist of our lives.

"I have to see him again. Sara, I really feel possessed by him."

"I'm giving you another week to get your rocks off to Mr. Not Happening and then we're sneaking out to a club with my brother and his friends and hooking up with random guys ... deal?"

"Deal," I agreed reluctantly. I didn't think I'd ever lay eyes on anyone who could hold a candle to Mr. Not Happening.

Every night I couldn't fall asleep until I climaxed to his image in my head. In my dreams, Louis Bruel was doing all kinds of things to me. The things I only knew about from books and movies I probably shouldn't have been reading or watching in the first place. Just saying his name out loud would make me excited and dampen my panties. I could feel his lips kissing me, and his talented fingers touching me everywhere. I could visualize him going down on me and using his tongue to taste me down there. I would sometimes even orgasm in my sleep. I could only pretend to know what all those things felt like. I'd wake up drenched in sweat and even more aroused than when I went to sleep. I was beyond pathetic.

I couldn't ask Jenna about Louis. She wouldn't understand why I was inquiring about one of her clients. A real man not a boy, a man who had nothing to do with me. So, naturally I went to her husband, Mike. Jenna and Mike had been married for three years. They owned the event planning company together. Mike did all the marketing, booking, and logistical things for their company, Crown Affairs. Jenna had a creative flair for putting together spectacular events. She had a knack for transforming any given space into a beautiful backdrop to create a memorable affair. I came to visit them at their Lexington office in midtown under the pretense of taking my overworked sister out for lunch. Of course, I knew that every Tuesday afternoon was when Jenna got together with her friends—a.k.a. employees—to go over the events they have coming up. Mike was in his spacious office and greeted me with a big smile, immediately hanging up on whoever he was chatting with.

"Hey, you, what brings you down to our humble establishment?"

"Do I need a reason to come see my hard working sister and my favorite brother-in-law?" I asked, making my way over to him.

"Emily ... I'm your only brother-in-law," Mike snickered.

"Ha-ha. But you're still my favorite," I said, coming closer to give him a hug and kiss.

I loved Mike; he was the big brother I never had. I'd known him as long as I could remember. Jenna was lucky to have such an amazing guy as both her husband and business partner. I hoped one day I'd find someone who'd love and respect me the way he did my older sister. When Jenna walked into a room, Mike stopped breathing. The same was true for Jenna. They were both beautiful, with light blond hair and light colored eyes. Jenna and I have our mother's aqua colored blue eyes. Mike, on the other hand, has intense piercing green eyes. I could only imagine how gorgeous their kids would be when they decided to multiply.

Mike started telling me that I'd just missed Jenna; she'd gone to Balthazar to have lunch with Maya and Anna.

"They have a big couple of weeks coming up. We have some last minute functions we're scrambling to put together. My good buddy from business school runs this real estate firm uptown. Maybe you've heard of it, Bruel Industries?"

I stopped breathing when Mike mentioned Louis' firm.

"So he booked us for four events back to back. He can't stop talking about the last party Jenna put together for his company. About a week ago, I think it was."

"Nine days ago," I corrected him. "I was there helping Jen-Jen out, when two of your waitresses called in sick at the last minute, remember?"

Mike smiled and said, "Yeah, Jenna told me you really bailed her ass out that night. She said you were pretty good. You know, Emily, if you'd like a summer gig before you start NYU we'd love for you to work here. We're always hiring."

Wow, this was better than just talking about Louis; this would ensure I'd actually see the Adonis live.

"Really? Thanks," I said as calmly as I could, considering I was jumping up and down inside. "Maybe that's not a bad idea. I am free all summer."

I then asked Mike very nonchalantly, "Tell me about your friend who owns that real estate company. What did you say his name was again?"

Tea in Louis land...

That Friday I was once again wearing the Crown Affairs signature uniform consisting of a black stretch mini skirt with a white tank top and black heels. The wait staff was predominantly female. Lined up, we'd look like a Robert Palmer video clip.

My heart was beating in my throat all day. I was breathlessly awaiting Mr. Bruel's appearance. He occupied so much of my thoughts. I felt as if I knew him ... intimately. After talking with—or more like interrogating—my brother-in-law earlier that week, I had a little more insight into Louis' life. I knew two things for sure: Louis Bruel was straight and definitely not married.

"What does Louis' wife do?" I'd asked Mike, fishing for some personal info on Louis. Mike snorted before answering my question.

"Louis married! That's a good one. I've known Louis for a long time and he doesn't do the one-woman thing! He's the type of guy that needs a few women in his life. My boy always used to say when we were back at school that it's not fair to other women if he settles down with just one girl. Hahaha! He's a real character."

Yeah, so funny. I was laughing with Mike on the outside but inside I was dying a slow, painful death. It wasn't Mike's fault;

he had no idea that Louis and I had a full-fledged monogamous mythical relationship in my head. I was right about him and those two blondes, I thought sadly to myself. Hearing Mike talk about Louis with other women gave me a pang in my gut.

Mike said his friend Louis was a great guy and that they went to NYU business school together and were roommates for a year. Mike also told me how much he respected Louis as a businessman, and how hard his friend worked to get to where he was. It was admirable to hear how Louis had built his company up from nothing and that he came from humble beginnings in Connecticut.

Why was I doing this to myself? Maybe I was a closet masochist. Why else would I subject myself to inevitable rejection by my fantasy boyfriend? I knew why, because his eyes definitely weren't rejecting me two weeks ago. Deep inside, I still had hope. HOPE! Did I really think there was hope? I must've been crazy. Something was most definitely wrong with me. I was eighteen years old; I'd kissed two guys and went to second base with only one of them. And there I was, trying—no, obsessing—about getting the attention of the sexiest man I had ever seen outside the pages of *Vogue*. What could I possibly do with him even if I did get his attention? I needed a reality check. Maybe I needed to tell Jenna about this. I could always count on my no-nonsense older and wiser sister to give me a good dose of the real world.

At three thirty in the afternoon, Louis Bruel finally walked in, or shall I say floated in. The way he carried himself was a dream to watch. His body moved smoothly, as if each body part was being put on display for me to appreciate. He pranced in looking fresh out of one of my wet dreams. There must've been a song playing in his head to help him move with such frictionless rhythm. I think it was "Start Me Up[11]" by The Rolling Stones.

He was wearing a dark gray, tailored, single-breasted suit that looked molded to his body. I could see a crisp white button down shirt peeking from under his suit jacket, with the first two buttons undone. *Yum*, I thought. I could make out a small part of his smooth upper chest. I wanted to lick my way up his neck, stopping only to suck on his Adam's apple and finally make my way to those succulent lips.

That face ... it wasn't normal how heart-stoppingly beautiful this almost perfect stranger was. His hair was wet, as if in the middle of a workday it was a perfectly normal occurrence for him to take a shower. All I could think of was how I'd like to take a shower with him. I guess I should've thanked him for the visual he provided me for that night's installment of *The Emily & Louis in La La Land Show*, which included a new steamy shower scene.

I had the advantage of being hidden in the kitchen arranging little cucumber tea sandwiches on silver platters for the tea party that was about to start. The event took place in an ultra-modern loft in SoHo that was up for sale by Bruel Industries. The whimsical tea soirée that Crown Affairs designed was in such sharp contrast to the cold, modern apartment that it worked brilliantly. Jenna had us all walk around with three-tiered silver platters containing tiny little morsels of food. Every teacup and saucer were a different pattern. It felt like Alice in Wonderland[12] came to have tea.

The beautiful state-of-the-art kitchen in this loft was set behind a one-way glass wall. The kitchen staff could see out into the house and yet the guests could only see themselves in the huge floor-to-ceiling mirror. I could see through the glass that my imaginary boyfriend seemed suddenly preoccupied. I would even go as far as to say he looked a bit frazzled. Louis Bruel was looking around from person to person like a possessed man. *Was he looking for Jenna?* I asked myself. He found Jenna and was talking to her animatedly, but was calmed by whatever it was she had said to him. I was so jealous that Jenna got to talk to him; she even got to put her hand on his arm while they were talking. I wish I knew what had him so flustered. Half an hour later, the party had officially started. The servers, including me, were all ready to start passing out trays of food to guests of Bruel Industries.

To be quite honest, I couldn't describe any of the guests in attendance that day because I had tunnel vision and could only make out one set of dark sensual eyes—which I felt on me at all times. Every time I passed within a few feet of him, I could actually smell his very subtle, yet intoxicating, cologne. His scent was faint but manly. I'd read books describing what sex smells like; I think I finally got it. Louis Bruel reeked of sex and every woman within sniffing distance knew it.

After a while, my insides would clench just getting a whiff of Mr. Bruel nearby. I could swear I was having the same effect on my dream boyfriend, or maybe it was wishful thinking. I do know that at one point during the party, I looked up to meet his hungry gaze from across the room. As my eyes traveled over his body, I could clearly see him still watching me and blatantly adjusting his crotch. I was mortified after that incident and I avoided looking at him for the rest of the party.

My sister, at one point toward the end of the function, pulled me aside into the kitchen and discreetly asked, "How do you and Louis Bruel know each other? Spill it."

I looked at her with horror and felt my face turn a deep shade of red. I had no idea what she was talking about. I only knew Louis Bruel from my dreams.

"Jen, why would you ask me that? I haven't said one word to him."

Jenna assessed my response the way only an older sister could and said, "The two of you have been staring at each other nonstop all afternoon. It's obvious something is going on. When he first came in earlier, he was very upset with me. Louis demanded to know why we didn't provide him with the exact same staff as the last event. He said Mike promised him the exact same waitresses. The only thing that placated him was when I assured him that our staff was all in attendance today, including my little sister, who by chance helped me at the last party."

Wow! No way, that's so interesting, I thought to myself.

My sister mirrored my thoughts by muttering, "Very interesting, Emmy," under her breath. "This guy is Mike's age you know. He's way over your head, if you know what I mean. You're not his type of girl. Trust me, Sis, don't play games with rich boys—you'll lose," she added.

I nodded. I knew exactly what she meant. I felt way over my head and totally out of my league around him. Not that what I felt really mattered. My phantom boyfriend had yet to utter a single word to me.

Don't wake me up...

The tea party finally came to an end three hours later. I was exhausted; all I wanted was to finish cleaning up, get home, and go to bed and have my delusional relationship with Don Juan the mute. We would first take a naughty shower together and then he would carry me to bed and finger me until I screamed out his name. After that, we'd sleep happily ever after. THE END.

Dreaming of Louis and I showering in sin made me smile to myself. However, my dirty fantasies would have to wait until I finished the dirty work at hand. I was still at work and the loft was a total mess. My sister's staff was running around trying to quickly finish up for the night. I loved helping Jenna and pretending to mingle with adults at her catering events, but I could do without the yucky cleanup. I couldn't imagine Mr. Big-Deal wanting anything to do with someone who was scraping his guests' dirty plates.

I was cleaning in the kitchen, blissfully withdrawn to yet another one of my Louis Bruel daydreams, when it happened. First, I smelled him, then my body sensed him, and then I saw two large tanned hands placed on either side of me on the granite countertop. He essentially caged me in. I didn't need to look back to know who was behind me. His scent alone added another milliliter of arousal to my underwear. I couldn't turn around, he was leaning into me so close. I could feel his heat as his wide muscular chest pressed against me, enveloping me. *Heart, don't fail me now. Please don't stop beating*, I kept repeating to myself as my heartbeat started increasing to presto speed.

"Are you trying to make me come in my pants in front of all my clients, little girl?" he asked.

Fuck, I need to breathe. He continued whispering into my ear, making every hair on my body stand at attention. "I've been jerking off to the vision of your tits in that white top for the last two weeks."

I think I officially stopped breathing when he said, "your tits."

"Please tell me you're at least eighteen. I really don't want to go to jail. But I think it might be worth it even if you're not."

Okay, Emily, snap out of it. Say something adult and memorable. This was my chance.

"Yeah, I'm eighteen…" I finally said, a little breathlessly.

He got a little closer as his whole body shook, laughing at my pathetic comment. I could faintly feel something hard bulging out and grazing my lower back. I was afraid of having a spontaneous orgasm if he got any closer.

"Thank … you … God. So you must be Jenna's little sister?" he asked, sending chills through my overheated body. My underwear was soaked by now. Even I could smell how aroused I was.

"If Mike knew what I wanted to do to his hot little sister-in-law right now, he'd have my balls."

I still hadn't turned around. My legs were shaking, my brain was drawing a blank. I was much braver in my fantasies. Thank God there was no one in the kitchen to see us. *WAIT!* Reality hit me—where was everybody? Shouldn't the other staff members be helping me with the clean up? *Oh my God, can somebody see us?* I thought. I remembered the one-way glass and started to turn my head around to check just in case anyone else was there.

That's when Louis Bruel's lips brushed my cheek as I turned my head. I guess that was the official moment I stopped breathing. I gathered all my strength and turned to face him inside his loose grip. I looked up at him, trying to seem in control of the situation. After what felt like twenty minutes of me craning my head up to his towering height, he broke our silent stare-off.

"I can't believe how beautiful your eyes are, little girl. They remind me of the water in Turks and Caicos. Your hair is the color of the sand there."

He was smiling the most beautiful smile I have ever seen, showing off that glorious dimple and his perfect white teeth. I still was not breathing. This had to be one of my daydreams. Surely, I was about to wake up wet in my bed panting. Is this the part in my dream where Louis Bruel asks me to join him and a few other girls in a hotel room?

He continued talking. "We have a property on the market right now that we're selling in Turks. I have a private showing tomorrow. I'd like you to come with me this weekend, so I can show it to you. What do you say, Jenna's little sister?"

The first thing that popped into my head was, "I'm not really looking to buy anything in Turks and Caicos at the moment." He stared at me silently, assessing my response.

"Touché, little girl, but just to be clear my offer still stands. I was only planning on showing you the bedroom, not the whole house," he said with a mischievous smile.

Was he crazy? I'd barely said two words to him! He hadn't even introduced himself. He didn't even know my name for God's sake and he wanted to take me to bed in Turks and Caicos. Wow, he was a real arrogant dick, I concluded. If my sister knew what he'd just proposed to me, if she walked in and saw us like this, she would have my head. Mike would have Louis' balls. My mother would have a stroke and my dad would just shoot him point blank.

I collected myself and answered his slimy comment. "My

name is Emily Marcus, by the way. It's a pleasure to meet you, Mr. Bruel, right? I usually don't leave the country with men that don't know my name or I haven't at least had coffee with." That elicited yet another panty dropping, dimple showing smile. That smirk should've been illegal. He really was too gorgeous to be real.

"Emily, call me Louis. Mr. Bruel on your lips makes me sound like a molester," he said, almost into my mouth.

He was so close that if I moved even to take in a breath, I would've collided with his mouth.

"I accept your coffee offer. Let's go, little girl."

Oh. My. God! Louis Bruel wanted to have coffee with me! His dark eyes had the sexiest little sparkle when he smiled. He was even more beautiful up close and personal. I could definitely get used to that smile and that face. If this was a dream, I didn't want anyone to wake me.

Coffee at the Grand Hotel lobby was spent mostly in comfortable silence. The feel of the place was chic, sophisticated, and exclusive—very Louis Bruel. Even the music filtering in was like nothing I've even heard before; it was smooth and sexy but you could still dance to the underlying beat. This place was definitely not my cup of tea, or coffee, in this case. The tables were tiny. I was sitting next to him trembling on the inside, yet desperately trying to appear calm, cool, and collected for his sake. I was even sitting on my hands, to stop myself from fidgeting with the cappuccino. Clearly that was the dumbest move ever; I only managed to shove my boobs forward and accentuate my raised nipples. He was trying hard not look down, but he failed miserably. I think I even saw him salivating. I released my hands from under me and went back to playing with my beverage. I was struggling to figure out *what in the world am I doing with Louis Bruel alone at a hotel?*

We were sitting close together and smiling quietly, drinking in one another. After two hours and two cups of coffee, Louis finally asked, "Emily, would you let me take you to dinner upstairs? I'd love to know what's been floating around in that pretty little head of yours."

I didn't feel in a hurry to part from my dream boyfriend. I didn't know any more about Louis than I knew two hours prior. I wanted to accept his dinner invitation, but first I had to make sure of something, "Louis, you want to have a real dinner with me, like in a restaurant with food, not go up to one of the hotel rooms, right?"

He smiled, got up, extended his hand to me, and said, "No bed, just food." As I got up and took his hand, he added lasciviously, "For now!"

I really wasn't that hungry, and even if I were, I don't think I could've eaten a thing with Louis Bruel watching my every move. I needed to grow up, find my confidence, and ask him everything that was spinning around in my mush of a brain.

Once he ordered us a few dishes to share, I asked him, in a very prim and proper tone, "Louis, tell me a little about you."

He hadn't yet looked away from me. Still smiling, he answered, "Nothing really to tell. What you see is what you get. Do you like what you see?"

The smile plastered on my face since we sat down dropped and died. I didn't like the feeling I got in my gut from his reply. He suddenly felt as genuine as a used car salesman. I realized that maybe I should stick with my "make believe" version of Louis Bruel. Make believe was more my speed and was also set to mute most of the time. I smiled my fake smile and nodded at his generic line. *Time for me to pack my cards up and go,* I thought sadly. I didn't sleep around with random boys or men. I wasn't one of those girls, as much as I would've loved to be a slut with this hot man sitting so close to me ... I just wasn't. My sister was spot on as to the type of guy Louis Bruel was. As gorgeous as he might have been, he was just another rich playboy always getting whatever he wanted. I broke our staring game and finally spoke up to the vain, beautiful stranger still wearing a triumphant smile.

"It's really getting late. I think it's time for me to go catch a cab. I need to get home. Thank you so much for coffee and dinner. It's been very nice meeting you, Louis."

The way he visibly sobered at my remark and, for the first time, looked uneasy made me rethink my last character assessment of him. He dropped that fake smile, sat up straight, looked down at his hands on the table, and after a few deep breaths said, "Emily ... you can't go ... not yet! Let me try this again."

How could anybody say no to him? After that, Louis Bruel got comfortable, dropped the sly pretenses and started to really talk to me.

"What do you want to know about me?"

I think that round went to a Ms. Emily Marcus. That would serve as payback for our kitchen encounter. Had I just humbled Mr. Louis Bruel?

"Tell me about your family ... your parents, your brothers or sisters..."

He smiled at my question. Louis seemed a little surprised. I'm sure most women just wanted to know about his money and status.

"No brothers, no sisters, just me. I grew up in Connecticut with my mom."

"What happened to your father?" I don't know how I had enough nerve to ask him that.

"My dad lived across the street from us my whole life. But my parents never married each other, or anyone else. I guess marriage just wasn't for them."

I sighed at his description of his parents' relationship, trying to imagine my mother and father not living together. He picked up on the sympathy that flashed in my eyes.

"Emily, don't feel bad for me. I had a normal childhood, except for living on both sides of the same street."

I wanted to ask him why his parents never married. Did he not believe in marriage either? That would explain why he dated so many women. But I just couldn't get my nerve back. It was quiet again. He wasn't really volunteering any information. If I wanted to know more about him, I had to talk. What should I ask him? Why did he have to be so intimidating when he looked at me? I forgot how to put words together and make sentences, for the love of God. I was just about to ask him about his company when he started talking.

"Five years ago my dad died of a heart attack. So imagine me at his funeral. I'd just lost my dad. I was still in school back then, getting my MBA from NYU. I was in a state of shock, to put it mildly. An attorney walked over to me and informed me my dad had a will. I figured he left me his house and his prized classic Jaguar." He stopped talking and looked up at me. "I hope I'm not boring you, talking about all this. Are you still with me, Emily?"

I was hanging on to each word like a lifeline. How could he ask me if this was boring? He could've been describing a bio-chemical reaction and I would've eaten it up. "Yeah, of course I'm with you. I like hearing about your life. I'm sorry to hear about your father, Louis."

"Thank you. I like telling you about my life. Okay, back to my story. So, the next day I go with my mom to the attorney, Mr. Waxman's, office, for the will reading. He informs me that my mom and I are the sole beneficiaries to my dad's estate. I inherited two-thirds of everything, which, to my mom's surprise, was a shit load. My inheritance included over twenty huge buildings around New York City. Emily, my mom and I were flabbergasted. It was a whirlwind; we went from middle class to nouveau riche in the blink of an eye. We never knew about any of his stocks or properties. Eric Bruel was loaded. We knew my dad as an accountant who lived a pretty middle-of-the-road kind of life. His only big splurges were a classic 1952 Jaguar XK120 Roadster and paying for my college. I found out he'd acquired these amazing properties in the early '60s and '70s, which today are in some of the most sought-after areas of New York. I knew then that real estate was my calling."

I was shocked by all the information he was divulging. I was afraid he would stop talking so I listened silently.

Louis continued, "When I graduated business school, I formed my real estate company with the savings I'd accumulated over the years. I have yet to touch any of the money my dad left me. That's my rainy day fund," he said with a sexy wink.

It was interesting to hear Louis describe how he was *a nobody* in the New York real estate world and how he couldn't get a listing to save his life. If I had a house, I'd let him sell it—hell, I'd let him do anything he wanted at this point.

"After not getting any major listings or making any money after a year, I decided it was time to finally start selling a few of my dad's buildings. Putting them on the market was hard. It was like selling a piece of me."

His voice was deep and commanding. Could something actually be hard for this larger-than-life superman sitting beside me? When he said *a piece of me,* I wanted to reach out and touch him. I could listen to him talk for eternity. All he was doing was telling me about himself and there I was, becoming more aroused than I'd ever been in my life.

"In the last three years, my firm has sold over five hundred and fifty million dollars worth of real estate in New York, and half of those sales came from the buildings my dad left me."

I'd be lying if I said I wasn't impressed. Louis, sensing that all of this information was starting to intimidate me, suddenly changed the course of conversation and started to ask me questions.

"I should've known you were Jenna's sister."

"Why? Do you think we look alike?"

"Nope—it's the eye color; it's very rare. I remember Mike always raving about his girlfriend's beautiful eye color when we were rooming together at school. But your eyes are even more amazing. I've been sitting here babbling about myself. Why don't you tell me a little about you and your family? All I know is that you have a sister named Jenna and Mike is your brother-in-law."

Okay, Emily, your turn. You can do this. All I needed to do was form coherent sentences without looking like a fool.

"My life is kind of boring. I grew up in the city on the Upper East Side. I just graduated from high school two weeks ago. I was accepted to four out-of-state universities but I decided to stay local and go to NYU like Jenna and Mike. I haven't decided yet what I want to be when I grow up." I moved my body to face Louis, getting a little braver.

"I'm glad you decided to stay here for school. Tell me about your parents." Louis also shifted his body to face me getting a little closer.

"My parents met in medical school and got married right after they graduated. I only have one sibling, Jenna, who's older than me by seven years."

"Do you have a boyfriend?" Louis asked and then brushed my arm with his hand, accidentally or not.

My breath got caught in my throat from the jolt of electricity I felt and I couldn't even remember my own name. It was magic. He took my reaction to his touch either as *No, I don't have a boyfriend,* or *If I have a boyfriend then I'll break up with him immediately,* because he continued the journey with his fingertips up my arm and lingered at my exposed shoulder. I still had all my hair pulled back in a low ponytail from the party earlier.

He leaned in closer and whispered in my ear, "Could you

make my night and release your hair? I've been imagining it down for hours."

I took a long breath and like a marionette doll, did just that. I released my long blond hair—per his request; it came down in waves around my shoulders and his lingering fingers. Louis was the one to stop breathing now. I smiled at his response. I really couldn't believe I could affect this beautiful man like that. He moved his fingers from my shoulders where he was drawing imaginary circles. He placed his hand at the base of my neck and then brushed his thumb over my swollen, half-opened lips. We were looking at each other's lips when he drew his tongue to wet his. My heart was beating out of my chest. He leaned down for the softest kiss I've ever experienced. I'm not really sure our lips even touched. He tore his gaze from mine, threw two one-hundred dollar bills on the table, and without another word, led us out of the restaurant.

When dreams come true...

Louis led me down the stairs to the hotel's underground garage where he informed me his car was parked. I was trying hard to keep up with his fast paced strides; for every one of his steps, I took two. I was still wearing my black heels; well, technically they were Sara's heels, which she swore would get me noticed. In actuality, what Sara really said when she brought the sky-scrapers over earlier that day was, "If these puppies don't get you laid, nothing will." Looking down at my aching feet, I wished he opted for the elevator. I needed to calm myself down or I'd hyperventilate before we even reached the bottom of the staircase. Why was he in such a rush to get rid of me? Did I say something wrong?

"I don't want to scare you, Emily, but I'm being a really good boy and restraining myself from ripping that poor excuse for a top off you. I'm regretting my promise to not take you to one of the rooms upstairs."

It's a good thing he wasn't looking at me as he said those words because I could feel my skin take on a magenta tint. My brain was taking extra time in explaining to the rest of my body that this was not a dream. All of a sudden, my feet didn't hurt anymore, my left hand, which Louis had a crushing grip on, stopped throbbing, and all I felt was my heart beating out of my chest.

Once we got to Louis' car, he pulled me flush against his hard body and pressed his lips against mine. He kissed me with everything he had. The kiss was so desperate and rough that I couldn't catch my breath. I was making little moaning sounds into his mouth. His tongue was probing and digging so deep inside me I was sure he could feel where my tonsils used to be. It felt like nothing I had ever done in my life. If this was what just a kiss felt like with Louis Bruel, I was in very big trouble. His neck must've hurt from bending low to reach my lips, because he suddenly lifted me like I weighed nothing and placed me on the roof of his car so he could stand between my parted legs and continue to kiss me without craning his neck.

We enjoyed about ten minutes of nonstop, hard-core kissing, with him running his fingers through my hair and down my back. He moved away from me to remove my black heels and lifted me off the car, then commanded, "Wrap your legs around my waist, baby, and hold on tight."

I obeyed like the rag doll that I was slowly turning into. He opened his car door with one hand, holding me tight with the other and sat us both into the driver's seat with me straddling him like a primate. He adjusted the seat as far away from the steering wheel as possible. His crotch was nestled perfectly between my parted legs. I was panting and couldn't stop myself from shamelessly rubbing against his erection like the horny teenager that I was. He was along for the ride, gyrating with me and enjoying every second of it, moaning and groaning with satisfaction. Louis Bruel was into me. I actually felt like I was the one driving *him* crazy and not the other way around. How was that even possible?

I remember every detail of that evening. We were insatiable, as if the world's end was looming and our touching, kissing, and sucking would single-handedly save it from destruction. While I buried my head at the back of his neck, I inhaled his heady cologne. The air inside the car was laced with the scent of him, me, and new leather. There was no backseat, but behind him, I could make out stacks and stacks of files and papers. The tiny sports car looked like his mobile office.

I'd had some practice fooling around before with boys, but this was different. Louis Bruel was a real man, not a boy. I felt wanton and brave sitting in his lap. His large beautiful hands knew exactly what they were doing. He was touching me everywhere, making my body hum. His lips were soft and yet he kissed me with such force that I felt he couldn't get his tongue deep enough into me.

"Emily, let's get out of here. I want to take you to my apartment," he said, out of breath, into my mouth in the now steamy car. "There I could just spread you out in bed and take my time touching every part of your sexy little body."

I moaned into his ear hearing those words. I wanted him to do just that. I also wanted to explore every lean, smooth, tanned muscle I was feeling under me. I wanted to feel his hot, pulsating penis in my hands rather than just dry rub him with my drenched underwear in his tiny exotic car.

After not getting any coherent response from me, he pulled away from our heated embrace and looked up to meet my swooning eyes. "That's probably not a good idea for a first date, right? I need to go nice and slow with you. I don't want you running away from me, little girl. It feels like I've been with you since that first time I saw you a few weeks ago. God, I feel like such a little shit around you."

I smiled at his cute confession. I drew my hands to touch his face and traced his sexy lips with my index finger. He closed his eyes and pushed his head back against the headrest, letting me explore.

"Emily ... Em ... where did you come from? And what are you doing to me? I'm too old for you, but I can't stop. I can't think. I can't even play it cool. I want to be inside you so fucking bad ... I think I'm gonna explode."

Could dreams really come true? I asked myself. They did for me right then and there. This was exactly what he said to me in my dreams, minus the *too old for you* crap. I was never into boys my own age and now I knew why. I was waiting for a man like Louis to find me. I wanted more of him that night, but I was out of my element. I managed to say, "Louis, I'm sorry. I've never done this before," in a small whisper into his neck.

"I'm starting to guess that much, little girl," he answered while kissing my swollen lips.

Wait, what? How did he know I didn't go around humping random men in underground parking lots? *Oh God, was I a bad kisser? Was I doing this all wrong?*

He must've seen my flustered, panicked look because he cupped my face with both his hands and added, "Baby, I meant you're amazing. I didn't know there were women like you out there. I've never wanted anything as much as I want you right now. I'm about to blow my load in my pants like a horny little teenager." He kissed me and then looked at me with his intense gaze. "You have these big blue, innocent eyes that I'm slowly drowning in every time I look into them. Your lips and these fucking tits will be my kryptonite."

With a mischievous smile, he pulled my white tank top down, dipped his index finger into my bra cup, and pulled out my hard nipple. He pushed me back against the steering wheel and lowered his head, never breaking our eye contact. He put my engorged bud into his wet mouth and closed his lips around it. I felt those lips all the way to my sex. He moaned his appreciation and started sucking. He closed his eyes and said, "Em, you taste so sweet. I may have to suck these tits all night."

I clenched my thighs hard to get some much-needed relief. That made Louis jump. I couldn't stop moaning and running my fingers through his now messy mane. After covering every inch of my breasts with his tongue, he then squeezed them both together and nuzzled his whole face between my aching boobs. He started taking in deep breaths, almost as if trying to inhale my breasts. Then he groaned. "One day soon I'm going to fuck these big tits and come all over them."

With those words, I started climaxing in his lap. My orgasm tore through my body and sent me into another universe. I was now floating in space. My body was still convulsing and I could hear myself somewhere in the distance shamelessly screaming out Louis' name over and over. He was sucking and lightly biting my nipples as I cried and whimpered his name. I could hear him encouraging me with, "Fuck, yeah, baby, come hard for me."

I finally came back down from my earth shattering orgasm a few minutes later. I opened my eyes, beyond mortified at what had just happened. I had never had an orgasm in the presence of someone other than me, myself, and I. I found Louis staring at me with a huge smile on his face like he'd just found the magic beans.

"I'm changing my career for you, Emily Marcus. My new job description from now on will be to make you come all ... day ... long. I need to put that freshly fucked look on your beautiful face as often as you'll let me."

Who was I? What happened to the prude who didn't straddle perfect strangers, even gorgeous ones, in some unknown underground parking lot? During prom, I didn't even let David Steinberg feel my boobs when he tried to kiss me. My parents would not be very proud of their slut of a daughter. But honestly, the feelings I was having for this man didn't feel wrong or dirty. Louis Bruel felt right; he felt like a piece that was missing from my life.

Once the lust cloud lifted, I realized it was approaching midnight and I needed to get my eighteen-year-old butt back home if I didn't want my parents to elicit the help of the NYPD to find their whore of a daughter.

"Louis you need to take me home, it's really late," I said between kissing his neck. He smelled so good.

"Aurggg, I can't let you go home, that's not an option. I need to make you come again, using my fingers first and then my tongue."

"I thought you already made me come with your tongue," I joked with a big smile on my face. I was feeling high on the sex hormones flooding my veins.

"No, my tongue needs to taste your pussy, which I'm sure is dripping wet for me. If you leave me right now, I'll need to go home, take my pants off, and suck them dry, until I get every ounce of wetness you left behind. You wouldn't want to reduce me to that, would you my sweet, beautiful Emily?"

Was he really asking me that? I started laughing. We both did. I got off him and gave him my home address. We drove in silence just glancing at one another every couple of minutes and smiling. Louis held my hand the entire ride home. Twenty minutes or so later, we pulled up outside my parents' Upper East Side townhouse. Only then did it dawn on me that this was probably the end of my allotted short romantic fling with hotshot Louis Bruel. He didn't need a "little girl" like me, as he kept referring to me. He'd have a new, real woman who would probably put out by the next day. Or maybe, he'd have a girl waiting for him in his bed when he got back to his apartment that night. Surely, this beautiful god didn't sleep alone.

I looked up into his impossible sexy dark eyes and asked, "Was this a one night stand?"

Louis looked at me as if I'd just insulted his mother. *Shit!* Why did I feel like the wrong thing always comes out of my mouth? His beautiful face, that only a few seconds ago had a huge smile all over it, was now somber and troubled.

"Emily, please have breakfast with me. I won't make it to dinner tomorrow. I need to see you. We can be in a public place if you want. I'll only touch your hand. I promise."

I nodded, knowing I couldn't wait a whole day to see him

again either. It was physically hard for me even to leave his car. I was so happy he wanted to see me again. There was hope!

"I'd like that. I'm sorry I didn't give you any pleasure tonight. I'd like the chance to make you have an orgasm too. I feel like a tease. It wasn't fair to you."

His mouth just dropped open at my comment. Louis then took my face in his hands, fixing my long, messy blond locks behind my ears and kissed me so softly that I melted and sighed right into his mouth.

"Emily, you should really go now or I'll kidnap you for my pleasure. I'm very close to driving away with you still in my car."

I kissed his dimpled cheek, adjusted myself, and left his car as quickly as I could. I didn't look back, and didn't really believe what had just happened. Sara was going to flip when I told her that Mr. Not Happening just became Mr. Happening for sure.

Once I got inside, I ran upstairs and dialed Sara breathlessly.

"'Get Outta My Dreams, Get Into My Car[13]' by Billy Ocean."

"Bitch, shut up!"

"I hope this is really happening to me and not one of my dreams. Sara, if I wake up tomorrow and this didn't happen, I'm just going to find him and rape him."

"Emily Marcus, you fucking slut. Is your hymen still with you?"

"Sara, for shame! I didn't sleep with him. We just made out a little in his car."

My friend couldn't stop laughing on the other end of the line.

"Emily, you forgot to add ... yet."

Good morning, beautiful...

I couldn't sleep all night. I kept rewinding and replaying every word, every touch, every expression and laughing out loud like a psycho. *Emily, you did it! You had a fantasy that was slowly proving to be even better in real life.* I guessed that was what it felt like when people fulfill their desires. I was elated and euphoric about being with Louis Bruel only a few hours prior.

Lying in bed, recapping our tryst, I dismally realized that Louis never mentioned a specific time when he would come to pick me up for breakfast. He never even asked me for my phone number. I pessimistically concluded that he most likely wouldn't show up at all. I really was a stupid little girl.

I couldn't sleep that night, and when the sun finally emerged, I got out of bed. I looked outside my window at six thirty in the morning to find a very familiar, exotic red sports car parked right across the street by the curb. I danced a victory dance. I couldn't believe he was there waiting for me. Did he not leave last night? I quickly ran to shower and make myself as presentable as I could for someone who stayed up and worried all night. I had a blush that just refused to disappear. He was here; he was really here. I left a note telling my parents that I had plans with Sara for the day and promised to call them later. I was hoping breakfast with Louis Bruel would turn into lunch and maybe dinner.

I walked outside thirty minutes later in a white, cotton lace-trimmed dress. My dress was short in the front and long in the back, all the way to the floor, very bohemian chic. I wore my nude wedged espadrilles that laced up my leg and reminded me of my ballerina days. I didn't have time to do anything with my damp wavy hair, so I just left it cascading down messily.

Louis was leaning back against his car, which was parked across from my house. He was wearing a tight V-neck t-shirt that left no muscle to the imagination, and washed out, low-waisted blue jeans that hung off his hips enticingly. I made my way down to his black flip-flops. I never would've guessed a man's feet would be a turn-on for me. But clearly, anything involving Louis Bruel was becoming a turn-on for me. He was smiling at me with his arms folded across his chest, displaying his incredibly big bulging upper arms. He removed his aviators as soon as I approached and gave me a look that made my heart, among other things, clench.

"Beautiful…" was all he said.

I smiled back and gave him a quick kiss on the cheek just in case one of my neighbors was watching us and decided to report back to my parents. I quickly got into the passenger seat and couldn't wait for him to drive us away.

"Look around you; this area may look dirty and industrial but in the next ten years, if my gut instinct is right, this all around us will be the hottest piece of real estate in New York. The land here is on fire," Louis explained to me before parking us by an industrial looking dock.

What he said about the neighborhood we were in was hard to believe but hey, what did I know?

We had breakfast at a small bistro in the heart of the meat-packing district. He chose a cute little corner nook with a tiny little metallic table. It all felt very Parisian.

"How did you sleep?" Louis asked, raising his perfect eyebrow at me.

"I didn't!" I answered with a little smirk between bites of my eggs Florentine. He smirked back.

"Me neither. I know this may seem forward and I'm not saying this to get you to sleep with me, which, I do want very much. But, I feel very juvenile and borderline obsessed about you, little girl. All I could think about and see, and taste and smell all night when I closed my eyes was you." He leaned in and ran the back of his fingers down my cheek. "How do I make sure you're only mine, Emily?" Louis had his left hand laced with my left hand under the table so we could both still eat and hold hands. He continued, "I've had a few girlfriends in my past but I've never felt so possessive about any of them. My head keeps thinking that you already belong to someone else. That you're not real and you're going to disappear on me any minute. Like some cruel joke that the universe is playing on me as payback for being a player."

I stiffened when he said the word "player." I needed to stop being a naïve little girl and smell the coffee. Louis Bruel didn't need an eighteen-year-old prude. He needed a six-foot tall model that put out and didn't mind sharing him with her other beautiful model girlfriends.

"I don't belong to anybody and I'm not going anywhere, Louis, but are you playing me right now? Are you saying what every girl wants to hear, to get me to go to bed with you?" I asked as sweetly as I could without sounding like the scared little girl that I really was.

"Emily, I'm not gonna lie to you. I want to fuck you so bad it hurts. But I won't sleep with you until it's your idea … I can't jeopardize this. Scaring you away is not an option," he whispered in my ear. "I will wait as long as you're mine and no one else's ... I'll wait. We both know I don't need my dick to make you come. I would love nothing more than to sink deep inside you, but I promise you, just a touch from you will make me blow my load," he said, flicking his tongue in my ear, making me impossibly wetter. "I waited almost thirty years for you little girl, what's another couple of weeks, months, or years between us?"

I stopped chewing my croissant and looked up to meet his lust-filled eyes. I swallowed and smiled into his mesmerizing gaze. "That won't be necessary, Louis. I'm not that cruel ... or innocent."

Louis kept brushing his long fingers over my crossed legs under our table. He knew exactly what he was doing to me, that bastard. After what proved to be the longest breakfast I've ever had, we continued our carefree date. We took a stroll to a nearby park. He pointed out in the distance to what looked like an elevated, decrepit train track.

"Look up there. That is the Highline. Bruel Industries is going to build an urban park suspended in the air—right there. It used to be an old railroad track but we're going to be part of a project to convert it into an oasis in this concrete jungle. What do you think?" he asked.

I think you're perfect, I thought to myself, but said, "I think that's the coolest thing I've ever heard." That produced a full dimple-showing smile from him. We walked hand-in-hand, still hungrily assessing one another.

"Tell me, what's your favorite book?" I asked him.

"That's easy, *Great Expectations*[14], and as of lately it's my favorite movie too," he quickly answered.

"Okay, Pip, what about your favorite color?" I continued to ask.

Louis started laughing and said, "This feels like I'm back in high school, but I love it, so here goes: as of yesterday I thought my favorite color was red, hence my red Ferrari ... but after last

41

night it's whatever shade of pink your nipples are."

That made me blush. I playfully pushed at him, only to have him come back at me with a kiss to the tip of my nose.

"Two things you'd take with you to a deserted island?" I continued my barrage of silly questions.

"Another easy one. I'd take one sexy Emily Marcus, of course, and a life supply of Twizzlers."

I was laughing so hard that I started hiccupping. Once my hiccups subsided, I needed to know, "Why Twizzlers?"

We finally decided to sit on a nearby empty bench. Louis pulled my legs over his thighs so he could run his finger up and down my exposed skin while we lounged in the sun. All his answers thus far were making me giddy with laughter. He was looking down at his hand caressing my skin, and causing goose bumps to form up and down my body. He then lifted his yearning gaze to meet my eyes before answering me.

"I can't live without them. My dad got me hooked on Twizzlers when I was probably like three years old. I don't think I'd survive more than a day without them. Don't you laugh at me! I don't smoke or drink as much as I used to, so I need me a little Twizzler. Cut me some slack, woman."

I just added cute to his long list of attributes. I asked about his longest relationship, and all I got was, "Pass, next question please." His response made me happy for some unexplained reason.

"If you had to lose one of your five senses, which one would it be and why?"

He took a minute to think about his answer. "Okay, Miss Twenty Questions. Let's start with the process of elimination. If I couldn't see your beautiful face again that would be awful. If I couldn't touch every inch of you, that would be a calamity. If I couldn't hear you cry out my name like you did last night while you were coming deliciously in my lap that would be a fucking travesty. If those lips and tits are any indication of how sweet you'll taste everywhere else, I have to be able to taste you. So, although your scent is intoxicating, Miss Marcus, I'd have to give up my sense of smell."

WOW, that was not the kind of reply I was expecting. I bravely gave him a light kiss on his lips.

"That was a very sweet answer, Louis; a little R-rated, but still sweet."

He kissed me on the lips softly for the first time since last night and I almost had a full-on seizure on that park bench. Since I've established that I'm a glutton for punishment, I had to ask him the next question.

"Why didn't you try and talk to me a few weeks ago at that first party? I thought you didn't like me." That question made him drop the permanent smile he'd had since picking me up that morning. For the first time he looked at a loss for words. I was starting to regret asking him that question. If he told me about his ménage à trois, I'd start crying and die.

"Emily, you know I couldn't keep my eyes off you that whole night. I just didn't have enough balls to bring myself over to talk to you." He stopped, ran his hand through his thick hair, and continued, "I kept waiting for the right moment to get you alone somewhere in a corner away from my clients and colleagues. I had all these people I needed to schmooze. But you kept going in and out of that damn kitchen. I kept losing my nerve. You looked so young. I was worried I'd scare the shit out of you. When the party started winding down, I was coerced into going to see a penthouse in the building next door. One of our new clients was thinking of having us put it on the market for her." He took another deep breath and looked into my eyes. "I thought for sure I'd be back in time to still catch another glimpse of you. I was hoping to get you alone. When I came back, the party was over and you were long gone. Only the florist staff was still there taking apart the arrangements."

His rendition of what really happened that night was so

much better than my twisted imagination. I ran my fingers through his thick wavy hair. Louis leaned into my hand and ran his lips along my inner arm.

He continued his explanation, "The next morning I called Mike and booked Crown Affairs for four more events that I didn't even have planned ... I had to see you again. I couldn't stop thinking about you," he said, kissing his way up my arm. "You were wearing that tight white tank top. I could see the outline of your nipples. When you'd get close enough to me, I could tell how hard they were under that thin top. Your tight little ass in that short mini skirt with those heels. I wanted to bite it and have those beautiful legs wrapped around my neck." He made a rough sound in the back of his throat. "You've been on a loop in my mind ever since. I think I jerked off at least three times that night, imagining sucking your perfect tits."

I blushed at his crude description of my body. But I loved every word. I leaned into his ear and whispered, "Before I fell asleep that night after the party, I imagined you in my bed and that made me have my first orgasm ... EVER." I left out the crying part.

He looked at me with an, *Are you shitting me?* face and I nodded to his silent question.

"Okay, little girl, I think we've been in public long enough. It's time for me to show you where you'll be spending the majority of your time from now on."

Standing up, he took my hand in his and led us back to his little red sports car.

Home sweet ... Lord of the Flies...

Louis drove very fast. I was holding on for dear life. He was a man on a mission. I asked him, "Where are you taking me now?"

To which he replied without taking his eyes off the road, "Bed."

My heart stopped. Oh my God, was I ready for bed? No, definitely not ready for his bed.

"Are you taking me to see your apartment?" I was trying to ask questions to calm my nerves down and not think about what *bed* really meant. He finally looked at me while stopping at a red light. He reached for my hand and kissed my fingertips.

"No Emily, definitely not my apartment. I'm taking you to my place ... to my home."

I was too nervous to understand what he was talking about—his apartment, his home; it all sounded the same to me. It all added up to us ending up naked in his bed. Fuck, what now? I couldn't keep teasing him like this. If he took me to his bed, could I stop him or me from going all the way? I didn't even take notice which direction we were driving. I tried to make myself aware of my surroundings. If this gorgeous man was kidnapping me, I wouldn't even know where the hell he was taking me. I looked up and noticed that we'd just passed Houston Street and then he quickly pulled up to an old building that looked like an abandoned warehouse. I was too anxious and petrified about going *home* with him that I hadn't even taken the opportunity to let my mind try and picture where a guy like Louis Bruel would live and call *home*. I looked over to find my handsome kidnapper smiling from ear to ear.

"Are you ready to see my lair? Ha, ha, ha," he said in his best impression of Dracula.

I must say my heart skipped a beat but this time from sheer fear. He pressed a button in his car and a huge metal gate that looked like a loading dock entrance started to pull up. He drove his car right through the gate and into the dark unknown. The gate lowered slowly behind us, blocking out any remaining light from the street. We were now in total darkness. I was starting to have my life flash swiftly before my eyes. All of a sudden, the lights came on and the car started moving up. We were in an oversized elevator for cars, apparently. I heard a ding and then I saw numbers illuminating one by one: 2, 3, 4, 5, and then stop on the fifth floor. Louis got out first and came to my side. I felt faint. My legs were shaking. My heart was beating out of my chest, and my mouth was wide open trying to gasp as much air into my lungs as possible. This is how horror movies began, with naïve, stupid girls like me going to unknown places with gorgeous men like him—and nobody knows where the hell they are. I should've at least told Sara.

"Baby, relax, breathe. Please don't be nervous. I promise I won't make you do anything you won't be begging me to do."

That didn't make me feel better at all.

"Louis, this is a little crazy. We just officially met last night and I don't really know you and I'm at a warehouse with you, alone. Nobody knows I'm with you." Maybe I shouldn't have told him nobody knew I was with him. Now he'd definitely kill me.

"Emily, I promise I don't live in a warehouse. I don't want to hurt you. I just really need to be alone with you. I want to kiss you and taste you. I need to touch every inch of you. I don't want to worry about looking like a pervert in some public place. I'd go back to your place, but if your parents knew what I plan to do to their daughter, they'd have me arrested. This is just a comfortable place for us to explore each other privately and intimately … don't be scared, baby."

I took a very deep, overdue breath.

"You technically haven't even set foot in my house, just my car lift."

Okay, this is it. It's time to pay the piper. I smiled, took another deep breath, and bravely walked through the huge drawn iron gate that Louis was now holding open for me.

When I walked through Louis' gate, I wasn't prepared for what I saw. I guess because we hadn't yet had the opportunity to really get to know one another; I didn't know what kind of style he preferred. Was he into ultra-modern or Art Deco design? My brain really didn't let my head conjure up what kind of house a thirty-year-old, successful bachelor living in New York would have.

Maybe it was my traditional upbringing. I lived in the same townhouse my whole life. My mother designed our traditional five-story home with lots of warm earth tones. My house always seemed warm and very pleasant. That is what I considered normal.

Louis, on the other hand, wasn't kidding when he said his *lair.* Since we entered from the side, the whole space seemed to just sprawl out indefinitely in both directions. It was like Crocodile Dundee[15] called Indiana Jones[16] and asked him to design his New York City bachelor pad. I could sense Louis watching me for some kind of verbal reaction: *wow, beautiful, great.* Any of those words would've worked. I was so shocked and unprepared for this visual feast, that I really couldn't produce any coherent acknowledgment of my feelings. My eyes did all the talking for me by enlarging to the size of plates.

I was in the biggest tree house on the planet. Everywhere I looked, I saw raw wood, leather, animal skins, and rope used to hold things up. The staircase was suspended in midair in the middle of this huge loft space. It looked like a flattened out and then coiled ladder, made of wide, highly polished tree planks that were held together by thick rope. I think I'd be scared of falling trying to walk up that thing. The room had such high ceilings that the staircase seemed to just float right into the sky. I have to admit, the effect was breathtaking.

There was a wall on the left side full of old worn out books that made the New York public library seem small. The books seemed to reach all the way up to the thirty-foot ceiling. I craned my head up to find at least ten chandeliers. They were all made out of some kind of tusks. Never in a million years would I envisage Louis Bruel, playboy millionaire, living in a tree house. Louis stood quietly holding my hand and letting me slowly drink it all in. I finally landed back on his dark searching eyes. I could tell by his weak smile that he was nervous of my reaction to his so-called *home.*

"So, Emily, what do you think? Is it a little too wild for you?"

I exhaled and nodded. "Yeah ... wow, it's not what I expected. Not that I've known you long enough to have any expectations. It's just that I don't think I've ever seen anything like this. Louis, it's tremendous and unreal. It almost looks like a movie set."

"Are you disappointed?" he asked me, his smile weakening.

"No! Not disappointed, just overwhelmed and surprised ... it's so huge and very masculine. I just need a minute to take this all in. But it's the most spectacular thing I've ever seen."

He finally smiled. I could feel him relax when he released the death grip he had on my hand.

"It used to be a pen factory before World War Two. It was the first building my dad bought in the early sixties. I suspect it was already run down when he purchased it. I couldn't bring myself to sell this place. I knew in my gut my dad would've wanted me to keep it. I turned the whole factory into my dad's favorite book, *Lord of the Flies*[17] by William Golding. He started reading me that book as a bedtime story when I was six or seven years old. Emily, I was enamored. That's the book that did it for me and started my love of reading."

I was staring up at him in awe. Could a red Ferrari driving millionaire really be so nostalgically idyllic? I didn't even know he liked to read. He continued telling me what I suspected was not at all common knowledge.

"My dad and I would spend lots of time together analyzing that book. I woke up one morning all grown up and was told my dad was gone. I read that fucking book over and over; it helped me remember our heated debates about that paradisiacal country. Years later when I was showing this place to some asshole investors, they were talking about turning this building into condos. I thought, no way! My dad, if he were alive, wouldn't sell it to be turned into some overpriced condos. That's when I turned one of my favorite memories of my eccentrically romantic dad into a fantasy world."

I was looking at him, floored by his private revelation, when he drew me into a hug, resting his chin on my head and continued talking. "This place helps me keep him close since I never got a chance to say goodbye to him. If he could see me now, if he could see all this, he'd know I love him."

I pulled away from him so I could look at his face. I was really falling in love with this man, one word at a time.

"Come, I want to show you the upstairs."

He was trying to change the somber mood that had descended upon us. I followed Louis up the hovering stairs, still fearful of falling. Although the stairs looked flimsy, they were anything but. He was taking two stairs at a time. I had to run just to keep up with him.

"What's upstairs?" I asked in a breathless voice half way up the stairs.

"My bed," I heard him say right before my heart dropped back to the bottom of the stairs.

Pay or play...

When we got up the stairs I was winded from the run, but then I was breathless from the sight. In the middle of what seemed like a black, still lake, stood a huge wooden platform, almost like a manmade raft. The structure appeared to be floating in water. His bed was covered in a white cloud of sheets with at least twenty scattered pillows. The same birch wooden branches that made up the base of the bed were also entwined and molded to form four thick bedposts that held up a translucent gauzy fabric. The floor looked wet and shiny. It was composed of black, polished river rocks. Blackout curtains were drawn shut all around the colossal room. The only light was emanating from the soft sprinkle of tiny lights covering the entire ceiling. The countless little twinkling lights above us looked like a galaxy full of stars. The whole clever design gave the illusion of walking at night on water. I was flabbergasted.

Before I could recover and voice my awe, Louis lifted me off my feet and, in a very groom-like manner, carried me to his bed. I wrapped my arms around his neck and inhaled his heady scent. When we got to the bed, he didn't put me down. He was just standing by the bed with me nestled in his strong arms as he calmly watched and assessed me. He didn't have to ask with words; his knowing eyes were silently begging me for permission.

I ran my hand over his face and moved my lips to his ear and whispered, "Louis, I'm so scared ... but I want you so much right now."

He let out a suppressed throaty sound from deep within. He then walked us up steps on the side of the bed that I hadn't yet noticed. Louis gently lowered us both into the floating cloud and started ravaging my mouth like a caveman. He knelt between my parted legs and we kissed each other fiercely. Tongues lapping, teeth biting lips, lips sucking face. Every once in a while his fingers moved between our lips, almost as if his lips and fingers were in competition for contact with my mouth. He was making these sounds in the back of his mouth that I could feel resonating all the way to my stomach.

"Emily, you here ... in my bed ... feels incredible ... thank you," he said between kisses. "I know you're a little over-whelmed but please, baby, I need you to touch me. I need to know you want this as much as I do."

That's when I realized I'd been holding myself propped up on my elbows, virtually immobile and rigid for the last few minutes of our heated commingling. I let go with one of my propped hands and started touching his chest. He pulled back and removed his V-neck t-shirt in one swift move and threw it out of our floating barge. I took in my first view of Louis Bruel shirtless. I didn't even want to blink for fear of missing a nano-second of this view. It wasn't fair for someone to look as good as he looked. His perfect body was a sight to behold. I couldn't take my eyes off his ripped chest, the bulging biceps. Oh God, the lean torso. Every muscle was defined and strained. His broad chest rose and fell, trying to take in deep breaths. I just wanted to keep touching and feeling him until my alarm clock finally went off and I needed to wake up. There was no way this was my life! He decided I'd touched him enough. He climbed back over me and laid me down flat.

"You like what you see, little girl?" he asked me cockily.

I don't think there's a woman, man, or child alive who wouldn't like the sight of Louis Bruel half-naked. He also decided that I'd seen enough and started kissing me again. He was kneading my swollen breasts with his long, adroit fingers. I knew that all he had to do was find my nipples and I'd come apart for him. A few minutes– or hours– later, he pulled away from my lips. Very slowly and softly, he moved his lips down my neck and then found my breasts. Running his tongue over the fabric of my dress, he lingered between my breasts.

"Nobody should smell this good. You're going to fucking drive me crazy."

He was inhaling my scent and then continued his journey down my stomach. He was breathing and nibbling through my cotton dress. I found that extremely ticklish. I immediately started giggling and drawing my legs up to stop his heavenly torment.

"You think it's funny what I'm about to do to you, little girl?"

That comment sobered me up, and trepidation crept in. He cocked an eyebrow and smiled sensually at me. Louis ran his fingertips from my hips down my now fully exposed bare legs.

"Relax, baby. I won't hurt you … I just need to worship at your altar for a little bit or I'll lose my mind."

His voice was so deep and sexy. His touch sent goose bumps all over my body. When he got to my feet, he very smoothly untied my espadrilles. One by one, he removed my shoes. He took each of my feet, which fit completely into his large hands. Very slowly, he started running his finger up and down my arch. I was ready to come just from that act alone. But no, that would've been too easy. I closed my eyes in pleasure and moaned out a rendition of his name. I then, very unexpectedly, felt his tongue on my feet where his fingers had just finished their delicious assault. This was insane. This feeling was like nothing my body had ever felt before. His hot tongue licking my feet and sucking my toes felt incredibly erotic.

"Louis, stop!"

"Stop what, baby? Doesn't this feel good?"

"It feels too good," I managed to exhale.

"Then I won't stop. I'm tasting every inch of you, Emily. I've dreamt this scenario in my head all night."

He ran his hands, followed by his tongue, up my legs. I was clenching my legs close together to try to give my throbbing clit some relief. He gently ran his hand in between my thighs, slowly ascending to his final destination—my now soaking panties.

"Open your legs for me; I won't bite," he said, and then added, "well, not yet, anyway."

Liquid was pouring out of me. My heart rate was at a steady two hundred beats per minute. My eyes were swimming with desire. I opened my legs a few inches apart. Louis stroked up and down my wet panties. He was watching my reaction to his seductive touch. I looked down and could see how hard he was. All he had on were low-rise, faded Levi's. His jeans now had a huge bulge against the button fly. God, I wanted to touch him, but I felt so out of my league. I felt as if my limbs were heavy, almost paralyzed. I just lay there, panting like a sacrificial lamb awaiting its slaughter. I was lost in my momentary reverie when I felt his hot breath against my wet panties. I gasped and started to lift myself up.

"Shhhh ... baby, don't move, not yet. Lie back. I'm about to taste your sweet pussy. Feel free to come in my mouth," he said in a deep, low, hypnotic voice. Louis then lifted my skirt up and over my hip. He continued with the gentlest of touches, removing my white lace G-string. He climbed and knelt in between my spread legs. Seeing this sex god of a man crouched between my legs, watching him take in my half naked form was incredibly erotic. His smooth rocklike chest rose and fell. Every muscle on his torso was defined. All of it adding to the potent sexual fuel feeding my lust for this man. A trace of hair starting right under his belly button and traveling south was visible. I took a deep breath, trying to drink this all in and not go crazy with passion. He gave me a half smile and lowered himself all the way in between my legs. He ran his finger through my very trimmed pubic hair. He lowered his nose into my folds and inhaled. I felt like this was it; all the hype was about this right here, right now.

"I take it back, there's no way I'm giving up my sense of smell. You smell too fucking good." He lapped his tongue from where my hole started all the way up to my clit. "Delicious ... better than any of my dreams," he moaned into my crotch.

He inserted his long middle finger inside me. We both stopped breathing and looked at each other, momentarily in shock. When his finger entered me, it sounded like a rock plunging into a pool.

"You're dripping, little girl; this is all for me. God, you feel so tight. Tell me, Emily, how am I supposed to not fuck you and survive?"

He had his finger all the way inside my pulsating sex. He then started massaging my clit with his thumb in fast circular motions. I was breathing heavily and clenching my sex walls so tightly around his finger that I was afraid I'd snap it. Louis added another finger and brought his mouth down for a better taste. When his tongue flicked against my clit right under where his thumb was circling, I couldn't take it anymore. I stared to let out a cry that came from somewhere so deep.

"Louis, I'm gonna come ... Louis ... Oh ... God ... Please, I'm coming."

He kept a steady pace with his fingers deep inside me. I rode the wave of my orgasm. I was clenching his fingers inside me as if by letting them go I'd fall off a cliff. He was frantically licking and sucking every ounce of liquid heat pouring out of me.

"You taste like you were made for me," he mumbled, still

buried between my shaking legs. He lifted his head to look at me a few moments after my tremor finally stopped. "You coming in my mouth and riding my fingers like that is the hottest thing I've ever experienced in my life." He moved up my body to kiss and nibble my exposed lower stomach. "Let's get you out of this dress. I need a dose of those big tits and then I can die a happy man." He lifted me up to remove my dress. My bra followed my now discarded dress.

I was lying on Louis' bed, totally nude except for my tiny little belly ring, which Louis had yet to discover in the dimmed light. He came back to assault my swollen lips, and make sure I was still drawing breath. I could taste myself on his lips and found that so taboo but still hot. He asked me, "Did that feel as good as it looked for you?"

I nodded. "That was incredible. I can't believe I let you do that to me. You must think I'm a total slut."

He smiled that sexy teeth-twinkling, dimple-showing smile and then started laughing. "You're an eighteen-year-old virgin, I suspect. I'm officially going to hell for borderline molesting you and fucking you in my head for the last two weeks. The only slut here is me, for not being able to control myself around you."

I looked up to meet his dark eyes and ran my fingers into his messy, sexy hair. I ran my fingers all the way down to his neck and smiled. "You aren't molesting me if I'm old enough and give you permission. I obviously want you as much as I think you want me. I just feel very self-conscious with you. I want to do all these things to you in my head, but I've never actually done them with or to anybody."

Louis brushed my cheek with the back of his fingers. "I will make sure that I'm the only person who will ever get to do those things to you."

It was so hot when he pretended to be possessive of me.

"Emily, you know every time you open your mouth to speak, I want to fuck you even more."

"Thanks, I think," I said. We both laughed until it wasn't funny anymore and our laughter turned into a look of pure lust. I ran my fingers down his shoulders and stomach feeling his washboard abs. I didn't stop there. I ran my hand all the way down to the big bulge straining at his jeans that was begging to be let out to join our party.

Louis took a deep breath through his nose and held his breath. I rubbed the length of his hard cock up and down. He was now lying flat on his back, propped up with some pillows, giving me full access to his erection. I knelt by his tented crotch and started to unbutton his jeans. I met no barrier to his cock. *Note to self, Louis Bruel likes to go commando.* I lowered his jeans a touch and his cock sprung out to meet me. He lifted himself up to help me remove his jeans. His jeans now mingled with our growing pile of discarded clothing already on the floor. In a brave move, I straddled his left knee, settling on it with my wet, still throbbing sex. He groaned with appreciation.

I then began to acquaint myself with his most impressive intimate part. I ran my hand along his smooth shaft from root to tip. I'd never touched a man's private part before. It was so velvety smooth—like a baby's skin. But underneath the smoothness, it felt like pure steel. I lingered at the top of his cock to caress the mushroomed head. I was using both my hands to try and encompass every inch of him. He was either very large or my hands were just too small. I tried to squeeze my fingers around his hard cock but couldn't quite touch my fingers together like I'd seen in the pornos I occasionally watched on late-night cable. *How could something so big possibly fit inside me?* I thought with trepidation. My clit was still pulsating as if I were touching myself and not him. Louis was taciturn, which started to scare me. Maybe I was doing something wrong.

I asked him in a small voice, "Louis, am I doing this right? Does it feel okay? You're being very quiet, I'm getting nervous."

He exhaled loudly. "Baby ... I'm trying to calm myself

down. I don't want to come all over your hands. This feels incredible. I'm hoping I can last until you at least taste my dick."

I smiled, and with the added confidence that I now felt, I lowered myself to do just what he'd asked me. I licked the top of his moist tip. Tasting a man, especially this man, for the first time was a feeling that will stay with me until I die. I left his delicious smooth head and descended with my lips kissing down his cock, giving his whole length a taste. I made my way back up with my tongue. I then opened my salivating mouth, and took him in as far as I could. I got about a third of the way down his cock when I heard him cry out.

"Baby, stop! I'm gonna come in your mouth ... you don't want that ... don't suck anymore."

Why should I stop? I wanted him to come in my mouth. Isn't that what all men do after a blowjob? Ignoring his plea I continued trying to swallow Louis' cock whole.

He belted out a loud curse, "Fucccck," before holding my head in place with both his hands. Louis jerked up and then started pumping his hot liquid into my mouth. The sounds he was making, and me riding his knee up and down made my sex squeeze so hard I started coming with him. He was still pumping into my mouth when I stopped clenching my pussy onto his knee. He let go of my head and I licked him clean.

"I'm never letting you go Emily, that was ... God, what was that?" he wiped my mouth with his thumb. "I can't believe you never did that before. That was the best blowjob I've ever had."

He pulled me up so I could lie on top of him. I could still feel his semi-erect cock between us. I had my head on his chest. We were still both panting, trying to return our bodies to earth from somewhere in outer space. I could feel his heart racing in my ear. He was stroking my hair as we both drifted off to sleep. My last thought was a plea for all this to be real as Belinda Carlisle's song, "Heaven Is A Place On Earth[18]" played in my dreams.

Salty but sweet...

It was around five o'clock when I finally came out of my post-orgasm coma. I was completely naked under the covers. I must've been so out of it I didn't even remember climbing under the sheets; I was deliciously depleted after my introduction to multiple orgasms with Louis Bruel. I felt around the dark bed to try and find my wonderful orgasm instructor but felt nothing. I was most definitely alone in bed and in the dark. I started to look around for my underwear and my discarded dress. I found none and panic started creeping in.

Where was Louis?

Why would he leave me alone in the dark?

I called out, "Louis." No answer, I tried a little louder, "Louis!" Still nothing. I grabbed the white sheet tousled around my naked body and covered myself before tippy toeing out of bed. I started making my way down the staircase to the fifth floor when I heard Louis' deep voice somewhere from above and tried to follow it and find him.

The sound of his voice was coming from what seemed to be a glass room on stilts. The glass cube was held from the ceiling by metal cables. It was hanging over a sunken floor with a fire pit in the middle. Round wooden benches surrounded the fire pit. Most people need to go to the beach or the woods to have a bonfire, not Louis Bruel; he can make s'mores right in his own living room in SoHo. A metal ladder led up to that glass cube. I gathered my resolve and started to climb the ladder. I heard voices I didn't recognize and almost fell down in panic. I waited and listened until I could make out Louis talking to someone on the speakerphone. The room, which I deduced was his office, didn't have a door. I peeked in as soon as I made my way up the ladder. I was greeted by his signature panty dropping, dimple showing, full teeth-baring smile. Louis was talking on the speakerphone and eating a Twizzler. He stretched out his hand and beckoned for me to come join him.

"Bernadette, thank you again for showing the property. I will make sure to be there when the client brings his wife back to see the house."

"No worries, Mr. Bruel, just doing our job."

"I'm in your debt."

"Any time, we know how busy you are in New York," the woman on the line said. Louis pulled me closer to stand by his side.

"Yeah, I had a very pressing matter come up this weekend. I'm still taking care of it actually," he said, raising his sexy eyebrows at me.

How could any woman resist him? Just his voice and words made me excited.

"I'm glad I was here in New York to handle the matter personally, but I have no doubt you and Peter did a great job showing the Villa."

"Again, any time; that's why we're here. Take care, Mr. Bruel. We'll keep you updated."

"Thank you, Bernadette. We'll be in touch."

He pressed a button to disconnect the call and pulled me into his naked lap. I took a bite of his Twizzler and we both laughed. I can't believe I wasn't embarrassed to sit on him while he was gloriously stitch-less. He lowered the sheet that I'd secured around my chest and ran his finger between and then under my breasts.

"How'd you sleep, little girl?"

God, every time he spoke, I'd get aroused.

"Very well, thank you. I didn't hear you get out of bed. Did you fall asleep, too?"

"I've never slept better in my life. How am I ever going to sleep without you stretched out by my side? I don't know ... I'm getting slowly addicted to you, Emily Marcus."

His roaming fingers reached my stomach and he dipped his finger into my belly button and pulled on my small belly ring. He gasped out loud.

"How did I miss this?"

He lifted me off his lap, and sat me down in front of him on his desk, sheet-less and naked. He was trying to get a better look at my belly ring.

"Fuck me, Emily; are you trying to kill me? I don't think my dick can handle any more from you. You are like my wet dream come to life. If I wake up and this was all a dream, I'll be ruined forever ... but I'll come find you! If it's the last thing I do, I'll find you!"

He parted my legs and started to lower me back slowly down on his glass desk. I looked him up and down as he stood, towering over me. It was undeniable that Louis approved of my belly ring and I approved of everything Louis. He was hard as a rock again. I could just imagine how good he would feel all the way inside me. *No!* I needed to stop teasing him like this. I knew that I wasn't ready to let him go all the way with me ... we'd just met. We needed to stop before we reached the point of no return.

"Louis, we can't do this. You won't be able to hold back and I'm not strong enough to stop you either. I've never gone this far with anybody before. I'm scared."

He kissed me chastely on the lips and pulled me back up and into his arms.

"Okay, you're right, let's try to cool down. I'm being a shit host anyway. Let me feed you. What are you in the mood for?"

I nodded my gratitude and appreciation for the time-out.

"I'm thirsty; some water would be nice."

I still wasn't sure how I'd make it through the rest of the day with my virginity still intact. "Where did you put my clothes? I couldn't find them on the floor."

"I put them in my closet. I was hoping to keep you naked as long as I could."

He grinned and lowered his head to lick my belly button and pull on my small ring with his teeth. We both got down from his glass office. We were still fully naked as we got into the elevator to go to the kitchen. I lost my sheet somewhere between there and the office. God, he was huge everywhere. It was bright in the elevator and we were exploring each other shamelessly, one titillating body part at a time.

The kitchen took up the whole fourth floor. Every inch of space was covered in stainless steel. The space felt utilitarian; I felt like I was in a sci-fi movie. If I didn't know it was the kitchen, I would have thought it was a hi-tech operating room. He opened a huge metal door that proved to be his refrigerator and walked right into it and got us a few bottles of water. Louis then went back inside the refrigerator to get a pre-made cheese and grape platter.

"Louis, what happens now?" I asked him as he was setting our snacks down on the table. He looked at me, obviously not following my line of questioning.

"What happens now as in...?" he asked, slightly baffled.

I guess I needed to spell this out for him. So, I clarified. "What are we to each other after today? Are we going to start dating? Will you be dating other girls, I mean women, while you're seeing me? If you still want to see me after today, that is.

Can I tell my parents and sister about you, about us? I'm an idiot. I'm way ahead of myself … I'll understand if this was just a one-time thing for you. Mike told me you don't like to be with only one girl or the same girl twice. I shouldn't have asked all that … I'm sorry … forget I said anything," I said all that in one breath. I was mortified when I looked up at him. Louis raised his eyebrow at me and popped a grape into his mouth. *Lucky grape,* I thought.

"Emily, let's go through this slowly. I'm completely and madly obsessed with you, if you haven't noticed. I don't want to see or date any other women. I only want to see and date you right now. I certainly hope you don't want to see other men. I obviously want to be your lover … as in your first and only lover. I would be honored if you let me meet your parents. I can't wait to take you to meet my mom; she's going to love you! First thing tomorrow I promise to call Mike and let him know of my intentions toward his beautiful little sister-in-law … and I'd like you to move in with me tonight … any other questions?"

"Yeah, just one," I said, giggling. "Do all your women fall for this romantic stuff when you bring them to your lair?"

He took my arm and jerked me up off the stool and in between his legs. I was staring at the floor and at our bare feet when he cupped my face. He lifted my chin with his finger so I could look into his beautiful caramel colored eyes. "Besides my mom, and my housekeeper, you are the only woman who has ever seen my lair, little girl." He then kissed me. "And I've never asked a woman to move in with me. So, you'd be the first to fall for this romantic stuff."

I was shocked. I couldn't say anything. I was still trying to make up my mind if this was a head game for Louis to try and get me into his bed. Well, he'd already gotten me into his bed. So that's a moot point.

"In the past, I've always brought my dates back to an apartment I keep on Park Avenue, never to my bed," Louis continued.

I was speechless; he had a *fuck pad!* Didn't he ask me to go to his apartment last night?

"Why did you bring me here and not your apartment?" I asked, not sure what answer would soothe me.

"It felt dirty to bring you there. I know in my gut that you're not just another woman I'm going to fuck. It's different with you. I don't want to just fuck you and never see you again ... I want to fuck you indefinitely in my real bed and wake up with you still next to me in the morning."

Did I really captivate the attention of this gorgeous man? I put my arms around him and kissed him slowly, starting at his neck and then his chin, making my way up to those soft talented lips of his. He hooked one hand under my knee, and then brought my leg over his thigh and then repeated the same move with my other leg having me sit, sprawled out on his lap facing him. I could feel his growing erection pushing against my ass ... I reached behind me and started playing with his now fully-grown cock. When I got to the base, I reached under and gave his balls a gentle squeeze that made him lean forward. He roughly grabbed one of my nipples with his teeth and bit down in retaliation. He got up from the stool we were sitting on. With his arms supporting my naked ass, he walked us back into the elevator pressing the B button. While I was holding on to him and nibbling his face I asked, "Where are we going now?"

"I have a surprise for you."

"Louis, this whole day has been bordering on fantasy. What else could you possibly have to show me?"

"Close your eyes and don't open them until I tell you to ... promise?"

"Yes, I promise," I said, closing my eyes and resting my head on his shoulder. The elevator stopped and we exited into a place that felt very warm. The air had a salty ocean-like musky smell to it. Louis' every step and breath was echoing off the walls.

"Not yet, baby, keep those beautiful eyes closed until I tell you to open."

I nodded my head and then felt us slowly descending a set of stairs. I could hear water lapping very close by. A few seconds later, Louis lowered us both into what felt like a huge warm bath. I held him close from the initial unexpected water dip.

"Can I open my eyes now?"

"One more minute, baby. Not yet."

He kept his grip tight on me and walked us in deeper. I was now fully submerged in warm water all the way up to my shoulders.

"Open!" he commanded.

I opened my eyes to see us standing in the middle of an Olympic-sized pool. The place looked like a tropical oasis. The ceilings were all concave and covered in iridescent emerald tiles. The tiles merged seamlessly into the pool that filled up the entire floor—wall to wall. The pool smelled of ocean rather than chlorine. There were spots of bubbling jets all around us. I tried to convince my head that this was all real and in the basement of Louis Bruel's house in SoHo. I heard Louis saying something in my ear while holding me flush against him ... I tried to clear my head and pay attention.

"I never asked you if you could swim, so I won't let you go, baby."

I looked around in utter shock.

"I can swim, I love to swim," I said as I kissed him, smiling. I was so excited I actually felt like the little girl that Louis kept referring to me as.

"It's beautiful, Louis. I can't believe you have this hiding down here. What else do you have here? A movie theater, bowling alley, a shooting range, maybe a golf course?"

Louis laughed, amused by my giddiness. He dipped his head all the way back in the water to wet his thick wavy hair. Then he ran his wet hands on my still dry hair as he said, "I'm happy you like this. I designed this pool myself. I had the mosaic brought in from an amazing little place in Italy. I should take you there—you'd love it. It's a small family owned factory on the outskirts of the city of Torino. They make each tile by hand. If you look at each one, it's a slightly different shade of green, but when they assemble the mosaic, it takes on a life of its own. And to answer your question about what else I have: yes to the movie theater, yes to the bowling alley, no to the shooting range and definitely no to golf. I hate golf."

We swam around enjoying our surroundings. I showed off my diving skills. Louis then pulled me in for a kiss and whispered in my mouth, "After I deflower you and we finally have sex, I want to bring you down here and fuck you in the water. At the other end of the pool, there is a beach-like entrance point, where the water is shallow for a few feet. I'm going to lay you down and shove my dick in that tight little pussy and fuck you until you come screaming my name."

"That promise just made me very wet," I told him in a whisper back into his mouth.

"I know I can't use my dick to fuck that wet little pussy ... yet. So, my fingers will have to do ... for now."

He turned me sideways and lifted my legs to rest on his outstretched arm so I floated in the water in front of him. He let his arms go from under me and I was floating on my own. He nibbled at my lips before he inserted two long fingers deep into my sex roughly without warning. It was a welcomed intrusion but I was startled at how much I loved having him be indelicate and crude with my body. My breasts were floating on top of the water, begging to be sucked. Pumping his fingers very slowly in and out of me, he lowered his head and fulfilled my silent wish by sucking at my hard poking nipples.

"Salty but still sweet," he said with my bud between his teeth. Without stopping his sexual assault, he walked us over to the other side of the pool where the water got gradually shallower. With me still in his arms, he cradled me closer and positioned me on his lap as he sat down. Louis continued pumping his fingers in and out of me. When he brought his lips to mine and began kissing me he also increased the speed of his finger fucking and added his thumb on my clit to the mix. I was close; I could feel the orgasm building deep inside. I started to clench my vaginal walls, and Louis, sensing my impending release, began talking into my mouth during our heated kiss.

"Come, baby, I need to see you come in my hands. I love doing this to you."

"Oh ... Louis, I'm so close," I moaned.

"I know, I can feel your pussy closing in on my fingers ... so tight ... so fucking perfect ... fuck, Emily, let go."

I was floating. I was gone. Waves of pleasure just kept coming and ripping through my core. I didn't know what was up and what was down. I was in a suspended state of ecstasy. All that was left after the tremor was a limp body. When I joined this world again, I managed to say, "Louis, that was incredible. It felt so deep, that was the most intense orgasm I've ever had."

He kissed me and with a smug smile added, "Wait until I fuck you with my dick."

God, I can't wait.

Louis gave me some privacy, and left me to shower on my own at the spa adjoining the pool. I was still not allowing myself to fully accept what was transpiring between us for the last couple of days. Two hours later, we were showered, dressed, and back on the fifth floor eating Chinese food on a cow skin rug. I took out my mobile phone to see a message flashing from Sara and a missed call from my house. I dialed two to retrieve Sara's message first.

"Thanks for the warning. Your mom called asking to speak to you. I told her you went around the block to get us pizza and forgot your mobile, so call her back pronto. All I have to say is

... 'Baby Did A Bad Bad Thing[19]*' by Chris Isaak. Rule number one of lying to your parents: You always need to keep the accomplice informed ... love ya, slut."*

I smiled, thinking how I totally got caught up with Louis today and forgot to give my alibi a heads-up about my secret rendezvous. I'd deal with her later. I needed to call my parents to let them know I'd be home around ten o'clock.

"Yes, Daddy, Sara's brother will walk me home. If he can't, I promise I'll call you ... okay thanks ... I love you, too." I'd just disconnected with my parents when Louis came to hug me from behind.

"Who's Sara? And more importantly, who's her brother?" Louis said while biting my earlobe playfully.

"Sara has been my best friend since kindergarten. My mom and her mom have been friends since they were in high school. Her older brother Eddie is great; he always keeps an eye on us and drives us around. That's why my parents don't mind me spending so much time with her. They know Eddie is a good chaperone."

My earlobe was still lodged between Louis' scrumptious lips. He let my ear go to probe farther. "How old is Eddie? I don't think I like the idea of him keeping an eye on my beautiful girl."

Did Louis just refer to me as his "beautiful girl"?

"Louis, don't be silly. He's twenty-five years old and he's graduating law school. He thinks of me as his little sister, not as a beautiful anything."

"Do you not own any mirrors? Emily, look at you. Unless he's blind or gay he wants in your panties ... trust me."

"I promise you you're the only one who has been anywhere near my panties." That seemed to make him happy and relieve his delusions of my universal attractiveness. I thought he had this all wrong. I should be the one worried about him being God's gift to women. Not him being worried about me and Eddie, of all people.

"Em, stay with me tonight. I still didn't get to fuck those tits like I promised. It will be amazing to wake up in the morning and see those two blue oceans when you open your eyes and beg me to finally shove my dick inside you. So you see, little girl, I can't let you leave yet."

"Louis, I can't stay. I have to go home ... my parents think I've been over at Sara's house all day. Sara only lives a few blocks away from me. We'll see each other maybe next weekend ... if you still want to see me. When you have some free time and I'm not working for Mike and Jenna, we could meet up. We could have coffee," I said while turning around in his arms and bringing my hands around his waist to draw him in closer to me. His scent was becoming familiar. It was both comforting and arousing—what an interesting mix.

"You think I'm waiting until next weekend to see you? Em, first of all, you are never wearing that white tank top in the presence of others again. You don't need a job. I can give you whatever you want. Second, call your parents and tell them you're sleeping over at your friend Sara's house tonight."

Everything he'd just said to me was wrong on so many levels. "Louis, I promised Jenna and Mike I would work for them this summer. I actually took the job so I could see you again. I most definitely don't want your money. I'm not your employee or some kind of whore ... is that what you think of me?" I was getting myself all worked up. He opened his mouth to say something but I stopped him ... I wasn't finished yet. "My parents don't let me sleep over at anybody's house; so me asking them would be ridiculous. Even if I could, I wouldn't sleep over at your house, Louis. That's not who I am. I wasn't raised that way. I'm sorry I gave you that impression ... we went too far today."

Louis hung his head like a defeated child. "Okay, you're right. I love what happened today and last night. Em, I don't think of you as easy so please don't get upset with me. I just don't know what to say to make you stay with me. Can I at least see you tomorrow?"

He looked at me with sad eyes. I could bet my life Louis didn't plead with any girl for a date. Tomorrow, however, was Sunday. I always spent time with Jenna and my nana on Sundays. We usually had brunch until at least three o'clock at Sarabeth's, a few blocks from my house.

"Louis, I have some plans with my sister and grandmother until late afternoon. Maybe we could go see a movie in the evening if you're free."

He looked like I'd just informed him that his winning lotto ticket was from last week's drawing.

"So I won't see you for what—at least twenty hours? I'm not sure I can agree to that."

"You'll be fine, by tomorrow morning you won't even remember me. You'll be like, Emily who?" I playfully added to make him laugh and lighten up our mood.

He smirked and said very crassly into my ear, "If by the morning you forget about me, little girl, I promise you, I'll come over to your house. I'll find you in your room and when I find you, I will fuck you so hard and long that you'll feel my dick between your legs for at least a month."

I swallowed and looked up at him, not quite believing he'd just said that to me. My look must've scared him.

"No, baby ... fuck, don't look at me like that. I was just kidding with you. I would never be rough with you. I just got carried away. I'm a stupid dick. I'm sorry, I shouldn't have said that."

I nodded, took a deep breath and looked away. He grabbed me in a bear hug and lifted me off the floor.

"Emily, look at me, I'm sorry. I don't know what got into me. I couldn't fuck you hard if I tried. All I want is to hold you in my arms all night ... you've got to know that. Please forget I said anything."

"Louis, it's fine. You just scared me a little. No one has ever spoken to me like that."

"If someone ever spoke or speaks to you like that, tell me who it is and I swear I'll beat them to a bloody pulp."

Great, I'm falling for a caveman.

When we got to my house, he said, "Thank you for spending your whole day with me. It was by far the best day of my life. What would you like to do tomorrow? Dinner or see a movie at my house ... we could do both."

I let go of his hand and ran my fingers through his soft sexy hair pulling him in for a kiss.

"It's your choice. I'd spend time with you in a cardboard box and I'm sure it would still be amazing."

"When I pick you up tomorrow, can I meet the folks? I don't want us to sneak around behind their backs. This shouldn't be a secret. I want everybody to know how I feel about the most beautiful girl in the world."

I nodded at his sweet words.

"Pick me up at six, Pip, and wear real shoes."

Wake up and smell reality...

I slept like a baby all night. I woke up Sunday morning later than normal. My sister Jenna was already over. She was chatting with my parents in the kitchen when I came down from cloud nine.

"Hi, working girl," my dad said with his cup of espresso in midair. "Jenna just told us she has a new summer employee."

I smiled and gave my dad a good morning kiss on the cheek. My daddy, up until a few days ago, was the only man I ever thought I'd love. I could totally understand why my mom fell madly in love with him thirty years ago. He was handsome with salt-and-pepper hair and kind gray eyes. My mom once told me that he was hot stuff back when they were in school together.

My mom wasn't too bad herself. She looked well kept and much younger than a woman who'd just turned fifty. Her long, dirty blond hair was always pulled back into a low chignon. Her skin was obviously perfect. She could still pass for Jenna's older sister. My dad loves to tell the story of being hypnotized by my mom's blue eyes while they were trying to study for exams in med school. Apparently, he almost failed every test he tried to study for in her presence.

"I miss my sister; this way we get to hang out together ... and it will give me something to put on my résumé," I explained, trying to diffuse my parents' curiosity over my sudden employment.

My mom cleared her throat. "I didn't know you were looking for a job, Emmy. We could've arranged for you to intern at Daddy's practice or at the hospital with me for the summer."

My parents are both dermatologists. My dad owned a very busy private practice on the Upper East Side, close to Mount Sinai Hospital where my mom was the head of the dermatology department. They always thought their daughters would follow in their footsteps and join the medical field. Neither Jenna nor I have any interest in the medical profession, to their great regret. My mom had been trying to lure me to work for one of them since I turned sixteen.

"Mommy, I wasn't looking for a job. I just covered for one of Jenna's workers a few weeks back and Mike mentioned that he and Jenna thought I did a great job. I just figured it was a good way to see more of my busy sister."

Jenna wasn't buying my pile of bullshit. "Does it have anything to do with a very gorgeous Mr. Louis Bruel?" Jenna asked with a cat-that-ate-the-canary smile.

I could feel the flush rising from my chest, up my neck, and turning my whole face bright red.

"Emily, are you all right? You're flushed … here, honey, sit down."

"Yeah Daddy, I'm fine. It's just a little hot in the house. Is the air conditioner on? I'll go check." I left the kitchen for a few minutes and tried to calm my treacherous body from blushing at just the mere mention of Louis' name. When I came back a few minutes later, Jenna continued making my life as difficult as she possibly could.

"Emmy has the hots for a big shot real estate developer, Louis Bruel. He went to NYU with Mike. Judging by the way he couldn't stop looking at her at the party on Friday, I think he likes her, too."

"Emmy, who is this boy Jenna's talking about?" my mom started her inquisition.

"Ma, I just told you he went to school with Mike. He's not a boy; he's a man ... and a beautiful one at that. He was named one of NYC's most eligible bachelors two years in a row," Jenna added while giggling.

I needed to shut her up.

"Jenna, enough. I can tell Mommy and Daddy about him myself," I managed to belt out.

"So you have what to tell then?" she retorted with a questioning stare.

Fuck. Emily, think before you speak, I admonished myself.

"I ... I ... I saw him after the tea party you put together for his company. He invited me out for coffee ... to talk ... we talked," I added. *Shit, I must be beet red.* "He's very nice. He wants to take me out to dinner and a movie tonight ... I think."

"Well, he should come in and introduce himself if he wants to date you," my dad said.

"He will. He asked me last night. I mean, Friday night after coffee ... if he could meet you guys before he takes me out tonight."

I could already hear my mom's mind working against me before she even opened her mouth.

"Emmy, don't you think this Louis is a little too old for you, if he's Mike's age?"

I was silent. I knew she had a valid point. Louis was older and way more experienced than me.

"I mean, what will you two have in common?" my mom continued with her justifiable concerns. Her questions were making me want to tell her just how much in common Louis and I actually had. How I couldn't stop thinking about him. How I was helplessly falling in love with him with every second we spent together. I knew what I wanted and what I needed to tell my parents were two different things.

"Mom, I'm not marrying him! It's just a date." I thought that lie seemed to pacify both my parents. If they knew the truth about how intimately I'd gotten to know Louis Bruel in the last few days they wouldn't be so keen on letting me go on a date with him tonight, or in the next five years.

My mom also added, "Honey, before I forget, Sara called this morning while you were sleeping and asked you to bring her the disc that has the song ... wait, I wrote it down on the pad ... okay ... 'Don't You Forget About Me[20]' by Simple Minds."

The girl was crazy—how could I forget about my best friend? Even around Mr. Sex on a Stick. I needed to call her before her brain exploded with X-rated scenarios, which probably wouldn't even come close to what really happened last night.

At noon, Jenna and I walked out of my parents' house to go meet our nana at Sarabeth's for brunch.

"I spoke to Mike about Louis after I saw the two of you making goo-goo eyes at each other. He had some pretty interesting stories to tell about their college days together," Jenna said, watching for my reaction. I said nothing, so she continued her verbal tirade. "He's not a good guy for you, Emmy; truthfully he sounds like a real dick to me ... Mike was saying he once walked into their dorm room and found Louis in bed with three girls. He asked Mike if he wanted to join him. Mike said he had a date, as in, he was meeting me later. Can you imagine him in bed with three girls? And that was back in college before he made his millions."

My insides just dropped at her words. She didn't know what I'd already done with Louis ... oh my God, was I a total dumbass? What was I thinking? Panic started to descend.

"Emmy, breathe, what's wrong? You're very pale, are you okay?"

No, I'm not okay, I was screaming in my head ... you just told me my dream man has orgies and I can't get that image out of my mind.

"I'm just a little hungry," I managed to lie. I even added a little smile to make it look as genuine as I could, considering the war waging inside of me.

"I don't want you to get hurt by Louis Bruel. He's not boy-friend material ... I don't want you to have high expectations of him. He'll want to sleep with you right away. I know you're still a virgin. You need to be going out with someone nice, your own age. I don't want you to be in a vulnerable position tonight..." Jenna finished her speech.

Oh Lord, if Jenna only knew what kind of positions I've been in with Louis Bruel already, I thought sadly, still berating myself for being a stupid ninny with this whole Louis thing.

"Emmy, you need to understand. For a man like Louis, go-ing after a young girl like you is a high. He needs to feed his ego; it's the chase. Rich men want to prove to themselves they can get anyone into bed ... especially someone young and innocent like you."

I might've started puking if she didn't stop talking.

"JenJen, don't worry, I'm not stupid. I won't do anything with him I don't want to do; I'm just having some fun ... he's re-ally cute and I like the attention," I said. *What a lie!* I thought as those words were coming out of my mouth.

I was stupid. I wasn't just in lust with Louis Bruel; I was head over heels for him. I couldn't stop thinking about him. Was he playing me just to get me to sleep with him? Was this just a rich-boy game to see if he could have whomever he wanted? Oh God, I hoped not, because I would give him whatever he wanted in a New York minute. I wouldn't survive this if this was just a game for him. Maybe I was getting in way over my head. This man was incredibly attractive, had more money than sense, and had the biggest cock I'd ever seen. Not that I'd seen many, but compared to the few boys I'd made out with, Louis' cock seemed ginormous in comparison. Louis could've had any woman he wanted. Models, actresses, successful businesswomen, and from what my sister and Mike already told me, he could've had a few of them simultaneously. What the hell was I thinking? I was a silly little game for him—a chase, a distraction. I wanted to puke after all.

Our brunch was just one big blur to me. I kept floating in and out of my thoughts and then back in to catch a few words of whatever conversation my sister and Nana were having. I kept smiling and nodding so as not to raise any red flags. Around five o'clock, I debated calling Louis and canceling our date. Why would I do this to myself? Set myself up to get hurt. I couldn't just have fun with him, like I told my sister. I'd always imagined I would give my body and heart to someone who'd love me. We would one day get married like Mike and Jenna. If I didn't let Louis have sex with me, he'd just stop seeing me. Worse, if I went ahead and have sex with him, he'd just have gotten what he wanted and stop seeing me anyway.

Shit!

I looked at the clock; it was ten minutes to six, for the love of God. I'd been going back and forth with this in my head for hours. Now it was too late to call him and cancel. I looked outside my window and, of course, saw his red Ferrari parked right in front of my house. I ran and grabbed the first thing I saw, which happened to be a pair of ripped up jeans I used for bumming around the house. I pulled out the first top I could find in my drawer: a black Guns and Roses[21], washed out, off the shoulder t-shirt. I looked very *Flashdance*[22] with one shoulder and a bra strap showing. I pulled on my beat-up Converse tennis shoes and ran down the stairs just in time to open the door as the bell rang.

Louis looked devastating. He was wearing a beautiful, sharp navy suit with a cream button down shirt and a brown tie. As I made my way down his body, I saw he was wearing expensive looking dark brown shoes. His hair was slicked back, giving him that Wall Street bad boy look, which I loved.

He smiled, melting my insides and said, "When you said to wear real shoes, I just assumed you wanted me to take you somewhere nice."

I managed a half smile back. Help me, God, this man was beautiful. How was I going to do this?

Goodbye Mr. Wonderful...

I still hadn't uttered a single syllable to Louis. I walked out to him, closing the front door behind me. I needed to tell him this was all a mistake. I was not doing this to myself. I might be innocent when it came to boys but I wasn't a fool. I couldn't get sucked into his game. I knew if Louis and I started playing games, the loser would be me.

"Em, what's wrong? I thought I was meeting your parents before we go out."

I took a deep breath. "Louis ... I don't want to do this with you..." *Okay, Emily, so far, so good. Keep talking. You're a strong, smart girl; you don't need his head trip. You don't need your heart broken into a million pieces by the most beautiful man in the world.* I continued, not giving Louis a chance to say anything.

"Yesterday was ... amazing. I will never forget it as long as I live. But I know what you want from me and I'm not that type of girl." I took a much-needed breath and continued concentrating on my shoes. "I should've called you before you showed up. I just lost track of time. You don't need to meet my—" My front door opened before I finished my goodbye speech to the most beautiful man I'll probably ever know. My dad was standing there, looking at us with a big smile.

"Emily, don't you want to invite your friend in? So we could meet him?"

Fuck, bad timing. No, Daddy, I don't want to invite him any deeper than he already is, I thought. If he knew what kind of friend Louis Bruel was, he wouldn't be inviting him in either.

"Yeah, Daddy. We're coming right in."

I turned around to see a smiling Louis. I had no choice but to gesture for him to follow me in. My dad had his hand stretched out to shake Louis' hand.

"David Marcus, Emily's dad."

"Louis Bruel, Emily's ... friend. Very nice to meet you, sir."

This was so awkward ... I'd just told this magnificent man I didn't want to see him again and now he was meeting my dad. My mom heard us talking and came running in from the kitchen.

"Oh, Emmy, your date is here."

My Mom got her first good look at Louis Bruel and almost tripped over her own feet. She finally stopped power blinking and gave me that *oh my God, is he really your date* look. She stretched out her hand to shake Louis' proffered hand. He cupped her hand with both of his and smoothly said, "Louis Bruel ... it's a pleasure to meet you, Dr. Marcus. Now I know who to thank for Emily's stunning eye color."

My mom was visibly melting and blushing. "Another One Bites the Dust..."[23]

"Adele Marcus, how lovely to meet you, Louis." My mom turned her attention to me. She took in my outfit and almost fainted. "Emmy, don't you need to go upstairs and change for your date?" she said with a giggle, sounding embarrassed for me.

"No, Dr. Marcus, Emily is dressed perfectly for our date. I just didn't want to be late picking her up and meeting the both of you. I came straight from my morning meeting that ran late. I'm afraid I'm the one a bit overdressed for the movies." Louis was searching my eyes for some kind of silent acknowledgment.

"Okay then," my mom said, giving me a fake smile and

added to Louis, "By the way, please call me Adele." Great, my mom loved him, too. Was there a woman out there who didn't fall in love with Mr. Wonderful?

I said goodbye to my parents and followed Louis outside to his car. He opened the passenger side door for me and I turned to look at him.

"Louis, you don't have to do this. I can just go to Sara's house for the evening. Thank you for being so nice to my parents."

"Get in the car, Emily," he barked at me. "I don't know what happened in your head between last night and right now. All I know is that if you think I'm letting you go just like that, you really don't know me at all. Get in the car and we'll talk."

I got in the car, trying to practice in my head what I needed to say to him without losing my confidence. He gave me a deadly look as he got in, shook his head from side to side, pressed the gas, and the car flew.

"Louis where are you taking me?" I asked, my voice cracking a little and betraying my air of confidence. Even to my own ears, I sounded like a scared little girl.

"We're going back to my house. I shouldn't have let you go home last night. We need to talk this out."

He wasn't looking at me. I could feel how angry he was. "Louis, there's nothing to talk about. I won't sleep with you. I know that's all you want. I'm not interested in being one of your conquests ... please take me home," I said with tears threatening. He stopped the car in the middle of a busy Fifth Avenue intersection and looked at me like I'd just stuck a knife into his stomach.

"Emily, what did I do to make you feel this way? Did I pressure you last night in any way? Baby, I'm sorry, I didn't mean to scare you or make you feel like you need to sleep with me ... yesterday was a little intense. I just can't stop myself around you."

I could hear horns honking in the background. Louis was

just staring at me, not affected by the loud noise growing all around us. He reached out to take my hand in his. I let him.

"Please Em, talk to me. Tell me what you're thinking."

"Louis, can you please drive? The cars are making me nervous."

Without letting go of my hand, he used both our entwined hands to shift the gears and the car started moving again. "Can I please take you to my house so we can talk this out? Please tell me you trust me enough not to hurt you," he pleaded with me. His voice sounded panicked. I couldn't refuse him. I doubt anyone could. I nodded.

I think I love you...

We got up to the fifth floor. While still seated in his car, I closed my eyes and felt my impending agitation. What can he possibly say to me to make this whole relationship not feel far-fetched and wrong? Why would he want me? What do I have to offer him? Well, besides adding my virginity to his running tally.

"Em … I can see that brain of yours working. What have you already convicted me of?" Louis asked while we were still seated in his car. I found my voice and looked up at his impossibly beautiful brown eyes. They weren't smiling at me tonight. He looked worried.

"What do I have to offer you? I just graduated high school … I'm nobody … I'm not tall or skinny or beautiful. I don't have any sexual experience to offer you, besides what we had the last few days together. I won't let myself sleep with you or anybody until I know it's serious and not some kind of game. I already feel that we went too far." My tears decided they couldn't stay in any longer. "Louis, I have never been as attracted to anyone as much as I am to you. Who wouldn't be? You're gorgeous, charming, successful, and not to mention, really good at seducing girls … I mean, women. I know you're just playing with my head. I'm weak and naïve. I've never even had a serious boyfriend. You're a man who's been with so many women. Multiple women at the same time, from what I hear. I know you'll hurt me after you get what you want. Can't you just take pity on me and let me be? Please, Louis, don't crush my heart—it's very fragile. I know being with you for the last few days will damage me and I won't soon get over you. You ... you are way out of my league and I appreciate and I'm flattered by your attention but I need to be realistic, I need to be smart ... just take me home please."

He stared at me while I talked. When I finished, he closed his eyes and dropped his head back. "Emily, you're right," he said. My heart dropped. I took a deep breath thinking, *I guess now he can drive me back home.* How did a fantasy turn into a nightmare so quickly? With his eyes still closed, he continued talking, "I don't deserve to be with someone like you. I've had my share of girls and women and I deserve whatever low opinion you, Mike, and everyone else has of me..."

He took a deep breath through his nose and opened his eyes turning to face me.

"You're the most beautiful woman I've ever seen. Every time I look into your eyes, I feel like I'm home. I can't explain what I'm feeling. I've never felt this way. You're right ... that first time I saw you at that party, I just wanted to lift that short skirt and fuck the shit out of you right then and there in some dark corner. But now all I want is to lie with you in bed all day and make love to you for the rest of my life. Please, Em, give me a chance to be a good guy. I know I don't deserve a chance with you. I can't let you walk away from me. I'm a selfish prick, but I won't let you go. I promise I won't do anything to hurt you. I ... I haven't found out what your favorite color is or your favorite movie or book ... I don't know what songs you listen to when you're happy or sad. Don't sleep with me, just please stay ... baby, don't leave me."

He ran his fingers across my wet cheek and his thumb over my quivering lower lip. I looked up at him with eyes full of tears. He brought his lips close to mine, searching my glazed eyes for permission to let him kiss me. I nodded silently. His lips descended on mine, he rained soft little kisses all over my mouth, then my cheek, then down to my chin. He cupped my face with both of his hands and continued kissing my nose, my eyelids, and then back to my lips for a deeper kiss. His tongue kept a steady pace, slowly dancing together with my tongue round and round. After what felt like a good hour, we pulled away from each other, panting and breathless.

"Baby, you still haven't said anything ... does this mean I get a chance with you?"

I looked at him and needed to know once and for all. "Even if we won't sleep together, you still want me?" I was looking for a clue; any sign that *this* was not for me. That all this was a mistake, a delusion I had about us but I couldn't find any clues. I was just happy to be close to him.

"Em, I want to be with you so much, I'll take you any way I can get you. I don't want anyone else and I don't think I ever will; as crazy as that sounds. You've ruined me for all women ... forever."

I smiled as he got out of the steamy car and walked over to my side to open my door and get me out. We walked into his house and he left me sitting on a huge brown leather couch on the fifth floor while he went upstairs to change. He came back a few minutes later, barefoot in soft black cotton sweatpants and a white, tight ribbed tank. He smiled and asked me playfully, "Better?"

I laughed and said, "Perfect."

He sat next to me, propping his right leg so he was facing me. With his right hand extended over the back of the couch, he started playing with my loose hair. Louis took my hair and lowered his head to inhale my scent then said, "I spoke to Mike this afternoon. I let him know we were going to start dating each other. I hope to still have the chance to date you." He stopped, took a breath and continued, not looking me in the eye. "He wasn't thrilled when I told him I was trying to pursue you. He actually begged me to just walk away. He said, and I quote, 'Can't you find women who are not related to me to fuck around with?' I deserved that, I've never had honorable intentions with women in the past."

"And your intentions are honorable toward me?" I asked, lifting my eyes to meet his and pinning his gaze.

"I told Mike he could bet his last dollar that I'm going to marry you someday, so he has nothing to worry about."

So, Louis Bruel was a comedian, too. I figured after that ludicrous comment everything was fair game.

"What did Mike say to that?" I asked, still not believing my ears.

"He said he's not a gambler and he doesn't know what game I'm playing, but if I hurt one hair on that beautiful head of yours he'll rip my balls out."

We both started laughing at that.

"I hope you get to keep your balls, Louis. I know you're very attached to them," I said, still laughing.

"I intend to walk out of this with my balls still attached and you by my side." We stopped laughing. He got serious and fixed my hair behind my ear. "I don't want to freak you out any more tonight, but you need to know that I'm pretty sure I love you, Emily Marcus. I'm prepared to spend my whole life proving that to you. All I needed was one day with you to know I'll never want anybody else."

That didn't play out the way I imagined. I was supposed to call Louis' bluff and keep my blooming emotions to myself. "Louis, I think I'm falling in love with you, too," I said and climbed into his lap, which somehow felt like the natural thing to do.

"Oh, baby, this feels so good," Louis inhaled my hair, and nibbled on my bare shoulder. "Please don't do that to me again. I'm an old man; my heart can't take that shit."

"What shit is that?"

"I really thought you were ending things with me. I thought I'd fucked it all up. Em, don't let me fuck this up."

With his face still in my hair, I looked up at him, kissing him softly on the neck and asked, "So are you my boyfriend now?"

"I asked you to move in yesterday. I met your parents today. I told your brother-in-law I want to marry you and I just confessed to you that I love you. It's safe to say I'm whatever you want me to be."

"My favorite color is green, my favorite movie is *The Blue Lagoon*[24], I read *Pride and Prejudice*[25] like eight hundred times ... and I'm obsessed with '80s music," I said all in one breath.

"So you're a big romantic then. When is your birthday, Emily?"

"July 21st and I'll be nineteen," I answered. That got a big dimple-exposing, teeth-showing smile out of him.

"How about you—when is your birthday?"

Louis was still grinning like a wild man before he answered me, "Very nice, July 21st."

"No, I mean when is your birthday? Not mine."

"July 21st."

"Wait ... your birthday is also July 21st? We have the same birthday?" I asked in complete shock.

"It would appear that we share a birth date, my lovely Emily. You see, you were made for me. You're my *bashert*, as my dad would've said."

I smiled. "My grandma says that, too." Hearing him use a word that I heard my nana use a million times felt like an omen from above. It felt like, *this, us,* was somehow written in the stars, even before we met. It was what Nana Rose always said: *Bashert is Bashert, no running away.* This was the sign I was looking for.

"You know, when I was little my dad used to tell me of how

before a soul is born into this world it gets broken into two pieces. He said that for a soul to ever feel whole again it needs to find its missing part. Baby, you have to be my missing half."

We didn't visit his bedroom that night or see a movie in his movie theater. We just spent the night talking and laughing. I sat in Louis' lap all night. I think he wanted to prove to me that what we had between us wasn't just a physical thing. He wanted to show me that we could spend a whole evening in each other's company fully dressed and abstain from any sexual activity.

Louis drove me home at midnight. We were quiet on the ride home. We were both replaying and trying to absorb everything that unfolded between us that night. My phone started ringing, disturbing the silence. I looked down to see Sara's name flash on my screen. I couldn't talk to her now in front of Louis. I had a lot of explaining to do for going AWOL on her for the last few days. I just let it ring and ring.

"Aren't you going to answer that?"

"Nope, it's Sara. I'll call her back tomorrow."

Louis raised a suspicious eyebrow my way but said nothing. A minute later, the phone started ringing again. *Fuck, Sara, give me a break.* Louis still had his eyebrow raised, trying to figure out why I was dodging my best friend's call.

"Hi, I didn't forget about you. Let me call you back when I get home."

I closed my phone before giving Sara a chance to answer, only to have the little bitch call again as soon as I hung up. I knew what she wanted.

"Hi, Sara. Sorry, I'll return your Roxette disc with 'Listen to Your Heart[26]'first thing in the morning." I heard Sara trying to mumble something before I disconnected. I looked over to find Louis trying to stifle a grin. I wasn't about to explain this to him or anyone else. When we got to my house, he unhooked his seatbelt and got out of the car to help me out. I was already out waiting for him. He pulled my hips close to him with both hands.

"I love you, Emily. God, it feels so good to say those words to you." He lowered his lips to mine, shutting me up before I had a chance to respond to his declaration of love. I had to get home and compose my emotions. We pulled away. I ran halfway up my parents' steps before I heard Louis humming one of my favorite songs. I swear I wasn't imagining this, but as I looked back, I could hear him whistling a familiar melody while he moved around his car to the driver's seat. He lifted his head and winked at me, still whistling as he got into his car and drove away, leaving me dazed and confused. I stood leaning on my front door, watching his car take off as I finished the song he started. Perhaps this thing between us was a once in a lifetime thing. Louis Bruel just sang Christopher Cross' "Arthur's Theme[27]" to me ... *maybe we will get married!*

I called Jenna that night when I got home.

"Emmy, I know," she said, before I even got a chance to say hello.

"What do you know?" I asked her, not sure how this conversation was about to go down.

"Louis called Mike today. He told him that he loves you. He promised that he would never hurt you. Mike said he sounded very serious. Like marriage serious."

"Am I crazy, Jen? I love him too, I think. I've only known him for a few days, but I feel so right when I'm with him. He makes me feel like the most beautiful girl in the world. It feels genuine, the things he says to me. I don't know why but I really feel safe with him. Am I being naïve? Is this how all men are?" I asked my sister, a little scared and lost in my growing emotions for Louis.

"Emmy, from what Mike told me about him and other

women, I think he's fallen for you hard. I mean, you need to be smart, obviously, and take your time. It seems you both have strong feelings for each other. You have to see where it goes. Listen, just because he was a total dick with every other woman before you, doesn't mean he will be like that with you. Every relationship has risks; there are no guarantees. No one can promise you that it will work out for you guys. But I hope it does."

"Do you think I'm special enough for him? I mean, he's so much better looking than me. You know, he's the total package." I needed someone other than Louis to reassure me that I was pretty enough and worthy of him.

"Emmy, he's the one who doesn't deserve you. You're young, beautiful, smart, sweet, and innocent. Please don't sell yourself short. You're not some slut or a gold digger who's just after his money. You come from a great family that supports and loves you. He knows and acknowledges that. I'm sorry about what I said today at brunch. I didn't think he was so serious about you. I just didn't want you to get hurt and get your hopes up over him ever committing to you. But I was wrong and I take it all back."

"Thank you, JenJen. I really needed to hear that from someone other than Louis."

"I love you, Emmy. Mike and I are always here for you. I can't believe my little sister is dating *The* Louis Bruel. Go big or go home."

My next middle-of-the-night phone call was to Sara. She picked up on the first ring.

"I'm not talking to you until you tell me everything. The one time you actually get some and what do you do, Emily Marcus? You shut me out. Don't forget I was there helping you pick out the dildo version of Louis Bruel."

"If you want to hear about my crazy weekend, stop talking

and listen." That finally shut her up. Let's see, where should I begin? Oh yeah: "Louis Bruel told me he loves me tonight. He asked me to move in with him last night, and told Mike this morning he's going to marry me. Any questions?" Silence ... holy shit, I've rendered Sara Klein speechless, no '80s songs required.

True to his word, Louis didn't once try to coerce me into having intercourse with him. He never even asked me to sleep over at his house after that night. I was only back on the sixth floor and in his bed once. I sat, very innocently, on the edge of the bed, waiting for him to change into a suit for a party we were attending together. I worked for my sister during that month, but only on events for Louis' firm. "Coincidently," Mike and Jenna changed the Crown Affairs uniform to a white button-down shirt instead of the tight white tank top. Jenna said it was Mike's idea, but I think Louis talked him into keeping me clothed and on the unemployed side. I can't say I minded. I only agreed to that job because I wanted to see him in the first place.

I remember a party that summer that his company was having at a penthouse on Central Park West. The apartment took up the entire top two floors of the building. Louis asked Jenna if it was okay for me to be his date and not have me work that night. He wanted to introduce me to some of his colleagues. He told me no one believed that he had a girlfriend. I knew they couldn't believe it was only one girl filling that post.

"Once my business partners get a glimpse of you, they'll know why I haven't been at work for the last two weeks."

That statement made me feel guilty. "Louis, I hope you hadn't been missing work because of me." In those last couple of weeks, we'd spent almost every waking hour together. I blissfully and naïvely accepted the time Louis dedicated to me as the norm.

"What's the point of being boss if I can't allocate my own time as I see fit? Em, I spent the last five years of my life working like a dog day and night. I just realized I was preparing for you. I clocked in enough overtime to spend as much time with you as you'll let me."

Who says things like that? And why hadn't someone more qualified than me snatched him up already? I loved the attention I was getting as Louis Bruel's girlfriend. He wouldn't let go of my hand all night, introducing me to all as *his girlfriend*. Louis knew how to work a room. He commanded the attention of every eye; especially of the female variety, which followed his every move. The women were always a little covertly catty toward me, sending me sideways glances. They were no doubt thinking, *What's so special about this little nothing of a girl?*

The men obviously wanted a better look at the girl who was able to capture the attention of their embodiment of Casanova. People who knew him were well aware of the kind of women Louis Bruel could have with his looks and means. I knew only a little of his reputation around town from what Jenna and Mike had told me. I'm sure that the reality of Louis Bruel as a bachelor was so much worse. I decided that ignorance was bliss when it involved my boyfriend's past transgressions.

I was, however, worried about him having slept with so many women in the past. Had he been safe with all of them? Probably not! I asked him once about it and that prompted a full physical an hour later. Complete with blood work, urinalysis, and sperm count. Louis Bruel never did something half way. He told me he had never had unprotected sex with anyone. He said how excited he was that when we did finally make love; it would be the first time for him without a barrier. I also took a blood test that day, more as a show of solidarity than an STD concern, since I'd never been sexually intimate with anyone except him.

Louis knew he had nothing to worry about when it came to STDs and me.

Treetop...

During our short courting period, one of my favorite dates was the 4th of July. Louis promised my father that evening that he'd have me back home by midnight. My father told Louis he had until two o'clock in the morning to bring me back, before they'd send the cops to find me. My parents really loved him; it's a good thing they knew nothing of his past dating habits, or the fact that he had deflowered their daughter with almost every part of his body.

That evening we went to his house.

"I feel bad that you stayed in the city with me. All your friends are hanging out at the Hamptons. I really wouldn't mind if you wanted to go be with '*The Boys*' for a few days."

"I respect your parents for not letting their daughter spend the night anywhere but home. And trust me, Em, I'd rather be with you watching the fireworks than hanging out with a bunch of strangers on some beach alone."

Yeah right, Louis alone. That's a good one. I knew he'd have every woman within a mile radius bobbing for his attention.

"Louis, your friends must hate me. I haven't left your side for more than five minutes. You haven't hung out with them in weeks. I feel like I'm monopolizing you. You're going to get sick of me very soon."

"I don't want to be away from you for a minute. Do you honestly think I'd leave you and go to the Hamptons? I don't think I could explain what I feel for you even if I wanted to. I can't imagine my life without you, Emily."

"Ditto."

I was secretly ecstatic that Louis stayed home with me. I'm no dummy. I knew what happened in those Hampton parties. Louis' friends threw a huge party every summer and invited ten girls for every guy. That was not the ratio of women to my boyfriend I liked him to be around. We still hadn't slept together. I'm sure with just the right amount of alcohol in his system, if the right girl came along Louis would forget all about the nothing-special eighteen-year-old he had back in the city. Jenna and Mike spend almost every 4th of July with their friends in the Hamptons. So I was pretty well versed on what took place outside of city limits.

We rode in the car elevator to the seventh floor of his building. I hadn't yet seen the seventh floor. Louis hadn't given me a full tour of his house. He thought the element of surprise was needed in every relationship. I figured he had more bedrooms, or a gym, perhaps. I was certainly clueless to what was waiting for me up there.

When Louis drew the metal gate up, my mouth dropped open and refused to close. If Louis' house was a huge exaggerated treehouse, then the seventh floor was the top of that tree. Stepping on that terrace that evening felt like we were hovering in the sky, looking down on a lush park. All I could see was a field of green and wide-open sky like a blanket all around us. The bright lanterns spanning the rooftop terrace blotted out the sight of any building around us. It felt like we were the last two people on top of the world. In the middle of this sea of green, I saw what looked like a really big arc—a hammock covered in pillows.

Louis broke into my dream state and said, "Seeing all this

through your eyes gives me the most content feeling I've ever had. Whatever I achieve and accomplish from now on will be for you, baby."

"Thank you, Louis, that's the most beautiful thing you've ever said to me. I love you so much."

The two of us made our way through the bushes and lay down in that hammock. We kissed each other hungrily with our eyes open for what felt like ages, swaying back and forth.

"Take your shorts off ... I'm going to make you come so hard you won't even notice the fireworks above you," Louis whispered into my ear.

"I can't take my shorts off; someone will see us," I protested, not being of the exhibitionist type.

"No one can see anything. The walls around us are pretty high. We are nestled between bushes and those lights all around the building are virtually blinding. So unless someone flies over in a helicopter and then shines a light directly on us, we're invisible," he said with a wink, already crouching down to where my fingers had started unbuttoning my white shorts. I wanted what my gorgeous boyfriend was offering. "I'll cover you with a throw anyway, so you won't get cold."

Getting cold with Louis Bruel within a foot of you is an oxymoron. He was already working me out of my underwear. He laid himself between my parted legs and with both hands under my buttocks, lifted my crotch up off the hammock and into his face. Louis closed his eyes and dug his nose inside me, inhaling me in like a drug. He took the cover and threw it over his head. It blocked my view of him and my naked torso. The hammock swung from side to side. All I could see was Louis' covered head moving up and down under the dark green cashmere blanket. I could feel his flattened out tongue lapping at my already oozing opening with long lazy strokes that started close to my rear and came up to my clit. When he would reach my clit, I could feel him draw his lips together and suck hard.

"Oh God, Louis, that feels so good," I groaned.

"Baby ... I'll make it feel even better," he promised. He bit down on my clit softly. That bite sent a bolt of electricity down my legs. To finish me off, he blew on my over sensitized nub. He was doing that to me over and over. I was feeling a delicious tightness start to grow in my groin. Louis continued licking and flicking his tongue at my lips until his tongue found my rear. He circled his tongue around my puckered entrance. That foreign sensation had me clenching both my rear and my sex from the unexpected decadent intrusion.

"Mmmmm ... you like it when I tease your asshole, don't you? Baby, I need you to relax. Stop thinking and only feel me..." Louis said in a muffled voice under the covers.

My head needed a visual. I pulled the covers off to see the most beautiful man in the world on his knees, squatted down on a shaky hammock. He was supporting my rear with both hands and feasting on my mound. I put my hands through his long, now dampened hair, moving his locks back off his face. Louis looked up at me smiling and plunged two fingers inside my sex. He slowly started to pump them in and out. After a few minutes of being assaulted by Louis' long fingers, he added yet another finger to my already quivering hole. It almost looked like he was putting me on like a glove through my open slit. I was stretched out and filled to the brim.

"Fuck, baby ... I want you to come hard and squirt all over my hand ... I want you dripping all over me."

As he looked at me and said those words, I could see the raw lust on his perfect face through my half closed eyes. I couldn't hold on anymore...

"Louis, I'm letting go ... it's coming ... oh God, Louis, I'm coming."

My climax ripped through me with such force that I was sure the spatter of bright light behind my closed lids was my brain having convulsions. When the sound of my heart pumping began to dissipate in my ears, New York City came crushing in all around me. I finally opened my eyes to see a black sky bathed in red, blue, and green bursts of lights exploding above our heads. The lights I saw in the midst of my euphoric state were actually the 4th of July fireworks. The loud shooting sound wasn't my heartbeat but the pyrotechnic display. I could swear it felt like they were being shot out of my crotch. I looked at my lover nestled around me like a vine. He was watching me watch the fireworks. I kissed his nose.

"Thank you, Louis; that was amazing."

"Baby, you're amazing, I wish I could watch you explode like that all night."

"You could watch me swallow your cock whole with fireworks in the background." He liked it when I spoke dirty back to him. He said hearing the word *fuck* and *cock* leave my lips was a treat.

"Em, I made a vow never to say no to you … swallow away, baby…"

Boys will be boys...

"**I**f you tell the guys how pussy whipped you have me, I'll withhold all forms of orgasm for a whole day," Louis warned me while on our way to meet his infamous group of friends.

I had yet to meet anyone other than people Louis worked with. I was very anxious to finally meet *The Boys* as Louis referred to them: Max, Phillip, and Andrew—his so-called best friends.

"I'm so nervous. Promise not to leave me alone," I asked, no begged, Louis before we got to the club.

"Em, I promise to not let you more than six inches from me at any time tonight. Relax, I love you and they'll love you."

Famous last words!

We walked up to Phillip's club, Lunna, at around eight o'clock that evening, which was not yet open for business. The club scene in New York only got going at around midnight. The club was located in a converted old church in an area of the city called Hell's Kitchen. Lunna looked very hip. It gave off an exclusive vibe. It was massive, occupying a whole corner and taking up most of the block.

I would never have come to a place like this by myself. I would've felt too intimidated walking up to the door and afraid of not being granted entry. I'd only been to one club in my whole

life. Sara's brother, Eddie, took us out with his friends to celebrate his college graduation. My best friend and I were fifteen
years old so Eddie had to slip the doorman some money to let us
both in. Eddie, being a great older brother, kept us within arm's
reach all night. He wouldn't let any guys get near us. He had a
protective barrier around me all night, while his best friend, Jeffery, was safeguarding Sara. I remember begging Jenna to let me
tell Mom and Dad I was with them that night at some fundraiser.
I got home at two o'clock in the morning, which was way past
my eleven o'clock curfew. Eddie and Jeff left the club early to
drop Sara home and then Eddie walked me home.

But that night, having Louis hold my hand, I felt like I
could walk on the red carpet at the Oscars and not feel an ounce
of intimidation whatsoever. Being out with Louis meant that everyone was always looking at us. He put his hand at the small of
my back and led me to the entrance. I was wearing a sexy, black,
long halter dress. The dress looked like a black sheet that I'd tied
up at my neck. My back was completely bare. No bra for me.
The deep plunge in the back was so low that I couldn't even wear
underwear. I'd chosen open toe, black sandals to help me close
the ridiculous height gap between us, and because Louis loved
seeing my bare feet. He said to me that after sucking my toes,
just seeing my feet was a major turn on for him. Louis noticed
my lack of bra but he had yet to discover my panty-less state.
Louis knocked on the door and after a few minutes, a big burly
looking guy with a shaved head and a goatee opened the massive
door.

"My man, Louis. It's about fucking time. Where have you
been, motherfucker? We thought you died somewhere."

The bouncer obviously knew Louis well.

"Joe, it's good to see you're still here. I've been keeping
busy," Louis said, giving my hand a squeeze.

"Where are The Boys?" he asked the bouncer, who then
looked behind Louis and spotted little scared me.

"Very nice, Louis. I see you brought a toy as a peace offering for The Boys to enjoy tonight. Boss-man won't like you taking away his job. But he'll like her, no doubt," he said laughing and running his eyes down my body. I could feel Louis recoiling at his words and then he visibly stiffened.

"Joe! Right here, look at me. Watch your mouth in the presence of my girl," he said briskly. He then added through gritted teeth, "Nobody plays with her except for me, motherfucker. You should keep your stupid comments to yourself." With that, we walked past the now flustered Joe.

As we made our way inside the club toward the bar, Louis whispered apologetically in my ear, "Don't pay any attention to Joe, no one else does. He wasn't hired for his wits." He lifted our clasped hands and kissed the back of my hand. I gave him a very brave smile and was rewarded with a wink.

Phillip was the only one of Louis' friends at the club when we arrived. He was very attractive with a dominating air. He was not as tall as Louis but nicely built. Short, curly black hair framed his heart shaped face. His thick dark eyebrows emphasized deep-set blue eyes. When he saw Louis and me approaching, he gave us a Cheshire cat grin. My heart was beating fast. I could only imagine Louis and The Boys breaking hearts everywhere they went. I took small, shallow breaths and tried to relax. I wanted to seem confident. I didn't want his friends to see a scared little girl. Phillip walked over and sat on a divan and watched us as we approached him.

"Lou, really, this is what the most beautiful woman in the world looks like?" Phillip said with a confused look on his face.

My fast beating heart stopped and dropped to the floor. My face probably blanched white. I took a deep, wheezing breath to try and keep my tears down. Louis squeezed my hand so hard I thought my bones would shatter.

"You say another stupid comment like that to hurt her feelings tonight and we're done Phil. Consider yourself warned. You can tell The Boys the same," Louis said, seething with anger. Somewhere in the back of my mind, I agreed with Phillip and wanted to hand Louis back to his friends where he belonged.

"I get it. Her pussy must be really tight, man. For you to go MIA on us and choose this 'ho over your bros–"

All I saw after that was red. Louis let go of my hand and launched himself toward the couch Phillip was sitting on. Phillip didn't even flinch. I had yet to see the man I loved this angry. Louis lifted him off the couch and held him dangling in midair while Phillip was still laughing.

"Lou, relax, put me down," Phillip, still cracking up, told my very angry boyfriend. "If you wanted under-aged girls, I'd have three on their knees sucking you off before this night is over. We pay them once and then they're gone. This little cock tease will milk you for everything you're worth. Let me call Julie, she's the one you really like. It's the Asian blonde that likes your dick up her ass and my dick in her pussy. Ha-ha-ha ... put me down, bro. I'm doing you a fucking favor. Trust me."

Angry was too gentle of a word to describe Louis. His face was red and veins popped out of his neck. He looked as if his forehead might burst. I was scared. He looked capable of murder. I could feel myself start to faint. I needed air. I needed to go ... I had that fight or flight feeling. I turned around to start walking, or maybe I was running, toward the door.

I heard Louis yell his answer to his so-called best friend, "We're done! You sick fuck. I told you how much I care about her. I told you I don't want this shit anymore and this is how you disrespect me, you worthless scum. You're only my friend for sharing pussy. I love this girl. If you ever want to see me again, you'll apologize to Emily. Even then I still won't forgive you for what you just fucking said."

I heard a crashing sound. I assumed Louis must've either let go of Phillip or thrown him into something. Louis ran to catch up with me before I got to the door. Joe was seated by the exit looking flustered and confused. Louis took my shaking hand in his and walked us right out of that club, forever. Fresh, cool air hit me and I took in some much-needed gulps. My tears, which I couldn't hold back any longer, rolled freely down my cheeks. Louis jerked my hand for me to stop walking. He swung me around into him for a silent embrace. My silent tears turned into loud sobs.

"Emily, I'm sorry, baby, that was so fucked up. I don't know what I was thinking. I should've never trusted Phillip to be anything but the animal that he is," he said on the verge of what sounded like tears himself.

I felt small and worthless, but mostly scared. I was out of my league with him and his friends. I looked up to meet his guilt-ridden eyes.

"Is that what you want, Louis? Have I been keeping you away from your friends and the hordes of sluts? This is what you really need? Then just go ... leave me alone." I took a strangled breath. "Why are you doing this to me? I told you before; I won't survive you disposing of me once this gets boring for you. I'm not some gold digger who goes from guy to guy. I'm scared. I've never felt this way. I'm in love with you. I don't think I'll ever get over what we have together. For the rest of my life, any man I will ever be with after this will have to compare to you ... and I don't think anyone will ... ever." I couldn't stop the well of tears my emotions had unleashed.

"Emily, listen to me. I love you, too. If you think I want to go back to being scum and waste my time with men who are not my friends then you have no idea how I feel about you. If I could, I would give up all the women I've ever known for you. Phillip is dead to me. The nameless women were all empty fucks. I just want this, I want you, and I want us. I need to know my words are getting to you. I have been alive for twenty-nine years and my life just started three weeks ago. I would do anything for you. Please trust that I'll never hurt you." He took a long, drawn out breath and continued, "I'm dying inside watching you get hurt by this. I can't see you cry. Please, baby, stop crying."

It took me a few minutes to collect my ego and my heart off of the sidewalk. People passing us on the street were starting to stare at our lovers' quarrel playing out for them like one of Shakespeare's tragedies. We walked quietly to his car. He opened my door and lifted me, almost childlike, and placed me into the passenger seat of his very low sports car. Squatting down, he buckled me in with a serious expression on his face.

"Are you afraid I'll run away?" I asked playfully, trying to lighten the gloomy mood we were both in.

"I'm not taking any chances with you. I fucked up enough for one night." He bent to kiss my puffy cheek. He closed my door, got behind the wheel, and took off in a flash.

Making up is fun to do...

We spent that night in Louis' house, lying on a plush, white wool rug listening to some smooth music. I had my eyes closed, sprawled out on my stomach. Louis lay sideways facing me and soothingly ran his fingertips up and down my bare back. When we were like this, alone and together, nothing else mattered. Not his stupid friends. Not the thoughts of people judging my intentions or his. Right there on the floor with that man was all I ever needed.

"Louis," I said with my eyes still closed.

"Yes, baby."

"You know I don't care about your money ... right?"

"I know, Em," Louis choked out. "I never thought you did," he snorted and added, "I just realized you haven't once asked me for anything. I'm a stupid prick. This whole time we've been together, I've never gotten you one damn thing. A normal boyfriend would at least buy his girl some kind of gift. Let alone me with all my fucking money."

I opened my eyes. "I don't need anything. I have everything I need. I just want to be with you. All this stuff you have around is amazing. But please know that's not why I love you."

"It's not that I'm some cheap bastard. I'm not just using you, Em. I love you, and I should be spoiling you. Lord knows I can.

I've never done this before. I never needed to buy a woman a gift. I would pay for whatever they wanted and that was it."

"Louis, you don't need to buy me anything and I don't care about what you did with other women," I said, hating the pang I got in my chest every time he mentioned other women.

"Em, I'm sorry. I know I don't need to, but I want to. I want you to have everything. You're a beautiful young woman. I'm the man who's courting you. I should be showering you with flowers and jewelry. I've just been lost in you, in us."

I ran my fingers through his long hair and then placed my hand on his heart. I looked up at him. "I know I'm young and I don't have much to compare our relationship to, but when we're together I feel like you're mine and that's all the gift I need from you. I can't explain it. I know you don't really belong to me. But when I look at you, I know I'll never need anyone else. I don't need anything. I'm just happy knowing you're mine."

He smiled, kissed the tip of my nose, and pulled me up toward him. I was now almost fully resting on top of him. He kissed the top of my head, inhaling my hair. "You own every cell in my body, Emily Marcus." He ran his hand down my bare back until his fingers grazed my bare bottom. "Are you kidding me? You were naked all night under this dress?" Louis asked as he continued with his fingers spread out going down to cup my butt.

"Surprise," I said, smiling into his dark eyes.

He urged his middle finger down between my butt cheeks until he felt my wetness. He dipped his fingers into my crotch before bringing it back up to play with my other hole. He lightly pushed his finger against my rear hole and I cried out.

"Shhhh, relax … I promise to make it feel good … tell me you trust me."

I was lying with my upper body on top of him. My face was on his chest and I nodded.

"I want you to forget all of tonight's bullshit … it's just you and me … I wish I could be buried deep in you and make you forget everything but me. Not tonight, little girl. Tonight I'll be making you come with everything except my dick. Are you ready for me to make you forget the world?"

I was wet from his words and ready was the understatement of the year. "I'm always ready for you."

I opened a few buttons on his white shirt. I started kissing his bare chest, making my way down. I ran my tongue around his hard dark nipples. I knew he must've liked that when he closed his eyes and took a deep breath. He caressed my butt cheeks under my dress with both hands. He lifted my torso off the floor and laid me flush on top of him. I was sprawled flat on him like a prized cat. He gathered all my hair with one hand. I think he wanted a better view of my tongue teasing and playing with his erect nipples. He let go of my hair to place his fingers at my swollen lips. Louis was outlining them hungrily. I looked up at him from under my lashes and slowly parted my lips. He smiled at me and inserted his probing finger into my mouth. I closed my lips around his long, middle finger and drew it deep into my throat. Louis was watching me suck his finger in and out slowly.

"Baby, if you could see yourself. So fucking sexy. You're not even sucking my dick and I'm already done."

I was lying flush on top of him and could feel his erection build against my sex. He was working me with his other hand from the backside, dragging my wetness up toward my puckered hole. He unexpectedly and crudely pushed his wet thumb into that hole. I was sucking his finger and bit down from the unexpected invasion. He moaned from my reaction on his finger.

"I'm going to finger fuck you in both holes tonight," he said as he slipped his index finger inside my empty slit. He was simultaneously filling me at both holes. It should've felt wrong. I wanted to tell him to stop, but honestly, I couldn't. It felt too good. Louis was frantically moving his fingers in and out of both of my holes. I felt like a hand puppet in his masterful hands.

"Oh, baby, yeah, I knew you'd like that … don't even think

of telling me to stop ... I won't," he said with a strained voice. His hand was jerking me up and down the length of his erection. He was rubbing me into himself and grinding me hard against his cock. It was so desperate, so rough. He withdrew his finger from my mouth abruptly. He strained his neck toward me to give my lips a hard kiss before he put both his middle and index fingers into my mouth. "Suck," he said bluntly.

I was beyond turned on at his commanding tone. I was inflamed from his rough talk and his rough deeds. I was giving his fingers a thorough blowjob. His raunchy double holed finger job was driving me crazy. I felt the panic start to build and spread. I knew I was moments away from detonating. I needed the release. I was so close. Louis then stilled his fingers inside me.

"Don't stop, please," I cried out with my mouth still full of him.

"Baby, you begging me is so hot. Tell me what to do to make you explode on top of me."

"Louis, I'm so close. Please, just don't stop."

"I won't stop, I'll never stop. I'm going to make you come like you've never come before."

"Yes, don't stop ... please, harder, Louis. I need to come," I begged the puppet master.

"God, you're so tight everywhere. I don't think my dick will ever fit inside your ass." He pressed his submerged fingers even deeper. He was moving his hips up and down, pounding my clit with his hard rod. I could feel my climax begin to build again.

"Ohhhhhh," I started moaning with his fingers still rammed deep in my throat.

"I can't wait for your little pussy to feel my big dick. I'm going to fill every inch of you." He started thrusting his cock in upward motions. He removed his wet fingers from my mouth and added them to my already overfilled crotch. I was on sensory overload. I felt like I was high. I couldn't control my panting and screaming. I was yelling loud.

"That's right, fucking come, baby. Come hard. I can feel it; you're so close. Don't hold back, I want it all, every drop."

I was there. I was falling. I was his! "Louis ... yes ... Louis, I'm coming!"

He didn't stop; he kept driving his fingers hard into me. He pushed my orgasm on and on. I was still clenching around him while he rubbed his cock shamelessly against me. I was convulsing with him, gyrating my body on top of his cock. He was using me like a rag to polish his dick. When I started to reemerge, I heard him yell out my name.

"Emily, oh God, Em ... baby ... FUCCCCKKK!"

I then felt hot liquid spread between us. Louis was coming hard with his pants still on. He came all over himself and my dress. The realization that I just made this sex god come did wonderful things to my wounded ego. That night was also the first time Louis and I did laundry together.

I called Sara as soon as I got home that night. I couldn't tell her what had really happened at the club because I'd break down again, and deep down I kind of agreed with Phillip's assessment of me. I was going to give her a brief overview with our secret code, which required few words and even fewer explanations.

"I had sex with Jeff again," was the first thing Sara said to me as soon as she picked up the phone.

"What? Doesn't he have a girlfriend?"

"No, he doesn't have a girlfriend. He has a fiancée, silly. I was horny; he came by to hang out with Eddie. Eddie wasn't home; he was with Michelle ... blah, blah, blah ... bang ... bang ... bang ... everybody is happy."

She could make all the jokes she wanted; I knew she had feelings for Jeffery, the asshole. I just couldn't understand why she was selling herself short and fucking around with someone who obviously had no respect for her or the woman he was supposedly marrying.

"You happy, Sara?" She didn't need to answer that. It was a rhetorical question. We both knew there couldn't be anything resembling happiness after doing something so fucked up.

"Let's not rehash my affairs and let's discuss your evening with Mr. Too Good to Be True."

Sara still hadn't met Louis and I couldn't blame her for sometimes doubting his existence. All she knew of him came from our Internet research and the stories I'd been telling her.

"Sara, I had one crazy night. It started with 'Careless Whispers[28]' by Wham and ended with 'Nothing's Gonna Stop Us Now[29]' by Starship ... I'm not elaborating ... your turn."

"Well, my evening started with 'You Keep Me Hanging On[30]' by Kim Wilde morphing into AC/DC's 'You Shook Me All Night Long[31]' and now I'm at 'I Want To Know What Love Is[32]' by Foreigner ... I think I win the crazy night contest."

We were just silent, contemplating one another's emotions through song lyrics. I knew she was really hurting about Jeff and hiding behind jokes.

"I love you," I said to my slightly damaged and wounded best friend.

"I love you back ... goodnight."

After that night, thanks to what happened with Phillip, I never met the rest of *The Boys*. I think Louis didn't want to commingle his past life with me after that night. I was actually willing to give Phillip and the other guys I'd never met another chance. But Louis never gave any of them the opportunity to get within speaking distance of me.

We were having an early outdoor dinner a few nights after that dreadful evening at a restaurant on the Upper West Side when a man walked up to our table smiling at Louis as if he knew him. Louis straightened up, clasped his hands together, and looked up at the man approaching. Before the stranger had a chance to greet him, my livid boyfriend said, "Walk the fuck away." The man was struck speechless and did just that.

I asked him confused, "Louis, who was that? Do you know him? Why were you so rude to him?"

He retorted dismissively, "No one you need to know. I thought I knew him but I was wrong. Believe me, he deserves much worse than what I just said."

Many years later, I recognized the man in some pictures I found of Louis when we were packing boxes and moving his stuff. The pictures I found were of Louis with *The Boys* posing on a yacht. The stranger I almost met many moons ago at that restaurant on the Upper West Side was none other than Max, one of his friends. He told me a few times he wasn't proud of some of the things he'd done to, and with, women in his past. I got a feeling those friends of his played a big role in his promiscuous way of life B.E ... *Before Emily,* as Louis always referred to his life before we met. Louis started hanging out with my brother-in-law Mike more and more after that night. Jenna and Mike were always championing my relationship with Louis so it felt right to be around them.

After that regrettable night at the club, my boyfriend never made an effort to find another group of guys to hang out with again. When you have the kind of money that Louis Bruel has, good friends are hard to come by. Louis was running a huge firm and his free time he allocated only to me. I also wasn't a social butterfly; my only close friends were my sister Jenna and Sara. Even with Sara, I felt we were moving in two different directions. She was just starting to enjoy her life as an adult. She wanted to go out and meet people and be a normal college student. I'd already met the love of my life and only wanted to be with him. Louis was my air. I went from being a girl to becoming a woman in his arms. Being apart from him was not an option. I wanted to be there for Sara as a friend, and I tried but I was too invested in Louis Bruel to have much time for anyone but him. Looking back, maybe I shouldn't have let Louis dominate my whole life. But then again, how could you tell your body you can't have air when you need to breathe?

The pissing line starts here...

"**H**ow cool is it that the weather is perfect today?"

I bounced up and down in the car, giddy with excitement en route to Bruel Industries' annual picnic in Central Park. Jen and Mike had been at the park with all the vendors since six o'clock that morning. Every year, Louis apparently put together a summer outdoor party for all of his employees and their families. He also invited some of his business partners and top clients. That year, the party was huge. Louis' company had over sixty full-time employees plus their families, which equaled well over two hundred people.

Jenna and I had come up with the idea of a carnival theme for that year's shindig. They had rides, games, music, and street entertainers. There were stilt walkers, balloon sculptors, and caricature artists, just to name a few attractions. Food carts were catering to all palates from burgers to hotdogs to falafel and even my favorite, Chinese food. I couldn't wait to see it all and the weather was incredible. My parents were also coming to say hello a little later. Louis even encouraged me to invite my best friend, Sara, who had yet to meet him. I was looking forward to having them finally meet each other. Sara had asked me many of times if Louis Bruel was my imaginary boyfriend. It was hard to assure her because I still sometimes felt he was a hallucination.

I knew Louis would be busy once we got to the park as the host and the man in charge. He didn't look so intimidating that day. Once out of his suit and tie, he actually looked like a regular guy. He was still very much as beautiful and sexy as ever, but in his jeans and white t-shirt, he looked more approachable. Before we exited his car, he cupped my face and brought his lips in for a very passionate, slow kiss. I pulled away, reminding him that people were waiting for him.

"I'll miss you while I mingle out there. Come find me if you get bored."

He gave me another kiss, this time on the cheek, and went off to welcome his guests. I saw several very zealous women follow my boyfriend as soon as he left my side. That's what I got for dating Mr. Wonderful. I couldn't be upset with women's reactions to Louis or let it bother me. He never even looked in the direction of another female while we were together. I knew what I was getting into when I agreed to date "The" Louis Bruel. I didn't like the attention he got, but I loved the attention he gave to me.

I wanted to find Jenna and Mike to see if they needed any help with the event. I came as a guest that day but I knew how pressured my sister got during these events, especially one the size of that one. I found Sara instead, standing by the face painting station. I ran over to her, beyond excited to have her here with me. I didn't even notice Eddie standing right by her. I gave them both a group hug once I ambushed them. I was used to seeing Sara every day. Since I'd started dating Louis, we probably hadn't seen each other in close to three weeks. But we did speak at least every couple of days.

"Thank you for showing up. This is going to be so much fun. I can't believe we haven't hung out in so long ... you look so pretty today. Is this that new dress you ordered online?"

"My new dress is not important! Where is the horrible boyfriend who stole my best friend away? I wish he had a brother or some hot friend of the British variety for me!"

I loved this girl; it was as if we hadn't been apart for weeks. Sara and I could always pick up right from where we left off.

"Sorry, babe, definitely no brother, and awful friends. I wouldn't wish them on my worst enemy."

We were both laughing. I hadn't even noticed that Eddie had his arm around my shoulders. Innocent embraces between us were like second nature. Just like I wouldn't notice if Mike or my dad put their arm around me. There was zero sexual undercurrent in our relationship.

"Emma, you're coming to my birthday party next week. Right?"

I had no idea what Eddie was talking about. He shot a deadly look over to his sister.

"Don't tell me you didn't invite her? I asked you weeks ago to make sure Emma knows about the party."

"Relax, dude, I haven't seen her in weeks. She fell off the face of the earth after meeting Mr. Rich and Famous. I was going to invite her today."

Sara and Eddie were so cute; they reminded me of Jenna and I. They would always quarrel in public but they loved each other to pieces. Sara could've told me a thousand times about Eddie's party; it just wasn't a priority for her.

"Emma, please come to my party. It won't be my birthday without you. I need you there to—"

Before Eddie could finish his pleading birthday invitation, I saw Sara's face drop. I didn't have to turn around to know Louis was standing behind me. Mr. Rich and Famous should also go by the name of Mr. Drop Dead Gorgeous. Seeing him on the computer screen didn't hold a candle to seeing him live.

"Her name is Emily and she can't come to your party because she has plans with her boyfriend indefinitely."

The hairs on my neck stood up in fear. I'd heard him use that tone of voice before when things didn't work out the way he wanted them to at work. Why was he talking like that to Eddie? He pulled me away from Eddie's grip before kissing me hard on the lips. That kiss felt so forced I had to take a step back and look up at him. My eyes tried to assess what was going on inside that thick head of his. Eddie immediately flinched at the sight of Louis possessively manhandling me.

"Emma can speak for herself ... Mr. Bruel ... I gather," Eddie seethed, ready to pounce.

The air turned from hot to freezing in a matter of a nanosecond. Eddie calling me Emma must've rubbed Louis the wrong way. Eddie has been calling me Emma since I was three years old. I wasn't sure what this ego showdown between my boyfriend and my best friend's brother was all about.

"You can call me Louis. I'm not your boss ... yet!"

What had gotten into him? I had to jump in and diffuse this before it went from bad to sad.

"Louis, let me introduce you to my best friend, Sara Klein, and her brother, Edward Klein."

He finally tore his gaze from Eddie to look at my awestruck best friend. Sara was so cute. I fell in love with her every time I saw her. She looked so sweet and innocent but was the complete opposite. She had chin length, dark blond hair and elegant little pixie features. Her skin was über white and her long skinny limbs made her look fragile. Her personality, on the other hand, wasn't fragile at all. She'd tell you how it was whether you asked her to or not. That girl didn't have a shy bone in that skinny body of hers. She had been my very good friend ever since I could remember. Our moms had a picture of both of us sitting on the potty together when we were two years old, holding hands. So we've been dealing with each other's shit for a long time.

"Sara, I'm Louis, glad you could make it today. Emily talks about you all the time. I couldn't wait to finally meet my ... GIRLFRIEND's best friend," Louis said, emphasizing the word girlfriend as if he was talking to a bunch of second graders. He wanted to make sure Eddie didn't miss the sumo grip he had me in, either.

"Yeah well, you kidnapped her from me so I wanted to finally meet you, too," my vivacious, smart-mouthed partner-in-crime shot back to my still frothing-at-the-mouth boyfriend. We were both laughing a little, nervously aware of the awkward aura surrounding us. Louis was ignoring Eddie. He didn't even shake his hand. Eddie was such a great guy. Why did Louis feel so threatened by him? It was absurd. Louis Bruel was gorgeous, successful, and beyond wealthy. Why would my best friend's twenty-five-year-old brother be a problem for him? I'd actually thought that Louis and Eddie would hit it off.

"Louis, Eddie just graduated from law school. He'll be working in his dad's law firm. He's going away to Europe for two months, isn't that so cool?" I smiled lovingly at Eddie; I was very proud of him. I really did feel as if he was my older brother. We grew up together and our families have always vacationed and celebrated everything with one another. I wasn't happy about Louis treating him so callously.

My sister found us and gave Sara and Eddie a big hug before trying to grab Louis away from me. He needed to make a speech and thank all his colleagues and associates. He still had a death grip around my waist when he spoke quietly into my ear.

"Come with me, Em. I want you close by. Walk with me."

"Louis, why are you acting like a caveman? Go make your speech. You don't need me there. I'll be right here with my friends. I'll wave to you."

"I'm not leaving you with that guy you think is your brother. He wants you, and not in a brotherly way. Trust me! I can tell by how he was looking at you. He's totally in love with you, Em. Don't be naïve."

That was why he'd been acting like a jerk to Eddie. He thought someone other than him wanted me. Maybe he was the delusional one in our relationship and not me.

"Baby, I'm very flattered you think I'm so desirable. However, as adorable as you are when you're all jealous over me, I promise you Eddie is very much like a brother to me. The only man I want not in a brotherly way is you. If he looks at me with love, it's because he's known me since I was wearing diapers. You're the one with a harem of women at your beck and call. I could go all jealous bitch on you every time you leave my side and get swarmed by your female fans. It won't be pretty ... I promise. Go make your speech. I love you."

He smiled and kissed the top of my head before he went off with Jenna toward the podium where the band was still playing. I guess even beautiful millionaires have insecurities like the rest of us. I knew I had some explaining to do to Sara and Eddie who must've thought I was dating a madman.

"He's not used to having a girlfriend. He's usually very nice. Sorry, Eddie, that he went all green-eyed monster on you."

"No worries, Emma. If that ape makes you happy, knock yourself out. I'm not sure what women see in him, anyway."

Sara and I both laughed. Sara gave me a knowing look. Louis was one gorgeous ape. He was appealing on so many levels that Eddie's sarcastic comment was hysterical.

"I'll try talking Louis into coming with me to your birthday party. If we have plans I'll see if we can change them around," I promised Eddie before I bid them farewell on that beautiful day.

An hour later, I went to find my man before he realized he could have any woman he laid eyes on. I found Louis stuffing a hot dog into his mouth while laughing with Mike and my dad by his side. He seemed so domesticated. I let myself imagine what it would be like if he was really mine. I was eating him up with my eyes when he caught me staring. He gave me a raised eyebrow smirk that said it all. We hadn't yet fully consummated our love affair but our minds had been making love to one another countless times.

I walked over to all my favorite men, enjoying how easily they all fit in together. I walked over, kissed my dad on the cheek, and gave Mike a hug. Louis was just standing there waiting for his turn at my affection. I didn't want to be disrespectful in front of my dad so I just stood by Louis' side and slipped my hand in his. He looked down at me with so much love it gutted me. That soft knowing look would stay with me until the end of time. When our gazes locked, the whole world melted away.

"We're not making it all the way back to SoHo later. If I don't taste you soon my body will go into shock. Let's go visit The Plaza and rate their amenities," he whispered in my ear.

I couldn't wait to have him all to myself after that long day. I squeezed his hand and that was all the affirmation he needed.

Let there be peace...

My Louis and Eddie drama needed to stop. I arranged for all of us to have lunch before Eddie's birthday party, which was a few days away. I wasn't going to let Louis talk me out of attending a good friend's party. I also had no desire to go to a party without my boyfriend. I wanted Louis to get along with Eddie. There was no reason for them not to be at least civil, if not friendly, toward one another. I did everything I could to make sure Louis was in a good mood before our rendezvous that afternoon.

It was summertime and Louis assured me it was perfectly normal for him to go into work every day in the late afternoon, since it was slow for them during the summer months. He was really spending every second of his free time with me. I loved that he came to pick me up every morning and we'd have breakfast together. That day he brought us back to his house for croissants and coffee. We had breakfast on the glass-enclosed balcony on the fourth floor off the kitchen. It was like our very own mini greenhouse on that balcony overlooking SoHo.

"What do you have planned for us for today ... boyfriend?" Louis loved it when I called him *boyfriend* out loud. We were sitting across from each other admiring the view. He grabbed my foot under the table and placed it in his lap. He removed my flip-flops and started expertly massaging my feet.

"I was thinking we could fly over to Rhode Island for lunch and relax on the beach. I can have you back home before midnight."

"We can't leave the city. I made us reservations at I Tre Merli for lunch with Eddie and Michelle. Did you conveniently forget?"

"Baby, I don't forget anything. Let's not go and fly over to Rhode Island instead. Call him and tell him something came up," he said with a mischievous smile, placing my foot against his straining, growing erection. I was not going to let him sidetrack my plans with his seductive innuendos.

"How about we go to Rhode Island another day, and today, instead of going to the beach, we take a relaxing bath together before lunch. Doesn't that sound nice?"

"Nice? You and me naked in water is going to be way better than nice and definitely not relaxing. I'll have to do all kinds of meditation techniques to restrain my dick from attacking your wet pussy."

"Lead the way; I'm ready for a not-so-nice tense bath with my sexy Zen boyfriend."

We were both in a great mood heading to the sixth floor master bath. Louis' bathroom was just as sexy as the man himself. The room was huge with a cylindrical glass shower that could easily hold ten people in its center. My favorite part was the sunken bathtub by the window with a fountain like faucet cascading from the ceiling. Every inch of the room was covered in black granite slabs with little reflective blue specks. Louis once told me the granite was called blue eyes and every time he went to the bathroom, he thought of me and my eyes.

I told him I wasn't sure how I felt about him thinking of me while he's taking care of business. He assured me that the only business the thought of me helped him take care of was some much needed relief for his underworked penis. He described to me how he woke up with *morning wood* from dirty dreams of me, and that he stood in the shower imagining me staring back at him and very quickly, the business of dick relief took care of itself.

"I'll fill the tub ... you strip. I'm washing your hair today. I've never done that to anyone before and the thought of washing your hair, little girl, is very intriguing to me. I have this unexplained need to tend to you."

"I want to wash your hair, too ... I once read that cutting a man's hair will ensure he's yours forever. So I may give you a haircut after I wash your hair."

"You want me to be yours forever, baby?"

"Forever to infinity. I will never want anyone else. You have become my whole life in such a short time that I don't even remember my life without you. That scares me, Louis."

"Emily, I'm never going to leave you. You have me. Until I met you last month, I wasn't really living my life ... I was just existing. You are my life now. I can't wait for us to be together all the time."

"Louis, thank you for saying such nice things to me. But the truth is we've spent every day together since we first met. We haven't been apart for more than twelve hours. I'm sure I'll get old for you soon."

"I don't even want us to be apart for twelve hours if I can help it." He kissed me softly and pulled my yellow knit dress over my head. I was just wearing underwear; the dress had built-in bra cups. He got on his knees in front of me and started sucking at my aching nipples one at a time. He was twirling his tongue around and around and then flicking it at my sensitive buds. Watching Louis latch on and suck my boobs was hot. He had his eyes closed and I ran my fingers through his thick, wavy hair. He looked up at me with those incredible soul-piercing eyes and said, "I love you ... but I have a special kind of love for these tits."

I smiled while enjoying those words washing over me, and

wishing I could give myself to him. Not just with my words but wholly with my body. It was getting harder and harder to abstain from sex with Mr. Drop Dead Beautiful every day. Louis lowered his head farther down to suck my belly ring. He removed my underwear and got up to undress himself. We were both naked and about to get into the overfilled tub when Louis walked away from me to go lay down naked on the plush gray rug by the tub.

"Come here. I want you to sit on my face and let me taste you before we get into the tub."

I was a little shocked at his bluntness. He was usually very gentle with me, but when Louis used his no nonsense, command voice it really was a major turn on. He really didn't need to say anything to turn me on; just a glance at him was enough to send me for a change of underwear. But him describing what he wanted to do to me or telling me what to do to him was enthralling.

"Em, stop looking at me like that. I'm not going to be ashamed at how much I want and need you. That pussy is mine and I want to feast on it ... NOW!"

I walked over to where he was sprawled out and got on my knees next to him. I placed each knee at the side of his head and lowered myself shamelessly on his face.

"Come on, baby, don't be shy with me. I want you riding my face with that sweet pussy. Sit all the way down. I want to suffocate my senses with all of you."

I was excited and couldn't wait to be sucked, bitten, and probed by the most beautiful man in the world. I still couldn't believe he found me as attractive as I found him. He urged me farther down onto his mouth and started tongue fucking me with no mercy. In, out, in, out. He was moving his tongue so fast you'd think he was battery operated. He would occasionally lift me up a little off his lips to blow air across my over sensitized slit. I couldn't just sit there; I had to taste him too. My mouth was salivating just looking at his massive erection. I needed to be filled somewhere by him.

"Louis, can I suck your dick?"

"Ohhhhhh ... baby, you can do whatever you want to my dick. You're the boss; it's your dick. It only works for you."

I lowered my body to ingest Louis' cock. The angle I was in helped his long, hard dick fit into my mouth and down my throat perfectly. As soon as I encompassed his girth with my wet lips, he let out a cry that rippled through my depths. I closed my lips and hollowed my cheeks around his shaft. I opened my eyes to catch a glimpse of our reflection through the shower glass door. The site was hard-core X-rated. Me straddling his face with my ass swaying up and down in the air, and stretched out over his hard body while sucking his cock. Seeing Louis pumping himself into my hungry mouth and kneading my swinging breasts was the most visual sexual feast my eyes had ever seen. I started coming as soon as I saw our pornographic, vulgar image. Louis followed shortly after, ejaculating all over my mouth. I was covered in his semen and lying flat on his stomach, still arranged in the infamous 69 position.

"Em ... baby ... if you don't get off my face I'll start eating you out again. Your scent after you come should be bottled. Let's get into that tub before the water overflows."

"Mmmmm..."

"Em, I gave you fair warning."

Louis started flickering his tongue at my exposed entrance. I needed to find the strength to get off him. I couldn't handle another orgasm from this fiend. My legs were already shaking. I reluctantly rose a bit and crawled on all fours toward the tub. The sunken stone tub was already filled to the brim. I slowly submerged myself completely, head included, into the hot water. Louis got into the tub and sat facing me, sighing contently at the feel of the hot water lapping all around him. I came up for air and moved toward him for a kiss. I arranged myself on top of him and placed my head on his chest before closing my eyes. I wanted to enjoy and feel this moment. This man under me had to be my other half. There was no way anyone else on the planet could make me feel this way. I don't remember any hair washing that morning.

After spending another hour in the bathtub and Louis bringing me to another screaming orgasm, I was content I'd done all I could to ensure he was in a good mood. After the things I let him do to me, I couldn't imagine him having any insecurities about my feelings toward him.

I was excited for Louis to meet Eddie's long time, on-again off-again girlfriend from law school. Eddie and Michelle walked into I Tre Merli restaurant in SoHo a few minutes after Louis and I were seated. I waved them over to our table.

Eddie really was a very attractive man. I don't remember ever thinking he was a man until that moment. He was close to six feet, lean, with jet-black, short hair. He had that preppy look going for him. I could definitely see his appeal. He just wasn't my type; he wasn't Louis Bruel. I saw his warm, pale blue eyes take in the sight of Louis sitting beside me and become instantly cold.

"Hello, my beautiful Emma ... you remember Michelle?" Eddie said, just to get a reaction out of Louis. I never knew how catty men could be.

"Michelle, it's nice to see you again. Let me introduce you to my boyfriend, Louis. Eddie, you and Louis already know each other."

Louis extended his hand to Michelle and gave Eddie a raised eyebrow greeting. The *my beautiful Emma* comment didn't go unnoticed by my possessive beau. Michelle was very sexy in her own way. She was about the same height as Eddie with a toned, lean body. Eddie once told us she swam every morning. Her black, wavy hair was long and she wore it loose. Her feline shaped, dark green eyes gave her a very exotic look. She and Eddie made a striking couple. Michelle was holding on to Louis' hand and looking into his eyes waiting for acknowledgment from the demigod. I guess every woman unanimously agreed on the appeal of Mr. Louis Bruel. Louis finally landed on Michelle's face and nodded his hello. He let go of her hand, pulled me close to him, and almost urged me to sit on his lap rather than the chair I was occupying. He was trying to position me between Michelle and him, away from Eddie.

"This place makes great pizzas and the best penne alla vodka. Louis and I eat here at least twice a week."

I wanted this lunch to flow smoothly and be fun for all parties. My boyfriend clearly wasn't enjoying himself. He had a serious constipated look going on that even started to make me feel uncomfortable. I needed to make him understand that there was zero sexual chemistry between Eddie and myself.

"Eddie, do you remember when Sara and I were twelve years old and you were like nineteen? Our parents took us on that fancy European cruise to Italy where you and Michelle first met. Sara and I kept trying to sneak up on the two of you making out. You threatened to throw us overboard and we believed you and cried. Wasn't that when the two of you decided to go to law school together after college?"

"Yeah, that was when I fell for Michelle. I can't believe it was that long ago—over six years. I remember it like it was yesterday. I've been trying to make this stubborn girl mine practically my whole adult life. I told our parents on that trip that I fell in love with a girl and our mothers were destroyed. Our parents always thought Jenna and I would end up together but we couldn't stand each other. Adele kept asking me to tutor Jen with the hopes of sparking our romance. I mean, don't get me wrong, Jenna is gorgeous but I couldn't imagine dating a Marcus girl. That's borderline incest. The two of you were like extra annoying sisters I never wanted. I wished you had a brother so at least I would have had someone without PMS to hang out with during our holiday vacations."

We were all cracking up, including my now less constipated looking boyfriend. Michelle and Eddie shared a sweet kiss after that cute story. I hoped that maybe Louis would finally drop the *everybody wants to fuck you* bit and actually get to know Eddie. I didn't think Eddie would fuck me if I were the last female on earth.

"Louis, why don't you tell Eddie about the hotel you're building in Chelsea."

"Em, I'm sure Eddie isn't interested in my business."

Eddie looked up at Louis and passed him the hypothetical olive branch. "Louis, I'd like to hear about that hotel. Chelsea is an up and coming area. My dad's law firm has been doing lots of real estate business there lately. I've recently heard him talking about closing on a few condo sales in that area."

"Eddie, I actually know your dad well. Robert Klein was the buyer's attorney for the last two apartments my company sold. We are currently in the process of creating a new legal department within Bruel Industries to handle our growing business at Chelsea. Besides the hotel, we're also breaking ground on a new residential one-hundred-unit condominium building. Your dad and Em keep raving about how good you are; so if you're as good as they say, perhaps you should send over your CV and come work for me, if that sounds like something you'd like to pursue."

"Yeah, man, that's definitely something for me to think about. Thank you for the opportunity. So we're cool? I hope to see you both at my party this weekend, right?"

"Yes, Eddie, we're cool. I may have overreacted last weekend. I tend to get very possessive with the things I love. I may have channeled my macho emotions on the wrong person. I can't wait to do some dancing with my girl."

Hallelujah … I thought I diffused that situation nicely if I do say so myself. Louis and Eddie could be friends or even work together. That lunch went better than expected. I would definitely be attending Eddie's birthday party after all. Go me.

Louis Bruel meet my friend Pinky...

That weekend we were heading to Cheetah Club in midtown to celebrate Eddie's twenty-sixth birthday and graduation from law school. Eddie didn't know yet, but that night, Louis was going to offer him the position of a lifetime with Bruel Industries. Louis showed up early to pick me up. My parents were out of town at a medical convention for the whole weekend. It was just me at home when I answered the door. He was a good hour early; I'd just gotten out of the shower and wasn't dressed yet. I was wearing my black silk robe and nothing else. Louis looked delicious, as always. He was wearing black jeans with a black V-neck t-shirt and a gray blazer.

"Are we alone?"

"Well, hello to you, too," I said mockingly.

We hadn't seen each other all day. He had important meetings that he couldn't delegate to someone else to attend in his place. I had plans, too; I was helping Jenna and Mike set up for a posh baby shower on the West Side. I knew why he was early–Louis needed a private dose of me before we went out in public. He seemed a little on edge and was looking around to make sure it was just the two of us before he pushed me to the entrance floor.

"I need you to do something to me ... maybe you could ride

me. I haven't come since Thursday night and I'm about to explode. I'll be in my boxers; I just need to feel your naked body on top of me."

"How could I say no to such a romantic request? Come on, it's time for you to see where I do most of my Louis dreaming."

He followed me up the stairs like an obedient puppy. We got to my room and I locked my door just in case someone unexpected decided to show up. I had a pretty good idea how we would be spending the next hour, and it wasn't appropriate for an audience.

"Emily, how did you manage to enslave an almost thirty-year-old, grown man, self-sufficient in all aspects who up until four weeks ago, never had to ask a woman for anything? I will do anything you tell me. I will take whatever scraps you offer me and I've never been happier in my entire life."

"Louis, I don't know. I ask myself that every minute—"

"Shhhh ... Em, this is not about me telling you I don't think you're good enough for me. This is about me telling you that you have me completely enchanted. I am yours. I never want to stop being under your spell. I've never been happier just to have a woman agree to dry-rub me. Even if you only let me hold your hand, I'll take it."

"I'm yours, Louis. You have this all wrong. If you want my body, I'll give it to you. I love you. I will do anything for you."

If he'd asked me to sleep with him right then and there and take my virginity, I would have gladly given it to him. But I knew he loved me too much to ask or push this topic. I loved him wholeheartedly, but I wasn't ready to have sex with him, yet, and he knew it. I was still worried that he would wake up from my bewitchment and— abracadabra—all this between us would go away. That Louis might finally realize he didn't need me in his life. That he had willing, beautiful participants for sex lining up by the busloads. If that day came, I would still have a part of me that I didn't give to him. I would know that he didn't take with him all of me: heart, body, and soul. My chastity wasn't so much of a physical entity, but more of a spiritual virtue I was holding on to.

"I want you to feel secure enough in our relationship and my love for you to want to make love to me. I don't want us having sex because you think I need it. All I need is you close to me."

I walked over and backed him into a chair. He looked like a giant sitting on a baby chair. Come to think of it, Louis in my room looked out of sorts and funny. He was too much for such a feminine, small space. He was watching me intently. I hadn't realized until that moment that the ball really was in my court. I was the puppet master for once. That feeling was empowering. I untied my robe, dropping it to the floor. His pupils dilated and his caramel colored eyes turned black. He ran his hand through his hair. I could sense his need to touch me. I took both his hands and brazenly placed them on my aching breasts. He smiled, exposing that delicious dimple and started to take over. His long fingers spread and squeezed my tits hard. It was almost too painful. He pulled me closer and sucked on one nipple while pinching the other. He quickly got up to remove his blazer, shoes, t-shirt, and unzip his jeans. He sat back down only in his boxers.

He turned me around, away from him, and then pulled me down to sit on him. I could feel how hard I made him. I started rocking back and forth on his lap. We both needed the sexual relief we offered one another. He was cupping and kneading both my breasts. There was a silent rhythm we both moved to. I wanted to be so much closer to him. To think that only six weeks ago, I'd had my first orgasm and now I couldn't survive without at least a few of them a day.

I brought my hand behind me and reached into his boxers to free the beast. I positioned his cock between my legs and squeezed both thighs and started to milk him. I was already leaking wet and my juices were lubricating his long shaft lodged between my legs. He was so quiet. I turned my head to see what kind of expression he had on his beautiful face. His eyes were downcast and I could see him watching his dick rub against my butt cheeks and disappear towards my sex. I felt the need and the yearning in his silence. I just couldn't give him all of me, yet.

"Where should I come? I'm almost there."

"Come anywhere you want. Should I suck your dick? Are you asking me because you want me to swallow your cum?"

I didn't get a response. He pushed me off him briskly, lowering me to the floor on all fours. He ejaculated all over my back.

"Shit, baby, I'm sorry. I'll clean you up."

Sorry? There was nothing for him to be sorry about. Knowing that I could make him lose control in a matter of minutes was a very potent aphrodisiac. He ran to my bathroom and came back with tissues and a small wet towel. He cleaned his cum off my back and picked me up off the carpet and carried me to my bed.

"Now we need to take care of you … how do you want me to make you come?"

I had an idea; I just hoped he wouldn't be against it or think less of me.

"I bought a vibrator a month ago. Will you use it on me to make me orgasm?"

What would he think if I told him that he was the reason I went with Sara to buy the stupid thing?

"Did I tell you that every time you open your mouth to speak I want to fuck you for the rest of my life?"

"You've mentioned that a few times … should I stop talking until we're ready to start fucking?"

"Yes, stop talking and go get your vibrator. I want to see what I'm up against."

We were laughing. I ran into my closet and took my pink, silicone dildo out of an inconspicuous shoebox. The vibrator was about half the size of Louis' cock now that I looked at it in my hands. When he saw my battery-operated companion, he almost fell off the bed laughing. It was kind of hysterical having my real boyfriend meet my rubber boyfriend.

"Louis Bruel, I'd like you to meet my friend, Pinky."

He took the toy out of my hands and placed it against his semi-erect penis. It was much thinner and smaller than his. I'd bought it a few days after I had my first orgasm. It was after that night I first saw him. The night he didn't say a single word to me and left. I needed that vibrator to get me through my Louis Bruel obsession. When I saw it in the store, it looked huge. Sara called it a good start. Now, looking at it compared to the real thing, it was comical.

"Pinky, it's a pleasure to meet you. Thanks for making me look good ... your days are numbered. Once our girl over here gets a taste of the real thing ... you'll be history, my friend. Enjoy her while you can."

Louis Bruel, having a serious conversation with Pinky the pink vibrator was priceless. He powered up Pinky and proceeded to take care of me. I lay back on my queen-sized bed surrounded by pillows. He spread my legs out and started teasing the oscillating tool between my folds. He was spreading my moisture all over the pink dick. The act was so sensuous.

"Are you dripping for me or Pinky?"

"I bought that thing so I could pretend it was you ... oh ... and now here you are in my room using it on me. Louis this is so much better than any fantasy. I'm wet for you 24/7."

"What did we say about you talking? I'm hanging on by a very thin thread around you, little girl. Have some mercy on me and stop talking."

The more he spoke, the more aroused I got, too. He still hadn't penetrated me with the vibrator. He was just leisurely teasing me. Louis was on his side, facing me with his arm bent and head resting in his hand. He lowered his lips to mine to absorb my whimpering moans. Those full lips and that talented tongue engulfed my whole mouth. I forgot all about the sex toy he was using on me and closed my eyes, succumbing to our deep, passionate kiss. The fake dick was definitely smaller than Louis' cock but longer and wider than his finger. He unexpectedly inserted the artificial penis all the way inside me, in one, crude thrust. I opened my eyes in shock. He was watching me to see my response to his vulgar manipulation with a huge smile. The vibrator was fully lodged inside my sex. It was vibrating at a persistent speed. I had never actually inserted it all the way. It felt so deep. Louis lowered his head to make sure my clit wasn't feeling left out. He was flirtatiously poking his tongue lightly at my peak.

"I think I just lost my virginity to Pinky."

"No way, baby. When you have me inside you, you'll know who your virginity belongs to."

"Oh yeah, that feels so good. I'm close … I can feel it … don't stop…"

"Don't come! When I start sucking your clit then I give you permission to let go…"

"Louis, I can't hold it, I want to come."

What did he think I was, a trained porn star? I can't come on command or not come on command for that matter.

"Not yet, it will feel even better if you don't let your body climax … I promise."

He was licking at my clit. I was waiting for him to suck it like he promised. I needed to come more than I needed to breathe. I could feel the flush and the tremor start to spread over my body. He pulled the dildo all the way out and then he aligned it back at my entrance and started pumping it in and out of me as if he was screwing me. Every time he pulled it out, I thought I would come. But my mind was obedient to its master. I was holding on and not coming like a good little girl. He placed the round base of the vibrator in his mouth, holding it between his teeth, and continued to plunge it in and out of me, touching his lips to my slit with every thrust. He brought his hand up to my mouth. He let go of his mouth around Pinky while it pounded inside me. He needed to give me orders to make sure I knew who the boss was.

"Suck my fingers and then spit. I need them wet."

I would do anything he asked of me as long as he would let me have some relief. I licked his index and middle finger and then closed my mouth over them, sucking them in. He withdrew and I slowly spit on them as instructed. He gave me a sexy mischievous smile. He moved his wet, saliva covered fingers from my lips down to my butt. He rubbed my spit over my puckered hole and started to slowly insert his index finger.

"Oh yeah ... baby, relax and just enjoy what I'm doing. Don't think about anything except how good I make you feel. This will feel so good, baby. Don't fight it; just breathe into it. I want you to come harder than you ever have in your life."

I don't know how deep he got that finger in my rear canal. He was trying to distract me by telling me what to do to myself.

"I'm out of hands Em. Squeeze those beautiful tits the way I would."

I was concentrating hard on not coming. It was the hardest thing I ever had to do. I had the vibrator pulsating inside me. I had Louis' finger halfway up my ass. I was rubbing my nipples and then he closed his lips around my clitoris and sucked. My brain got the green light and sent a signal to my body to start exploding into a violent orgasm. One spasm turned into another and then a few moments later, I was climaxing again. Rapture is the only word that I could use to explain how I was feeling. During the whole raunchy scene, my boyfriend kept pumping and sucking me vigilantly. I thought Louis Bruel needed to do this professionally if real estate didn't work out for him. That was the orgasm that we have been trying to replicate for the past ten years. Still trying...

I promise you...

We needed to leave and pick up Sara for the party. We were already half an hour late. As far as I knew, Louis only had one car: his two-seater red Ferrari. When I told him that we would need to give Sara a ride to Eddie's party earlier that week, he apparently got another car for the occasion. Not just any car, he got the sexiest car I'd ever seen. When I came out of my house and saw this black beast waiting at the curb, I almost had another orgasm. I'm not into cars at all; I didn't even know what kind of car it was. All I knew was that it was the equivalent of sex on wheels. If Louis Bruel were a car, this would be it. Dark and dangerous and oozing sex appeal. I was shocked at how much I loved the look and attitude of this car. I was hoping Louis didn't just buy this car, but rented or borrowed it for the night. I should've known better.

"Did you get this car because I asked you to drive my friend tonight?" He just shook his head. "Louis, we could've just taken a taxi."

"I don't take taxis and neither will you. Do you like it?"

"Like it ... I love it. It's so sexy. The black and the red interior make such a hot combination. What kind of car is this?" I asked as I ran my finger along the smooth curvature of the car. He was so excited that I liked his choice of transportation.

"This is a Maserati Gran Turismo. It won't be available for sale anywhere for another three years. This is one of four demos. Only Italians know how to make sexy cars. I bought it ... for you."

I stopped breathing at his words and looked away from the car and towards his grinning face.

"What do you mean you bought it for me? You ... you bought it so you can have a car with more room for someone else to sit. Right?"

He was enjoying driving me crazy. I could tell by the fact that his dimple stayed plastered on his face while I tried to deal with his outlandish gesture.

"No, baby, I have a car. I don't need anyone but you and me to fit in my car. This is your car."

"Are you crazy, Louis? I don't need a car. I can't even drive."

"I know. Once I teach you how to drive you can drive your own car if I'm not around to drive you."

This man was certifiably crazy. Who buys a woman a car after four weeks? A woman he hasn't even slept with. Louis Bruel apparently lived by a different set of rules than the rest of us. Most girls get flowers and chocolate as gifts; I got a sexy Italian sports car.

As soon as Sara saw my face when we pulled up to her house, she started shaking her head at me. "Hello, children, it's nice of you to remember to pick me up."

Louis and I shared a conspiratorial look. If she only knew why we were so late she'd be so proud of me.

"Nice car," Sara said to Louis as she climbed into the back seat. Louis gave me a raised eyebrow look.

"Aren't you going to thank your friend for complimenting your new car, baby?"

I gave him the hairy eyeball. I did not need to start explaining to Sara that my crazy boyfriend just gave me a car.

"Wow ... nice, Emily. Only you freaking get a car before you can even drive."

My stupid friend was enjoying torturing me, too. I should've also mentioned that I got myself a sex god before I was ready to have sex, so what else was new? She continued to harass me by adding during our ride, "Emily, do you know which song I hope they play tonight?"

Oh fuck, I'm not playing this game with Sara. I'm not going to bait her. I don't care which song they play tonight. Louis, however, wasn't privy to my plan of ignoring Sara's heckling. He took the bait.

"Sara, tell me which song you'd like to hear. I'll make sure the DJ plays it."

"It's an old song by The Police called 'Wrapped Around Your Finger[33]' ... I love it; I can't stop singing it in my head."

The bitch will pay.

We got to the club and made our way to find Eddie and his friends, already two sheets to the wind. I'm not a club rat. After my last experience with Louis in a club, I was feeling a little tense. This place was packed with people. I saw Sara already talking to a guy by the bar and Jeff was watching her while holding his fiancée's hand. Michelle and Eddie were dancing by the table.

Louis pulled me close to him and whispered in my ear, "Half hour we stay to be nice and then let's go back to your room. Pinky and I would like an encore with our leading lady."

I looked up at him already wet just from his words. I was thinking *yes, please,* but I had to cool down to make it through the next thirty minutes.

"Let's dance a little. I need to see if you got the moves,

Pip."

Without another word, he pulled me up, forcing me to wrap my arms around his neck and my tight jean-clad legs around his waist. He pushed us through the sea of people to the middle of the compact dance floor. Louis pulled me a little lower so I was aligned with his lips. He kissed me slowly and gently at first until I opened my mouth to welcome his tongue. It was just us again. He made everything and everyone just disappear. There was no music, no people, just Louis and Emily. Louis was swaying us to his own tune. We were still passionately kissing as we moved from side to side. I felt like Baby dancing with Johnny for the first time in *Dirty Dancing*[34]. I still had no idea what song Louis had us moving to in his head. I cut our kiss short and pulled away breathlessly. I begged into his ear, "Sing to me. I want to know what song is playing in your head."

He pushed my head closer to his lips and started singing the most beautiful song in the deepest, most erotic voice that sliced right through me and found my heart. The music in the club was deafening, and yet, I remember being able to clearly hear every single word he sang. He was serenading me with his mouth to my neck how I never needed to doubt or look for anyone but him, that he promised to always be there for me. He nibbled my ear lightly before he continued crooning into the space below my jaw that he promised to make me fall for him. Silly man; didn't he know how far I had already fallen? My world had officially stopped spinning with each word coming out of his mouth. "The Promise[35]" by When in Rome was the anthem to my existence. How was I supposed to not make love to this man immediately?

"How did you know about this song?" I asked, somehow knowing the answer already. He looked into my eyes, giving my lips another taste.

He pulled away to whisper in my ear over the loud music. "I made a new friend. Her name is Sara Klein."

That little slut! I knew it. Should I kiss her or kill her?

139

"Take me home ... I'm ready to leave."

Only God knows how we managed to not sleep together that night. Louis didn't even sleep in my bed while my parents were gone. He kept telling me our first time sleeping in the same bed and waking up together would be epic. He didn't want it to be a ruse.

I wish I was sixteen...

"**I**'m so nervous, I changed my mind; I don't want to meet your mom. What did you tell her about me anyway?"

"I told her you have the most delicious tits and the sweetest little pussy I've ever tasted," he said, grinning from ear to ear.

"You proud of yourself? You think this is funny? I'm hyperventilating as it is Louis, stop joking around."

"Em, my mom can't wait to finally meet you. She asks about you when she calls every fucking day. She's been begging me to bring you over to meet her."

I smiled but then got nervous again and asked, "Has she met any of your other girlfriends? How would she think I compare to any of them? Do you think she'll also think I'm with you because you're loaded? Do you think your girlfriends dated you because of your money? God, Louis, I'm so nervous."

We were pulling into a driveway of a non-descript house. I'd imagined Louis growing up in an affluent Connecticut neighborhood. All the houses on this street kind of looked the same. They were all ranch style, dark colored brick homes with green-shingled roofs and wrap around porches. The house we pulled up to had a huge grass covered front lawn. I was drinking in the scenery trying to picture my boyfriend growing up in such a humble dwelling.

"My mom met one of the girls I used to date back when I was in grad school. I didn't have what I have now so I can't tell you if she was with me because of the money. I can tell you that my mom knew I wasn't serious about that girl," Louis told me while we pulled into the driveway.

"She was probably with you because you're hot. If you had money on top of that she'd never let you go," I said playfully.

"You don't compare to her. You don't compare to any of them. It was always about sex for me with women before you, Em. After a while, I couldn't understand why it was never enough, even when the women were gorgeous. With you, it's still very physical, but I also want to be a part of everything you do and I want you to be part of my whole world."

He was now completely turned toward me and while holding both my hands, he continued, "I wake up every night thinking you're right there with me, and when reality hits, I try to go back to sleep as quickly as possible to make the night go by faster so I can see those incredible eyes again. Emily, you erase all the rest. You're my life and you have my heart. So how could you possibly compare?"

He leaned over to kiss me when a loud knock on the car window made us both jump. I looked up to see his mother smiling in at us. I probably turned multiple shades of red. Louis came out of his car and gave his mother a huge bear hug. The way he was lovingly interacting with his mother made me remember what my nana always told me about boys: *You know a boy will treat you right if he loves his mother and treats her well.* My nana knew her stuff. I didn't wait for Louis to come get me out of the car. I got out, quickly adjusted myself after our two-hour commute, and walked around to meet the most important woman in Louis' life.

"Emily, it's so wonderful to finally get to meet you. My baby boy has been talking and raving about you nonstop. I couldn't wait to finally meet the love of his life."

Oh my God, no pressure, I thought, still feeling my blush spread like wildfire. Louis' mom came in closer to give me a hug, to which she then added a kiss. *Wow,* she was so nice. She reminded me of Louis, especially when she smiled; she had dimples on both cheeks. They had the same skin tone. She was small compared to her giant son. Louis' mother was sweet with kind hazel eyes that had a slight downward crinkle. She looked like a free spirited artist with dark hair falling down loosely to her mid-back. She was a beautiful woman now and I'm sure in her youth she was stunning.

"It's a pleasure to meet you, too. I was very excited when Louis mentioned we would be making the trip to come see you," I tried to sound mature and smart. I didn't want her to think I didn't deserve to have her son's love.

"My baby boy was right; your eyes are special, they're the most incredible thing I've ever seen ... that color is mesmerizing, sweetie."

It was one thing for Louis to be saying things like that to me, but to hear his mother give me a compliment felt overwhelming. I was melting and blushing simultaneously.

"Thank you, Mrs. Bruel."

"Oh, no ... oh, honey, never call me that—just Elizabeth or Liz. I've never been Mrs. Bruel; that's Louis' dad's last name and we never married. Eric and I could only take each other in small doses. But when Louis was born and his dad took one look at his beautiful baby boy, he decided he couldn't live his life more than a few feet away."

I felt like a total idiot, I should've been asking Louis questions about his family and not his ex-lovers. "I'm very sorry, Elizabeth," I said, feeling more awkward than humanly possible.

"Don't be silly, my baby boy must be too mesmerized by those lovely eyes of yours to brief you on his strange family antics."

She led us inside. Louis took my clammy hand and started

kissing the back of it in the hopes of calming my nerves down.

"Relax, she loves you. Who wouldn't?" he whispered in my direction.

I could name a few people who didn't love me, one being his stupid friends and two, the entire female population of Manhattan.

The afternoon spent with Louis' mother was sweet. I really had nothing to worry about. Elizabeth didn't have a judgmental bone in her body. After seeing his mother and some of his family pictures, I gathered that Louis actually had more of his father's features. I saw pictures of Louis as a baby that melted my heart. He looked like a sweet boy, not at all the heartbreaker millionaire the world must've seen. Louis caught me studying a picture of him and his dad placed prominently on the fireplace.

"I'm sure you would've liked him. I wish he were alive to meet you and see how happy you make me. If he knew I found a woman like you, he would've been really proud of me."

"I wish I knew him too. Both you and your mother only have nice things to say about him. So I can't imagine him not being wonderful. You look a lot like him."

Elizabeth walked into the living room announcing that lunch was ready and on the patio. We followed her outside, helping her carry a few more trays of food and a pitcher of fresh lemonade.

Half way through our delicious lunch, Louis' mobile phone rang and he excused himself from the table. I was left at the table with his mom when she laid her hand on mine.

"I haven't seen my boy this happy in a long time, Emily. After Eric passed away, Louis was completely focused on finishing school and starting up his business. It was his way of trying to make his father proud of him for the way he took care of his dad's legacy. I always asked him why he never tried finding a nice girl to share his life with. He told me on many occasions to not get my hopes up on him ever settling down and having his own family. I always worried that my unconventional relationship with Eric gave Louis a distorted view of love and marriage. Eric and I loved each other terribly; we just couldn't integrate our love for one another into a traditional family life. I never loved anyone after I fell in love with Eric, and him moving across the street only confirmed to me he felt the same. In a way, I guess that was our way of professing our love and committing our lives to each other. I'm so happy he found someone wonderful like you to love."

I listened to Elizabeth's candid heart to heart, understanding and acknowledging another layer of Louis' life.

Elizabeth continued, "When I look at the two of you, I don't feel like a failure. Emily, you give me hope that my baby boy and you will perhaps make the family Eric and I couldn't."

"I love Louis very much, Elizabeth. You should be very proud and know that you and Eric are responsible for all of Louis' many accomplishments. Judging by everything Louis told me, you and Eric were great parents; he adores you both." I sighed and continued, "I hope very much for us to one day have a family together."

She gave me a hug and a kiss on the cheek and said, "Thank you, dear. I know you'll take good care of him for me."

We were still embracing and nodding at each other, wiping our tears away when Louis returned, looking at us a little confused.

"What did I miss? This looks very deep."

"You didn't miss anything, my dear boy, and to answer your earlier question. I say yes, without the shadow of a doubt," Elizabeth said to Louis, getting up and hugging him lovingly.

After we finished clearing away our dishes from lunch, I asked to him jokingly, "Louis, can you show me your room? I'd like to see where my inamorato grew up."

"Little girl, do you want to take advantage of me in my own room? Have you no shame?" he asked mockingly before biting my earlobe.

"Definitely no hanky-panky while your mother is here," I answered, swatting him across his arm with a kitchen towel. He raised one eyebrow and smiled mischievously.

"Watch this," he said, walking over and opening the top freezer door of the refrigerator.

"Mom, I can't find my favorite ice cream. Emily really wanted some too."

My mouth dropped open. His mother came running into the kitchen inspecting the freezer contents.

"Louis, why don't you keep Emily entertained while I go around the corner and get some cookies and cream ice cream?"

I was shocked. I started to protest but Louis' mother was already out the door. I turned around to find my very mature boyfriend laughing uncontrollably.

"How old are you?" I asked, not finding this whole scenario amusing.

"Right now I wanna be sixteen years old and relive my wettest fantasy with you in the starring role."

He lifted me up, threw me over his shoulder like a rolled up carpet, and swatted my ass for good measure. He walked us to the back of the house where his room still looked as if he were sixteen.

"Ah, home sweet home. My right hand got a lot of action in this room," he said, flipping me down on his twin-sized bed. Louis began fumbling with his stereo. "I know my friend Def Leppard's 'Love Bites[36]' will put you in the mood to jump my bones, little girl." He walked over to lock his door and then turned, coming my way with a look that liquefied my insides.

Since it was his wet dream we were reenacting, I got up off his bed and proceeded to take both his hands, guiding him to sit down on the edge of his mattress. I ran my fingertips over his hard chest, descending farther down his rock hard abs, feeling every ripple beneath my extended fingers. I reached the bottom and with a swift upward jerk, pulled his red t-shirt off. Louis shirtless was always one of my favorite sights.

I took my flowery silk top off, doing a little sensual strip-tease for him, followed by removing my bra. I was still in my jeans, but topless, as I started slowly and seductively to undulate my hips on his muscular thighs. I arched my back, holding on to Louis' knees with both hands. I was presenting my full breasts for him to devour. He slid both hands up my back and brought me closer to him so he could nuzzle my breasts with his face.

Letting go of his knees, I cupped his face, feeling light stubble starting to form around his jaw. I could imagine the friction his beard would cause between my legs and closed my eyes in a state of bliss. Louis squeezed my breasts together with both hands, causing my semi-dormant nipples to wake up to full attention. He lifted his face to watch my slightly ajar lips await his next move. He then opened his lips and drew one nipple into his mouth, sucking and closing his eyes in pleasure. I could feel his cock harden and push against my butt. At the feel of his thickening cock, I shimmied off his lap and made my way to the floor, kneeling by his parted legs.

"Since you're sixteen years old right now, that means I need to travel back in time. I made this trip to the past to see you for a reason. You need to be a good boy and take your pants off for me so I can suck your cock so hard that you'll wanna wait for me for the next thirteen years until you're twenty-nine and I'm eighteen and legal for you to play with."

He took his pants and briefs off so fast you'd have thought I had a gun to his head. I ran my tongue around the base of his saluting cock and then twirled my tongue up and around his length like a spiral lollipop, coming up all the way to the tip. When I got to the top, I closed my mouth around the crown of his cock and moaned appreciatively. I was trying to take him in as far as he would go. I used both hands to pump him, squeezing him from the root upward, meeting my lips. After fucking him with my mouth for a few minutes, I loosened my lips from around his swelling cock. While still pumping him with both hands, I brought my face down to inhale his titillating scent. His musty sex-infused aroma sent a surge of lust straight to my crotch. I was starting to have a Pavlovian response to his distinctive scent. I licked his scrotum and closed my mouth around one of his balls. Louis shut his eyes so hard I thought he was in pain. I was about to open my mouth and let go.

Just then, he wailed, "Oh fuck, baby, that feels so good. Don't stop ... please keep sucking my balls. Fuck, just like that."

That comment was all I needed. I went to work on him like a gluttonous beast. I was giving both balls the same royal treatment. Louis was now breathing strenuously. He put both hands in my loose hair and cupped my skull.

"Em, suck hard. I'm going to come in your mouth."

I came up and lowered my mouth over his thick, throbbing cock. I angled his big, thick rod into my mouth, pushing him deeper than ever before. His heavy breathing encouraged me to push my limits and take more and more of him in. He was lodged in my throat so deep that I started making gagging sounds. They must've sent him over the edge because he yelled out my name and pulled his cock back a little and then started jerking and spouting hot semen into my mouth. He was still gripping my head and milking himself into my mouth, when we both heard his mother call out our names.

"Mom, we'll be right out; just showing Emily my signed balls. *Fuck*, I mean my signed baseballs."

He looked down at me with my mouth still full to the brim with his cock and said, "We need to get the fuck out of here."

Ice cream was perfect and just what I needed for my sore throat, thanks to the enormous cock that was lodged down my esophagus less than ten minutes before.

"Louis, I keep forgetting to mention that Robert Harris keeps calling me. He has a serious buyer for your dad's house across the street."

Louis paled and without looking at his mom, said monotonously, "How many times do I have to tell you, that house isn't on the market, Mom? Tell Robert I'm not interested in selling it … EVER!"

Elizabeth continued, clearly unperturbed by Louis' apparent discomfort. "Emily, maybe you can talk some sense into my stubborn son. Why spend money on the upkeep of a house you have no intentions of ever using? He needs to just sell it."

I looked over to see my typically vivacious boyfriend start to visibly withdraw.

"Louis, it's getting really late. We should start heading back; it's at least a two-hour drive to the city. You promised my parents we'd join them for dinner, remember?" I said, trying to change the course of conversation. Louis nodded in solidarity and started to bid his mom adieu. I thanked Elizabeth for graciously welcoming me to her home and gave her a warm hug goodbye.

The first forty minutes of our car ride back to the city was spent in utter silence. I knew his mother had touched a soft spot. Him holding on to his father's empty house after so many years was unusual. I just didn't want to push him to open up to me. He needed to be ready and willing to talk about this on his own. I glanced over at him, sensing his mind being somewhere far away. Without warning, Louis finally broke the silence and started talking.

"My dad and I used to always try to come up with a plan to

get him and Mom back together. I spent most of my childhood fabricating romantic schemes with him. Every night when he'd come to tuck me in, he would say, 'Maybe tonight's the night I get my family under one roof.' He died and we failed. Our plans to get Mom back didn't happen. Em, I can't sell that house. That was where my parents were meant to come together and become a real family. He loved her so much. He could've lived anywhere. God knows he had the means. He could've found another woman, had more kids, but he just wanted her and me. Growing up, I didn't understand him ... I get it now. I would wait for you for thirteen years. I'd wait till kingdom come, no questions asked, even if I only had a glimpse of what we have. I would wait for you my whole life, Emily."

It wasn't possible at that moment for anybody to love another person as much as I loved Louis. I knew then that everything I'd ever need for the rest of my life was in that car.

Not on or in a car...

"Sara, London sounds amazing! I wish I could go with you. My parents would never in a million years let me go away for that long alone to a different country. Your parents are awesome."

I was beyond ecstatic for my best friend. Her graduation gift from her parents before starting Brown University was a three-week, organized trip to England in August. It was a very expensive sleep-away camp in Europe for young adults. I would've loved to experience that with Sara and see where some of my favorite authors came from. But who was I kidding? I couldn't be away from Louis for more than a few hours without going crazy. That man had become my addiction.

I hung up with Sara and was about to call Louis and ask what time he was planning to pick me up that night. It was only three o'clock and he'd just dropped me off at home a few hours before, after our morning breakfast ritual. I called his private office line. The phone rang five times before going to his answering service. I hung up. He must've been busy.

I was considering finding something else to do when I heard cars honking outside. New York City gets crazy in the summer with all the tourists and taxis everywhere. Living so close to one of the world's greatest museums had some drawbacks. The honking outside didn't subside.

I walked downstairs to head for the library, thinking I might read Jane Austen's *Emma*[37]. *Ha, no way,* I thought. I needed me some Mr. Darcy until a Mr. Bruel decided to grace me with his voice or presence. It was either *Pride and Prejudice*[25] or me and Pinky.

I heard those damn car horns again and walked over to the window to see what all the commotion outside was about. Double parked outside my house and virtually making it impossible for anyone other than a motorcycle to pass, was my Mr. Darcy. Louis was sitting inside a vintage two-seater convertible, hair all messy from the wind and aviators covering those sexy eyes. He looked like a '50s Hollywood actor. He seemed too big for that car, but the effect was nonetheless shattering. I ran to the door to see what was going on. Why was he there? We had dinner plans for later that night, it was only a little after three o'clock. I locked my front door and sprinted toward him.

"What are you doing here?"

"Your street is impossible! I've been trying to park this fucking car for the last half hour."

"Where did you get this car? It's gorgeous." God, I hoped he hadn't bought me another car. One car for a person who couldn't drive was more than enough.

"Thank you, baby. I love this car, too. It was my dad's. Get in, let's go for a ride."

I climbed in without having to open the door and was giddy with excitement. I was just wishing I could be with him again and there he was. I was so pathetic; I couldn't even be away from Louis for a few hours.

"This is a 1952 Jaguar XK120 Roadster. I just had it delivered this afternoon after its new paint job. Do you like the color?"

"I've never seen this color on a car in my life. It's stunning. It's amazing, Louis. You have incredible taste."

"I'm glad you approve. You were the inspiration for this color. Well, your nipples, to be exact, were the muses for this shade."

I was speechless. He had to be kidding, right? There was no way Louis would paint a priceless vintage car the color of my areolas.

"Did you think I was kidding when I told you that the lovely shade of your nipples is my new favorite color? I meant it. I was going to paint the Ferrari this color, too, but I know how much you like the red so I wanted to make sure it was okay with you first."

"You want to know if it's okay to paint your exotic red Ferrari the color of my nipples?"

"That, or turquoise to match your eyes. Your choice."

"Are you insane? Please tell me I didn't fall madly in love with a crazy person. Louis, don't you dare paint anything else to match any of my body parts."

"I love your body parts. If I can't have you with me all the time, then I need a reminder of all your delicious body parts."

"I can remind you if we go somewhere less public."

"Fuck yeah, now we're talking."

I must've been just as insane as that wild man. That car could drive. It took Louis less than twenty minutes before he had me spread-eagled on the roof of the nude colored Jaguar. We were devouring each other inside his underground car garage in SoHo. Well, I was the one being consumed. Louis did most of the eating. My breasts were a weakness for that man. He just couldn't seem to get enough.

"Let me come all over your tits."

"You can come anywhere you want."

"Don't say that to me when all the blood in my brain went south to my dick. Baby, you know where I really want to come."

"So stop wanting and do it!"

He stopped stroking his hard cock over my sprawled body

and grabbed my face harshly to bring my eyes to his. He was breathing hard, pupils dilated, veins bulging in his neck. He looked furious.

"The first time I make love to you, little girl, will not be on the hood of a car or in a car! GOT IT? Don't you dare belittle what you are to me."

That was so crass and so beautiful at the same time. Just like the man himself. Rough and smooth all in the same breath. I got up off the car and pushed him on the hood in my place. I took hold of his magnificent, thick, throbbing shaft and lowered my mouth onto him to finish what he'd started, one lick at a time. I was becoming accustomed to having his big, beautiful penis down my throat on a daily basis. I craved the look on his face right before he detonated in my mouth. Louis got that vulnerable look that I knew nobody else got to see but me. The look that told me that I owned this powerful man. Just before Louis came violently in my mouth, holding my head in place and pumping himself into me like a jackhammer, he looked down at me and muttered, "I love you so fucking much, Emily. So fucking much … fucccck." That was just how I loved him—scummy and sweet wrapped up neatly in one beautiful package.

After having an orgasm in and on every one of Louis' cars, including my new car, I was finally back home at six o'clock to get changed so we could go out for dinner. Louis had some phone calls to return so he stayed in the Jaguar while I went inside to change. I came out half an hour later to find my dad chatting it up with my boyfriend.

"This is the most beautiful car in the world. I always dreamed of owning a vintage Jag. The maintenance on it is crazy, though, and we don't have a proper garage to keep such a classic beauty. But this is amazing. The condition you keep this beauty in, Louis, is incredible. Say, what color is this anyway? I have never seen a more fitting color for this car in my life."

I could see my pompous boyfriend trying to stifle a laugh.

He spotted me coming toward them and begged me silently with his eyes to be rescued from my father's line of questioning. I should've gone over there and told my daddy that Louis just had his prized Jaguar painted after his daughter's nipple color. That should teach my boyfriend a lesson. My nipple color should be for his eyes only.

"Hi, Daddy, nice car, right? It was Louis' dad's car. Louis just had it repainted after the color of a sunset we saw together last week. It's different shades of pink, peach, and golden nude. Gorgeous, huh?"

"Whatever color this is, it is stunning. Just perfect."

Louis smiled his boy-next-door smile at me, the one that stops time and my heart. He was nodding his head, agreeing with my father's assessment of my nipple color.

"David, I couldn't agree more that it's the most beautiful color I've ever seen in my life. I needed to share it with the world."

I raised myself on my toes to whisper in Louis' ear, "You owe me big, Pip."

"I am in your debt indefinitely, little girl."

Surprise...

After dating for a little over a month, one evening during a stroll in Central Park, Louis asked, "Our birthdays are coming up next week. Can I make plans for the both of us? I already asked your parents and they said no problem as long as it's okay with you."

"Of course it's okay with me. What did you have in mind?"

"Now what kind of surprise would that be if I told you what we were doing?"

"Just tell me. I'll act totally surprised. I promise," I said, laughing.

"Nice try, slick. No way. I'm surprising you if it's the last thing I do."

"And how will I know what to wear?" I retorted, trying to reason with the most unreasonable man I knew.

"Jenna will dress you."

"So my sister knows about the surprise and I don't?" I asked, trying to sound as wounded as possible.

"Don't feel bad, your parents and grandma also know." That earned Louis a hard slap on the chest. "Don't hit me, woman, you know how sensitive I am when it comes to you."

Our birthdays were three days away so I made sure I was ready for anything. I treated myself to the works: a haircut, manicure, pedicure, and even a facial. I went a little crazy and opted for a Brazilian bikini wax that left me completely hairless. I had picked up Louis' birthday gift and worked on the rest of my surprise for him.

Jenna called me a day before my birthday on July 20th and asked if I'd like to go and have coffee with her at Yura's, which was down the block from my house. I jumped at the opportunity to try and extract as much info as I could from my sister about my upcoming birthday surprise. Jenna, however, was tougher to crack than 007.

"Did Louis pay you, Mom, and Dad to keep quiet? JenJen, can you at least tell me what to wear tomorrow?"

"Yeah, sure, Emmy … whatever you're wearing now is perfect."

"Jen, stop being silly. Is Louis closing down some fancy restaurant for us? Make sure he invited Sara; I've been such a shitty friend to her lately. She's leaving for London in a few days so I have to see her on my birthday."

All I got was a big nod and a laugh. I could tell my sister was enjoying torturing me. I didn't get much out of her. When we got home an hour or so later, a black limo was pulled up at the curb right in front of my house. As soon as I walked up the stairs with Jenna to go inside, Louis came out of the limo, smiling that familiar, beautiful smile at me. He was so gorgeous; every time I saw him, it was like the first time all over again.

"Hi, baby, are you ready to go?"

I looked over at my smirking conspirator of a sister and walked back down the stairs to the main culprit.

"Ready to go where, Louis?" I asked, a little thrown off and a lot curious.

"It's a surprise ... we need to get going; go say goodbye to your family."

I was very confused. I looked up to where my sister was standing and was now joined by both my parents, all wearing huge smiles on their faces, ready to send me off. I ran up the stairs.

"Mommy, Daddy, what's going on? Where is Louis taking me?"

"Enjoy, honey; it's a surprise," my mom said, giving me a big hug which was followed by a kiss from my dad. My sister also came in to give me a hug and then whispered in my ear.

"You are one lucky bitch."

They all waved to Louis while I got into the limo as clueless as ever.

Thirty minutes later, we pulled into JFK airport and into a private jet terminal.

"Louis, we're flying somewhere? I don't have my passport; I didn't pack anything. I don't even have a pair of underwear on me. These shorts were too tight for underwear."

He took my hand and put it on his semi-hard cock. "Please don't tell me about your lack of underwear because we won't make it to our final destination."

"Which is?" I asked.

"For me to know and you to eventually find out." He must've seen the discombobulated expression on my face, because he took a small amount of pity on my nerves.

"Don't worry; Jenna and your mom packed for you, and whatever you'll still need I'll buy you. I also have your passport and underwear is actually strictly prohibited where we're headed."

"My parents know you're taking me away on an overnight

trip and they're okay with it?" I asked him, feeling as if I'd just entered a parallel universe where my parents let me smoke pot and get tattoos.

"Your parents have given me their blessings. They said, and I quote, 'Louis, what a wonderful idea.'"

I was officially speechless.

We boarded a private jet that only had eight seats. The aircraft interior was decorated in a beautiful royal blue and gold color scheme. The plush recliner seats were upholstered in rich, navy colored leather with burled wood tables separating every pair of seats. We sat down, Louis buckled me in, and smiled his glorious, dimple-showing, loving smile at me. The flight attendant walked over and welcomed us with champagne.

Louis held my hand as we took off and kept our clasped hands next to his mouth, giving the back of my hand soft kisses every once in a while. He was reading and signing some paperwork during the flight and I guess I must've dozed off. We landed about two or three hours later. Louis had the shades drawn while I napped. I had no idea where we were.

Over the loudspeaker, our pilot announced, "Mr. Bruel and Ms. Marcus, I hope you enjoyed your flight with us today. Let me be the first to welcome you both to the beautiful island of Turks and Caicos."

Louis turned his head to me and smiled. "Surprise."

This is not real. Things like this don't really happen to girls like me. How could he be this perfect?

Louis informed me that we'd be staying in Turks and Caicos for the weekend to celebrate both our birthdays. The house we were staying in was one of the properties he still had on the market. He said it was the same house that he wanted to bring me to with his indecent proposal to me during our first kitchen encounter.

During the ride to the house, I called my parents to let them know that we'd landed safely. I promised to call them every day to check in. The ride to the house was lovely. The lush country-side and the cloudless sky were just beautiful. I couldn't wrap my brain around where we were together. I was drinking in my sur-roundings when Louis said, "All the villas on the island have names. You see, that home over there is called *Stargazer* and if you look over there, hidden behind those palm trees, that's the *Coral House.*"

"What's the name of the house we're staying in?" I asked.

"Tell you what, ask me the same question tomorrow. You will appreciate its name once you get to experience the villa first hand."

Louis went all real estate broker on me and started selling me the property we were slowly approaching.

"The estate we'll be staying on is located on Grace Bay beach in an area of Turks called Providenciales. It's a stunning eleven thousand square foot, beachfront villa with full-time staff. It is set on ten acres of land with three hundred feet of white sand beach frontage. Emily, wait until you see this place. It exudes Caribbean charm and oozes romance; it should be right up your alley. There are six bedrooms and seven bathrooms and any amenity you can think of. I think I've said enough. Baby, I can't wait to see your reaction to *the Blue*—I mean the villa."

The place he described sounded spectacular. I quickly add-ed, "I'll take it. It sounds perfect for me and my nonexistent budget." My gorgeous boyfriend smirked at my reply and kissed me softly.

Fifteen minutes later, our chauffeured SUV pulled up to a gated property. Louis got out and punched some numbers into a keypad and the gates parted for us. We drove ahead onto a wind-ing driveway that led to a stunning, white Mediterranean villa with a red terra cotta Spanish roof. The sprawling estate was set amidst lush palm trees and yellow hibiscus bushes. The carved, arched front doors were at least ten feet tall.

Louis unlocked the front doors and led us both inside. I walked in behind him and gasped. A row of glass French doors lined the entire wall facing us as we entered. As soon as I walked in, all I saw through the glass wall of doors was turquoise ocean stretching out indefinitely. I was drawn to the windows like a moth to light. I didn't notice the beautiful crystal chandeliers or the marble double staircase framing the wall of doors or the fact that the house was totally empty; I was entranced.

"I hope you don't mind that we're staying in this empty house. We could go to one of the hotels on the island if you want. I just thought it would be romantic to spend the weekend alone, just the two of us in paradise. Blue Lagoon-style," Louis said, while walking over to me and engulfing me from behind.

"Louis, I'm speechless, this house is the most beautiful thing I've ever seen. Will we be sleeping on the beach or in a tree?" I asked, laughing. He moved my hair to the side of my shoulder and nibbled up my neck.

"Tree, of course," Louis said with a straight face looking down at me. "Come, little girl. I need to show you the color of the ocean."

Louis did prove to me that my eyes indeed matched the color of the clear blue water in Turks and Caicos. The view was straight out of a postcard. The sand was powder white and the turquoise colored water seemed like a man-made pool; it didn't look real. The villa had a rectangular shaped, long pool with an infinity edge extending seamlessly into the blue ocean. It was as if we were the last two people left on a deserted island in the lap of luxury.

The sun was beginning to set. We had our dinner brought in and set outside on the patio by a sweet lady. She left so quickly I didn't even get a chance to say hello. We were having whole, steamed, black lobsters, which, according to Louis, were locally caught.

"Louis, this place is amazing. What did I do to deserve this and you, and when am I waking up?"

"Shouldn't I be asking you that?" Louis countered. Taking my lemon drenched fingers, he sucked the juices of each one profanely. I could feel the fire and the need growing deep in my core. I was yearning to be somewhere entangled in Louis. I thought it would definitely be the night I would bid my hymen farewell. The wooer beside me had been nothing but patient with me, willing to endure celibacy to prove his love. That night, I would give him the only gift I had to prove my love and devotion. I just hoped he'd still want me after I gave it to him.

"This is the best surprise I've ever had. I still don't know how you talked my parents into letting me come with you."

"I can be very persuasive. Especially when something is as important to me as you. I had to make it happen."

"Did you promise my dad I'd have my own house with a drawn up moat?" I asked, laughing. Louis took a piece of lobster meat, dipped it in lemon, then hot butter, and brought it to my lips. I opened my mouth for him to feed me. When his fingers came in contact with my lips, I had to suck them. Lobster with Louis was my new favorite delicacy.

"Em, I negotiate for a living. But truthfully, this was the hardest negotiation of my life. Just so we're clear; I was bringing you here even if I had to smuggle you out of the country."

I had no doubt he was dead serious.

"Thank you for bringing me here, I'm sure it wasn't easy but very much appreciated." I got up and moved to stand between his legs. I put my hands in his hair and pulled him into me for a hug. He tightened his grip around my waist and rested his head on my chest.

"It was worth the effort. Tomorrow morning I'll get the best birthday present of my life when I get to wake up with you in my bed. This is not what I imagined when I invited you to come with me to Turks six weeks ago in that kitchen. Who knew that I would be madly in love with you? Emily, what I feel for you is indescribable. I have never been happier. You, little girl, have become my whole life."

God, I loved that man and thanked the heavens for whoever decided that I deserved to have him.

I really wasn't expecting a trip. I didn't know when I left with Louis in the limo earlier that day that we wouldn't be going back to our respective homes before our birthdays. I was upset that in the morning I wouldn't have his birthday gift to present to him. I knew that a man like Louis could get himself anything. Money was no object, and there wasn't anything that he wanted that I could possibly afford to buy him. I wanted to give him something that was special and meaningful. I had hidden a gift for Louis in his bed, under the pillow. My plan was to call him first thing on the morning of our birthday and tell him to reach under his pillow for his gift. My plan had failed miserably. The gift wasn't extravagant; it was more sentimental. I had a long, silver chain made for him with a small, round disc hanging from it. The disc was engraved with a quote from his favorite book, *Great Expectations*[14]. Now I felt silly being empty-handed on his birthday when he'd gotten me a trip to paradise for mine. Since my body was the only gift he'd get, I hoped it was enough for him.

"Let's go upstairs ... I bought a bed for us and had it brought in earlier today," he said.

I smiled. *Of course he did,* I thought.

"What? Don't look at me like that. I didn't want the first time we actually slept together all night in the same place to be on the floor."

"This romantic thing of yours is getting old," I told him sarcastically as I climbed a few steps ahead of him to reach his lips for a playful peck.

"Are you calling me old, little girl?" he asked while lifting me off my feet and carrying me up the stairs.

Happy birthday to us...

The circular master bedroom was as completely empty as the rest of the house, except for the white rococo, ornate carved bed in the middle of the room. It was covered in crisp white sheets and a sea of pillows. The hum of the ceiling fan high above the bed kept a steady hypnotic pace. The scent of seawater and exotic flowers was incredibly intoxicating. The wide-open French doors led to a balcony overlooking the ocean and let in the night breeze. Louis was quietly observing my reaction to yet another one of his well-orchestrated plots.

"The way you take in your surroundings is awe-inspiring," he said while watching me and pulling me close.

"The inspiring surroundings you provide for me are awe-worthy," I answered, looking back at him from under my lashes.

"I'll never stop trying to put that look on your beautiful face, Em."

I looked up at him, waiting for his soft lips to make contact with mine. I was his completely: heart, body, and soul.

I took my overnight bag to the bathroom to take a quick shower and freshen up. Louis said he'd be downstairs making a few phone calls while I showered. I suspected he wanted to give me some privacy. I unpacked my bag, pleased to find underwear, bathing suits, and some light summer dresses. My sister packed a toiletry bag for me with all my favorite products. I also found a wrapped present that said in big bold letters *DO NOT OPEN UNTIL YOUR BIRTHDAY! Love, Nana Rose.* I guess even Nana knew about my romantic getaway with lover boy turned Prince Charming. I showered, washed my hair, and felt refreshed but still a little spent from our long journey. I put on a dusty rose-colored silk camisole that my sister had packed for me and came out of the en-suite bathroom. The room was empty. I could hear Louis still on the phone talking animatedly to someone downstairs. I climbed into the tantalizingly inviting, soft bed and lay down. I was engulfed in a sea of gossamer sheets and satiny soft pillows. I rehashed the day's events and waited for my love to join me for our first, uninterrupted slumber party.

"Sweet, Emily ... wake up, my love."

I could hear Louis calling me. *He sounds so close,* I thought to myself, still in a fuzzy dream state. I could feel him kissing my décolletage.

"Wake up, sleeping beauty. Open your eyes and let me see my birthday present."

What? Where am I? I need to get up, I thought. I opened one eye to see Louis lying down next to me in bed in a sun-drenched room.

"Happy Birthday, Emily Marcus," he said with the most heart stoppingly beautiful, perfect teeth-displaying smile I'd ever seen.

"Happy Birthday, Louis Bruel," I said back to my dream man.

I propped myself up sideways on my elbow facing Louis,

mirroring his position. I focused on his smiling sexy eyes and those long lashes. Lord, I could watch that man all day. I ogled my boyfriend's too-beautiful-for-his-own-good face and hadn't yet drunk in his naked form beside me. He ran his fingertips down my shoulder and along my arm until he reached my hand. He laced our fingers together and drew my left hand to his lips and kissed the back of it. I still hadn't torn my gaze from his.

Louis was still nibbling on my hand, clasped in his, when he started to say between kisses, *"I love her against reason ... against promise ... against peace ... against hope ... against happiness ... against all discouragement that could be.*[38]*"*

My breath caught. I recognized that line from *Great Expectations*[14]. I took our entwined hands and brought them now to my lips and kissed the back of his hand. I said to him, teary-eyed and in between soft kisses, the quote that I had engraved on the chain under his pillow back in New York, *"You are part of my existence, part of myself. You have been in every line I have ever read since I came here.*[39]*"* Louis stopped smiling; he looked as though he was about to cry. He lowered our clasped hands, urging me on my back and lowered himself on top of me.

"Emily, I will love you for the rest of my life. I will only exist knowing you are mine. I will respect you and obey you. I will never look at another woman as long as I live. I will make you proud of me. I will dedicate my whole life to you and the family we will have. I know you're still a baby but I promise to give you a great life. You and our children will have a need for nothing. I will show you the world, and I can't wait to see everything anew through your beautiful eyes. You will not find a man who could love you more than I do."

My breath caught in my throat again at the words coming out of his mouth. I was floating in a state of suspended consciousness when Louis reached one hand beneath my pillow and pulled out a small red leather box. He opened the box with trembling hands and asked, "Emily Marcus, will you marry me and let me love you and take care of you for the rest of my life?"

I couldn't tear my eyes from his and I didn't even look at the contents inside the box before I nodded my head. "Louis ... oh, God ... yes ... yes. I love you; of course I will marry you," I said, sobbing in a tear filled haze.

Louis was visibly crying, too, and while trying to wipe my tear stained cheeks, he took the ring out and slipped it on my finger.

"Em, I love you so much. You are the most beautiful, captivating woman I have ever met. I don't want us to ever be apart ... I never want to wake up without you."

I finally broke our staring session and looked at the ring he slipped on my finger. "Louis, this ring ... is magnificent," I gasped, finally inspecting the jewel. It was a princess cut, colossal blue diamond with large round yellow diamonds surrounding it.

"All shades of blue remind me of your eyes, and the canary diamonds just really made the blue pop. I couldn't bring myself to get you any plain old diamond. If you want to change it, we can go back to Cartier as soon as we get home and they'll find you something you like more. I just saw this blue diamond and couldn't stop thinking of the eyes I'll get to see for the rest of my life."

"Louis ... I love you and I love this ring; it's incredible. I don't believe any of this is happening, let alone to me." I couldn't stop crying. Only six weeks earlier, I was having childish fantasies about that beautiful man. I thought to myself, how could this be happening to me?

Start at the beginning...

After a good hour of us crying and talking about what had just happened, I noticed Louis had a long silver chain around his neck. I yanked the chain from under the covers to see the disc with my inscribed quote. I looked up at him, not quite connecting the dots.

"My housekeeper found it under my pillow and gave it to me. Thank you; that was the best present anyone has ever given me, besides getting to wake up with you." He nestled me into his chest. I took a deep breath inhaling his familiar scent and relaxing into his grip.

"I feel like such a dork. I can't believe I fell asleep on you last night."

Louis took a whiff of my hair and said, "I ain't gonna lie, I had some great expectations for us last night. But walking in and seeing you draped on those sheets with your hair spread over the pillow like a veil ... that sight made me gasp for air. I didn't know if I'd be able to make it until morning to propose. I watched you sleep for hours last night ... you're breathtaking, you know that?"

"Oh no! Louis, my parents! They'll flip—they won't understand. I'm only eighteen ... they're going to kill me when they find out about us," I said, sitting up as reality and panic finally made an appearance.

"First of all, you're nineteen and second, your parents already know."

What? Come again. Was this Louis' idea of a joke? I needed a better explanation. "What do you mean they know?"

"I've known that I wanted to marry you since that first day we spent together in my house."

"Louis, I'm still confused. Can you start at the beginning? My parents knew you were going to ask me to marry you, as in, not in two years from now but now, today?" I asked, trying to slowly comprehend this crazy situation. He sat up in bed, too, and faced me. The panic and disbelief on my face must've prompted him to start filling in the blanks.

"Jenna and Mike have known for about a week now. Jenna even came with me to Cartier to help me pick out your ring. Sara knows, too, by the way. But I didn't tell her until yesterday before I picked you up. I couldn't decide if she'd be able to hold that kind of information back from you. I wasn't about to chance it."

My sister had known for a week that my life was about to change drastically, and she didn't tell me anything. Sara knew that I was being proposed to.

Louis just kept rambling. "I had Jenna and Mike arrange a meeting for me to talk to your parents privately. They came to the Crown Affairs office a week ago. I explained to your parents that I love you very much. I told them I want to spend the rest of my life lost in those eyes of yours. I made it clear that I can't and won't live without you. I also told them I'm old enough to know you are IT for me. I assured them that I have a successful business and that I would provide for you like a queen."

This was really happening? Was there a hidden camera somewhere? I frantically looked around the room.

"Your dad asked 'What's the rush?' He couldn't understand why we couldn't continue dating and then see where it led us a few years from now. I told him that whatever we feel for one another wouldn't change because of time. Your mom then said that she thinks you're too young to get married. She worried that we wouldn't be able to handle living together. I told her living together is not our problem—it's the living without one another that is unacceptable. She then asked me if I'd gotten you pregnant. I assured both of them we haven't had intercourse ... in the Biblical sense," he said, winking and smirking at me.

"Jenna and Mike were there, too, so they told your parents that you and I are in love. Mike even told your dad that he's known me for years and has never seen someone more serious and in love than me and you. Jenna told them she thinks that your age is irrelevant. That age only comes into play in a serious relationship like ours when two people are too young to support each other financially. This meeting of ours took over two hours. By meeting's end, I had your parents' halfhearted blessing. I think it was a big shock for them. They needed some time to process it all."

I was trying to picture this scary meeting in my head. I'd kill to have been a fly in that room. I couldn't even imagine what my parents were thinking during this Louis Bruel ambush.

"Your parents and Nana came to see me the next day at my office. I did a small rendition for Nana Rose from the meeting she missed the day before. I told her that I would love her beautiful granddaughter for the rest of my life. I told her that you and I are soul mates. I walked her around my side of the table and showed her a picture of us."

"What picture?" I asked, entranced by his story telling.

"Baby, you've never seen it. It's from that party the night we first saw each other. *Architectural Digest* was there that night. There was a photographer taking candid pictures of the space for an article they were writing on that particular property. They took a panoramic picture of the party. It was an aerial shot. I saw the picture in the magazine two weeks later. I found myself in the picture staring at you while you were passing me by. Seeing that picture confirmed I was already in love with you then. I had the picture blown up and framed. I said to Nana 'Bashert is Bashert.' She pulled me down and gave me a kiss on my cheek," Louis said proudly, pointing to his dimpled cheek. "She then said 'zol zein mit mazel' which you know means *you are the most handsome man my granddaughter will ever meet.*"

"It does not mean that, you big buffoon," I said, pushing him back down. He pulled me down with him.

"Your parents, including Nana, gave me their full blessing that time. That's when I told them about Turks and Caicos and your birthday surprise."

I couldn't believe he went to battle for us like that in front of my parents without me. Wow, even my nana gave him the green light. That was huge!

"What about your mom? Does she know?" I asked curiously.

"She knew even before we came out to see her that day. I speak to her every day. She knows what you are to me. After meeting you once she told me that she approves of you, of us, without a shadow of a doubt."

"God, I can't believe you did all this for me, for us. I know hands down that I am the luckiest girl in the whole world to have you."

"Thank you, Em, for giving me and us a chance. I know I don't deserve someone as beautiful and sweet, and pure both on the inside and out as you. But I promise I will make you proud to call me your husband."

"Louis, I love you but I hate to disappoint you. I'm not so pure," I said, getting on my knees and removing my satin camisole. His eyes traveled up to my bare breasts as I sat naked in his lap. I then asked him, "Will you please make love to me as my future husband?"

"Yes ma'am." He saluted me and flipped us both on the bed

so I was now pinned under him. "I don't have any condoms and I never want to wear one with you," he said while hovering over me.

"Louis, I know. We spoke about this already. But what happens if I get pregnant? I'm not on the pill."

"Well, I guess I'd have to marry you then."

We both laughed.

"Emily, seriously I don't want to hurt you. I know how petite and tight you are. First, I'll need to make you very wet. Then I'll need to stretch you out with my fingers. I will not penetrate you until I make you come at least three times. Is that understood?"

"Yes, sir," I retorted, saluting my sex commander at his well-laid plan.

Worth waiting for...

He lowered his head to give me a lazy kiss that quickly morphed into the most desperate kiss I have ever experienced to this day. His lips were swallowing me whole. I was swimming inside his delicious mouth. I could feel every bump of his demanding tongue. We would alternate taking in deep breaths and then once again plunge into each other's mouths. Our kiss was so lustful you'd think we hadn't seen each other in years.

Louis made me feel wanton and unapologetic for my animalistic response to his touch. I was running my fingers through his hair, down his lean back, and over his bulging muscular arms. I wanted to touch every inch of his beautiful smooth skin. I slipped my hands under his silk boxer shorts and cupped his firm ass in my hands, pulling him and his stiff cock down onto me. I could feel myself moisten.

Louis nestled himself between my parted legs, and pressing against my mound only added more wood to an already burning fire; no pun intended. He suddenly left my lips as though someone had torn him from me by force. Still panting hard, Louis grabbed my breast and squeezed, giving one of my engorged nipples a wet lick while squeezing the other between his fingers. He continued lapping his tongue down my shaking core and licked into my belly button, finding my small ring and tugging it with his teeth. He then sucked at it, making me cry out. His hands were still kneading my breasts when he positioned his head at my entrance.

"Your pussy is calling my name, baby." He proceeded to part my labial lips and push his tongue all the way in and then out of me.

"Ahhhh, Louis, I want your cock inside me, not your tongue. I can't wait anymore."

"Baby, don't say that to me yet, please. I'm trying so hard. God, you're so ready; your pussy is soaking. Fuck, Emily, I won't last; I need to fuck you ... now."

With that, he straightened up and took his massive erection in his hands and started to guide himself into my dripping hole, blowing his well-laid plan to hell. I was so wet that the first few inches of Louis slipped in effortlessly. I could feel the imminent pain building and felt my vaginal walls constricting around his bulge.

"My God, you're so tight, Em, I don't want to hurt you."

I didn't answer; I was too focused on the feeling of his cock finally penetrating me.

"Em, open your eyes, if it hurts, you need to let me know ... okay?"

I silently gave him a nod. He was too big for this not to hurt.

"Baby, I'll go slowly. I'll feed my dick into you ... little by little until you get used to me inside you."

He was now halfway inside me. Louis was undeniably in pain himself from having to hover over me motionlessly, while my body acclimated to his gargantuan cock. He moved in a little more.

"Ohhhhhh," we both cried out.

"Are you okay?" he asked, with a scared expression on his beautiful features.

"Louis, I'm fine. Stop worrying and try to move," I said,

braver than I felt.

He moved a little deeper in and stopped and stilled like a statue. A few seconds later, he let out a deep breath. He changed his position and sat back on his knees. He opened my knees as far apart as they would go and plunged the last couple of inches into me. The pain of the last thrust made me scream out. I looked down between us to where his root connected with my sex and clenched hard around his cock at the erotic sight.

Knowing his whole cock was buried all the way inside me was almost enough to make me come and forget the pain and discomfort. We looked up at each other simultaneously. I gave him a small, pained smile. Louis started rocking into me very slowly. It was both pleasure and pain I was feeling. I was so high on everything that had occurred between us in the last few hours. The surge of endorphins dulled most of the pain. I needed him to just let go and take me the way I knew he wanted and needed to. I would deal with the ache later.

"Louis, harder."

"Em, I know you're in pain. We'll take it slow today. We'll have our whole lives to fuck hard; right now I need to go slow."

"I need you to shut up and fuck me. Move your cock. I won't break, please make me come, I'm so close," I almost barked out.

He pulled completely out of me with a wet slurp in one swift move that made me wince from the burning sensation within. He took hold of my knees, bringing them together and then extended my legs straight up in front of him. He kissed my calves and licked up all the way to my feet. Louis lowered himself and parted my outstretched legs so they were now wrapped around his neck. Without any warning, he pushed himself into me hard. We both screamed out at Louis fully penetrating me with so much force. He lowered and pushed himself on me so that my knees came flush against my breasts. He was driving his cock in and out of me hard. He was so deep inside me that I could feel him in my stomach. Louis picked up the pace with each thrust.

I cried out, "Oh God!" This time he was even deeper, and with increasingly hard shoves, I could feel an unfamiliar part of me contract and tighten.

"Baby, I'm close. I won't last, please tell me you're close. I want us to come together."

All I managed to say was, "Ohhhhhh LLLLouisssss!" and then I fell and fell. I was somewhere far, far away. I don't even remember Louis coming or what he said when he finally came inside me that first time. I was feeling my sex pulsating so hard it was as if my heart had left my chest and immigrated to my crotch. When my body finally stopped convulsing some minutes, or hours later, I pried my eyes open to see my fiancé lying beside me naked, face down, and fully spent.

I ran my fingers down his back and asked, "How was that? Do you still want to marry me?"

He opened his eyes smiling. "I think I blacked out at the end. I never came so hard in my life. That was worth waiting for."

I smiled, pleased by his response. "I can't believe I had sex for the first time." My first time having sex was with my future husband, Louis Bruel.

"Emily, I hope you enjoyed the feel of my dick inside you because I'm not just your first, I'm going to be your last. There is no way anybody else on this planet is ever going to know how your pussy feels or tastes, as long as I'm still drawing breath. Just so we're clear."

I kissed his naked butt and quickly tried to get off the bed to visit the bathroom. Before I could get off our bed, Louis grabbed my hand and jerked me back in.

"Let me go. I need to pee."

He sat up and cradled me in his arms. "Are you okay? More importantly ... did I hurt you?"

"Louis I'm perfect; the pain is a delicious kind of pain. I can still feel you inside me, it's incredible."

He smiled his stop-the-world-and-look-at-me smile and added, "I love you. Thank you for all my birthday gifts, I think this one is my favorite."

"Ditto."

I had to agree. Best birthday ever!

More surprises...

After a quick joint shower, we got dressed and started to make our way downstairs. It was a little past noon and I was famished after all our strenuous morning endeavors. I was excited to finally call my parents, sister, and Sara and tell them what they already knew.

As we were exiting our bedroom, Louis said, "I totally forgot, Em, there are a few more surprises I have for your birthday."

"Are you trying to spoil me?"

"I haven't spoiled you nearly as much as I should've. You have carte blanche from now on." We briefly embraced and stole a few kisses walking down the grand staircase.

"What other surprises do you have up your sleeve, Pip?" I asked, giddy with excitement.

"Remember I told you your parents were okay with me bringing you here?"

"Yeah, I remember, so…?"

"So, your parents had one condition to their dispensation."

"What was the condition, Louis?"

"I can't remember. I definitely agreed to it or they wouldn't have let me bring you. I just can't remember what it was. I *am* thirty now. I guess I'm not as sharp as I was at twenty-nine."

I stopped walking down and placed my hands on my waist and stomped my feet like a four-year-old.

"Louis Bruel, I will not take another step unless you stop playing around and tell me what the condition was."

"Let's keep walking down the stairs and I'll tell you." I agreed and then Louis pulled me close to him and whispered in my ear, "The condition was they'd be the first ones to congratulate their baby girl."

"Oh, Louis, you scared me. I thought you'd promised to coerce me into going to medical school. I'll just call them before I call Jenna or Sara," I said, relieved.

"In person," he added and smiled as we approached the end of the staircase to see my parents beaming at us.

I'm not an overly emotional person but seeing my mommy and daddy there to share this moment was one of the happiest memories of my life. I ran over to my parents and hugged them like an eight-year-old who'd just come back from summer camp. I couldn't stop crying. I was elated that my parents could be there and see first-hand how happy I was. I was too wrapped up in the moment to notice that Louis had walked over to hug Mike and Jenna. They were sitting on the couch in the living room waiting for us to come down. It dawned on me a few moments later, after my eyes officially dried and I was all hugged and congratulated out, that the empty house I had entered yesterday evening was now fully furnished.

"Louis, when did you do this?" I asked. "I mean the furniture."

He smirked my way and said, "I had most of this brought in last night. I must say, the movers were pretty loud, but you were out cold."

The same woman wearing a gray and white uniform from last night approached and introduced herself as Trisha. She gave us her best wishes and playfully mentioned that she came with the house.

We had a beautiful lunch set out on the patio by the pool over-looking the ocean. Louis got up to give a toast. "I would like to first say that this is the best birthday of my life, and that I'm the luckiest man to have the most beautiful girl in the world agree to be my wife. I would also like to thank Adele and David for creating and raising the most incredible girl I have ever met. Thank you all for being here to share one of happiest days in our lives. Emily, happy birthday, baby, to you and to our beautiful life together."

There was a big round of cheers and glasses clinking and us smooching. After Trisha cleared our table an hour later, Louis lifted me out of my chair and pulled me into his lap.

"Baby, I'm backtracking a little. While we dated, I didn't even buy you a single rose ... but I will make up for all that quickly. I hope you like this house, Emily, because it's one of your birthday gifts. I took the liberty and named it "The Blue Lagoon" for you. We can stay here as long as you'd like. I can do all my work from here. I don't have to be back in the city for the next two weeks, so I'm all yours."

"Louis, are you mad? You can't buy me a house! This is your house, not mine. I can't accept a house from you! You've already bought me a car. Jenna told me you had my whole family flown down here on a private jet. It's just too much," I said, trying to get off his lap.

Louis held me tightly in place, not letting me get up. "Em, everything I have is yours. You'd better get used to me giving you gifts. I have lots of money and I choose to spend it on the people I love. The person I love most is you. You won't ever have to think about money." He took my clasped hands in one of his and continued, "I don't want a prenup, either. We need to tell your dad I won't need the contact information of his attorney. Your parents were under the impression that there would be paperwork between us. I told them if you ever leave me it means I'm dead and I'd want you to have everything."

I started to tell him that I didn't mind signing a prenuptial agreement when he put a finger on my lips to make me stop talking.

"This is not a negotiation."

"Louis, you worked hard and built your company from zilch. Your father entrusted you with all his financial and physical assets. Eric would've wanted you to protect yourself. We've only known each other for forty-four days. If you were my son I wouldn't let you marry anyone without a prenup," I said.

He looked up at me smiling, still holding my hands in one of his and twirling one of my blond locks in between his fingers. "It's a good thing you're not my mom then. I wouldn't want to be dreaming of fucking my mom, that's for sure."

Oh brother, that's all he got from that whole conversation. *Men*, I thought.

"Louis, I know you're very successful and you don't need me to work, nor can I contribute to your wealth financially. I do, however, need to do something with my life. Besides being your wife."

He was listening but he wasn't really hearing me. All he said back to me was, "You can come work for me. That way I don't have to wait until I come home to bang you." He was smiling but it wasn't funny. He continued, "Em, you can do whatever you want, go to school, stay home in bed all day, or start your own business. I will support you in whatever you decide to do. I just want you happy."

I kissed him and ran my fingers through his brown, wavy mane. "Are you really mine? You are every woman's fantasy and you want me ... why?" I asked him while still sitting in his lap.

"Em, do you really not know how incredible you are? How can you even ask me that question? You're stunning. Besides that perfect face and your indescribable eyes, you have the body of a pin-up girl. You know I've become obsessed with your tits, and baby, you taste so sweet everywhere. You probably don't know this because I'm the only one who's ever tasted you. And I will never let anyone else have a taste of you. I've never met a woman like you, and I've met lots of women. You never complain. You're not a bitch or an Upper East Side spoiled brat. You love and respect your family. I don't have to go into all your virtues. You were a virgin until I deflowered you a few hours ago, for God's sake. I am snatching and taking you off the market to make sure you don't smarten up and find someone better than me."

"Louis, you're perfect. I will only ever want you for the rest of my life. There is no one better for me … just you."

I then asked the question that was in the back of my mind since we'd descended the stairs. "Did we make love while my parents were waiting for us downstairs?"

Louis laughed and finally said, shaking his head, "No, they got in around noon; we were already showering."

My birthday gifts were far from done that day. My parents gifted both Louis and I with beautiful matching Rolex watches. My daddy said it was a tradition for the parents of the bride to give a watch as an engagement gift. My sister, and less so my brother-in-law, I hoped, had bought me sexy lingerie. I blame my sister for starting me on my love affair with Agent Provocateur. My nana Rose had my sister pack her gift to me in my overnight bag. I unwrapped it to find a wooden jewelry box with beautiful in-laid woodwork. Inside were two silver colored wedding bands. She had a small note tucked under the rings.

To my wonderful little Bubbala,
I know what a beautiful surprise awaits you today. I would like to be one of the first to say Mazel Tov to you and Louis. I wish the both of you a great life together. Kina-ahora. May God give you a big beautiful mispocha. May only naches visit your

doorstep. I wish your Zeyde Nathan was alive to meet your wonderful boychick. Louis loves you very much. He's a smart boy and quite a big macher I hear. I am very happy you met your bashert. I am passing along to you our wedding rings for mazel. My Tatteleh had them made for us during the war. It was always one of my treasured possessions. Your Zeyde and I had a long, happy life together filled with wonderful kids and grandchildren, and I wish you two the same, if not better.

 Zie Gezunt
 Rose Goldberg

 God, I loved that woman.

 I showed Louis the rings and he said it would be an honor for him to wear something that precious. God, I loved him too.

Sex on the beach...

My parents and my sister stayed with us for the whole weekend. That first night after dinner when all our guests turned in for the night, Louis and I went to take a stroll on the beach to recap. I was wearing a chiffon, cream-colored flowing dress. Louis had on white linen pants and a button down, light blue, linen shirt. We were both barefoot, strolling by the water's edge hand in hand.

"Can I try again tonight? Is it too soon? I promise I can do better."

"Better than what?" I asked.

"Well, for one, I won't let myself come after doing you for only three minutes. Two, I want to fuck you harder and longer. I need to know I can make my future wife come repeatedly."

I swallowed loudly. "This morning was so amazingly intense that if it gets any harder I may become permanently impaled on your cock."

"I just got a mental image of you attached to my dick. Shit, I'm already hard."

I looked around at the deserted beach and brazenly placed my unoccupied hand on his swelling cock, for affirmation of his statement. I caressed his length in upward strokes and then squeezed to be rewarded with a, *Ohhhhhh.*

185

Louis let our clasped hands go and hooked both his hands under my arms, then lifted me off my feet to the level of his face.

"I don't even need to touch you to know how drenched your pussy is right now," he said into my panting mouth. "Once all our guests leave and it's just the two of us … I promise to spread you out on this sand and fuck you in every imaginable position. But right now, I just need to be inside you."

I wrapped my arms around his neck and my legs around his waist. "Yeah, that sounds good … cock attachment in progress," I said mockingly, feeling Louis tug at my moistened panties with both hands.

"Didn't I say underwear was prohibited here?" he asked, while shredding them in two with one hard tug.

"Mmmmm," I moaned into his open mouth at his barbaric yank. He held my bare butt with one arm and fondled his zipper with the other. I loved how feminine and weightless he made me feel. When his cock spurted from the confines of his pants and rested with a thump hard against my butt, I jumped from the jolt. Louis took hold of his hard cock and whacked it a few times against my bare ass.

"You like that, little girl?"

"You know I like it. That feels good." I bit down on his bottom lip and then gently sucked on his tongue.

"Baby, can you imagine how good it will feel one day when you let me fuck that beautiful ass?"

If it felt anything like him fucking my pussy, I would let him fuck any hole he wanted. He lifted me a little higher and navigated the tip of his shaft into my leaking hole. I was wet as he slithered all the way inside me with one hard thrust. I yelled out from the harsh blow. Louis stiffened instantly, sobering from his carnal entranced state. I was still sore and tender from this morning's tryst.

"Em, I'm sorry, was that too rough?"

"I'll be okay. I think I like it rough."

I wanted to calm him down and focus on the pleasure and not the pain. He liked my answer because he started pumping himself into me with even more force. I knew it would be hard to walk after that. With every one of his upward thrusts, he pushed me down on his shaft harder. I was panting and moaning so loud that it sounded like I had a few cocks working me, not just one.

Our bodies were flushed and Louis' hard grip on my rear made my pubic bone rub against his. All I could hear was the sound of our skin slapping and the wet slurp of his penis every time he'd thrust into me. I could feel my clit start to tingle from the repeated stimulation. Louis was breathing hard. We were still both dressed and his hair was getting damp from the sweat. I knew he was close; I could smell the scent of sex and sweat between us.

I felt him deep inside me in this position and there was an unfamiliar friction to the front wall of my sex that his cock was causing. I clenched my vaginal walls around his magnificent length and felt my labial lips drag up and down his rod. I was being stimulated in so many places that I couldn't hold on anymore. I let go of Louis' neck and started free falling backward.

"Shit ... Em, hold on, baby." He caught me with both hands outstretched in midair. Then he gripped me by my shoulders and held my body in front of him at an almost ninety-degree perpendicular angle. Louis was squatting with me in his arms and continued pumping into me with irresistible force.

"Fuck, Emily ... COME!"

I was already there. I was already shaking and convulsing around him while he continued to pump into me mercilessly. "Louis ... Louis ... oh, God ... ahhhh," I managed to sob out in between the waves of contractions that sliced through me.

He gave a hard jerk, "Oh fuck ... Emily, I love you..." and then another and then he stilled. I could feel his hot liquid spout deep inside me. He sat down on the sand with a big thump. He then lay flat on his back with his cock still buried deep inside me. We were both spent and felt limbless. A few minutes later, with his cock still twitching inside me, he moved my hair off my face and said, "That was earth shattering if you were wondering."

I was too debilitated for any coherent response. I just smiled and kissed his smooth chest. I was definitely not going to be able to walk the next day... or the day after.

The next day, Louis' mom joined our gleeful group. My new house—*Oh my God, my new house!*—*The Blue Lagoon* had six bedrooms, which meant everybody had their own nook. By the end of that weekend, the house was one hundred percent furnished. I also found out that Trisha and her husband lived on the property in a guesthouse and did all the maintenance and upkeep for the Villa. Trisha was a great cook and was a pleasure to have around. Elizabeth and my mom got along wonderfully. I was blessed to have such a welcoming future mother-in-law. I called my nana back in NY, thanking her profusely for the rings and was happy to know she approved of my love.

I excused myself and left Louis' side for the first time since we arrived at Turks and Caicos to give my best friend a much overdue call.

"Guess what?" I said as soon as I heard Sara's familiar voice.

"Let me do a timeline of your weekend for you. The way I've been imagining it: it started with 'Like A Virgin[40]' by Madonna, leading to Salt 'N Pepa's 'Push It[41],' followed by John Mellencamp's 'Hurts So Good[42].' But all that doesn't matter because Billy Idol is promising us a 'White Wedding[43].' How'd I do, future Mrs. Rich and Famous?"

"You cheated, Mr. Rich and Famous called to give you a heads up ... but I'm glad he did. He knows we're like family. Are you happy for me?"

"Emily, happy? Are you kidding? I'm ecstatic for you. When I think of you and Louis together, I feel like maybe one day I'll find someone to love and someone who wants to stop the world[44] and melt with me. I just hope that someone isn't married with children when I find him."

I wished with all my heart for her to find that person who would see how wonderful she was and love her. Only I knew how much she was hurting inside, even when she put on a big smile for the world to see. I hoped she wouldn't let someone like Jeff break her.

"I'm sure you'll find 'The One[45]' by Elton John..."

"Thanks, love. I'll accept that one even though we both know that 'The One[45]' is not an '80s song ... you're losing your touch, kid. Before I forget, I told Eddie; he asked me to tell you he wishes you guys a big congratulations."

I was with Jenna in the pool the morning before they were scheduled to leave, floating in a white inflatable love seat together.

"Do you think this is crazy?" I asked her, not really needing an in-depth explanation to my question. Jenna was not just my sister; she was also a kind of best friend for me, sometimes even more so than Sara.

"Yes, I think it's crazy and unbelievable. But I'm happy it's happening to you and Louis."

"I lost my virginity, or rather, gave it away willingly, on my birthday."

Jenna turned and looked at me, "And," she said with a hand motion.

"And … it was painful, but mostly amazing."

My sister cooed at my admission. "So now we can talk about sex to each other openly; and you will actually know what the hell I'm talking about. I can't believe my baby sister is getting married soon."

"I don't know when we're getting married yet, we haven't discussed that far," I admitted to Jenna.

"Is he as amazing in bed as he looks?"

"Better," I said, blushing and remembering our sex on the beach from the night before.

Jenna interrupted my daydream, saying, "Mike and I like Louis' idea about expanding Crown Affairs and bringing you in as a full-time partner."

What was going on? I knew nothing about my life anymore. "Jen, what are you talking about, more surprises?"

"What? Louis didn't tell you? He's investing a lot of money into our company. He thinks that it would be great for us to all work together. It will be like a family business."

I'd never really thought about what I wanted to be when I grew up. I guess it was time for me to grow up.

"I'm a little pissed for being constantly left out of the loop. But working and building a business with you and Mike sounds kind of awesome."

Jenna squealed loud enough that our men heard us all the way on the beach.

Rewind, erase, and change...

My surprises didn't end there. Once my family and Louis' mom left us, we had a few days to frolic in the sun, just the two of us. I really did feel like we were lost on a deserted island. We were naked most of the time, either swimming in the pool or making love in the sand. One morning after being alone for a week, Louis didn't let me go downstairs naked. Instead, he picked out a white bikini and cover-up for me.

"It's just us; I thought you liked it when my boobs were at your disposal."

We'd just had our morning shower sex and Louis was still drying me with a big fluffy towel.

"Baby, I love having your tits on display. But I need you dressed today. We're having company ... if they see you naked they won't ever want to leave."

"So it's my tits that keep you from leaving?" I asked, knowing that Louis needed to suck my nipples to start and end each day.

"Your tits are one reason, then there is your tight pussy and your talented mouth, and that juicy ass. But what keeps me glued to you is the package that holds all my favorite parts together. You have bewitched me since I first saw you. You are mine for life, baby. I can't wait to officially make you Emily Bruel."

"Who's our company today, Mr. Bruel?"

"Why don't you put your bikini and cover-up on and go downstairs to find out?"

I got dressed in a New York minute and ran down the stairs to see Sara and Eddie sitting in the kitchen having breakfast. Sara and I squealed and started jumping up and down like a couple of pre-teens at a rock concert.

"I thought you left for London," I said, still embracing my best friend.

"I'm leaving from here to England. Eddie will get me settled before he starts his vacation. I had to see with my own eyes if fucking made you more beautiful," the stupid ditz said to me right in front of her mortified brother.

"Congratulations, Emma."

"Thank you, Eddie." I let go of Sara to give her brother a hug. "I can't believe you guys are here. This is such a wonderful surprise. Thank you for coming. How long are you staying?"

"Thank you and your rich fiancé for bringing us here. My camp doesn't start until next week. We're all yours for the next three nights. Let's go *chica*, show me the ring. I can't believe that my best friend is getting married to the hottest, richest guy ever."

Eddie rolled his eyes. I guess he still wasn't sold on Louis' hotness. While Sara was inspecting my left hand, I realized I'd left my engagement ring upstairs. After hugging and kissing my friends over and over, I ran back up to our room to put my ring on. I found Louis on the phone talking quietly to someone, obviously unaware I'd come back up. I didn't want to interrupt his conversation. I snuck in quietly.

"Isabella, let me talk. You never fucking let me say two words. Why would you keep that from me? Yes, I'm getting married, but I want to know who the fuck told you? You're doing this to me because you want to punish me? I have a right to know. Well, it's too late now. I love her, that's the difference. I don't want her to know anything about you. She won't understand. If you try to contact her Isa, I. Will. Ruin. You! That's right ... the video. You know which video I have and I know you don't want your family to see it. If you jeopardize my marriage, I repeat, I will ruin you. No, she's all I need. I don't share her and I will never need anyone else in bed when I'm with her."

I felt my legs start to give out. I made an unconscious, pained noise, which Louis must've heard because he turned around in horror. I berated myself for letting my guard down and believing him. I'd heard his whole secret conversation with God-knows-who about God-knows-what. He tried so hard to keep me sheltered and as far away from the life he lived before we met, that every time those worlds collided it was cataclysmic.

"Fuck ... Emily! Let me explain."

My body had a déjà vu feeling back to that night in Phillip's club. It went back to that fight or flight instinct. I chose flight once again. I couldn't fight with Louis being in the state my head and heart were in. The air was still very much knocked out of me. I ran out of the room operating on autopilot and into another bedroom on the same floor. I locked the door behind me, fell on the floor, and started to cry. Who the fuck was Isabella and what didn't she tell him? Why did she want to talk to me? What kind of video did he have that could ruin her? He was knocking on the door like a madman. It felt like the whole house was shaking.

"Em, you don't know what you just heard. Let me in. I want to explain. It's not what you think. Fuck ... baby, please, I can explain."

His voice was angry but I could tell he was scared. *Good*, he should be scared.

"Louis, fuck off! Leave me alone. I don't want your stupid explanations. I don't need a husband who keeps dirty secrets from his wife."

"Open the door, Em, or I'll break it down. You have less than a minute to make up your mind; either way I'm coming in."

I wanted to avoid an ugly scene, knowing that both Sara and

Eddie were still downstairs blissfully clueless to what was happening in my broken paradise. I'd just finished convincing them a few weeks ago that Louis wasn't a Neanderthal and now here he was, breaking down doors to get to me. I got up off the floor and unlocked the door.

"Door is open; no need to be violent. I don't want to hear your stupid stories ... I want to go home."

He walked into the room and locked the door. He thought he could keep me confined to one place. He was always afraid I'd run.

"Isabella is an old friend. She was in love with me ... still is. I never loved her ... I ... I just kept her around because it was convenient. You have to understand, she came from money so I didn't think she was using me financially like a lot of other women." He looked down at his feet, choosing his words carefully before going on. "Her family kept trying to bribe me into marrying her. Her parents are very wealthy. They own hotels and resorts all over the world. I had no interest in her other than being her friend."

I didn't stop him so he kept talking. "Isabella was fun to be around at first but she started to cause trouble. I once found her in my apartment snorting cocaine with men she picked up in some bar. She always tried to get a reaction out of me. Emily, you have to believe me. I want nothing to do with her, but she won't leave me alone. Her father even tried to invest in my company with the hopes of entwining our interests. I refuse to have any dealings with anyone related to her.

"The last time I saw her, she was in a hospital recovering from a suicide attempt over a year ago. Her younger brother found me a few months ago with the intention of beating me up as some kind of revenge. He was under the impression that I'd ruined his crazy sister's life. He said that because of me and my sexual experimentations with Isa, she couldn't be with a normal man." Louis started nervously laughing, like a maniac. "I didn't even waste my time telling him the truth about his sister. I had security escort him out of my office. His parents obviously preferred to keep him in the dark about Isabella."

He pleaded with me. "There was nothing for me to tell you, Em. I've told you I'm not proud of the things I've done before you. Isa and I were friends. I slept with her once ... way before I met you. I was alone and horny one night and she was there. Sleeping with her was the biggest mistake of my life. She wasn't mentally stable and I shouldn't have fucked her. She made me look like a villain to her family. Now I look like an asshole to you."

I didn't know what to say. This was too much information coming at me all at once. I guess there was a lot I still didn't know about him. I still had questions for him that just didn't add up in my head.

"You said to her that she should've told you. What should she have told you?"

"Emily, she wrote a book; a memoir about her and me. My legal department has been trying to keep it out of print. But, as you know, sex sells. The media loves to make me out to look like a heartless pig. One minute I'm an eligible bachelor; the next I'm a sex-hungry douchebag. There is no question that even if she removes my name people will still know the book is about me. It's mostly lies. Some of the events did happen but she edited me into almost every sexual scenario you could imagine as the fucking culprit."

"Louis, who cares? It's just a book. It's not like you have a sex tape out there with her ... right? If you just tell people it's all a lie they'll believe you."

"No, definitely no sex tapes. But, baby, if you read this book ... I know you will never agree to be my wife. It will scare the shit out of you. Emily, what she did in my presence is nothing I'd ever want to come to light. She liked crazy shit. She needed crazy situations to get herself off and I was dumb enough to provide them for her."

"Louis, I don't understand."

"Baby, why would you? You're perfect and innocent. I was fucked up before I met you. I was empty. I was trying to find myself. I once arranged for ten men to fuck her in every hole imaginable at a private party. She asked me and I didn't even love her or care about her enough as a friend to stop it. I told her it wasn't a good idea at first but she begged me to make her 'gang bang' fantasy happen and I did. I was there; I watched. Now it all comes back to bite me in the ass."

I could feel bile rising into my mouth.

"Did you read the book?"

"Yes."

"What else does it say about the man I'm supposed to marry?"

"It says that she did all those things to please me. That she was in love with me. That she would fuck any man or woman alive just to turn me on and make me happy. She's a sick delusional girl. I never asked her to do anything for me and those things didn't turn me on. She was just entertainment."

"I guess you're the entertainment now. What do you want me to do, Louis? If this book comes out, how will I face my parents? They won't let me marry you if they find out."

"It won't see the light of day. I promise you. My lawyers are suing her father and his billion-dollar empire for defamation of character. I have a video of us in my apartment. On the video, I tell her that I don't love her and that as her friend, I don't want her to keep doing what she's been doing to her body. She told me that if I didn't continue having a sexual relationship with her she would kill herself or she would kill me. She promised to make up lies and ruin my career. That was when our friendship ended. My lawyers have been working with her father and his counsel to eradicate this stupid, filthy book. Hopefully they'll be able to get her out of our lives forever."

What if she tries to hurt him? Could she come after me? I thought to myself as fear ran up my spine. "Will it work?"

"Yes, my team is confident. I just didn't want her coming after you. Emily, I told you if I knew I would one day find my heart and soul outside my body, I would never have done the things I did. I never knew it was possible to love a woman the way I love and need you. Please, baby, you have to believe that I made stupid choices and had stupid friends, but you are my life now. I would never do anything to jeopardize what we have. I love you and I wish I could rewind, erase, and change my past, but I can't. You are my future and I want to live with YOU in the future. I don't want to live in my past. My past was what brought me to you; it prepared me for this, for us. I promise we'll get through this ... just don't leave me."

He looked scared that day. How did he not know that I couldn't leave him even if I tried? I couldn't imagine a second without Louis Bruel, let alone a life without him.

My life changed drastically after Turks and Caicos. Life wasn't as happy and carefree as I'd let myself imagine. There was a dark cloud quietly looming over our life now. I had a bodyguard at all times, shadowing my every move. The book Louis described to me never got printed and a few months after our wedding, Isabella was admitted into a psychiatric hospital shortly after trying to kill herself.

That was a big disaster that Louis and I were spared. Having a book like that forever circulating about the man who would one day be the father of my children was nauseating to think about. A few years ago, Louis informed me that Isabella overdosed and died while back home in London. Despite everything he told me, I knew that he had cared for her, seeing how depressed and sad he got after learning about her death. I was sad for him and for her family. They couldn't save their daughter; she was a lost soul. I forgave Louis for being an immoral, careless friend to that fragile girl. But I was also secretly relieved for my family that she was gone and would never be a threat to any of us again.

Our past was there to teach us to be better in the future, and my husband had learned his lesson ... I thought.

Life in fast-forward...

Our life after that point just seemed to go in fast forward. To make up for not spoiling me during our early courting period, Louis over-compensated by having fresh flowers delivered to me every day for a few months. I finally talked him into just getting me flowers once a week. Louis was generous in all aspects. He spoiled me with his love, his time, and his wealth; which, as he constantly reminded me, was my wealth, too.

I moved in with Louis shortly after we got back from Turks and Caicos two weeks later. My parents weren't thrilled about my decision, but Louis threatened to move into my room if they refused. He was so worried about me getting mad and leaving that he felt he could only diffuse those situations by keeping me within arm's reach. I honestly loved going to sleep and waking up in his strong arms every day. I couldn't imagine for a second living apart from him.

We had sex on every surface of his treehouse. My favorite place to make love to Louis had to be in the pool. The way the sound of our lovemaking echoed across the space, bouncing off the walls and the water only added to the impossibly risqué spectacle.

Between being Louis Bruel's fiancée and starting to run Crown Affairs with Jenna and Mike, I had very little time to go to school. We agreed that going to school part-time was still better than not going at all. My overachieving parents kept trying to push me to go to school full-time. I wanted to attend NYU full-time to be a well-rounded person, but the truth was, it only took away from my time with Louis. My subconscious must've known back then that my days with Louis Bruel were numbered and that every minute was precious. We were inseparable, insatiable, and omnivorous, sharing ourselves with no one but each other.

We decided to get married on our estate in Turks and Caicos on December 31st, with thirty of our closest friends and family. Louis told me that his New Year's resolution was for me to be Mrs. Bruel. That wedding was the first event that I executed as a shareowner and partner of Crown Affairs. The wedding was incredible and romantic. The festivities lasted for a whole week. We rented out several villas around Providenciales so that all of our guests had their own place to retreat to. I think Louis wanted our house to be just for us. He was unapologetic about not wanting to share me with our friends and family.

Sara and her entire family, including her brother Eddie and his girlfriend Michelle, all joined in on our festivities as well. She was my unofficial maid of honor. Eddie and Michelle also announced to everyone a few nights before the wedding that they were engaged, finally. Louis and Eddie very unexpectedly took a liking to each other in addition to having a good working relationship.

The night before our big day, we had our sorry excuse for bachelor and bachelorette parties. Mike promised me no strippers and Jenna promised Louis that we wouldn't leave the house. It was more like a relaxing pajama party with my favorite girls than a wild night out. Sara presented me with my something blue, which was a brand new, light blue, vibrating dildo. It was double the size of Pinky. My sister's gift was my wedding night lingerie, which consisted of a pure white lace bustier, that propped my boobs up even higher, and satin, ruffle and lace panties that hardly covered my butt.

Louis and I were supposed to spend that night apart from each other before we got married. That was the plan. Sara and I got a little tipsy on champagne and fell asleep in her room together. In the morning, I woke up in my bed and in Louis' strong arms. I knew he wouldn't spend the night away from me. I was admiring the view of my soon to be husband, not yet letting the anxiety of our upcoming wedding day get to me.

"Did you enjoy your last night of freedom?" I asked when I could tell he wasn't asleep anymore but just pretending so I could ogle him a little longer.

"The hottest part of my night was finding my sexy soon to be wife in bed with another woman. I should've stayed home to watch."

I pushed him away. He was laughing and trying to pin me under him. He was just about to prove how sexy the thought of me with another woman was when Jenna stormed the room and almost threw Louis off me.

"You can wait until tonight ... for the love of God, leave her alone for one night," she screamed.

He was holding a pillow over his straining hard-on. The scene was unforgettable and hysterical. The look on my sister's face was priceless. She was trying hard to look at him with disgust and contempt but those two emotions are hard to fabricate around Louis Bruel naked and smirking with that damn dimple plastered on his cheek.

"Can you please leave our room? I have a gift for your sister," Louis yelled mockingly back at JenJen.

"I know what kind of gift you have. You'll have to explain to your gift it has to wait until after the ceremony. Emily has to get ready."

"Jenna, please, we need some privacy unless you want me

to drop the pillow."

Jenna gave him the *I'm warning you* look and then she gave me the *be strong* look and stormed out. Louis dropped the pillow, giving me a glimpse of what would soon all be legally mine.

"I'm ready for my gift ... I won't tell, if you won't."

He jumped into bed and shut my mouth with a proper good morning kiss. He pulled me to him and straddled me on his hips. He pulled a box from his nightstand drawer. I guess he was serious about getting me a gift.

"Louis, I didn't know. I didn't get you anything."

"Em, you're marrying me today and you're sitting naked on my dick ... if you find a gift to top that ... I want it!"

I lowered myself to kiss my most prized gift of all. I didn't even want to leave him for a few hours to go get ready. I just wanted for us to stay in bed together forever. I'm sure the Rabbi could just marry us in bed. He pulled the square red box open to reveal matching blue and canary diamond earrings, a pendant, and tennis bracelet. It was magnificent and must've cost more than some people's homes. It was beautiful.

"It's incredible and I don't deserve it. I haven't done anything to earn this."

He looked at me, confused by my reaction. Whenever Louis bought me crazy expensive things, I felt undeserving. I hadn't worked for any of this. He didn't need to spend his hard earned money on me. I didn't need this.

"You deserve the moon, the sky, and the fucking stars. Once I figure out a way to get those, they'll be yours. If I can't buy you things, then what's the point of me having all my millions? Everything that is mine is yours. I didn't steal the money I have. I earned it! I earned it for us. Emily, please let me give you beautiful things."

I nodded. There was no point arguing with him. He loved me and he got me things that he thought pleased me. "Thank you. It's beyond stunning, I'll wear them today."

Jen and I decided to have a local designer supply the flowers for my wedding. Every inch of the beach was covered in pink peonies and lilacs. Our *Chuppa* was constructed over our infinity-edged pool overlooking the ocean. The pool was covered with a special Lucite stage with a sea of water lilies trapped under the glass. It looked as if we were walking in Monet's garden toward a flower altar. Once the sun started to set, hundreds of candles illuminated the night sky. My parents, my Nana Rose, and Louis' mom all stood with us under the *Chuppa*.

I was wearing a cream-colored, strapless, mermaid bottom, silk taffeta Carolina Herrera gown designed just for me. Louis wore a black Kiton tux that was hand delivered from Italy and fitted to perfection in Turks a week before our wedding. Holding his hands and listening to him profess his love to me, promising to take care of me in front of God and our family, was equivalent to having my heart beat outside my chest. It was indescribable. That night was perfect.

Louis had only one request for our wedding. He wanted to be in charge of the musical entertainment. I remember Jen and I agreeing but being slightly apprehensive. I wanted everything to be perfect. I should've known Louis Bruel couldn't do anything less than perfect. We had more musicians perform at our wedding than guests. You would think we were at Carnegie Hall attending a symphony. Our first dance still takes my breath away and chokes me with tears every time I let my heart relive that moment. A beautiful, older woman walked out on the illuminated checkered dance floor that was set up on the beach under a huge, white tent. With her soulful sexy jazz voice, she serenaded us to our first dance. She belted out 'What Are You Doing For The Rest Of Your Life[46]' by Barbra Streisand, and I stopped breathing. I was floating away with my husband and letting each word wash over me. The lyrics were incredible and said exactly what we both expected and hoped from one another; to just spend our whole lives lost in each other.

That song still plays in my subconscious as the background to all my dreams. Hollywood couldn't have scripted my wedding better if they tried. It was spectacular from beginning to end, just like my husband. Every song that played at my wedding had meaning. Louis, with Sara's help, chose all of my favorite '80s songs. He didn't want to let anyone except my dad dance with me. I had to beg his mother to make him dance with her for a few songs so I could sneak a dance in with Mike and Eddie.

Sara and I even had our girls' moment where we danced to Tina Turner's 'Simply The Best[47]' like we were back in my room and it was just the two of us. Louis enjoyed our little show, but came to claim his runaway bride and made sure I danced only with him for the rest of the night. At midnight, we toasted and wished each other a happy New Year with a private fireworks display as a surprise treat from my husband. He wanted to know during the light spectacle if we could have another 4th of July performance, but this time with penetration. He could do whatever he wanted to me from that day on and I would love every minute of it. We danced all night and made sweet love into the morning hours long after our guests had left. It was our fairy tale. I should've known the end would be closing in on my fairy tale eventually. Fairy tales aren't meant to last outside the pages of a book.

Happy V-Day...

Our first year of marriage was filled with many risqué sexcapades. On Valentine's Day, which was also a little over a month after our wedding, I decided to surprise my husband at work for once. After a quick trip the day before to Agent Provocateur, I came into his Upper East Side office. The über young, blonde receptionist told me my husband was still out in a meeting. She offered to open his office for me so I could wait for him there.

"Mrs. Bruel, right this way. I'm sure Louis will be happy to see you once he gets back."

So I'm Mrs. Bruel but my husband is Louis, I thought to myself with a ping of something that was bordering on jealousy and animosity.

"Stephanie, you can call me Emily, especially since I'm probably younger than you."

There we go, now I feel better for her calling her boss by his first name. She gave me a knowing smile and unlocked Louis' office.

I was wearing a Diana Von Furstenberg wrap around, red polka dot dress and I had on my black, satin corset with crotchless underwear hiding underneath. It was early afternoon. I had hoped Louis wouldn't have taken too long with his meeting, or I might've lost my nerve.

I walked around his office doing a little snooping. I found our wedding picture prominently displayed on his desk, which made me happy. He had a huge jar full of Twizzlers. He consumed an obscene amount of that confection every day. I also found a picture of a ten-year-old Louis with his dad in an open jeep. They were both wearing safari hats. God, he looked so much like his dad. I smiled to myself, thinking about what our kids would one day look like.

I began to wonder if I shouldn't wait for him to come back before I stripped, but instead, just wait for him in my sexy lingerie behind his desk or on his couch. I called Stephanie up front.

"Stephanie, when my husband gets back, make sure he's alone, and don't let him know I'm here. I'd like to surprise him."

"Okay Mrs.—I mean Emily. No problem."

Forty minutes later, I could hear the lock turn and the door start to open. My heart was beating out of my chest with anticipation. Louis walked through the door slowly, his eyes looking down at some paperwork he was holding, not yet taking in my presence. He looked preoccupied and deep in thought.

I was lying down in my tight, satin corset with my boobs pushed up almost up to my neck. I had my legs slightly parted so that my sex was peeking out of my crotchless satin underwear. I still had my black Manolo Blahnik heels on with my knees somewhat bent so that the heels dug into the green leather couch. He walked right past me and went to sit behind his desk, fetching a Twizzler. I guess I blended into the surroundings. The couch was positioned on his left against the window and across from the door. I started to touch myself by running my fingers down my satin corset. Louis noticed the movement and lifted his gaze. Our eyes locked.

Surprise, then shock, registered on his face. Still silently assessing my ensemble, I could see the beginning of what looked like a smile creep onto his beautiful lips. Not looking away from me, Louis picked up his phone and snapped his command, "Hold

my calls and cancel my appointments, something just came up."
No hello, no goodbye, no thank you, just point-blank like he always was: *wham, bam, thank you ma'am*. He dropped the Twizzler and got up, still not looking away from me. He walked over
and locked the door. He removed his jacket and threw it on the
floor. He then sat in a chair at the foot of the couch facing me.
His no nonsense attitude was beyond hot. My heart rate started
picking up. My hand had now made the journey to my exposed
crotch.

Louis leaned back, getting comfortable on the chair and
loosening his tie. He put his right foot over his left knee. He rested his chin on a propped up hand and just watched me. I was
incited to put on an erotic show for my indulgent husband. I
parted my legs marginally to give him a better view of my wet
sex. I played with my aching clit, rubbing my moisture into it.
He, just staring at me with no words, was a little unnerving. I
wanted to know if this was as hot for him as it was for me. I
slipped a wet finger inside my pussy. Louis' eyes widened and
his breath hitched with the sound of my finger entering my wet
slit; yes, he was affected by my brazen behavior in his office. I
brought my other hand back up and lowered the breast cup of the
corset. My boob jiggled out of its confines and a stiff nipple
emerged, saluting its master. I started squeezing the nipple between my fingers. I hadn't yet looked away from him.

Louis ran his dark gaze up and down my body, watching me
masturbate for him. That little display of mine felt very raunchy
and risqué with him egging me on. I started to moan in a low
voice. My own finger worked me to chase my climax. I was
grinding my hips into my fingers. Louis was with me. He was
taking in long slow breaths. He dropped his propped leg from his
knee and leaned forward with both elbows coming to rest on his
parted, outstretched thighs.

My boobs were big enough that if I wanted to, and I did
right then, I could reach down and suck my own nipples. I low-

ered my head and cupped my breast, bringing it close to my mouth. I started sucking my own firm nipple. When my lips closed around my rigid bud, Louis let out his first sound. "Fuck," was all he said before he took hold of his straining hard-on. Watching him touching himself was exciting. I started massaging my clit at warp speed. I was groaning like a caged animal from the sight of my husband finally losing control.

Louis jumped off the chair. He unzipped and freed his cock in the blink of an eye. He was working his shaft so hard it looked painful. He was now standing close, hunched over me. I looked up at him, releasing my wet nipple with a pop and leaned toward him, opening my mouth wide. We needed no verbal communication. Our eyes did all the talking. Louis positioned his cock at my mouth and cupped my jaw with his free hand. As soon as my lips came in contact with his tip, he closed his eyes. He was holding me with one hand and his cock with the other. He was feeding me his cock one inch at a time. I tried to take as much of him as I could without suffocating. The taste and the scent of him made me frantically massage my clit. Louis let go of my jaw and lowered his hand to test my arousal.

"Fuck, baby!"

We were operating on sentences composed of two words—max. His fingers found my sweet spot and he drove two long, talented fingers inside my drenched channel. His fingers did a much better job than I ever could. I clenched my jaw around his cock at his invasion. I was close. I could feel my body start to give in to the building eruption within my core. I started moaning with Louis lodged in my throat. I was still rubbing my clit and holding on to his submerged hand as I started to explode.

Our vulgar sight was playing out in the back of my closed eyelids, which only kept the waves of pleasure coming over me. I was still holding Louis' hand clenched deep in me when he stopped pumping his hips into my now lax mouth. He removed his fingers from my hole and let go of his cock. He grasped my head with both hands over my hair and pushed himself unbearably deep into my mouth. He belted out my name and purged his cum deep into my throat. When we finished our lewd display of passion, we were both ready to collapse.

"Nice to see you, Mrs. Bruel. What brings you to this neck of the woods?" he said as if we hadn't just gotten one another off in the kinkiest, most shameless mid-day booty call.

"It was the wood that brought me here, Mr. Bruel," I answered smugly. He dropped to his knees and finally kissed me hello.

"Is that really what I taste like?" he asked, making a pained face.

I nodded, "It's an acquired taste. I'm not sure I'd survive without it, much like you and your Twizzlers."

"It's a good thing you taste nothing like my cum."

We laughed. I finally got off the couch and sat on my husband's lap. "Happy Valentine's Day," I announced.

"Em, you're the only Jew I know who celebrates every goddamn holiday."

"What? Everybody celebrates Valentine's Day. It's the day of love."

"Baby, I'm not complaining. You can wear sexy lingerie for me for Christmas, Easter, St. Patrick's Day; I fucking love it. Wherever you got this outfit, go back and get more. Better yet, call them up and order one of everything in the store. I plan to watch the surveillance video of you getting yourself off in my office every day."

I blushed, realizing someone could see that tape.

"Relax ... I'm the only one with access to that footage."

I exhaled, relaxing at the thought of our crude act staying private.

"I can't go back to work after that," Louis said, running his fingers up and down my satin corset.

"Your receptionist calls you Louis and not Mr. Bruel.

Why?"

"I don't like when young girls call me Mr. Bruel. It makes me feel like a molester."

I shot him the look of death and got off his lap before he had a chance to stop me.

"Em, it's not like that."

"Didn't you tell me those same words before you humped me in your car?"

He got up to come after me. He wrapped his hands around me, engulfing me from behind.

"The only person I ever want to molest is you. Please, never think I could possibly want anyone but you."

I really believed him that day. I would never want another man and was certain that my gorgeous husband felt the same way about me. I guess it's true what they say about blondes; we're not the sharpest tools in the box.

Almost legal ... and pregnant

After being married a little less than a year, Louis and I found out we were going to be parents. I think we went through seven pregnancy tests, and even after that, we were both still in denial. Our plan was for it to be just the two of us for at least two years before we started thinking about kids. I wasn't on the pill and Louis refused to even look at a condom.

My sister and Mike were having trouble conceiving and we didn't think it could just happen to us without us trying. Thinking back, that was really silly of us. It wasn't like we were only having sex once a week. We were sometimes fornicating several times a day. Of course, we would inevitably make a baby.

I secretly told JenJen, Sara, and my mother, but Louis didn't know. I remember Eddie telling Louis once he found out we were expecting, that we'd have to postpone my twenty-first birthday party. My due date was July 1st, which would mean that on my twenty-first birthday I would already have a little baby in my arms. We had a big party planned out where we'd all congregate in Las Vegas for the weekend and get obliterated on alcohol. Sara and I were especially excited that we could finally drink legally. So what did I do? I went and got myself knocked up.

"You are such a stupid cow. First you marry the first gorgeous millionaire you meet and now you go and start having his beautiful kids." Sara always made me laugh. I was always shocked at the stuff that came out of her mouth. How could someone who looked elegant and sweet have such a colorful tongue?

"You're just upset about Vegas. You could still go and drink yourself into a coma without me."

"First of all, my birthday is before yours and second, Eddie promised to take me to Amsterdam where, no question, I'm getting high. Thirdly, the only way I'm going to Vegas is with my favorite bitch. I'm not interested in getting drunk on my own. I can do that in New York every day."

"Thank you for holding off on Vegas until we can enjoy it together."

"No worries; once you become a mommy, I promise Guns N' Roses and I will take you to 'Paradise City.[48]'" She smiled her mischievous, cute little pouty smile at me.

We were hanging out on my seventh floor, outdoor, treetop terrace, all bundled up in our jackets. It was a few days before New Year's Eve and my one-year wedding anniversary. Sara was back home from Brown University and we'd just had a Christmas tree delivered upstairs. We were both Jewish, but just like every Jew in Manhattan around holiday time; we too wished we could have a Christmas tree to call our own. We settled for having a New Year's tree that we got to decorate. That year, the theme was liquor. We decorated the whole massive, seven-foot tree in little chocolate, liquor filled bottles and tiny little lights.

"I can't believe Louis and I are going to be parents."

"You have been shocking me from the day we graduated high school. I would never in a million years have thought that you would fall so hard and so fast for the first guy who shoved his tongue, among other things, down your throat. It's like someone pushed a button and life just started for you. I wish I could find that same button. I'm sick of the losers I keep ending up with."

Sara had been serial dating her way through the last two years of her higher education. You couldn't tell by looking at her how promiscuous she really was. Sara lost her virginity at fifteen to her brother's best friend, Jeffery. I'm the only person besides Sara and Jeff who knows that. I promised to take their secret to my grave. Eddie, for one, would break Jeff's dick off. So would Jeff's wife, who was his girlfriend at the time he and Sara had sex. Well, I knew they secretly still fucked but Sara was tight lipped about that, knowing I'd rip her a new asshole for sleeping around with a married man.

"I'm sure you'll find a nice guy. Stop dating random jerks and your problems are solved."

"I don't want a nice guy. The nice ones are boring and suck balls in the sack. I need someone hot who knows how to use his big penis."

This girl had no filter. Even though I thought that, I would never say it out loud. That's why we were best friends; Sara could say what I thought better than me.

"Okay, Sara, I'm sure you'll find a hot, dangerous guy with a big dick who knows how to use it."

Of course, that's when my husband decided to sneak up on me from behind to check up on my New Year's tree-decorating progress.

"I hope you were describing me, little girl."

"Who else, Louis? You're the only dick I know."

"Very nice. And let's work on keeping it that way." Louis kissed the top of my head. He pulled Sara in for a group hug. "Sara, if you want, I can introduce you to a few dicks I know."

"Thank you, my wonderful friend-in-law. I think I will stick to fetching my own dick on my own time."

Louis then eyed our beautiful tree, raising his eyebrow at it. "Why is the tree covered in little chocolate bottles?"

"It is in honor of our upcoming twenty-first birthdays. But

thanks to you knocking me up, now I won't be drinking." I made a sad face at Sara for a full theatrical performance.

"You two are making a real meal of this drinking shit. Sara, you have been drinking since starting Brown and, Em, you hate the taste of alcohol. Who cares how old you are?"

"Louis, don't be a crab. It's just symbolic. You're just too old to remember turning twenty-one," Sara retorted, trying to stand up for our choice of tree ornaments.

"I see two Jewish American Princesses decorating a Christmas tree on New Year's. What does that symbolize?" Louis asked, laughing and pointing to our beautiful New Year's tree. Louis didn't get me at all.

"It symbolizes that I have an ass for a husband." I was about to storm off and go back inside when he pulled me into him. He put his hands around my waist and cupped my growing belly.

"It only symbolizes how much I love my crazy wife who celebrates every goddamn holiday under the sun." He leaned down to kiss the area right under my ear, which sent a jolt of heat right to my crotch. I could hear Sara groaning her disgust in the background. But I was already melting into my husband's touch. All he needed to do was touch me, and the whole world vanished.

"I'm out of here. I'm not into watching without participation!" Sara called out before I heard the sound of the elevator gate slam shut behind her. I said bye silently in my head.

"Why do you always make my friend leave?"

He continued nuzzling down my neck, moving whatever came in between his lips and my skin.

"I didn't make her leave, baby. She could've stayed and watched, but she said she wasn't into that. Now where should I fuck my wife?"

"Bed please..."

I loved being pregnant. Louis and I were both surprised at how sexy he found my body during pregnancy. It was spring in New York. We flew to our villa in Turks and Caicos to escape the city life a little. I was about six months pregnant. Other than my growing tummy and overfilled boobs, I didn't seem pregnant. My face and legs were still skinny, and I really didn't get bloated.

"How is it possible that I find you more attractive with a huge belly? It should be wrong for me to want to fuck my pregnant wife in the positions that I have you in my head."

I was just waking up from a restful night. My sleep position of choice pre-pregnancy was on my stomach. However, at six months pregnant, I became more of a back sleeper. Waking up on my back had its advantages. Louis always got up before me to run. While in Turks, he would run on the beach. Lately, I'd noticed he'd been skipping his running routine in order to administer the most sinful wakeup calls for his pregnant wife. A few nights earlier, I'd woken up to him halfway inside me. I was startled by the intrusion but my husband assured me that he had made sure I was dripping wet and ready for his needy cock. That morning, Louis was lying beside me, running his fingers up and down my naked blooming belly. I could tell he really was struggling with himself for finding my new body appealingly sexy.

"The doctor said we don't have to abstain from any sexual activity. So we could fuck away."

"Knowing that my seed did that to you is intoxicating. It gives me such a high to mark you like that for everyone to see. Em, I love how voluptuous you are everywhere. Will you let me do whatever I want to do to you?"

"My body is at your disposal. Lick it, suck it, and fuck it as much as you want. Just don't hurt the baby."

I was insatiable before I was pregnant. Now, the pregnancy

hormones definitely made me a total nympho. I wanted Louis to make love to me all the time. He was only too happy to oblige. My biggest craving was not for food these days, but for my husband's cock, preferably in my mouth. I did have to pee every hour, so that was the only downside to *being with child*, as Louis liked to say.

"Before you get too excited, I need to go take care of business. I don't want to pee on you or the bed."

"If you're not back by the time I count to twenty, I'll have you suck me off while you're peeing."

I ran to the bathroom. I could hear Louis counting out loud. I wanted to goad him a little, so after I finished, I just closed the lid and stayed there, waiting for him to storm the bathroom.

"...18, 19, 19 and 1/2, 19 and 3/4, 20 ... sweet Emily, ready or not, my hard cock and I are coming to get you."

I was sitting on the toilet over a closed lid. He came in dick in hand as promised. The vision of this beautiful, naked, virile man all tanned, smooth, and muscular standing before me wearing only a silver necklace that I gave him for his thirtieth birthday would be too much for any woman. His hair was a sexy mess and his unshaved jaw gave him that extra sexy edge that promised roughness. For the millionth time since I'd first laid eyes on Louis Bruel, I thought how it wasn't fair for one person to be this devastatingly handsome. He was stroking his long, thick cock from root to tip. I was innocently sitting, smiling, and minding my own business, just waiting for him to attack. I could see his eyes travel from my eyes down to my impossibly huge breasts, down to my growing stomach, and finally to my exposed sex. I could see my husband's trigger points; boobs, stomach, pussy, and go...

"Are you fucking with me, little girl? The only one doing the fucking here today will be me fucking your brains out."

He knew how hot I got when he talked dirty to me. Louis had never been anything but perfect to me in bed. He couldn't hurt me even if he tried. He walked over to me and kneeled down to kiss me tenderly. He left my lips to caress my aching breasts. He was handling them with such care you'd think they were rare jewels, running his fingers and lips all around them. He pushed them together and inhaled my scent. He squeezed both nipples between his fingers and I moaned in ecstasy. We really were obsessed with each other. He lowered himself farther down and kissed my belly, whispering his love to our little baby growing inside me.

He glanced back up at me from under his thick, dark eyebrows. I was cupping his cheeks with both hands, waiting for a full smile, dimple included. My wish was granted. I kissed my favorite dimple. Louis got up and took his massive erection with both hands. He was towering over me, his dick in line with my face. I could feel his asshole persona re-emerge. No more mister nice guy. I would now be dealing with Louis Bruel, Hotshot Millionaire.

"Suck my dick ... NOW!"

Wow, hello Mr. Asshole. Well, I guess we need two to play this game. "And if I don't want to suck your dick, Mr. Bruel?"

"Baby, I can see your mouth salivating. You would swallow my dick whole if you could. Don't be coy with me; open your mouth and take what's yours."

"Say please."

"Please suck my dick, Mrs. Bruel. Now!"

I went to work giving my husband what he likes to refer to as: *the best blowjob of his life.* I sucked him into my mouth so deeply I was afraid he'd get stuck in my throat. The cause of death would be *suffocation by spousal's cock.* I worked his shaft thoroughly, licking every inch and sucking every exposed surface, scrotum included. After he brutally came and poured himself savagely inside my mouth, he lifted me off the toilet. I was hoisted up with Louis' forearms sliding under my parted knees. I grabbed his neck as he effortlessly supported all my weight and carried me, spread eagle, back toward our bed.

Louis didn't put me down. He lowered me down his body before plunging his once again, hard cock inside my sprawled pussy. He was moving me up and down while I held on to him by his hair. My stomach was blocking my view. I needed a visual so I could let go and give in to the raging climax Mr. Asshole had ignited.

"Louis, I want to see you doing me. I can't see anything; my belly is in the way."

Still holding me suspended over his half submerged cock, he walked us into our mirrored colossal closet.

"How's that, baby? Now you can see me fuck you hard."

This was exactly what I needed. I could see us from every angle. I saw how his butt muscles flexed every time he plunged inside me. His balls were hitting my ass with each jolt of his cock. He was relentless, driving himself into me like a machine. I had our image imprinted in my head. I started to close my eyes and was about to let go.

"Open your eyes. I need to see your eyes as I'm coming."

I opened my eyes and my orgasm exploded around his pummeling cock. I was straining to keep my eyes open. My vision was blurry. I could make out Louis glaring into me and I could feel by his frantic pace he was seconds away from…

"Eee … ma … ly … fuck … baby … yes…"

Would this ever get old between us? Every time he entered me, it felt right. How was it possible that we were that perfect for each other?

Goodbye and hello...

I was eight months pregnant when I got the strangest call from my husband, saying we needed to talk. I was going crazy with the endless possibilities of what was that important for Louis to make sure I was home at one o'clock on a Tuesday afternoon. Maybe this was it; he'd found someone new, better looking and not pregnant. But then my mind went back to our weekend and how we couldn't get enough of each other.

Saturday night we'd blown off Sara and her man du jour. I lied to her and told her I wasn't feeling well. Being my best friend, she called bullshit and told me to say hi to my horny husband who she could bet her life was between my legs at that very moment. As usual, she was one thousand percent right. Louis and I bummed around in bed all day eating takeout and alternating giving each other X-rated body rubs.

Sunday, which I usually reserved for brunch with my sister and grandmother, had become harder and harder for Nana Rose to keep. Lately, Jenna and I bought French pastries and paid Nana a visit at home. My grandma had been feeling off-kilter all week and told Jenna, who told me, that she would just like to rest that Sunday and would see us the next week. Louis took advantage of having me available and made plans for us with one of his friends. I was way too comfy come Sunday afternoon to leave our warm bed. He took one look at me sprawled out naked in bed and called off brunch with his friend Henry.

Henry was someone Louis got to know while building his new hotel downtown. Henry Stanton owned a decorating firm and had been chosen by Bruel Industries to design and decorate the new Chelsea Hotel. Louis and Henry hit it off and had been hanging out from time to time. I was happy whenever Louis made a new friend. I think I always felt responsible for what happened with *The Boys*.

Henry was nice but I couldn't stand how his wife Lillian only had eyes for my husband. It was like I was invisible to her. Any conversation was always directed at Louis. *What do you think, Louis? Let's see what Louis says,* etcetera. Henry was a great guy and I liked hanging out with him as long as he left his stupid wife with her hungry eyes at home. I told Louis I hated the way Lillian was shamelessly eating him up with her gaze. My oblivious husband said that I thought every woman we met wanted him. And they all did. He couldn't be that blind to how the world saw him. I was only too happy to distract my man on that particular Sunday morning in bed while he cancelled our brunch plans with Henry and Lillian.

But now it was Tuesday afternoon and I knew Louis had a jam-packed crazy day at work. He couldn't even squeeze me in for a nooner. Why would he drop everything to come talk to me? I decided to call him and find out before I went crazy wondering what was going on. He answered before the phone even rang.

"I'm five minutes away. Don't go anywhere."

"Louis, you're scaring me. Why are you rushing home? What happened?"

"Baby, I'll explain everything in a few minutes. Wait for me on the fifth floor. I love you … just hold tight; I'm almost there."

He walked into our living room as promised five minutes

later with red brimmed eyes. His hair was messy and looked like he'd spent the last hour pulling at it in every direction imaginable. Something happened, something bad. He almost ran over to me once he spotted me on the leather couch. I'd already started shaking in anticipation of the bad news I was about to receive. I got up off the couch and then quickly sat back down, deciding I needed all the support I could muster up for what was coming next. My husband reached me in a few strides and sat on the floor at my feet.

"Emily," he had tears in his eyes. Louis almost never called me Emily; it's always Em, baby, or little girl. Emily was too long and formal for his lips. Emily was reserved for something serious. I looked into his eyes knowing the next few words would hurt like hell. "Nana Rose passed away early this morning."

I was already braced for the worst. I was physically detached. My first instinct was to grab my belly. I felt the baby move inside almost as if she'd heard her father's news, too. I wasn't ready to accept what Louis had just said. There was no way my nana would just die. She was supposed to meet my baby. She was supposed to tell me how to be a good mother. Louis was mistaken. Why would he say such a horrible thing to his eight month pregnant wife?

I shook my head, "No! No!"

I got up and started to walk up the stairs to our bedroom, leaving him on the floor. I didn't even have to look back to know he would be following me.

"Em, you're in shock. Baby, let's talk about this."

I would do no such thing. What he was saying was false and I wasn't going to let him say such a horrible thing again. I was going upstairs to call my nana.

"Emily, look at me. It won't go away if you ignore it. The funeral is tomorrow morning; you—"

"Stop it, I don't want to hear it anymore. My nana is alive and she will meet my baby. Why are you doing this to me?" I was screaming and the tears finally came out like a bursting dam. I was fighting with my head to disbelieve my husband's words. I was halfway up the stairs when I couldn't feel my legs under me. The next thing I remembered, I was curled up in Louis' lap in our bed with my cheek against his soaked shirt. My nana left me ... and I didn't say goodbye.

Last week she held my stomach and told me how she couldn't wait to meet my little angel. I was trying to remember the last thing she said to me. I giggled when it came to me; she called me a superwoman in Hebrew: *Eshet Chayil.* She then told Jenna that God gives us children only when we're ready. Maybe she was saying goodbye to us in her own way. I closed my eyes to try and absorb my reality.

"Em, baby, let's go take a shower; you'll feel better. I promised your parents we would stop by their house once I told you. Jenna is taking care of all the arrangements."

"What will I do now?"

"You will make your grandmother proud and continue to be my beautiful Emily; an amazing daughter, a great sister, an incredible wife, and very soon a wonderful mother. One day, like Nana Rose, you will be an awe-inspiring grandmother and great-grandmother."

I looked up into his tear-filled eyes, giving him a weak smile and kissing his beating heart beneath the tear soaked button down white shirt.

"She won't meet our daughter."

"Maybe she already has. Baby, she passed away at night. She wasn't in pain. This was her time. She probably decided she could help her family more from the other side. You and Jenna are lucky to have had such a great, strong woman in your life for as long as she was. Nana wouldn't want you to be upset. It's natural for kids to bury their parents and grandparents."

I was nodding. Louis was right; I have an abundance of great memories. I would tell our children all about their wonderful grandparents who risked their lives to survive during the war and give their kids a chance at a better life.

"Thank you for coming home to be with me. I love you so much."

"Where else would I be? I don't have anything more important in my life than you and our baby."

"I should go call my mom. I should be comforting her, not feeling sorry for myself. She lost her mother today."

"Your dad and sister have been by her side since this morning. They were all worried about how you would take the news. You're carrying their little granddaughter. They wanted to make sure you don't get too upset over this and put the baby through too much stress."

I understood I couldn't let my mind and body get too worked up, which would affect our baby. Louis wanted to make sure he was there to comfort me once I got the inevitable terrible news. He moved off the bed, still cradling me in his arms. He walked us into our bathroom.

"I'll lay you down on the bench while I draw you a bath. Then I'm feeding you before we go see your family."

"Okay ... thank you. Louis, I love you."

While we shared a hot bath, I started to wonder how hard it must've been for Louis when he lost his dad.

"When you told me about being told one day that you no longer had a dad, I felt sad but I didn't really get it. I never lost anyone close to me. I wasn't even born when Grandpa Nathan passed away. My dad's grandparents all died before Jenna and I were born. With Nana gone, it feels like time is standing still. I can't believe that tomorrow I will get up in the morning and she won't be around." I was calm but tears still poured down my face. Only the sound of my tears hitting the bath water betrayed my calm façade.

"When they told me my dad died, I felt like a worthless scumbag. I've never told anyone, but he had a heart attack and died alone in his bed across the street from the only woman he ever loved. The night he died alone like a dog, his ungrateful disgrace of a son was piss drunk. I woke up in bed that morning with too many bodies around me to count. I don't even remember sleeping with any of those women. My only comforting thought was that my dorm room floor was littered in used condoms. My mom had been trying to call me for over seven hours to tell me my dad was dead. I was numb after that night. I couldn't look at myself in the mirror for months from shame. I didn't know what was worse, knowing that he failed in reuniting with my mom or knowing that he now knew what kind of a lowlife his son really was."

I turned to see the love of my life look broken and far away. I turned sideways and rested my huge belly on Louis' stomach. He was shaking and crying and I didn't know what to say to make it better. I had never seen him break down like this. He told me things that night in the bathtub I had never heard before.

"Louis, you need to be strong for me. If you break down, I won't make it through the next couple of days. Eric loved you and your mom; he didn't fail. If he would've left the two of you behind and moved on then he would've failed. He was there for you for every milestone. The man tucked you in every night. He decided that he loved you and your mom so much that he was ready and willing to accept just having you both near him and he was happy. You had a loving family, Louis. Your dad loved your mom and she loved him and they both adored you. Whatever you did in the past, good or bad, is what made you the man I love today. You have to believe that all of your choices have brought us to the here and now."

He smiled through his tears, rubbing my belly. The baby shifted under his touch making us both jump and giggle.

"Little baby, wait until you come out and meet your wise-beyond-her-years beautiful mama."

I sat up to reach his lips. Louis turned me around so I was

sitting in his lap, straddling him with water lapping all around us. My belly was so enormous that it rose way above the water line. He lowered his head and kissed my protruding tummy. I knew then that life goes on.

My sister really was an event coordinator through and through. Jenna and Mike took the burden off my parents and arranged everything. I was holding on to Louis and drawing strength from him and the life growing inside me. I had to grow up that day and accept a future without my nana in it. Louis was there for me every step of the way. I had the solace of knowing that Nana Rose lived long enough to have at least met the love of my life before she passed away. Nana was so incredibly important in my life that it was hard for me to imagine going on and not sharing my life with her. I knew she and Grandpa Nathan were together again in heaven watching out for all their children.

I will never forget the look on Louis' face four weeks later when our baby girl was born. When Dr. Naderman gave Louis his daughter, I promised myself that I would endure anything to keep putting that look on his beautiful face. All the pain and suffering was worth the expression on my husband's face when he first saw his little baby girl. He was shaking like a leaf at the sight of this tiny person. When she opened her eyes and gave a slight smile at him, he broke down and wept. He turned to me and said, "Em, I love you more than I could ever express. I didn't think it was possible, but I love her even more. She's you and me together."

We named her Rose as homage to our beloved Nana Rose. Louis said that when he thought of our little baby girl bearing the name of my grandmother, he knew she would always be protected from above. That was one of the happiest memories I have of us.

Louis surprised me a few days later with our Upper East Side townhouse. We were bringing baby Rose home from the hospital. I gave birth at Lenox Hill, ten minutes away from where our new home was, unbeknownst to me.

"You didn't think we'd raise our family in a treehouse. That we'll keep as our love pad, this will be our home," he said as our precious-cargo-carrying SUV pulled into the driveway of an unfamiliar townhouse.

Life was always interesting with Louis Bruel. He was born to be a father. He was amazing and took off of work for three weeks, never leaving our side. He woke up at night to bring the baby over to me so I could feed her and then he would change her and put her back to sleep expertly. He always went to sleep thanking me for being his and giving him a family. My life was a dream.

La vie en Rose...

My life with Louis always bordered on fantasy. We were passionate lovers but we were even more passionate friends and partners. He taught me everything from how to drive a car to how to sail a boat. For our three-year anniversary, Louis bought us a one-hundred-foot yacht that we kept docked in St. Maarten. Before the boat was finished and named, Louis asked me in bed one night, "What do you think about naming the yacht *Great Expectations*?"

I leaned over to touch the necklace he never took off; the necklace that had our quote inscribed on it. "I don't want to share *Great Expectations* with anyone but you. Let's keep it between us. Why don't we name the yacht something that we won't have to explain to people?"

I could see him chew over my words before giving me that glorious dimpled smile.

"I like that ... I agree. I don't want anyone knowing about our love affair with Pip and Estella. No one knows me like you do and I like it that way. Sometimes I can't believe I found you. I can't even think about my life without you and Rose in it."

We ended up naming the vessel *La Vie en Rose*, which means *my life through pink- colored lenses*. But to me and Louis, it meant our life through my nana and our baby. It was a small dedication to the wonderful roses who'd blessed our lives.

Once our yacht was ready for sailing, we spent a whole week cruising from one Caribbean island to the next in our new extravagant toy. My parents stayed with baby Rose at home while we went off on a romantic getaway.

"I can't believe you know how to sail this monstrosity. Shouldn't there be a qualified captain?"

"Do you not trust your husband to get us to our next destination, little girl?" I hated when he did that. Always joking around, answering a question with another question. This was not the boardroom; we were not negotiating a deal.

"Louis, can't you ever answer a question rather than turn it all around and make me seem like an ungrateful, stupid kid?"

"Em, what the fuck? I was kidding around with you, why are you getting all bitchy on me? I just wanted to play with our new toy for a little bit before I give it over to Franco in St. Barts to navigate for the rest of the trip. I took courses for this. I'm trying to impress you, little girl, not piss you off."

"I'm sorry, Louis. I've just been freaking out about Jenna. She had another miscarriage. My mom told me this morning. I feel enormously guilty that we have a beautiful little baby and Jenna and Mike have been married longer than we have and are having tons of problems. They would make amazing parents. It's just not fair."

I started crying, trying to imagine how empty our life would be without our beautiful baby girl. Every time I looked into her little chubby face, I could see my husband, and I fell in love with her and him all over again. We had a great life before having Rose, but our bond became much stronger once we became parents. I really wanted that for my sister and Mike. Louis walked over to where I was leaning on the rail and wrapped his arms around me.

"Mike told me last night about the miscarriage. I didn't tell you because I thought Jenna would."

Louis always knew shit about my family before I did. I gave him the look. He knew that look. It's the *why didn't you tell me?* look. I was sure I was about to hear an explanation of why Mike could tell his best friend about his wife's miscarriage, and yet I was probably the last to know, as always.

"Jen knew we were going away and she probably didn't want to ruin our trip. Don't be sad, baby. Their time will come. I know how lucky we are for having Rose. But I'm sure Jenna wouldn't want you feeling guilty for having her beautiful little niece. They love her and I'm hopeful that they'll have their own baby one day soon. We should ask Nana to help them out."

"So besides being handsome, sexy, and smart you also always know what the perfect thing to stay to me is when I'm being a total bitch?"

"You forgot to mention that I'm a sex god … I also happen to know what the perfect thing to do to you when you're being a total hot bitch."

Only he could make me forget about the world around us. We kissed each other passionately for a few minutes before Louis remembered he was supposed to be the captain.

"Em, will you look down on me if I tell you I'm ready to retire as the naval captain of this vessel and resume my obligations as your little pussy whipped sex slave?"

"There is nothing little about you, baby … and you're too tall for me to look down at. As for the pussy whipping, I'm more into sucking than flogging."

He liked me being playful and sassy. Louis lifted me off my feet and swung me over his shoulders, swatting my ass before I could get away. He knew exactly how to cheer me up.

"I'm glad you mentioned sucking. I know just the perfect thing."

"I married a sex maniac," I groaned and tried unsuccessfully to escape.

"Don't pretend you don't love it, little girl."

"Louis, who's sailing the boat?"

"Franco ... I quit."

After that, Louis never tried to sail our yacht sans captain again. He decided it was too much responsibility. Our master bedroom on the *La vie en Rose* was bigger than most hotel suits so we could stay in bed and at sea for days.

I called Jenna the next day, giving her a chance to tell me herself about her latest miscarriage. This was number three.

"How's our little angel—a.k.a. home grown terrorist?" I asked Jen playfully when she picked up the phone at my parents' house. We'd set up my old room as Rose's new sleepover room at my parents' house. She had everything there; her crib, toys, and clothes. She loved spending time with my parents. My mom and dad melted at the sight of their only granddaughter. My mom kept telling me that Rose was my carbon copy.

"Stop, Emmy, she really is an angel. I don't know what kind of voodoo you spin at home but the kid goes to sleep at seven, like magic. Before we even leave the room she's out like a light."

I smiled, thinking back to how her behavior came to be. I'd read a book one of the nurses had recommended. It was almost like a recipe book for training and house breaking babies. People don't give babies enough credit. You can't let their minuscule size fool you. They are way smarter than we think. If we don't train them, they will train us to rock them, walk them all day and night. I had to fight Louis and my mom off the first couple of months. Every time Rose would make a peep, they would run over to try and make her stop crying by picking her up. I went all Nazi Mama on them and refused to let them near the baby or pick her up when she randomly cried. If she was fed and changed, it was time for her to sleep. I struggled at first, getting dirty looks from everyone. But now my husband worshiped at my altar every night when he put his little munchkin down after we bathed and fed her. Louis put her down at seven o'clock every evening and got a full night's rest before she woke us up at seven o'clock the next morning. No magic involved. Sara once told me if she ever found a dude to marry and have his babies, that I'm training them for her. Mike also said he'd be signing his babies up for The Emily Bruel Training Camp.

"So what's going on with you? All is well?" I was trying to sound as clueless as possible and to give Jenna a chance to tell me herself. I didn't do such a good job.

"Oh for God's sake, don't pretend to be stupid. I'm sure either Louis, Mom, or Mike told you about my useless uterus."

"Jen, it's not about someone telling me. You're my sister; why wouldn't I be the person you tell after Mike? Why does Louis know something incredibly intimate before your own sister? I feel like you hate me, Jenna. I even feel guilty for having Rose. It's like you resent me for being able to have a baby."

I could hear Jenna crying on the other end of the line. What's wrong with me? She just had another miscarriage and I was upset at her for not telling me first. I'm a fucking toddler.

"JenJen. Fuck ... I'm sorry. That was stupid and selfish. I don't know why I just said all that shit to you. This must be horrible for you guys. I'm sorry I can't be there for you the way you need me to. I'm sorry I don't know how to make it better."

We were now both crying on the phone. I was hiding in the master bathroom with the shower running so at least Louis wouldn't hear how childish I was being.

"Emmy, I didn't tell you because I'm embarrassed. I'm a woman; this is my job and I can't seem to get it right. If I could, I wouldn't tell anybody, Mike included. I just want to cry myself to sleep. I look at Mike holding and playing with Rosy and I want more than anything to give him a baby. Emmy, what if I'll never be able to give him that? What kind of worthless woman did he get himself?"

"How could you say that? Mike loves you so much. I have been reading your love story ever since I could remember. You guys will have a baby—if not naturally, then you'll adopt or find a surrogate. Don't ever call yourself worthless, Jenna. You are my sister and my role model. I love you and whatever is happening is not your fault. You can't blame yourself."

"Thank you, Emmy. I'm sorry; I didn't mean to ruin your first romantic getaway on the love boat. I'm sure you guys have already christened every inch of that cruise ship you call a yacht. Mike told me Louis has been preparing some new moves for you."

We both snorted at that comment.

"I hope he hasn't been practicing those new moves on someone else."

"Emmy, don't worry. I'd rip his dick off if he ever tried."

"Promise?"

"You know I'd do anything for you little sis…including castrate your cheating husband if need be."

The good, the bad and the sad...

When Rose was five, I gave birth to our little boy. We kept the sex of the baby a surprise this time. When Dr. Naderman told Louis, *Mr. Bruel, congratulations, you have a son,* I thought he would faint. I was holding our baby boy in my arms. I was amazed at how we managed to clone Louis into a 7lbs 3oz and 20-inch long baby. The only difference between Louis and his son was that the baby had my aqua-colored eyes.

"Louis, I'd like to name him Eric in honor of your dad and have my grandpa's name Nathan as his middle name..."

Kissing his son's little head, Louis nodded with tears in his eyes. "Thank you, my love. That would be perfect, just like my son."

I couldn't ask for a better father for our kids. Louis was the most amazing parent anyone could wish for. His whole life revolved around me and the kids. Our life was pretty wonderful and I always made sure to take a moment and thank whoever was looking out for us.

You couldn't have the good without enduring some bad. Unfortunately, I recall some low points, too; the worst being when Louis' mom, Elizabeth, was diagnosed with breast cancer. Rose was almost six years old and Eric was eight months. It was the first time since we got engaged that we spent a night apart from each other. Elizabeth had no one but her son and I couldn't blame him for wanting to spend every minute with her. Louis was by her side and got her the best possible care.

He came home one night after not seeing the kids and me for two days. His mom was going through a treatment of chemotherapy and he had stayed by her side 24/7. I remember looking at him and thinking that he'd aged ten years in two days. My defeated husband walked over to me and buried his face in my neck. He just stood there, breathing me in.

"How's your mom, baby?"

He started sobbing into my neck. I'm sure he was strong for Elizabeth and didn't shed one tear in her presence, but he needed to let it out. Elizabeth had to get through this; her son needed her. She had no idea how many specialists Louis flew in from across the country to make sure she got the latest and best cancer care money could buy.

"Do you want me to spend the night with your mom tonight and you can sleep at home with the kids?" I asked, knowing he needed someone to take the burden off him, even for a little bit.

"I can't be away from you another night. Could your parents come to stay with the kids and you'll sleep with me at the hospital?"

"Louis, it's too last minute for my parents to change their work schedule and Jen and Mike are away until next week, but I can call Sara. She'll stay over."

"Okay ... I need to go kiss my babies."

Seeing this bigger-than-life beautiful man deflated and dejected was pure anguish.

We spent the next two weeks in the hospital with Louis' mom. I slept by his side every night and came home first thing in the morning to be there before the kids got up. Only Louis Bruel could've arranged for us, including his mother, to have a private suite at the hospital.

Thank God for my best friend. Sara was a lifesaver and stayed at our house the whole time. We had a full staff but I always wanted a family member to be there when we didn't sleep at home.

Sara and I were having breakfast, just the two of us, one morning. I had just come back from the hospital when she sprung some very disturbing news on me.

"I'm moving to London next month."

I just looked at her. I was going to let her continue before I'd start ripping into her. I knew it wasn't just because she loved London. She loved New York more.

"I can't be around him and his family anymore. Every time we're together I feel like this is it ... I feel like he loves me and will choose me. But then after we fuck, he leaves and goes back home to her. Sex is not love. He fucks me and I think he loves me ... isn't that grand?"

I was still silent. That was the most she'd said to me about her and Jeffery in the last six years. She'd been dating random men but I had this feeling deep down inside she was making sure she was unattached, ensuring that she'd be available for that cheating scumbag.

"Do you love him?" I asked, which was a dumb question. Obviously, she loved him. I just had to hear her say it. She smirked at my question.

"I love me more," she answered.

Good, maybe there was hope.

"Why are you going to London? Just tell him to leave you alone. Tell him you'll tell Eddie if he doesn't leave you the fuck alone. Do you think his wife knows? Better yet, tell him you'll tell me and I'll tell Louis and Louis will ruin him and his law firm."

Sara always enjoyed when I got myself all worked up. She laughed at me and said, "Frankie Goes to Hollywood says 'Relax[49]'..." She knew how to diffuse my anger with jokes.

"'Tainted Love[50]' by Soft Cell is calling your name, Sara," I answered her back. This was us. When shit hit the fan, we went super '80s. It's how Sara and I always dealt with life.

"Eddie knows by the way. Jeff told him; he needed to tell someone, that selfish prick. Eddie fucked him up, I heard. It was Eddie's idea for me to move to London and start over. I got a job at an up and coming law firm. My dad and Eddie both think I'll be able to make partner in a few years." She closed her eyes, which was her way of stopping the tears. When she finally opened them, she was looking anywhere but me. "Emily, don't hate me for being a bad person. I know what goes around comes around. Some of us fall for good guys and some of us, like me, fall for assholes."

I stood up and walked over to where my delusional friend was sitting and engulfed her in a hug.

"I could never hate you. I just want you to be happy. You deserve to be happy. I know one day you'll find a good guy. 'Don't Stop Believin'[51] by Journey."

That made us both smile. I was losing my best friend to London, but maybe it was the clean slate she needed.

That night was the last night Louis and I spent at the hospital with Elizabeth. She was discharged the next day and we had her moved into our house until she was well enough to go back home. A few months later, the doctors gave us the good news that her cancer was eradicated; she was officially in remission and would hopefully live a very long life. Louis, during one of those nights after being told that his mom would be okay, told me the rest of his parents' sordid love story.

"I bet you didn't know that my mom was an orphan. She

doesn't like talking about it, but her parents died in a car accident when she was almost sixteen years old. Her great aunt raised her; and also died a few years after that. I think from a stroke. My dad fell in love with her at first sight, he used to tell me. He loved how confident and independent she was. When he found out she was all alone in the world and that she had no one, he promised he would love her and take care of her for the rest of his life. They were together for a few months before my mom got pregnant with me. My dad asked her to marry him the second he found out about the baby. He told me he would've married her with or without her being pregnant. She was proud and had her head filled with feminist ideals. She said she didn't need a man to marry her because he felt guilty for getting her pregnant. She wouldn't marry him. Wouldn't take one cent from him ... but she loved him and no one else. I think my mom was afraid he'd leave her like everyone else did, so she tried to beat him to it.

"My dad was loaded apparently. She had no idea how much he was really worth. All she knew was that he was an accountant from a good family who'd gone against his parents' wishes to be with her. He didn't care; he told his parents to fuck off if they didn't like her and me. I've never met my grandparents. Eric was their only child. His parents had him very late in life. My dad spoke very little about his family; all I knew back then were their names, Pauline and Isaac Bruel. They were deported from France right before the war and immigrated to America. When I was nine, I remember going to a cemetery with him and sitting inside a mausoleum. It was my grandparents' burial place. He chose to love a beautiful, crazy hippie and his son over his parents and their money."

"Do you think if your mom could do it all over she would marry him?"

Louis contemplated my question then shook his head.

"She wasn't that type of woman, Em. Marriage just wasn't for her. She told me in the hospital a few months ago that my dad died in her arms and not alone like I'd always thought. She was with him the night he had the heart attack. At least he died knowing she loved him as much as he loved her."

I kissed the love of my life. He was Louis Bruel: a successful businessman, my husband and the father of our children, but on the inside he was still Elizabeth and Eric's lost little boy.

When in London ... lie

While I was living my life and raising my kids, my BFF finally met a man in London and decided to get married after dating him for eight months. Sara and Gavin Masters were having one wedding in London for his friends and family and then they would be returning to New York for another, smaller wedding for Sara's friends and family. They decided they'd stay and live in New York after their wedding since Gavin had a law firm branch in the city, too.

Sara described Gavin to me on the phone as good-looking, wealthy, and British. Sara was working for Gavin's law firm in London. She told me as soon as she started working for him they started fucking and then dating and then they fell in love. That's my friend Sara; her modus operandi is always doing everything backward. I couldn't wait to finally meet the man who'd captured her heart. The way Sara described him, I was a little in love myself. Louis and I made plans to go to London a week before Sara's wedding; I'd have enough time to meet Sara's fiancé and get to know Gavin a little before they'd get too involved with the wedding and then leave on their honeymoon to France.

Normal people get a hotel room when they go away, not Louis. My husband purchased a condo for us in London on Tree Lane. He didn't ask for my opinion; he just informed me on our flight to England that we'd be staying in our own apartment. I'd been to London with Louis when we first got married for a weekend business trip. This time, we were staying for a whole week. I couldn't wait to see Sara. I hadn't seen her since she left me and made the big move to London to escape from Jeff. As soon as we got settled in our new beautiful apartment, I called Sara and she came to find me.

"One thing I need you to keep in mind when you meet Gavin is that he is not the usual kind of guy I've been with in the past. Behavior-wise, that is."

I didn't like where this conversation was headed. What did a statement like that even mean? I didn't like any of the guys Sara had ever been with, especially Jeffery the cheater.

"Sara why are you telling me this? Why don't you just tell me what you really want to tell me?"

"Emily, all I'm saying is that he's not a 'Take Your Breath Away[8]' by Berlin kind of guy. Don't get me wrong, Gavin is attractive and successful, but he's not like Louis. He loves me but you'll see he's not all over me and he doesn't look at me as if I have the cure to his disease."

What was I supposed to say to that? My best friend was basically telling me that she was settling for someone who wasn't head over heels in love with her. What the fuck did that mean?

"I thought you were 'Holding Out For A Hero[52]' by Bonnie Tyler. I don't get it. Wasn't that the whole reason you left New York to move here and start over?"

"Listen, this is as good as it's going to get for me. He's not married, no kids; he's not into BDSM, or some kinky orgies. He's not gay. You'll see he's really hot. We have similar interests, we're both attorneys, my parents like him, and he's British. It's just that your Louis is a '500-Miles[53]' by The Proclaimers kind of guy; he will do anything for you. Gavin wouldn't even walk one mile for me or anybody else; he'd just pay someone to do it. If I wait for Prince Charming, I may be too old and decrepit by the time he finds me. After Jeff, I don't think there are any chivalrous men out there anyway. Emily, I stopped holding my breath. I'm happy and that's enough for right now."

Wow ... I needed to meet this guy. I couldn't imagine marrying a guy who wouldn't jump into the fire for me. Maybe thanks to Louis and Mike, I'm permanently warped about how I think all husbands should be. We were only twenty-seven years old, Sara and I. Not sure if twenty-seven was the age one started settling, but hey, what did I know? I met my prince at eighteen for crying out loud.

While I was catching up with Sara, Louis was having beers with Gavin. I couldn't wait to hear his character assessment of this man who was starting to sound very lukewarm from his betrothed's description. As soon as Louis came back from the pub slightly buzzed, I pounced. I jumped into his arms like a dog waiting for its owner all day. If I had a tail, it would've been wagging.

"Tell me, tell me, tell me! I need to know everything about Gavin."

He walked us over to the couch and sat down with me in his lap facing him. He was trying to put his feelings into words. I could see the wheels turning. He wanted to say something and then he changed his mind, and then he wanted to say something else and then he changed his mind again. Louis was having a conversation in his head that I needed to be a part of—pronto.

"Remember when you and Sara were almost twenty-one and she said she wanted to meet a dick?"

I nodded, of course I remembered, I was pregnant and we were decorating our New Year's tree on the terrace.

Louis continued with a pained looking smirk on his face, "Well, she found him."

Okay, there was no way my best friend was going to marry a dick.

"Louis, why would you say that?"

He pulled my hair off my face and pulled me down for a deep kiss. He then laid me on the couch and got comfortable between my legs. He was trying to distract me. There was something he didn't want me to know about the man who would soon be my best friend-in-law. He knew my weakness. He liked exploiting my weakness any chance he got by seducing me into submission.

"Oh ... Louis, stop ... you need to ... first tell me ... about Gavin ... then ... you can do whatever you want with me," I tried to reason and negotiate with Mr. Drunk and Sexy. God, he smelled good and he was playing with my nipples through my robe. I couldn't win with Louis when he played dirty.

"I'll tell you all about Gavin the dick after I get some of my dick inside you. We're in London in our new apartment all alone. And as the activity coordinator for this trip, I planned for us to first fuck each other's brains out and then worry about Sara and her dick. Deal, little girl?"

Whatever Mr. Sexy Activity Coordinator wanted was fine with me. I couldn't even remember what I was asking him in the first place. I just needed the most beautiful man in the world to fill me and make me scream his name. He was already rubbing his hard cock onto me. He flipped me over onto my stomach and lifted my silk robe up so he could cup my ass. He lowered my panties and kissed my exposed bum before I felt his velvety smooth, hot cock glide between my butt cheeks. I got on all fours to get closer to him. He lowered his body to mine and put all his weight on me. I loved feeling his weight on me. I could feel his big dick hard against my lower back. He moved my hair to one side and whispered into my mouth.

"Will you let me fuck your ass today? We haven't had anal in a while. I have a need to be inside your derrière. Is that okay, baby? I bought lube on the way here. I've been thinking about it for hours. I promise to stretch you out first."

I knew this version of Louis Bruel. If Louis drank even a little bit he got into his kinky fucker mood. Where he wanted to fuck me as if I wasn't the mother of his children but some slut he'd just met. I liked this game, too.

"I want what you want. Make me feel good. I promise I won't tell my husband if you won't tell your wife, Mr. Bruel."

I chanced a glance back toward my kinky husband. He had one eyebrow raised, hair falling into his smoldering dark eyes. I could see the exact moment my words ignited his usually hidden alter ego. The dimple that I loved usually softened Louis' features and made him look sweet. That same dimple at that particular instant looked one thousand percent sinful. I knew sweet was not what I was about to get.

"Fuck yeah ... as long as we keep this between us, I'll make you feel better than good. Good is for when your husband makes love to you. I promise, you will not use the word 'good' to describe the way I'm about to fuck you. If I don't make you come at least three times, then I'm not finished yet."

I'd learned Louis didn't make empty promises. If he said I'd have three orgasms you could bet the farm I was about to have a wild ride. He unwrapped himself from me and stripped whatever clothing he still had on. He lifted my hips in the air and helped me out of my panties. He gently, but fiercely, lowered my head on the couch. I was on my knees with my butt sticking out. My face and boobs were pushed into the couch.

"Baby, stretch your hands up and hold on tight. Feel free to scream, nobody can hear you but me."

Oh God, I was going to start coming if he kept talking that way. I could feel him watching my exposed genitals. I knew without looking that Louis was stroking himself to the image of me in that erotic pose. With his free hand, he started touching my glistening pussy. As soon as his fingers made contact with my drenched core, he gave a loud hiss.

"Fuck, you're wet. You want me to fuck your ass, don't you? Oh yeah … I'm going to bury myself in every hole, baby. I want my cum inside you, dripping down your thighs. I'm going to fuck you all night. So keep calm and enjoy the ride. No getting off until morning."

Okay, if he even looked at my clit I'd start exploding. We could count this as orgasm number one; I was as good as done.

"Louis, you're talking too much. I need your cock inside me. Pick a hole, any hole, just fuck me already. I want to come around your dick, not around your words."

He lowered his head between my legs and began licking and parting my folds, inserting two fingers inside my slit. He moved to my puckered rear hole and circled his tongue around his point of interest. I was close. He knew how close I was. All he had to do was press hard on my clit and I'd be convulsing into his hand.

"I could make you come just by touching your clit. Is that what you want? You want to squirt in my hand or do you want to come while I penetrate your beautiful ass, baby?"

Oh God, how could he ask me to make any decision when I didn't even know my own name at the moment? I just made some kind of sound, which my husband totally accepted as a valid answer to his ludicrous question. He didn't need any store bought lubricant; he just rubbed my wetness into my ass. He inserted his cock into my drenched pussy to coat his length in my oozing juices. He then, just as quickly, removed his dick and started working himself into my rear.

"Relax into me. When I push in, you push out. First my fingers, then my cock."

"Ohhhhhh … Ohhhhhh…"

I could feel him spreading my moisture and inserting his fingers into my tight anal canal. I was aroused; melting with every stroke, with every touch. I needed more. I started having that familiar panicked buildup where I knew that if I didn't get some relief quick, I'd start rubbing myself off for instant alleviation.

"Louis, I'm ready. Don't play too long; I need you inside."

"I have a horny little girl on my hands tonight. What happened? Did your husband not make love to you on the plane ride over to London? If I'd been there, you wouldn't be begging me to fuck you in the ass right now. You wouldn't be able to walk. I want to be inside that tight hole more than anything in the fucking world. Oh, yeah. You are ready for me. You were made for me."

I had to physically stop myself from coming at his words. I was counting the seconds until he pounded into me. He aligned the head at my rear entrance and spit down into my ass. How did he still have this crazy effect on me? It was painful that first inch until I could feel his whole mushroomed tip fit in and then he slowly pushed in. The sounds coming out of Louis' mouth were intoxicatingly guttural. This kind of carnal satisfaction could only be achieved with rough, uninhibited sex. After the initial intrusion, I loved the feel of Louis filling me from behind. It felt different than vaginal intercourse. I started letting go again, giving my head a chance to catch up to my stimulated body.

"Louis, I'm coming. Come with me ... Ohhhhhh ... Louis ... I'm coming."

I was shaking and spasming around his stiff rod. I could feel myself contract around him. He wasn't even moving. He was just buried fully inside me and I could feel his balls against my pussy. He wrapped his lean, hard body around my small frame. He was so enormously broad that you couldn't even tell I was under him. It was like being swallowed whole by Louis. I was shaking and he was my human blanket. Once he felt my trembling subside, he lifted himself up and started punishing my ass. This wasn't my gentle, caring husband; this was a wild savage lover who was pummeling me with no mercy. His fingers were digging into the flesh on my ass with such force that I knew I would be wearing his handprints for days. It felt like he was trying to split me open to accommodate his ample girth. Sweat was dripping off him and onto my back. He was ready to detonate. I knew what would set him off to the land of ecstatic bliss.

"Touch my tits," I cried out breathlessly.

He instantly let go of my ass cheeks and brought his hands under me to cup my swinging boobs. He squeezed them and moaned his satisfaction. I let one hand go of the armrest I was gripping for dear life and started rubbing my clit. There was no way I would let him explode without me. He was using the hold he had on my tits to shove me harder into his pounding cock. My euphoric countdown had already started. I was just waiting for Louis to say go.

"Fuck .... Commmmme ... I'm coming baby, I'm there, please come ... Em ... Ohhhhhh..."

We were both in paradise ... Louis was pouring himself into me while Joe Cocker was crooning "Up Where We Belong[54]" in my head.

That ... Was ... Perfect.

"I love your ass. I love you ... every fucking inch of you. Only you, baby."

Were we still in London?

The next day, I still didn't get the answers I was hoping for from Louis. He told me he wanted me to make up my own mind about Gavin and that once I'd met him, we could compare notes. We met Sara and Gavin for lunch at the Ritz Hotel. I was dreadfully nervous—you'd think I was meeting my future husband. We were waiting in the lobby for a good ten minutes before I saw them come our way. Gavin was tall with jet-black hair molded to his head and perfectly coiffed like plastic. He was more pretty than handsome. He carried himself in a way that showed he knew he was good-looking. He and Sara were walking with a two-foot gap between them, more like business associates than lovers. They weren't even holding hands. I looked up to see Louis studying my reaction. He knew what I was thinking.

"Em, be nice and give him a chance before you annihilate him. I can see the jury has already read the verdict in that pretty little head of yours."

I was totally going to give him a chance before I tried to vanquish this love farce. He walked over to us, shaking hands with Louis before directing his two thousand megawatt smile my way, giving me the up and down glance over.

"E ... mma ... llly, nice to finally meet you. I think Sara only surrounds herself with gorgeous people. Louis, you did well. It's a good thing I didn't grow up in America or my knob would be on the pull for some of that fit arse."

I think I puked a little in my mouth. He was extremely fake; he kept looking around to see who was watching him. How could she possibly be with a man like this? Yes, he was easy on the eyes, but so what? He hadn't even looked at my beautiful friend who was wilting by his side. Gavin didn't even make an attempt to touch her. Yuck, this guy was not for Sara. I looked over at Sara and she picked up on the deranged look on my face. I had to tell her to run. I didn't need to get to know Gavin. I already knew at that point that I would rather her be with Jeff than this pompous dick. He didn't love her. He only loved himself. He was full of himself. I had to endure a whole lunch with him?

"Sara, could you please show me the ladies room?"

"Emily, I don't work here; go ask someone at the desk where the loo is."

You stupid cow, I need to talk to you about your stupid fiancé, I was trying to tell her telepathically. Louis offered to take me to find a bathroom. I told him it was fine and that I'd find one once we got settled at our table. Once we were seated, I looked at Sara, who was trying to avoid my gaze at all costs. She knew this marriage was not happening if I had any say in it.

"Do you know what song I just heard in the car coming here? It was that '80s song by Flock of Seagulls, 'I Ran (so far away)[55]' ... Sara, do you remember that song?"

She looked at me, obviously not in the mood for my song selection. We were staring each other down when Gavin opened his stupid mouth and said, "I hate '80s songs; they give me the creeps. I can't bloody believe some nutters still fancy those songs."

He was officially dead to me. I think I even saw Sara cringe. Louis squeezed my knee under the table to snap me out of the shock. I think he was making sure I stayed seated and didn't launch myself across the table to scratch Gavin's pretty little eyes out. I don't know anything else that was said during that lunch; I checked myself out. I do remember Gavin telling Louis he was invited to his *stag night*. Over my dead body would my husband attend this dickhead's bachelor party!

When we parted that day, Sara whispered in my ear, "Nothing you could say will make me not marry him. Let it go ... it's happening!"

As soon as we left the happy couple, Louis said, "Relax, I'm not leaving you to go to some bachelor party with guys I have no desire to ever get to know."

Thank God. The day before, I had been beyond excited to be in London, but after less than twenty-four hours, I just wanted to go back home to my kids and New York City.

"Why is she marrying him? I don't like him; he's not a good guy. I don't think they even said more than two words to each other..."

Louis stopped walking and pulled me in for a much needed hug. He knew I wasn't getting any love from my best friend.

"He may be really great in the sack." I looked up to see an adorable grin on my husband's beautiful face. "Em, we don't know what's going on in that crazy head of hers. Her best friend has been married with children for years. She wants that, too. I agree that what Sara and Gavin have doesn't come close to our relationship. But this is her choice and we need to support her."

"I can't lie to her. He makes my skin crawl."

Louis brushed my hair from my face and leaned down to kiss my lips. "Baby, the good news is ... you don't have to marry him. I believe you're already spoken for."

I let go of Gavin and Sara on that horrible London trip. They got married and I attended her wedding in body but my heart and spirit were somewhere else. Everybody except Louis and I seemed to be in love with this pseudo man. I truly wished them a happily ever after, although I knew there was no way in hell they'd get one. When we left London, I texted Sara: *"Right Here Waiting For You*[56]*" by Richard Marx.* She'd understand, and when the time came that she needed me, I would be there for her.

I wasn't part of her New York wedding. I heard from Louis, who heard from Eddie, that Sara's parents had a small family dinner to celebrate her marriage to the vainest man I had ever met. We still texted each other from time to time but it wasn't us. It was forced and cold and distant. I'd lost my best friend in London and I really wished I had her back. As long as she was pretending to love that idiot, we couldn't be friends and she knew it. She could pretend with him but she couldn't lie to me. We knew each other too well. I wanted to call her a million times over the past few years, but I just didn't know what to say.

The last contact we had was a text I'd sent her on her birthday four months ago. I texted her, *"I Just Called To Say I Love You*[57]*" by Stevie Wonder.* I was desperate to have her send me back any song title. I waited for a week and then sent her another text: *"We Belong*[58]*" by Pat Benatar.* I wanted to know what was going on in her life. I knew she was hurting ... alone. I also wanted to talk to her about what was going on in my life.

She finally texted me back two weeks later: *Thank you ... Ditto.*

It was like our old friendship had just vanished. I guess she hated '80s songs now, too. I had a language but no one to speak it with. Eddie told me about her divorce two months ago, before anyone knew about it. He made me swear I wouldn't tell anyone because even his parents didn't know that Sara and Gavin had filed for divorce. I wanted to call her but what would I say? I figured she'd call me when she was ready.

The honeymoon is over, little girl...

Louis made this deal with himself. For every one of our birthdays he would add another property for us to call home. We had so many homes that lately we only got a chance to visit them once a year, if we were lucky. We had a summer beach house in South Hampton; a gorgeous ski lodge on Mont Tremblant in Montreal; an ultra-modern condo in Miami's Bal Harbour; a beautiful historic château in the Champagne region of France; a breathtaking villa in Santorini; and in London, we had that condo on Tree Lane that Louis purchased when we attended Sara's wedding. We never needed to stay in hotels because we could always stay at one of our own fully staffed homes. I'd never asked for any of those homes. I'd have been happy living in our treehouse if given the chance. Louis would inform me that he'd bought *me* another house. Truth be told, all I needed was Louis and our babies...

My parents were doing great; they loved spending almost every available second with their grandchildren. Jenna and Mike finally had a baby after trying for years with fertility drugs. On June 2nd they welcomed a healthy little baby girl into all our lives. Baby Renée was now the official center of our family. So many amazing things happened in those early years of our marriage. I was blessed to be with the man that I loved and adored. I was the chosen one and I reveled in the knowledge and security of our life together.

I never had to worry about money. Louis made it clear that my job was to be his wife and lover and be there for our children. He never told me how to spend our money; I was told I had free rein. I had access to all our funds; I just never needed to use it. Louis took care of everything. I didn't make any decision concerning the financial aspects of our life. Looking back, I should've been more involved. What kind of person lets someone else do everything? The same kind of person who gets married at nineteen years old. I was David and Adele's daughter until I met Louis, and then I became Louis Bruel's wife. I never got the chance to just be Emily. I never had the opportunity to worry about making the rent or even paying for my own cup of coffee. I was a kept woman. I made my bed and I'd have to lie in it, or in my case, get kicked out of it.

I can't say the exact date or moment that I felt a premonition of what lay ahead. We just slowly started drifting apart like two icebergs in an ocean. Over the last four months my husband gradually withdrew; first sexually and then emotionally from our long love affair. My family didn't notice a thing. Louis was still a devoted father, a loyal friend to Mike and Eddie, and a dedicated businessman. He just stopped being my best friend and lover.

He would come home from work at ungodly hours. It started with phone calls telling me he would be missing dinner, then he would call and tell me to put the kids to bed without him and then he just stopped calling. He would come home and go to bed without even attempting to kiss me or touch me. I was lost; I didn't know this Louis Bruel. He even made sure to get up way before me to leave for work each morning. He would leave before the sun came up. He didn't touch me or talk to me and the only thing I could do, after getting his message loud and clear, was let him slowly abandon me. We were like two ships passing in the night. I tried to talk to him and figure out what was bothering my loving partner. Our conversations were short and always ended the same: "Baby I'm fine. Don't worry; just lots of shit going on at work right now." I could recite those words by heart I'd heard them so many times.

I wanted to get us out from under the black cloud that descended upon us. We needed to get away from the city. Louis needed to clear his head and I knew just the place that could do it. I decided to surprise Louis with a trip to our house, *The Blue Lagoon,* in Turks and Caicos. Out of all our properties around the world, that was the most sentimental place for us. That house was his engagement gift to me and where we got married. It was the place we took Rose as a baby on her first vacation. It was our little paradise; where we became a family. Maybe if I could bring him back to where it all started, we could get past our dry spell. I arranged the company jet to fly us there as soon as the kids were finished with their school year and I could become dispensable for a few days. When I finally told Louis of the surprise that I'd arranged for us, he was frantic and livid.

He yelled at me like a lunatic. "Em, I can't just get up and leave! I have a business to run. I have important meetings to attend. That needs to be my priority right now. It can't always be about you. Money doesn't just get deposited in our account, someone has to make it!"

That was a low blow. I stopped talking to him after he made that degrading comment implying I spent our money frivolously. I wasn't the one buying outrageous homes, cars, boats, expensive watches, and jewelry. That was all him! I never asked him for any of those things. I didn't choose to be a stay-at-home mom.

Louis chose that for me. He wanted me home raising our kids. He liked always having me available for him. Well, I guess as the cliché goes, after almost ten years of marriage our honeymoon was finally over.

I asked myself if it was someone else. When a man has the kind of money that Louis has, women are always circling around like hungry vultures. He gets new little realtors in *fuck me* heels and *do me* dresses parading around his office day and night. I never felt like one of those jealous wives. Louis always made me feel young and beautiful. He never looked at other women; at least not in my presence, anyway.

I thought our sexual appetites were on the same page. I wasn't an *I have a headache* kind of wife. I needed our sexual bond like I needed air. Louis and I had no inhibitions, no limits. I knew what made him hot. He knew which buttons to push to make me squirm. We were never argumentative. My personality was to please and I enjoyed bending to accommodate the love of my life. But how much could I bend before I broke?

It's been three months since we made love. Not due to lack of trying on my part. It was a gradual decline; it started with fast sex. Louis claimed that he was tired and would take care of me later, until he just stopped making promises altogether. On the few occasions we did make love, he sometimes couldn't even get himself to come and would just roll over and go to sleep.

Louis hasn't tried to make me come in months. Maybe I don't do it for him anymore! Maybe someone else does. It can't be that at twenty-nine, the best sex is behind me. I'm not even middle aged and I can't tell you the last time I had an orgasm in the presence of someone other than me. I know it's not easy to make me climax. I have to be both sexually and mentally aroused, but Louis used to pride himself on being able to make me come repeatedly on a daily basis. We would spend hours kissing and touching and getting each other hot so that once he entered me, I could erupt. Now I'd be content with a quickie for the sake of my peace of mind and deteriorating sanity.

I felt him emotionally withdraw from me, from us. When I would start to cry after he couldn't bring himself to have sex with me, he kissed me and told me how much he loved me and that all this was just a temporary hurdle he needed to overcome. He promised that it wasn't me; he was just mentally hung up on work related shit. I ate it all up. It was easier than facing the truth.

Time's up...

It's four days away from our birthdays and Louis and I are still not really talking. I had a horrible dream that night—more like a nightmare—where my husband was fucking another woman and didn't care about someone else fucking me. I tried to talk to him about it but he wanted nothing to do with me, and my so-called "stupid dream." Louis left in a hurry before I got up this morning. Well, I wasn't really sleeping but I had my eyes closed. I needed to just keep my mind from drowning in the what-ifs. I had to fool myself out of a state where all the walls closed in on me.

If it hadn't been for the plans I'd made with my sister last week and finally being able to drag her to lunch sans baby Renée, I wouldn't have even gotten out of bed.

Jenna and I meet for a light lunch at The Plaza Hotel. It's early afternoon, and we are sitting at the hotel lobby in plush blue velvet chairs, eating little croissant sandwiches and enjoying our afternoon champagne. I want to forget about my life's troubles for a few hours and try to get lost in Jenna and Mike's life as new parents.

I see Phillip first. I haven't seen that piece of shit in ten years but I would never forget the image of him. He, on the other hand, probably wouldn't be able to pick me out of a lineup. I'm sitting in an oversized wing chair facing the reception area and the elevator banks of The Plaza.

Phillip walks briskly out of one of the elevators. He has his signature repulsive smile that says *I don't give a fuck about anything.* After fixing his unruly hair, he walks out of the hotel. My sister is telling me a story about Mike falling asleep with Renée on his bare chest, but once I see Phillip, I blank out on what she's saying. Seeing Phillip is a momentary slap on the face. I remember that day we almost properly met at his club. It feels like yesterday, not over ten years ago. His words cut me very deep that night. I'm not sure I have ever fully let myself recover from them. As soon as Phillip leaves, I am able to take a deep breath again. I pretend I hadn't just missed the whole story Jen was rambling about.

"Emmy, can you imagine? She wiggled her way down to his nipple and started sucking."

When she starts laughing, I join her without missing a beat. After composing ourselves–my sister from her funny story and me from my disturbing sighting–I lift my gaze just in time to see my husband walk out of one of the elevators with a beautiful tall brunette by his side. He looks fresh as a cucumber and as gorgeous as ever. He has a huge smile on his face. I haven't seen a smile like that in months.

He'd left particularly early this morning; I didn't even see what he was wearing to work today. It is one of my favorite Etro suits; light gray with blue stripes, fitted single-breasted jacket with a crisp white button down shirt. He has on a coral colored tie. I picked out and bought him the whole ensemble he is wearing. The whole effect is right out of the pages of *GQ* magazine.

She is walking by his side, keeping up with his pace. She's stunning! She is wearing a short, white dress that looks molded on her body. Probably my husband's preferred brand, Alaïa, with high-heeled peep-toe nude Louboutins. She has sexy, bedroom messy hair that falls down around her shoulders. She looks young, about twenty-five. They look breathtaking together. Both tall and oozing sex appeal. They look like they belonged together. They look like they'd just had sex.

"Emmy! Emmy! Where are you? Did you just fall asleep on me with your eyes open?"

I look at my sister with shock and then back at Louis and that woman. Jen follows my gaze and turns to look at my field of view. She registers Louis and then I see her smile fall once she takes in his beautiful companion. Louis passes right by us. No sign of recognition. It almost feels like the last ten years of my life were all part of my overactive imagination. He seems far away from me ... untouchable. He walks to the door and holds it open for her to pass. I turn my head to the big wall of windows behind me to see them both enter his chauffeured Rolls Royce.

"Emmy, it's not what it looks like. It's not what you think. He was probably showing her an apartment. You know The Plaza has condos that they sell now."

I lift my empty gaze to meet my sister's panicked eyes. My sweet, supportive sister is trying to make excuses for the brother-in-law she adores. I know The Plaza Hotel like the back of my hand and I know that the elevators my husband and his long lost friend, Phillip, walked out of lead to hotel rooms and not the condos. I also know that my husband, who runs a billion dollar company, doesn't parade around Manhattan showing condominiums to twenty-five-year-old sluts. Words just don't come together in my brain to form sentences.

Seeing Phillip felt like being slapped on the face. Seeing the person I love and trust above anyone follow him out with a woman by his side was like being shot in the heart. I really believed Louis when he declared he'd cut all ties with his philandering friends. He told me that he and Phillip liked sharing girls before. I guess old habits die hard. What a fool I've been. I can't move. I can't speak. Even my tears are too shocked to fall. My life as I knew it just ended. Everything just changed and it would never be the same again. *Emily Bruel, I hope you enjoyed the ride ... time's up. Please exit on your right and don't let the door hit you on your ass. You stupid girl!*

I'd always believed I wouldn't be enough for "The" Louis Bruel. I remember Jenna telling me stories about Louis and his proclivities when she was trying to warn me off him. I was a little, stupid girl who fell in love with a fantasy. This day came ten years later than I'd initially anticipated. I am suddenly not Mrs. Emily Bruel, but once again, Emily Marcus. Out of high school, afraid of the future and wondering what life had in store for her. I am a nobody—a nobody and a fool.

"Emmy, can we talk this out? You're starting to scare me. Emmy, honey, say something!"

"Jen, can you do me a favor?"

"I would do anything for you, you know that. Just say the word."

"I need you to keep an eye on Rose and Eric for me."

My sister looks confused. She wasn't expecting this.

"You have a live-in nanny and a housekeeper. Why would I need to keep an eye on them?"

I take in a breath that feels like fire mixed with acid going down my chest.

"I'm going to go away for a little bit. I need to make sure you and Mom can be around for my babies while I'm gone. I need to know they're getting love from family and not just the hired help."

"Emmy, where are you going? And what's 'away for a little bit' mean? I don't know what's going on. This is not like you. Can't you just go talk to Louis? Let's call him now."

"Jenna, I didn't tell you but we've been having some problems. It doesn't affect you guys. I don't want you to get involved. I know you care about him and he's a big part of your business.

What's happening between us won't affect any of that. I don't know where I'm going or for how long yet. But I need to go. I have a lot on my mind. I need to try and make sense of my life. My world is about to change drastically. I need you to understand. Please make sure my kids are okay. Promise me?"

"Emmy, I promise I will take care of your kids, but you need to work this out with Louis and not take off somewhere."

I nod, leave some money on the table, and walk out before I break down and die at The Plaza. In hindsight, my nightmare last night night was just a pleasant interlude to the real nightmare that just manifested itself for me in full Technicolor.

I walk back to my so-called home in a haze. I don't know how long it takes me to walk those few blocks to my house. Once I get to the front porch of my townhouse, I just stand there like a pedestrian admiring someone else's beautiful real estate. I finally walk in. I go over to the playroom to see my blond-haired boy grin from ear to ear.

"Mommy, look what I made. It's a hand puppet. We used Daddy's sock and macawoni for eyes."

"Eric, that's very creative. Come here, my baby boy."

"Mommy, I'm not a baby. Wenée is a baby, I'm a man."

"Who told you you're a man?"

"Daddy said I'm a man."

I smile and the tears I've been holding back since I first saw Louis earlier come flowing down. Whatever happens to us, Louis Bruel loves his kids. He would never abandon them like he's done to me.

"Mommy don't cwy. I can be your baby if you want." I take Eric in my arms and inhale his delicious scent. "Don't cwy Mommy," my beautiful, sweet boy repeats into my neck as I hold him close. At this moment, I know that if eleven years ago, someone with a crystal ball had shown up and told me that Louis would break my heart and destroy me, I would still do it all over again. I would still fall for him and love him and marry him. Even knowing it would all end and hurt for the rest of my life. I would do it all over again, just to have my kids.

"Where is Rose?" I ask Marni, the nanny.

"Rosy is watching a movie in her room."

"Eric, Mommy is going on a trip tonight. I'll be back soon. Promise Mommy you'll be a good boy."

"Is Daddy going, too?"

"No, baby, just Mommy. Aunt JenJen and Nana Adele will come see you every day. Daddy will be home with you, too."

That seems to make him happy. He smiles, showing off his cute little dimples. God, he's beautiful, just like the man who made him.

I go to see my daughter upstairs. I walk up the stairs feeling like a stranger in my own house.

"Hi, Mama, I love camp so much better this year. Almost all the same kids as last year. I was picked first for the dance off group today. And do you know what Jake said to me at lunch today?"

"What did he say?"

Without missing a beat, she answers, "He said he wants to kiss me. Eewww, Mama, he is so gross. I would never kiss him."

"Good, no kissing boys."

Rose and Eric are both blond like me with different variations of my eye color. They have Louis' features, though; hence, you can't mistake who their father is.

"Listen, my love, I wanted to talk to you about something. I'm going away for a little while. I don't have all the details yet. I just know that it's very important that I go. Aunt Jenna and Grandpa and Nana will all be here for you and Eric. Daddy will also be here."

Rose looks at me, seeing right through my pain. I'm afraid she sees how scared and lost I am. I try as hard as I can to channel all my bravery, to make us both believe that I am a strong woman and not a hot mess.

"Mama, are you okay? Do you want me to come with you?"

"Thank you, baby. I need you to be my big girl and help with Eric."

"Why isn't Daddy coming with you? Are you mad at him?"

"Baby, Daddy is very busy. I love you all more than anything and I will come back as soon as I can."

I hug and kiss my sweet little child. I remember me and Louis bringing her home from the hospital when she was just born, and here we are, discussing kissing boys, and Louis is leaving me for someone else.

If I could call Sara right now, I would say to her, "Simply Red, 'Holding Back The Years[59],'" or maybe I'd say, "Cher, 'If I Could Turn Back Time[60],'" or better yet, I wouldn't say anything at all…

It must have been love...

I don't use our chauffeur or any of the company jets. I don't want anyone knowing my whereabouts. I am about to become Emily Marcus once again. I feel the need to purge myself from the life I'd become accustomed to. I take a cab to JFK airport. I have no idea where to go. I withdrew ten thousand dollars in cash from my personal bank account and am now standing at the Delta terminal, holding an overnight bag and the clothing on my back.

I look at my phone and see twenty texts from my sister. She was trying to talk some sense into me. I even got a text from Mike, begging me to go stay with them for a few days. Louis also sent me a text, which I can't bring myself to read. Maybe he wanted to tell me to not wait up for him. He won't have to worry about seeing me tonight—or maybe ever again. Whoever invented texting did a great disservice to mankind. Now I can go for days without uttering a single word to my friends and family. But as long as a text is sent, that somehow fulfills my communication quota with the world.

I want to call Sara. I need to talk to someone who knew me before Louis. Sara and I haven't been there for each other in years and she is going through her own breakup. I can't call her now. I have no right. I am in shock but I still can't hold myself back from sending her a text that I know only she would understand and not question: *"It Must Have Been Love[61]" by Roxette.*

I walk up to the Delta ticketing counter and ask which flight is leaving in the next hour and if I could buy a seat. Twenty minutes later, I am sitting in economy class, heading to St. Lucia. Before takeoff, I call my mother. I get no answer. She is probably still at the hospital seeing patients and preforming procedures. I leave her a voice message, telling her that everything's okay and that I just needed a little break. I asked her and Daddy to keep an eye on my kiddies while I am gone and not to worry. I promised I'd come back as soon as I could.

I didn't even grab a charger for my phone. It has ten percent left before it dies on me. I feel as depleted as my phone … almost dead. I close my eyes and all I see is a fool. Have I been delusional for the past ten years? Maybe he's been cheating on me from the start. God, how could everything I'd felt my whole adult life be a lie? I have never enjoyed drinking hard liquor. Champagne is as far as I have gone in the booze department, but on this flight, I need something to numb the voices in my head.

"Vodka on the rocks, please," I say to the flight attendant.

My husband has turned me down repeatedly in the past three months; maybe even longer than that. Maybe this is exactly what I need to finally wake up. Maybe I have been a naïve dimwit our whole fucking relationship. How can one person be enough for the insatiable Louis fucking Bruel? He is irresistible, tall, dark, and handsome, with a big cock and more money than sense. God, I hate him. No, I hate me. I should've known that someone who looks like my husband and can make a woman feel the way he made me feel would need to share his attributes with more than one woman. Having Phillip watch and join him fucking some girl was essential to the formula.

Why did he need to marry me? My virginity and my naïveté must've been incredibly enticing. He was willing to temporarily give up his womanizing lifestyle. He won't even know I'm gone.

Maybe in a few days my parents and sister will nag him about my whereabouts until he realizes I haven't been occupying my side of the cold bed. He won't have to suffer anymore. He'll finally be able to live the life he so desperately missed while pretending to be a loving husband. Phillip was trying to do us a favor that night at the club. Louis was just too stubborn to listen and I was just too blind. *Show me your friends and I'll tell you who you are*, my nana used to tell me. He had her fooled, too. I begin to cry again. Had I even stopped crying? I start blacking out.

"Ma'am, excuse me. Ma'am."

I open my bloodshot eyes to see an empty plane and a flight attendant looking sadly at me with pity in her eyes.

"Honey, are you all right? We need to exit the aircraft. We're in St. Lucia."

I get up, take my bag, and walk off the plane. Panic starts to set in. I have no idea where I am going. I have never been to St. Lucia. I have no plan. It's nighttime. I am the only person at Immigrations and I clear customs quickly. I find a wood bench and sit outside the airport like a lost puppy. I am still anesthetized from the three vodkas I'd downed on the plane. I close my eyes and black out again.

It is dawn when I pry my eyes open. I am lying down on a wooden bench, clutching my overnight Louis Vuitton bag for dear life. I'm groggy and disoriented. It takes me a few minutes to figure out where I am. I start having a nervous breakdown when I realize I'm in the Caribbean by myself. *Okay, Emily time to figure out what's next.* I get up and walk over to a baggage porter.

"Excuse me, sir, can I ask you a question?"

"Yes, lady, how can I help you?"

I try to smooth my messy hair and my wrinkled blue,

Lanvin silk top hoping to look presentable and not on the verge
of jumping off a cliff. I'm thankful for my wrinkle-free, tight
jeans.

"I'd like for you to recommend a place to stay on the island.
A nice hotel."

"There are many nice hotels on this island. What kind are
you looking for?"

I think about his question and answer, "I need a mental vacation ... something private and quiet."

"Lady, you need Le Spa," he says, pointing to a huge poster
on the wall. The advertisement has a photo of a naked woman
sitting on a ledge in a Zen like yoga position. It says, *Le Spa ...
Say goodbye to the real world and say hello to our perfect world.*
Well I could definitely say goodbye to my crumbling world. My
mind is all shades of fucked up at the moment. I need all the help
I can get escaping the real world. I need to be strong, if not for
me, then for my kids. I decide I am only going to give myself a
few days to feel sorry for myself and that's it. I need to get up
and off the floor, dust myself off, and start over. Shit happens
and life goes on. I look around to find that same porter.

"Sir, how can I get to Le Spa quickly?"

"Lady, the best way to get to the other side of the island is
by helicopter. You'll be at the hotel in fifteen minutes. Or, you
could take a taxi, which will take about two hours."

The helicopter sounds perfect to me. A few minutes later, I
board a small helicopter and get whisked away. The view is
breathtaking. St. Lucia is mostly a mountainous rainforest. The
sight of the beautiful ocean and lush green land momentarily
helps me forget the pain. The helicopter choppers are so loud I
can't hear the voices screaming in my head. I begin thinking of
that girl, Isabella, who'd died many years ago. She was in love
with Louis and he rejected her. At the time he told me the story
of her multiple suicide attempts, I couldn't understand how
someone could self-destruct like that. I would never hurt myself,

but for the first time, I don't find the act abhorrent. I have no idea how I could possibly go on living without him. How is it possible to love and hate someone simultaneously?

I get to the hotel after a short taxi ride from the helipad. A smiling man, who offers me a cold towel and Caribbean lemonade, instantly greets me.

"Welcome to Le Spa, miss. I hope you had a nice trip getting to us. What name is your reservation under?"

"I don't have a reservation."

My statement wipes the grin right off his face. I offer the kind looking man a weak smile.

"This was a last minute trip ... can I get any available room please? I need a room, any room would be fine."

The poor guy takes a better look at me and decides I need all the help I can get. I've been crying for the last twelve hours; I'm sure my eyes are puffy and red. I slept outside of an airport on a bench, for God's sake. I must look like a dirty bum. Seeing myself through this stranger's eyes, I know I look pitiable.

"Miss that may be a problem. We have a wedding this week and the hotel is completely sold out. Let me call one of the mangers to see what we can do for you; maybe they can recommend a sister hotel on the island. I'll be right back."

I wait a few minutes, looking around and trying to take in my surroundings. It's early morning and the sun hasn't started penetrating yet. The spa grounds are quite tranquil. I see a tall man approaching, followed by the man who greeted me initially. The new stranger is handsome in an Australian surfer kind of way. He is young, definitely in his early twenties. He doesn't look serious enough to be in charge of anything except hanging out and enjoying the sun.

Preparing to be turned away, I try to assess him as he approaches. I can make out a broad, lean body under his white polo top, and muscular legs in form fitting Bermuda shorts. He has on tan colored driving shoes with no socks. His straight, dirty blond locks fall to his chin. I observe how this man is the polar opposite of my husband. Well, soon to be ex-husband. That's the first time I've said that to myself. *Ex-husband. I will be Louis Bruel's ex-wife.* I look down at my hand. I still have my engagement ring on. The sight of that ring brings back vicious, taunting memories. I've lost the love of my life. Louis is my everything. I don't even know who I am without him. I've been entwined with him my entire adult life and now, I've lost everything. I am nothing but an empty, used shell...

I feel hands lightly stroking my upper arms. I pull myself out of the bottomless pit my mind has gone to and look up into clear blue eyes.

"Are you all right? Why are you crying? Are you in pain? Should I call the doctor?"

Crying. *Oh, my God*, I didn't even realize I was crying. He reaches out his hand and, very gently, wipes my wet cheek with his thumb.

"Sorry, I didn't mean to cry. I don't need a doctor. I need a room. I need a place to stay for a few days," I say in whatever audible voice I can command.

The handsome man with a slight British accent smiles at me kindly. He looks as if he knows me. I feel the flicker of recognition pass through those knowing blue eyes. He looks over to the man who first greeted me. He gives him a questioning look and pulls his smiling lips together into a thin line. I know that look. It's the *we need to defuse a crazy situation* look.

"Don't worry, I have money. I'm not looking for charity. I just need a place to stay. I'll pay double."

"Leo, can you ask Ashley to have room 5450 prepared and cleaned for me?"

"Yes, sir. Where shall I tell her to move your belongings? We don't have any available rooms. Where will you be staying then?" Leo asks.

The manager—I'm guessing that's what he is—shoots Leo

the international *shut the fuck up* look and quickly adds, "I'll figure that out later, mate. Let's get our beautiful guest settled first."

Did he just call me beautiful? Is this guy blind or just polite? I look back up at his unshaven, scruffy face to meet those knowing clear blue eyes.

"I don't want to take your room. I don't care which room you have. I'm not picky. I just don't want to take your room."

Leo is already heading toward the reception area. I feel guilty for putting this man out of his own room.

"Emily, can I get you anything while you wait?" he asks, adding an extra syllable to my name and giving me a crooked smile. My mind is operating at half speed, but I am positive I didn't tell him my name yet.

"How did you know my name was Emily?" I ask with dread starting to course through my veins.

"I know a lot about you, Emily, including who you belong to."

He has no idea what he's saying. I don't belong to anyone … anymore.

"You don't know anything about me; my name is Emily Marcus. I don't know what you think you know about me."

He steps back to assess my appearance and adds, "I take it it's a room for one then, Miss Emily Marcus."

I look down, feeling my emptiness spread like wildfire.

"Yes, it's just me from now on."

"Let me introduce myself. I'm William Knight; please call me Will. Nice to make your acquaintance, Miss Emily Marcus." He's still looking at me, probably assessing how long ago I escaped the loony bin. I need to find a nice black hole to wallow in my depressive sorrow alone. "Miss Marcus, I'll have Leo take your bags to your room. I'll show you around the resort and take you for some breakfast if that's acceptable with you."

My stomach likes the idea of having some much needed fuel. Will seems very well mannered; he probably is one of the managers. Maybe he recognizes me from an article he's read about Louis in *Forbes* or *Money* magazine. I nod at his offer. My choices are pretty nonexistent.

"Brilliant. Let's start with the beach and work our way to our sanctuary. Where did Leo put the rest of your luggage, Miss Marcus?"

I hand him my small, Louis Vuitton overnight bag that I've been clutching flush against my chest. He looks at me with something between confusion and pity. I need for him to stop looking at me like I'm a child who's lost a parent. Even though in some fucked up way that is exactly what has happened to me.

"This was a spur of the moment trip." I know I didn't need to explain myself, but this stranger has been nothing but nice to me.

"Of course, Miss Marcus. In case you forgot to pack anything, we do have some great shops for you to rummage through."

"Thank you. That's good to know, and please, Will, call me Emily."

Every ego needs a Knight...

The hotel property is beautifully set on a pristine beach. The Piton Mountains serve as a picturesque backdrop. The pools are very modern and sleek. I would never come to a place like this with Louis. There are too many people everywhere. Will explains that the hotel is sold out because of a wedding taking place in a few days.

"Will, if I took your room where will you stay?" I ask, feeling guilty.

"Don't worry, Emily, my parents are back in London for the summer, so I will be taking residence in their house. Right over there." He points to a magnificent villa nestled high in the mountain overlooking the resort. "My family owns a few resorts on the island. If you grow bored of this place I can take you to another property, if you fancy that."

I smile and hear my stomach make the loudest, most unladylike sound. Will must've heard it too; he quickly suggests we go and get something for me to eat.

"Emily, do you mind if I join you for breakfast?"

"No, I don't mind. Thank you."

After sitting down and sipping my first cup of coffee, it feels like maybe tomorrow would come after all.

Will breaks our awkward silence by saying, "Emily, why

don't you tell me why a beautiful American girl comes to a romantic island like St. Lucia alone and sad."

He got right to the point, and since he's a total stranger who doesn't know me and can't judge me or my choices, I decide to tell him the truth.

"My husband is cheating on me after almost ten years of marriage and two kids. I have known him since I was eighteen years old. He is my whole life. I only existed knowing he loved me. Now I'm almost thirty and lost. I don't know who I am and how I will ever move on from this. I came here so no one could find me. Not that he would even notice I'm gone. I need some time to compartmentalize my emotions and deal with the pain that I'm in. Thank you for giving up your room for me, I really need a place to stay." I have no idea why I felt the need to say all of that out loud to a perfect stranger, but I needed to get those words out of my head.

Will has the opposite reaction of what I would've expected from him. He is livid.

"That fucking bastard. Don't apologize, you are very welcome, mate. I would like to offer my services as a friend to you. If you need to talk to someone, I could listen. I just broke up with my betrothed because I found out she and my good buddy from school were shagging. Believe me, we can start our own support group."

That makes us both laugh. The cheating thing hit a nerve with him; that's why he got so mad. I fish into my pocket for my iPhone and see that it is completely dead.

"I didn't bring a charger. My family has no idea where I am. They can't reach me. I'm sure my sister and Mom are worried."

"Would you like to call them? Here, use my phone." Will hands me his cell phone. It's now nine o'clock in the morning. I call my house; it rings twice before my housekeeper, Pam, picks up.

"Bruel residence, how can I help you?"

"Hi, Pammy, it's me. How are the kids?"

"Emily, where are you? Your mom slept here last night. Jenna's been calling since last night. They're all looking for you."

"Why did my mom sleep over? Pam, are the kids okay? Where is Louis?"

"The kids are okay. They just want to know where you went. Louis didn't come to sleep at home last night so Adele came to sleep in the house. But your parents left this morning very early before any of us got up."

Hearing that Louis never made it home last night is like another nail in my coffin. Why should Louis come back home when he doesn't need to pretend to be a loving husband anymore? Now he can be the asshole he always promised he wouldn't be to me.

"Pam, I'm fine. Call my mom and tell her I'm fine. Tell Rose and Eric that I love them and will see them soon." With that, I hang up the phone. I try to avoid the clear blue eyes that are boring into me. I draw my eyes to his reluctantly. We've only known each other for a few minutes, but we are having a silent commiserating conversation with our eyes.

"Is it too early for tequila?" Will asks, trying to make me smile. "The bar is not open, but I have the keys."

"I could use some vodka. That may possibly knock me out again, if I'm lucky," I say, hoping to drink my heartbreak away. He gets up and stretches out his hand for me. I accept it and follow him.

I had never had so much to drink in my entire life. I don't think I left out one nuance of my life while talking to Will. I can't recall everything I told him but I do remember something about us acknowledging that we both love the '80s and enjoy anal sex.

Yeah, I was that drunk! My head has a special beat that won't subside. When I finally force my eyes open, I am in a beautiful room that I've never seen before. The bed is so massive that I don't notice I'm not alone in it until five minutes later. *Please God, don't let me have slept with whoever is in this bed with me,* I think to myself desperately. I may be soon to be divorced but I don't want to be an adulterer like Louis. I lift the covers to see that I am still in my panties but no bra.

"Emily, are you checking to see if you still have your knickers on?"

Fuck, that's Will's sexy, British voice. I am in bed with William Knight. No fucking way. He continues talking, "I'm not a bloody arse. I wouldn't bang you after that bender yesterday."

Fuck my life. I lost a whole day with no recollection.

"Will, why are we in the same bed together?"

"You don't remember? You begged me not to leave you. Emily, you were really pissed. I didn't want you to be alone so I offered to stay and rest with you. I had a few shots myself; a gentleman doesn't let a lady drink alone or sleep alone. We were both shitfaced. You do remember giving me the concert of my life ... right? The way you sang to me 'Only Time Will Tell[62]' by Asia was wicked. Then you stripped your clothes and got into bed. It was a brilliant night. Don't worry, we didn't shag." He looks up and gets his head off the pillow. He's even more handsome than I remembered. "Not because I wasn't up for it," he says with a sexy-as-sin smile.

I fucking sang, naked and drunk ... to a perfect stranger in St. Lucia. Will's voice brings me back to my current crazy situation.

"You are the sexiest thing I've seen in a very long time. I just didn't want our first time to be when we're both zonked."

I'm about to have another breakdown.

"Will, I'm not ready to jump into bed with anybody right now. My life is really fucked up. I don't want to complicate things further. Thank you for not taking advantage of me while I was piss drunk and thank you for calling me sexy. My ego is on life support right now so I'll take any words of encouragement— even if they're lies."

He's enjoying my discomfort. He lies sideways, facing me with his head propped up in his right hand. I swallow, which feels like rubbing sandpaper in my throat, then I continue my speech, "I came here to find myself, not to find another man. I obviously couldn't keep the attention of the man I love. I need to figure out what's wrong with me first."

He sits up on his side of the bed. He pulls the covers off and stands. I think he wanted to give me a better view of what I was turning down. He is gloriously naked and very well hung. I stare at his cock as if I've never seen one. In my defense, I haven't had sex with my husband for over three months. I must've forgotten what a big dick looks like. He was semi-hard and had the biggest balls I've ever seen. His body is all muscle. Tan, lean, defined washboard abs. He has a tattoo over his left nipple. It is a word or maybe a name, I can't make it out. He reminds me of a younger version of Sawyer[63] on my favorite TV show, *Lost*[64]. He puts his hands on his hips, enjoying me staring and taking him in.

"Not sure what's wrong with the bloke who's supposed to be your husband. But, luv, if you were mine, I wouldn't bloody let you farther than two feet from me and my cock."

I smile. It was crude but very much appreciated by my wounded, almost extinct, ego. Will is good for me.

"If your Louis has half a brain, he'll come find you before I pull every trick in the book to show you how a real man would treat a beautiful woman like you."

"I'm still in love with my husband. Even if he doesn't want me, I can't just turn off my heart. He is my soul. I've never been with anyone but him. You deserve to be with a nice girl. I have two kids and too many issues. Do yourself a favor, Will, walk away from me. I'm not worth the lay."

"I'm giving the tosser two days. If he's not here in forty-eight hours I won't be able to resist taking you for myself."

"Will, he won't come. He has no idea where I am. I didn't use our chauffeur or any of our jets to get here. I paid cash and my phone is dead. I've never been to St. Lucia before. Louis would never think that I would come to a place like this. I'm as stranded as Brooke Shields[65] was in *The Blue Lagoon*[66]. But the most obvious reason he won't find me, is that he doesn't want to. He doesn't want me anymore."

Knowing how true those last words are, I can't keep the fucking flood of tears from falling again. I don't even know how it's humanly possible to shed as many tears as I have in the last few days. Will walks over and sits on the edge of my side of the bed. He turns toward me and cups my face with his warm hands. He wipes my tear stained cheeks with his thumbs.

"Emily, how could someone not want you? I've known you for five minutes and I want you more than anything. I give him forty-eight hours; after that, fuck the bloody arse. I'll make sure you never have that look on your beautiful face again. I will teach him a fucking lesson on how to treat beautiful girls."

The Russians are here...

Two days earlier in New York City

Louis

"Sammy, keep the car up front. I don't think this meeting should take more than half an hour."

"No problem, Mr. Bruel, I'll be right here when you come out."

I can't believe I'm doing this shit. I haven't seen this cocksucker for ten years. He hears from our mutual business acquaintances that I'm in the hole and calls me. He fucking calls me as if ten years ago he didn't almost cost me my wife. If Em knew I even spoke to him, she would be hurt. Now here I am, on my way to meet the fucker.

I never thought it would be this bad. I need to get Bruel Industries in the black again. God, I've taken a beating. How could I have trusted that wealth management business with so much of my hard earned money? It was a big deal for Jonathan Stein to agree to manage Bruel Industries' investments. It was just too good to be true. For years, they were growing our money at inconceivable volumes, until six months ago when my world got turned upside down. Jonathan Stein was arrested and charged with securities fraud by the FBI. The fucker pleaded guilty to over twelve federal felonies, and admitted to turning his wealth management business into a massive Ponzi scheme that defrauded investors of billions of dollars. I fell for a Ponzi scheme! Well me, and thousands of his other investors. We were at least able to keep our name out of the news, but what a monumental fuck up. For years, I managed my own money and then I just got lazy and greedy. I learned my lesson and lost over seventy percent of my net worth.

If Em only knew how close we are to losing our townhouse, she'd think I'm a total loser. My job is to provide for my family and I'm about to lose everything. If the deal Phillip is proposing checks out, I can at least buy back from the bank our SoHo building–or as Em likes to call it, the treehouse–and *The Blue Lagoon* Villa in Turks. I promised Emily almost eleven years ago that I'd give her and our family the world. What kind of man am I? I gave her gifts and now I'm forced to take them back.

I'm ashamed of who I've become. I don't deserve to be her husband. I haven't even been able to make love to her in months. I'm worthless. People only see me for my wealth; once I lose that, who could possibly see me as anything at all? Will Emily be able to forgive me for losing all our memories? The *treehouse* is our love pad. Every room in that building is her; the bedroom where I had my first taste of her; oh God, the roof where I ate her out for hours under the 4th of July fireworks; the pool where we made love countless times; the theater room where we made out like teenagers while watching *Great Expectations*[14]. She told me we were having a baby while I had her spread out on the kitchen counter. God, how can I look her in the eyes and tell her I lost our first home? The place where I knew I would love her forever. I need this fucking deal Phillip came up with like I need my heart to keep beating. I need to sell five of my dad's buildings.

Here we go; it's time to make a deal with the fucking devil.

There he is with that smug look on his face. The last time I remember him, he was spitting venom at my wife. Saying all that dirty crap that made her cry. The last time I saw him, he tried to apologize by hijacking a private lunch meeting I had with Max. I listened to his bullshit about how he was just kidding. That we shouldn't fight over some girl, that once I worked her out of my system I'd want my old life back. He just didn't get me. He didn't know me at all. Max was listening to this shit and didn't say one damn word to Phillip. I told them I loved Emily. I told them I planned to marry her and these bastards still had the gall to invite some 'hos to our private lunch. One of the sluts, at Phillip's request, got naked and started sucking him off right at the table. Max came behind her and started fucking her from behind. I got a glimpse at the man Emily saved me from being. No one even noticed when I got up and left. That was the end of our long, fucked-up friendship.

I want Emily to be proud of me. I want to be the kind of man my dad was. He loved my mom and me until the day he died. I would be that kind of man. Thank God Emily and I found each other. I have a beautiful woman who's my whole world. All I need now is to be the man I promised her I'd be.

"Lou, man, look at you. Did I really not see your pretty face for ten years?"

You fucking douchebag, I think, *I could've lived without seeing that smug face for at least another ten years.* Why did I ever love this guy? Every memory I have of him involves something I could never share with anybody. I fucked so many women with him and in front of him. God, what an imbecile I was back then; too much money and no morals. After we do this deal, I'm done with Phillip Dashell forever, so help me God.

"Phil, good to see you." *Not*, I think to myself as I shake his hand. "Where are we meeting your friend?"

"What … no small talk? Is the little lady still keeping you on a short leash?"

What was I thinking? He just came to fuck with me, the son of a bitch.

"Relax, Lou, man, I can see she let you keep your balls on today. I'll be a good boy, promise. I know you think I only care about pussy. But I'll have you know that when I heard from Ronny that your company was headed toward bankruptcy, I was working hard to find you capital. I will always be grateful to you, man. You helped me open my first club when no one even wanted to take a meeting with me. You are my brother whether we share pussy or not."

Talk is cheap, I think. *Okay, motherfucker; time to show me the money.*

"Phil, it's good to hear you have my back. Even though you disrespect the most important thing in my life to my face."

"Lou, stop bitching! Did you grow a fucking vagina instead of that massive cock I remember? I'll let you bitch slap me later. Now let's go make you some money."

We head toward the elevators at The Plaza lobby. Emily loves to bring Rose here to have tea on Sundays. I remember Emily and I spent a whole evening in one of the suites when we were still dating because we couldn't wait to go all the way downtown to be alone. Once I pull us out of this mess, I'll bring them all here to celebrate. Phil presses the PH button and off we go to the make it or break it deal of my life. We exit the elevator into an elegant suite.

The Plaza had undergone a big renovation. It was my company that was given exclusive rights to sell the residential condos eight years ago, and look at me now! I'm at the mercy of a fucking club rat and a Russian oligarch.

"Miss Alexandra Ivanov will be right out to meet you gentleman. Please have a seat; she'll just be a few more minutes," a man informs us.

Alexandra? Wasn't Phil telling me about a man?

"Phil, what's this? You said we're meeting a dude?"

"Don't worry, Boris' daughter makes lots of deals for him. If he's indisposed, she's the one you'd want. Trust me. You'll see, she's a fucking knockout with balls of steel."

A throat clears behind us. We both jump up like little students caught talking about their teacher.

"Thank you *Phillipchik* for revealing my secret. Now how will I get a good deal from this handsome man if he thinks I have balls?"

Wow, Phil wasn't kidding, she is stunning. Her thick Russian accent actually sounds sexy and not butch. Dark long hair, tall and young, I mean she looks to be about my wife's age. If what the papers write about her father is even only half true, then they have more money than God. Fucking filthy rich. This Alexandra has an entourage of two bodyguards who put the guys at WWF wrestling to shame.

"Miss Ivanov, Louis Bruel. Pleasure to meet you," I say, stretching out my hand for a shake.

"You can call me Sasha. You, Mr. Bruel, don't need any introductions. *Moy* Papa has been romanticizing over some of your properties ever since I can remember."

She leaves me hanging and doesn't shake my hand. She's a wolf in sheep's clothes. This twat is trying to intimidate me. I've had girls like her for breakfast. I happen not to be the least bit sexually interested in this cunt. Any kind of mind fucking will be done on my end.

"Call me Louis. Mr. Bruel sounds old and too formal on your lips."

She lifts her green eyes to give me a sexy, *maybe we should fuck look.*

That's right bitch, let's see who will leave who hanging by the end of this negotiation.

Phil's voice filters in, saying, "Should I leave you two alone? I don't need to ask if you need a room because Sasha already has the whole floor." Sasha laughs at Phil's stupid comment.

That is not how I do business, fuckface. My family's future is depending on this deal. I don't need or want to touch this woman. I want to deserve to touch my wife.

"No, Phil, we won't need a room for what I have in mind."

"That's a shame," Sasha says and walks over to sit opposite me, pouting her red lips and very slowly crossing her long, tan legs to give me a peep show.

If only she knew what I have waiting for me at home. The sight of my wife's tits alone could make me come. Well, I haven't been able to fuck Em with all this shit pounding in my head. My brain won't let my dick do its job with all the crap eating away at me.

"Okay, Sasha, let's get down to business. I know the properties you and your father are after. My deal will be easy with a short expiration date. For every building you want that I don't want to sell, you buy two properties that I do have on the market. I will only part with these properties on that condition. Take it or leave it." I'm about to bluff and hopefully not piss my future away. "I have been talking to my friends in China this morning. If you even try to negotiate a dollar off the proposed deal I'm offering you, I will take the deal from right under your nose and gift it to them."

Sasha seems to contemplate my offer. I hand her the written proposal that Eddie and his team had finished drafting last night.

"Louis, you need cash very badly, I know. But lucky for you, the banks don't own everything you have … yet." She gives me that *I want to see you crawling and begging* look. She smiles with her bright red lips extending almost to her ears. "I need a few minutes to talk to *moy* Papa. I promised him I'd call before I turned down any deal with you."

She walks out into another wing of the suite. The bitch is swaying her hips from side to side and clicking her heels on the marble floors, giving both me and Phil a seductive show. As soon as she rounds the corner, Phil jumps out of his seat.

"Lou, are you crazy? They were only prepared for five buildings in Chelsea. Fuck, now you want them to buy fifteen? That's the most asinine move I've ever seen."

I don't even need to dignify that with an answer. I'd been making deals while this prick was still sucking his mother's tit. I know how much money I need to get my company back on the road to recovery. I took that amount and included in the bundle whatever was needed to make the deal sweeter.

Please God, I need help. I'm sweating my balls off. I keep picturing how I'll tell Em that the bank took away her house in Turks. If the Russians back off this deal, it's game over for me. Bruel Industries will be sold off in pieces to our blood-sniffing competitors. The bank won't give us any more loans. No investor wants to touch us with a 100-foot pole. My choices are very slim. I would have to sell our townhouse to pay the creditors. Emily decorated every inch of that place. We brought our children from the hospital to that house; it's their home.

Whoever is looking down on me: Dad, Nana Rose, my grandparents ... please, help me now. You were all good, no, amazing people; call in some favors for me. I already have the beautiful, healthy family thanks to all of you bringing me the love of my life. Now I need some luck. If Nana Rose were alive, she'd say I need a *bissle Mazel*. This reminds me of waiting for my kids to be born. I knew what outcome I wanted; I just had zero control. All I can do is pray.

We wait for that Russian cunt for a good half hour. She comes out wearing a different outfit. Fucking bitch just trying to keep us sweating while she does an outfit change. Emily would love her dress. I can't remember the name of this stupid designer, but I know my wife has a least five dresses by him. I do very vividly remember how hard my dick got when Em came out of the closet wearing a tight cream-colored dress. I think it was Alaïa because the last thing she said before I tackled her back into her closet and then lowered her on the floor was, *I can't believe I'm on my knees getting pounded in a fifteen thousand dollar Alaïa.* That image puts a smile on my face. Okay, dickhead now is not the time to dream about Emily on all fours. This is show time. Freddy said it best: "Show Must Go On[67]."

"Sorry, boys, right after our meeting I have to run to my lunch date with my attorney," our Russian princess finally says. *Stop milking us and spit it out,* I beg her in my head. I need this torture to end.

"I spoke to *moy* Papa," she smiles an *I will fuck you up* smile, and continues with her verdict, "and we should drink to our good fortune and our new business agreement. Well played, Louis. Boris Ivanov wanted that hotel in Chelsea since you first built it. You could've sold him the air rights to the Kremlin and he would've agreed."

Thank God, thank fucking God. Seven hundred and fifty million dollars is just what we need. I can't believe I won't have to sell our home, our treehouse, or *The Blue Lagoon.* I need to get out of here now and start the paperwork before they change their mind. I'll go home early today. I will make sweet, sweet love to my beautiful wife tonight. One day when this is all behind us, I'll tell her the tale of how close we came to losing everything.

"Pleasure doing business with you, Sasha. I hope to meet your father next time. I know he likes a few of my Fifth Avenue buildings. Maybe by next year he'll be ready for them. I'll have my attorneys contact yours to start drawing up the papers."

The man who greeted us at the elevator reappears with a tray of chilled Vodka. He fills the shot glasses and hands us some caviar on little blintzes. In Russia, if you don't close a deal with some kind of alcohol, then the deal isn't closed.

"Zah Vahs ... Na zdoróvye."

We all down our shots. I fucking hate alcohol. Haven't touched it in years.

"*Phillipchik,* would you give me a ride to Daniel's? I have a meeting there in fifteen minutes. It will take my driver twenty minutes just to go around the block to pick me up."

"Sasha, honey, I'd love to but I'm already late for lunch with the wife down in Tribeca."

I almost shit myself when I hear Phillip say he is married.

"Phil, you got married? To whom?"

"Don't look at me like that, asshole. She's great. Maybe one day I'll let you meet her. We can all go out with you and Emily. I'll apologize for being a dick and we could maybe start over."

I start laughing. Yeah right, I wouldn't let him near Emily if his life depended on it.

"Payback is a bitch, my friend. Wait until I tell your wife some interesting stories about her loving dickhead of a husband." I'm talking to Phil, totally engrossed in the new information I've just learned and forget all about the Russian Princess standing there, listening to our juvenile exchange.

"Boys, I hate to interrupt your moment but I need to go."

I turn to her, and since I'm feeling beyond elated from our deal, I say, "Sasha, I'm headed toward my office. My car is running out front. I can have my driver drop you off by Daniel's, it's on my way."

Phil says goodbye and heads into a waiting elevator. "Man, I got to run, if I'm more than five minutes late, Irene goes into bitch interrogation mode."

Maybe Phil grew up. Or maybe his dick finally had enough. I wait for Sasha to get all her shit together and we head toward the next available elevator.

She's gone...

I get to my office, lock myself in my private bathroom, and throw up. I've been nervous all morning. The coffee and vodka combined with my stress do some crazy shit to my stomach. I take out my phone to text Mike that the meeting went better than expected. He's the only person in my family who really knows about the financial problems Bruel Industries has been facing. I can trust that Mike won't blab to Jenna. It would get back to me faster than a speeding bullet.

I text Em that I'm sorry for being an ass and that tonight I'd make it up to her. I know my behavior the last few months has been detached and I've been strangely distant from her. I couldn't reward my financial deterioration and inevitable collapse with her love. I didn't deserve to enjoy myself and dull my anxiety in our love. Every time I looked in the mirror, all I could see was a good for nothing, inadequate, sorry excuse for a man. My wife deserved a winner. I was as big of a loser as they come. I was too much of a pussy to man up and tell her the truth. Emily never cared about the money. But these were our memories, our fucking roots that I was going to lose. I was her husband; I needed to protect and safeguard all the sentimentality she bestowed upon me.

At nine o'clock, I finally head home. I had Eddie and my legal department draw up all the necessary paperwork. I waited in the office to make sure that both sides started the negotiation process. I'm on cloud nine. This has been a momentous day. The weight on my shoulders has eased a bit. I want to go home and see my family. I want to kiss my kids and make love to my wife. I haven't tasted her in months. As soon as we're alone, I'll rip her clothes off and fuck her until neither of us can walk straight. Fuck yes, my dick is hard just thinking about those big tits bouncing as I pound her into the bed.

I'm a few blocks from my house when Adele, my mother-in-law calls. "Hi, Adele. How are you?" I say, still thinking about what I plan to finally do to her sexy daughter.

"Louis, have you spoken to Emmy today?"

"I'll be home in a few minutes. Should I tell her to call you? Her phone sometimes dies. Adele, just try calling the house; she should be home." There is a pause and I hear Adele take a deep breath.

"Louis, Jenna just told us that Emily left this afternoon. She called and left me a message a few hours ago. I was in with patients so I couldn't pick up. She said she's leaving for a little while and that I shouldn't worry."

Her words don't quite make sense to me. What does she mean, *Emily left*?

"Where did she go?"

"Nobody knows. She asked Jenna during lunch today to watch over the kids for her while she's gone. Oh Louis, I don't know what kind of problems you and my daughter are having, but we're very worried."

The sound of my mother-in-law crying, coupled with what she's saying, feels like being shot. I feel like the air is slowly being sucked out of my surroundings. I get home and stand in front of my house, looking up at the door, not really believing what Adele says is true.

"Adele, I just got home."

I walk up the stairs as Adele opens my front door to let me into my own house. I can see she's been crying. I'm still holding the phone to my ear … still in denial. Why would my wife leave without telling me? Why would she leave us? As a suspended state of slow motion and panic slowly come crushing in, I walk into my house to find my grim faced in-laws. My brother and sister-in-law are all waiting for me with questioning expressions. They're upset but I can feel the anger reverberating off Jenna.

"Jenna, where's Emily? Why didn't you call me earlier to tell me she was leaving?"

Jenna gets off the couch she was occupying, hands baby Renée to Mike, and storms my way like a caged beast. "If you weren't too busy screwing your girlfriend at The Plaza you'd know the whereabouts of your wife, you scum," she hisses at me.

I feel my whole world crushing down. I can't draw a much-needed breath. I'm sure that the pain constricting my chest is the beginning of a heart attack.

"Nothing to say big-shot? That's it? My sister's reign as your queen has ended. What happened? You only like them young, naïve, and preferably virgins? Can't just enjoy what you have … right, Louis?"

I can't talk; my brain is shutting down. Every word Jenna says feels like an axe cleaving me in two. I look up at Mike, who is looking down at his feet not meeting my gaze. *Fuck, snap out of it Louis. Tell them what's going on.* All I can think in this moment is, if I die right now Emily will think I cheated on her. How could she think I would ever want anybody but her? Emily. *Oh God, Emily.* I need to find her. I need to tell her. This is all a mistake. *Where is my wife?* I felt the rush of adrenaline hit my whole body like a punch. I take a deep breath and start to punch back.

"Jenna, I love Emily more than anything or anyone. I would never betray her or hurt her intentionally." *Think Louis … fucking think…*

I continue, "I was at The Plaza closing a deal with the second wealthiest man in Russia. His daughter Alexandra was negotiating the deal on his behalf. After I got enough money to save my fucking company from bankruptcy, I offered Alexandra a ride to a restaurant on the Upper East Side. It was on my way to the office, for fuck's sake! Where? How? Fuck!"

I look at Mike to get some much-needed backup. I'm not getting any help. He obviously has his doubts too. Fuck, I need to talk to her.

"Where did she go, Jenna? I need to tell her, it's not what it looked like. What did she say? Fuck, what could she have possibly seen?"

Jenna looks at her worried parents before answering me. "She saw you coming out of the elevator at The Plaza with that tall brunette. She also saw the both of you get into your car. Louis, I tried, believe me, I tried telling her it's not what it looks like, but I've never seen my sister like that. Her eyes looked panicked, lost, but she was strangely calm. She said she needed to leave for a while to work things out. Something about her life was about to change. She wanted me and Mom to be here for Rose and Eric while she was gone."

No. No. No. God, no! This can't be happening.

"How long ago did she leave? I need to find her."

I think I'm about to have a heart attack. My brain is drawing blanks. My heart is not beating properly. I need my wife. Jenna is talking again.

"Why are you acting as if you know nothing about this? Emmy said you've been having problems. I've seen her be off the last couple of months. I didn't say anything because I figured it had to do with the financial problems Mike told me you were having."

I look over at Mike. All I get is an *I'm sorry, man* shrug. Thanks a lot, dude.

"She doesn't know anything about the bankruptcy. I didn't

want her to worry. Jenna, we need to find her. She can't be out there alone thinking I did this to her."

I walk out of the living room to my office. I dial her number. I get nothing, just her voicemail over and over. I log into the surveillance camera, trying to see when she left. I page her personal driver. I see her on the screen hugging and kissing Eric in the playroom, cradling him like a baby. I zoom in and see she was crying. My tears start to fall. My wife left our children and me. She thinks I don't love her. How could she think I was with Sasha? Did she see Phillip, too? *Oh God, oh God.* She saw him walk out a few minutes before I did. No, she can't think that. I want to fucking die. This can't be happening.

I find her on the surveillance camera, lying on the floor in her closet. She is crying. I can't take this shit anymore. I won't survive her leaving me. I dial her number for the twentieth time; nothing, just her beautiful voice asking to leave her a massage. *Baby, please pick up,* I chant over and over in my head. Where are you Em?

I call one more person. If anyone knows what's going on with my wife, it's her best friend, Sara. My hands shake as I dial her number. Em wouldn't leave without some kind of communication with her evil twin.

"Sara, it's Louis. Do you know where Emily is? She left this afternoon and we can't reach her." Silence. Sara usually can't shut up and now she has information about where my wife is and she's fucking silent. "Sara, talk to me. I need to know where she is. I need to find her! I'm worried."

"Louis, Emily and I really haven't spoken in months. I didn't speak to her today."

"Bullshit, I know there is no way she left without telling you. Tell me the song."

"What song are you talking about? I just told you I didn't talk to her."

"Sara, I'm not playing games. I'm not stupid. You think I

don't know this shit you both do with naming songs instead of talking. Tell me the goddamn song!"

"'It Must Have Been Love[61]' by Roxette. She texted it to me. Louis, what happened? I didn't know she left. We just haven't really been talking to each other since my wedding and then my divorce..."

I punch the title of that song into Google to read the damn lyrics so I can at least know what the fuck my wife was feeling when she left me. The lyrics of the song appear on the screen and my world closes in on me for the umpteenth time today. The words to that song slice me open one by one. *I wake up lonely...* I'd left her alone this morning, I didn't even say goodbye. She woke me up during the night and I just dismissed her and her dream. I was nervous about the meeting today. I couldn't even touch her I was that wound up in my head. She asked me to touch her but I couldn't. I didn't deserve to touch her this morning. *It must have been love but it's over now.* Em thinks I don't love her; she thinks she lost my love. I have this pain in my chest. If I don't find her she will be out there somewhere, thinking I don't love her. Thinking that I cheated on her ... that we're over.

I'd spoken to her driver earlier. He hadn't taken her anywhere today. I see her on the video leaving the house at 4:10 p.m. She had a small bag. That's a good sign. She didn't pack a big suitcase. Maybe she'll be back by morning. I call her a few more times. All I get is her recorded voice. I would give anything to hear her voice live right now. I have to find her. I learn that our jets haven't been used, either. I call the credit card company to see if she'd used her cards to pay for a hotel room or plane tickets. Maybe she's at the Pierre hotel. Or maybe she's half way around the world. My lungs keep constricting. Taking enough air is becoming harder.

A few minutes, or hours, later, Mike comes in and sits in my office. I'm in a numb state. I don't even know how long he sits there.

"Mike, I fucked up. I need to find her. I'm not resting until she knows the truth."

He nods. "Let's go bring your wife back home, man."

I need to see my kids first. They have to know how much I love them. Eric is already sleeping. I walk into his room and quietly sit at the edge of his bed. He is sleeping soundly on his back with both hands over his head, not a care in the world. How could she think I would ever jeopardize this? My father lived across the street from me and my mom my whole life so he could tuck me in every night. I love my family so much. If Emily leaves me, I won't survive. This is my world. I only exist for them, because of them. I kiss my perfect little boy. I wish his eyes were open so I could see her eyes looking back at me. Eric's eyes are the closest to Emily's eye color. *Emily, baby, where are you?* I called in the wrong favor this morning. Whoever is watching over us needs to bring my wife back home to me.

I leave Eric's room to go find my daughter. I knock and Rose opens the door. She launches herself at me, hugging me and crying.

"Daddy, what's wrong?" she says between sobs.

"Honey, don't cry."

She looks up at me, with Em's eyes. "Are you and Mama getting a divorce? Monica's parents just got a divorce. She's moving to Long Island with her mother."

What? How could she think that? That word *divorce* hits me like a runaway train.

"Rose, nobody is getting divorced. Mommy and I will work this out. Nana Adele will be here with you. I will go find Mommy and bring her back home."

I lower myself to my knees to see her beautiful face. It was like staring at Emily as an eight-year-old little girl.

"Promise, Daddy?" she asks me with tears in her eyes.

"I promise, honey. I love you, Eric, and Mommy more than life itself. I won't let anything happen to our family."

What are you doing for the rest of your life?

We leave in Mike's car. I'm still calling everybody. Sara calls me back, frantic when she can't reach Emily either. She promises she'll keep calling and keep me updated. Jenna says she tried a few of her other girlfriends. I let Eddie and Michelle also know what's happening. I probably called every hotel in Manhattan.

I text Emily:

-Where are you???-
-I'm worried-
-I love you-
-Call me. It's not what you think-
-I'll tell you everything. It's not what it looked like-
-Baby I'm so worried, please tell me you're ok-
-Please come back to me-
-"Faithfully[68]*"- Journey-*
-"The Promise[69]*"- When in Rome-*
-"Please Forgive Me[70]*"- Bryan Adams-*

It's almost four o'clock in the morning. Mike has been driving me around the city for hours. We still have no clue as to my wife's whereabouts. She is somewhere out there alone. She would go to sleep tonight thinking we're over. I broke every promise I ever made her. I should've told her. She would've understood. I didn't want to fail her and that's exactly what I did. I don't even remember the last time we were intimate. I was so anxious about my stupid meeting that I didn't even say goodbye to her this morning when I left. She had a bad dream and I couldn't make it better. I'm such a coward. I have nothing to give her. I was so withdrawn into my trivial issues that I neglected her. I'm a fucking imbecile, I don't deserve her, and I never have. Oh God, the love of my life thinks I'm fucking some cunt. She saw Phillip. She must think I'm involved with him and then she saw me walk out with Sasha. My heart drops for the hundredth time today.

"Mike, pull over now!" I say as I jump out of the still moving vehicle just in time to hurl whatever bile I still have left in my stomach.

I imagine what Emily was feeling and thinking and I want to scream. I'm not going back home without my wife. We are on the West Side. I've already tried every hotel I can see. No reservation under Bruel or Emily or any other fucking variation of her name that I could come up with. I'm even showing them Emily's picture on my phone.

My phone rings. I jump, hoping it's my wife. Fuck, it's my father-in-law.

"David, any word from Emily?"

"No, we were hoping you heard from her. Adele keeps dialing her cell. You should come home. Tomorrow, if we still don't hear from her, I'll call a detective we know. Maybe he can help. He's been my client for years."

I snort … I don't have a right to come home without her. There is no home without her.

"David, I'm not coming home without my wife. I'd appreciate it if you guys could stay over tonight with the kids. I won't rest until I find your daughter." I hang up and think about how unreal all this is. Emily left me. We might have to track her down with the help of an investigator. She doesn't want to be found. I hurt her so much that she left her own children. She was that devastated over what she saw that she had to leave me. I'd thought I was a loser before for almost losing our memories. Now I may have lost my whole life and my future.

We drive all night. I keep begging Mike to let me do this on my own. He has his own family, a wife and a baby waiting for him. He says he wouldn't let me go through this alone.

"Louis, I've known Emmy since she was thirteen years old. I won't go home until I know she's safe and not in harm's way. If you think I can sleep knowing she's breaking down somewhere, then you don't know how much I love my sister."

If anything happens to her, I will never forgive myself. It will be my fault. It's almost morning; we're still driving.

I must've blacked out...

She was naked on our beach in Turks. She was smiling at me. Those eyes were beautiful, so clear. I could look into those eyes for infinity. Oh, I couldn't believe she was mine. The sand was all over her naked body. I was running my fingers, outlining the fullness of her beautiful breasts. The calm ocean brought in a low tide. The water wet her sun kissed body. Her nipples were the perfect color. I wanted to taste her. I needed to suck those tantalizing nipples.

Our wedding song was playing in the background: "What Are You Doing For The Rest Of Your Life[46]." She was laughing. Her laughter was washing over me. It was like a warm blanket. I could feel the heat coming from the sun. I could smell the scent of her hair mixed in with the salty water. I was in heaven. This is where I want to go once I die.

She was calling my name, 'Louis' ... Shit, where did she go? I think I lost her. 'Louis...' Emily, I can't see you. Where are you, baby? The light was getting really bright. I needed to go get my sunglasses. What was that sound? Fuck, the sound was getting louder ... I was very tired. I wanted to take a nap on the beach with Emily.

Where is Emily? The light is so fucking bright. I can't even open my eyes. It's so fucking blinding. I need some water. My throat feels weird. Shit, Emily, where are you?

I'm cold. Dad, why am I freezing? My hands feel numb. How do I make this sound go away? I need to just go to sleep.

"Louis ... Louis. If you can hear us, open your eyes. Louis, we need you to wake up."

I can't open my eyes. I'm too tired.

"Louis, it's time for you to wake up. Open your eyes."

I open my eyes. Where am I? Where is Emily? She was just with me. Who are all these fucking people here?

"Louis, welcome back, I'm Doctor Monroe. You are in Mount Sinai hospital. Can you hear me?"

Why am I in the hospital? How did I get here? Where is Emily? Is she okay?

"Louis, if you understand me, nod."

I'm nodding but nothing is happening. *Fuck,* why can't I nod?

"You suffered a heart attack two days ago. You have been in and out of consciousness for the last thirty-six hours. Your friends and family are all here. The nurse will let them know you're conscious again. Please nod if you understand me Mr. Bruel."

I want to nod so fucking bad but I can't move. I start looking around.

"Your brother brought you to the hospital. It was lucky for you he was with you. He said you were a few blocks away from the hospital when you collapsed. He started CPR on you. He saved your life, you know. Do you remember any of what happened?"

What is this man talking about? Where is my wife? I try

shaking my head from side to side. The last thing I remember is driving around to find Emily. I need to ask him if Emily was there. I just can't keep my eyes open or urge my voice to come out. It goes black again...

I open my eyes to see my mom holding my hand. *Mom, where is Emily?* I ask her in my head. She doesn't hear me. I try to squeeze her hand, but I'm too weak. She lifts her tear-filled eyes to me.

"Louis baby, thank God. Don't lose consciousness again; we need you to stay with us." She is sobbing. "I'm worried about you. The doctor said for you to not try and over exert yourself once you wake up ... I'll go get the nurse."

Mom wait, don't go, is Emily okay? I ask inaudibly. She is already gone. A few minutes later, I have a team of six checking out all my vitals. I just want to know if my wife is okay. *Emily.* I have to find my wife. If she were here, she would've been by my side. Where is she? I want my wife, somebody, please get me my wife. It's all too much again and then darkness...

It was fate...

Two days earlier in St. Lucia

Emily

"**W**ill, thank you for charging my phone. I'm a little scared to turn it back on. I'm sure I have like eighty messages from my parents ordering me to come back home."

Will smiles his now familiar, sexy smile at me. We're lying on the beach, watching the beautiful ocean and sipping our cocktails.

"Just tell them you're lost on an island with me. I can't believe your soon to be ex hasn't found you yet. One more day, doll, and you are all mine."

I'm not surprised at all. Louis must be making up for lost times, partying it up with *The Boys*. He could now go back to being the most eligible bachelor. I leave Will on the beach and head back up to my room to deal with my messages. I desperately want to talk to my kids and to make sure they know everything is fine. I power the phone up to find 159 missed calls, 35 voice messages, and 211 texts. *Holy shit!* I don't even listen to the voicemails or read any texts; I just call my mom. If I deal with her, I'll save myself lots of time. She picks up before the first ring.

"Emmy, is that you? Where are you? Are you okay?" She sounds tired and nervous.

"Mommy, I'm fine. What's wrong? Are the kids okay?"

I hear her take a shaky breath before she continues, "Thank God you're okay. Oh, thank God. There's a car, a helicopter, and a jet on standby to bring you back home from wherever you are. Where are you?"

"Mom, I'm not ready to come home. I'm not ready to face what's waiting for me."

She's crying. My mom is usually strong. "Mom, why are you crying? Please tell me Eric and Rose are okay."

"Emmy, you need to come back now! The kids are fine, but you need to be here!"

Did she already know Louis was leaving me? Maybe he announced to my family he has a new, young girlfriend. Maybe the tabloids broke the news of his affair. He's probably been parading around town with his new toy for all to see. How could I go back and face everybody?

"Emmy, please tell me where you are! I will send your father to come get you. We have something to tell you but it has to be in person."

My heart starts to beat rapidly.

"Is this about Louis?"

"Yes, baby, it's about your husband. You need to be here for your kids."

I knew it. He left me. Once I was gone, he stopped pretending and went public with his mistress. The reporters must have been all over the story. The kids; Rose, must've heard at camp from other kids. I take a deep breath. My mom is right. I can't hide away while my family deals with this public humiliation.

"I'll be home by tomorrow. I don't need the jet. I'll fly commercially. I love you, Mom. I'll be home soon." I hang up and fall to my bed, crying myself to sleep. I go to find Will three hours later. I find him in the clubhouse, the only place in Le Spa with a TV. He looks up as soon as I enter. No smile; just a worried look on his sweet face.

"Emily Bruel. I need to bring you back to New York."

How does he know my last name? Did I mention it to him in my drunken state?

"Why would you need to bring me home?" I ask, waiting for one of his funny, lighthearted remarks.

"Listen, luv, something happened while you were gone. Once you get home, you'll deal with it. But I can't keep you here, as much as I want to. You're not mine to keep."

I nod. Maybe it's all over the gossip shows—how a playboy billionaire was cheating on his wife of ten years. I look at his melancholy expression, which seems displaced on his normally cheery face.

"I know, Will, I just spoke to my mom. I'm flying out tomorrow. I just came to thank you for being a gentleman and a friend. I won't forget what you did for me." He walks over to me and embraces me in a warm hug. I melt into his arms, longing for the arms of another. I can't quite believe my love story with Louis has come to a screeching halt.

Will kisses the top of my head and says, "I have a helicopter waiting to take us to the airport. I've arranged for my parents' plane to bring us back to your home in the States."

I smile up at him, thinking he's going to make some lucky girl very happy one day.

"You didn't need to do that. I already called Delta and got myself a flight to New York for tomorrow morning. I don't need you to come with me. I'm a big girl. I'm almost thirty," I say, trying desperately to make him smile.

He pulls away from me and holds me at arm's length. "Emily, I won't bloody let you face this alone. I need to make sure you get to your kids safe." He wasn't negotiating. I knew that tone from Louis. I nod. He takes my hand and leads the way.

It's a little past six o'clock in the evening when we land at the private Teterboro Airport in New Jersey. I haven't seen my kids in over seventy-two hours. Will was giving me looks of encouragement throughout the plane ride. I could tell he was feeling sorry for me. He was probably thinking that I was the biggest idiot for believing I would be enough for a man like Louis Bruel. The whole world must know what a fool I'd been.

The seats on the plane fully reclined. I dozed off at one point. I'm woken up a few hours later with my head and hand resting on Will's chest. Both our seats were reclined into a flat bed. We were lying on pillows with a white, down comforter covering us both. I look up, momentarily expecting to look into my husband's caramel colored eyes. Will smiles his sad, defeated smile at me. He brushes a few stray locks from my face. He looks like he's in pain. We're both frozen, just looking at one another. I break our staring marathon by pulling myself off him.

"I'm sorry; I didn't mean to use you as my pillow." I straighten up.

"I enjoyed being used as a pillow. God, Emily, why are you this beautiful? I want to be your pillow or anything you'll let me be. I can't believe I'm bringing you back to him. I'm a bloody fool." Will straightens his seat and leans in to cup my face. "Promise me, if you need me, you'll call. I want to know that if something happens I can be by your side. I can't believe how lucky I was to be there for you. Out of all the resorts in St. Lucia, you walked into mine. If that's not fate, I don't know what is."

I can see he's struggling with himself. He lets go of my face and closes his eyes. I'm glad he didn't try to kiss me again. I know I have a shit storm waiting for me at home. I just need to have a clear head to deal with the unavoidable disaster awaiting my family and me. Since waking up together yesterday, he's been very respectful. The sexual tension between us is undeniable, but I would never entangle him in my mess of a life. This young, eligible man deserves a nice girl. One who won't lead him on while still madly in love with her philandering husband. I hope the look in his eyes is more compassion for a friend than longing for a lover.

Home is where Louis is...

A black Maybach brings us to my townhouse on the Upper East Side. This is incredibly awkward. Should I invite him in? Where would he go?

"Emily, go in. I'm sure your family is anxiously awaiting your return. I'm staying at a hotel a few blocks from here on Fifth Avenue. I'm here if you need me to talk or anything. Call me, day or night." He hands me a piece of paper with his cell number and the hotel information. He takes my hand and kisses my fingers. I feel sad letting him go. I've grown really fond of Will Knight. If Sara saw him, she'd jump his bones. *Shit. Sara.* I have to call her; she has probably been trying to contact me. I had my phone shut off; I still wasn't prepared to talk to anybody.

"Thank you, Will, for bringing me back home safely."

He gives me that sad smile that doesn't reach his eyes. "I wish you luck with whatever news is waiting on the other side of that door. You're an amazing woman. I hope to one day find someone who'll love me the way you love your husband."

I nod silently at him, content that he understands me, and got out of the car.

My front door opens before I even get a chance to get my keys out. My sister looks frantic. Jenna looks like she hasn't bathed in three days—not an ounce of makeup on her pale face, hair pulled back into a low ponytail. She doesn't say a word. She grips me into a hug and starts wailing.

"Jen, what's wrong? Why are you crying?" I have never seen or heard my sister this distraught.

"Thank ... God ... Emmy ... That ... You're ... Okay ... It's Louis ... Emmy ... He had a heart attack."

My world dissipated into ashes. Her words are floating around me like smoke. I want to wake up out of this perpetual nightmare that keeps getting worse. I just want to be home with my family. My life feels surreal. I snap out of my state of dismal consciousness. My heart is bleeding. I picture the love of my life all alone and suffering. A sob escapes my throat. I'm screaming before I crumple to my knees. My lament is for what Jenna would tell me next. If Louis was not of this world, if he died and I wasn't here, if my kids would grow up fatherless ... please, God, make this ordeal melt away. This must have been my subconscious, dreaming up horrible things because I was mad at him. He's young and healthy. My beautiful husband can't be gone. I feel strong hands lift me from my doorstep. But it all must've been a dream. I succumb to the darkness and it was finally quiet.

I open my eyes. My parents' best friend and my childhood pediatrician is here, hovering over me with a flashlight and smelling salts, I suspect. My parents are sitting at the edge of my bed.

"Oh thank God, she's up," my mom says to my doctor as she comes to my side.

I need to know what's happening. "Mom, where is Louis?" I beg her, "Please don't tell me I lost him again."

She looks much older than when I last saw her. My well-groomed mom looks exhausted and sad.

"Honey, Louis had a heart attack three days ago. Mike was with him, thank God. They were out looking for you all night. It was morning when Louis had the attack. He's at Mount Sinai in intensive care. He's been in and out of consciousness."

I take a deep breath that provides me no oxygen. My husband is alive. He would live. He had to live. He wouldn't leave me. He wouldn't leave us. I have to get to him.

"Mommy, I have to go to him. I need to be there when he wakes up."

She gets off my bed and starts pacing the room. "Emmy, you just fainted a few moments ago. Your friend Will carried you inside. You need to rest and be strong enough for you, the kids, and Louis."

"I want to talk to Jenna or Mike. I need to know Louis is okay."

My mom walks out of my room to get my sister. While Dr. Brennan takes my pulse and blood pressure, Jenna comes into my room. She gets in bed beside me.

"Where have you been?" she asks without an ounce of anger or accusation in her voice.

"St. Lucia," I say with a snort, feeling disgust at my trivial departure.

"He didn't sleep with her. Her name is Alexandra Ivanov; she's the daughter of some very wealthy Russian businessman. He was closing an important deal that day." She kisses my forehead like I was four years old and continues, "Mike told me a few months ago. I thought you knew, but didn't want to discuss it with me. Bruel Industries had some very serious financial problems. Louis was trying to save the company from bankruptcy. He closed a huge deal and just gave her a ride uptown to some restaurant. Emmy, he loves you so much. He was freaking out and driving around the city with Mike all night looking for you. Why didn't you pick up your phone?"

I start crying again. I was running away from my over active imagination. I probably caused his heart attack; all because of my own hang-ups and insecurities.

"Jen, I'm such an idiot. I'm sorry. My phone died and I didn't have a charger. I should've been home. I need to be there with him now. He thinks I left him. I just want to be with him. Jenna, oh God, what have I done?"

My sister seems past exhaustion; she can't even pretend to be strong for me. "Mike has been at his side for the last three days. Everybody is praying. We have the best doctors trying to pull him through this."

I feel weak. I want to know if Eric and Rose know about their dad. I'm about to ask Jenna when someone knocks on the door. I look up to see Will's handsome face and his knowing blue eyes. He gives me a weak, melancholy smile. I can't even offer him that in return.

"Nice to see you're back with us," he says with that sweet British accent. "I didn't want to leave until I knew you were okay." He looks down at his feet, clearly feeling out of place.

"Thank you for catching me. You keep rescuing me from myself. I owe you."

He looks up to meet my eyes. In another place, in another time, I would've been lucky to have someone as sweet and caring—not to mention gorgeous—give me his attention. But at this place and at this time, I am one thousand percent possessed and in love with my husband. Will must've seen our pictures in the news. He knew who I was married to, and what Louis and I shared. He understood how much I loved my husband. No one could compete with that. He walks over to me, kneels at my bed, and lowers his head to kiss my cheek.

"Emily, I hope you get your family back. Louis is very lucky to have you. He'll be okay; he won't leave you. Nobody who knows you could ever let you go. He's fighting for you right now. I promise; if you were mine, I'd fight for you."

A lone tear escapes and rolls down the cheek he just kissed. Will wipes my tear and continues, "It's not the right time now, but we need to talk. I have something important I need to tell you. I haven't been completely honest with you. You and I need to have words. Once all this works out, promise you'll ring me. I'm staying in New York until I hear from you. I'm not leaving until we talk. Good luck, luv."

Will gets up and leaves. I say a silent farewell to him. As much as I grew to like him as a friend, I don't think I'll ever see him again.

I'd forgotten about my sister, who was watching this whole exchange of ours play out. I look over to her and have a silent, telepathic exchange. I shake my head *No* to the question her eyes asked me. She gives a loud sigh of relief. I know she's proud of me for not cheating on Louis. I would never cheat on him, even if I believed he was cheating on me. He's the only man I've ever loved. He was my first everything. I need to be there with him, holding his hand and helping him find his way back home to us.

An hour later, I'm sitting in the back of my chauffeured SUV with my sister holding my hand. Mount Sinai is only twenty-five blocks up from our townhouse. I start shaking from the cold chill running up and down my spine. I can't remember being this scared since driving to the hospital to give birth to Rose. But I was also excited back then. Now, I'm just petrified. If I close my eyes, I can practically feel Louis' hands on my belly that early June morning eight years ago.

Em baby, breathe. Everything will be okay. By the end of today, we'll have a little baby girl. You and I will be parents, Em. You're very brave. I love you so much.

I remember him by my side every minute on that long, scary day. I was yelling through my contractions, waiting for my epidural to kick in. Louis held my hands, rubbing my back, and whispering in my ear how he would take away all my pain if he could. I love him so much. I would trade places with him right now in a heartbeat. I wouldn't be able to walk this earth knowing he wasn't with me. If Louis dies, I'd die, too.

We get to the hospital at a quarter to eleven. Visiting hours are long over. However, Louis Bruel isn't just another patient at Mount Sinai. Besides being a benefactor of the hospital and a New York icon, he's also Dr. Adele Marcus' son-in-law. My mom, as the head of dermatology at Mount Sinai, could pull strings. We take the elevator to the sixth floor ICU unit. Jenna knows where Louis' private room is, so I follow her like a ghost; not really alive, more like existing in an in-between state. As we walk toward his room, we pass other rooms in the hallway, and I hear the beeping sounds of the heart monitors. I see Mike standing up ahead. He's leaning his head back against the wall. He sees us coming and almost leaps over our way. Before he even speaks to his wife, he pulls me into a hug. He wipes away tears; I have never seen my handsome brother-in-law cry before. *Please, God, let Louis be okay.*

"Emily, I'm so sorry," he cries out, half sobbing.

"No ... No ... No ... don't be sorry, Mike. Please tell me he's alive."

Mike pulls away to look at me.

"Louis is still unconscious. The doctors are saying he needs time. His heart is better. I shouldn't have let him deal with all his shit on his own. I'm his best friend. I knew he was hurting. I should've given him better advice. He didn't want you to worry."

I nod, still replaying my silent litany in my head. *Please God, let him survive this. Please God, let him live.* Jenna comes over to hug both of us. We all walk hand in hand to see my love. I take a few steps toward Louis' room. I hadn't noticed the people sitting against the wall. I look around and realize the corridor is lined with benches and people occupying almost every available seat. They aren't just random people. They are our friends, and many of Louis' close business associates. The rooms in this wing of the ICU are all empty.

I first see Louis' mom. "Elizabeth," I say almost inaudibly as I run into her arms. Fresh tears start falling again.

"Emily, you're here. Don't cry, honey. Louis woke up yesterday. The doctors are with him now; his prognosis is good. I'm sure he'll wake up for you soon."

I look into her eyes. I'm not sure if my mind was playing tricks on me, or if she actually said that. She nods at my shocked expression.

"He'll come back to us, sweetie. I was begging Eric not to take him. We need him more than he does. He needs to be here for you and raise his beautiful children."

Hearing her say that Louis was conscious yesterday is the best news I could've received. It's almost midnight on July twentieth. Our birthdays are tomorrow and I just want to hold my husband close. Everything else is secondary—his business, his friends, and our misunderstandings. The only thing that matters is that he's alive.

"I want to go see him. I miss him so much, Elizabeth. I'm sorry I wasn't here for him. I've been stupid and childish." I manage to say between my loud sobs and hiccups.

Elizabeth looks at me and kisses my wet cheeks. "I wrote the book on stupid and childish. If I could turn back time, I would've let the love of my life have the family he always wanted. You're here now. I'm sure you're the only person he wants to see. Go to him."

I leave her side and start walking toward his room. Eddie runs over to me before I make it very far. He pulls me into his chest.

"Emma, we have been worried about you. My sister has been visiting every hospital in New York City looking for her best friend. She thought you had an accident. She didn't believe that you just got up and left without telling someone where you were. I'm happy to see you're okay ... Look at me Emma. Louis! Will! Be! Fine! Now that you're here, everything will go back to normal."

"Eddie, I'm sorry. Call Sara. Tell her I love her and I'll explain everything when I can. I know she's going through a lot of shit without me making her life even crazier."

My former best friend has been going through a messy divorce. Her marriage lasted for less than two years, and truthfully, I hadn't even thought it would last that long. Gavin has declared he's moving back home to London with or without her. Eddie told me that Sara refuses to go live with him in London and she decided that if London was more important to him than her, then they really didn't have much of a marriage to begin with. I had to agree. I was never a big fan of Gavin's from the get-go. He always seemed too in love with himself to truly love anybody else.

I let go of Eddie and make my way to Louis. Three men are standing ahead, blocking my way. When they see me inch closer, they all walk toward me. I recognize Phillip instantly, and then Max. I've never seen or met Andrew in person, but standing next to Phillip and Max, I know it's him. Phillip walks over to me first ... God, I hate him.

"Hi, Emily. I don't know if you remember me, but I'm a friend of Louis."

Friend. Yeah right, with friends like Phillip, you don't need any enemies, I thought to myself.

"Yes, Phillip, I remember you very well, unfortunately." He looks downright ashamed and saddened by my comment. But he deserves it and he knows it.

"What I said to you back then in my club was disgusting. I didn't want to lose my best friend to a woman. When I saw you and him walk in that night, I was furious. I knew I'd lost him the second I saw you. I was a prick ... forgive me. I love Louis like a brother. I don't want to lose him again. I just want him to walk out of here and for me to get a second chance to be his friend. I'm not that same guy I was before. I grew up. Emily, I know how much he loves you. I should've been a good friend to him then. I was supposed to be happy for him. I was jealous and scared." With tears in his eyes, he extends a hand for me to shake.

He actually looks sincere. I accept and put my shaking hand in his. I just want him out of the way so I can go see Louis. He pulls me into a hug, which makes me cry even more.

"Don't cry, Emily, he'll be okay. He's the strongest man I know."

I move away from his friends and finally go to see my husband.

Louis, come back to me...

Taking those last few steps have to be the scariest moments of my entire life. Louis Bruel, the most alive man I've ever known, is lying helpless beyond these closed doors. He has been fighting for his life without me by his side. He almost died thinking I left him because I thought he cheated on me. Will he ever forgive me for not trusting him? How could I think he could've done that to me? He would never do that to our kids. Louis knows exactly how hard it is not to have both parents under one roof. I take a deep breath and brace myself for the man on the other side.

My heart is beating in my throat. My right hand shakes as I hold on to the door handle. I almost don't have enough strength to push the door open, but I summon all my power and nerve and force the door open. The room is huge and all I can see are lots of white coats around a lone bed in the middle of the room. A nurse sees me come in and walks over to me crossly.

"You can't be here, Miss. You can wait outside with the others. One of the doctors will let you know his progress."

I try to catch a glimpse of Louis, but there are too many people around him.

"Miss, was I not clear? If I get security, they will escort you out of the building, not just out of this room."

One of the doctors looks away from Louis and over at us.

"Nancy, it's okay. That's Adele's younger daughter. Can't you tell by her eyes?" the young doctor says to the livid nurse. "She's Mr. Bruel's spouse."

The nurse gives me a questioning look and walks back to where the other attendings are congregating. The doctor who recognized me moves over to give me a better view of his patient. I see him lying on a propped hospital bed. My heart squeezes tight in my chest and my lungs refuse to take in any air. He looks small and weak. All six foot three inches and two hundred pounds of lean muscle lay motionless. Eyes closed. He has several tubes coming out of him. Screens everywhere. I'm not even sure he's breathing on his own.

I want to run to him, climb on top of him, and shake him and kiss him until he wakes up. I need to see that dimple. I want him to know how stupid I've been. He needs to know I love him. My legs, however, have a mind of their own. In my head, I'm running, but in reality, I am frozen; paralyzed by fear.

"Mrs. Bruel, I'm Dr. Monroe. I was here when your husband was brought in to the ER. He was real lucky he wasn't alone when he had his heart attack. He would've died if it wasn't for his brother."

I look up at this young doctor with a blank look. Louis would've died if he hadn't been with Mike. If I'd been with him, would I have been able to save him, too? What if he had been home alone? Who would have saved him then?

"Louis suffered a myocardial infarction. Your husband had a blockage in his coronary artery that deprived his heart muscle of blood and oxygen. This caused injury to the heart muscle. As soon as he collapsed, your brother started CPR on him and had someone call an ambulance. Your husband got to the hospital very quickly, which was fortunate for everybody. As soon as he arrived we did an emergency angioplasty."

I look at the doctor like he's speaking Chinese. I wish my parents were here; at least they'd understand. He continues trying to explain to me what happened to my husband while I had been breaking down on a beach, halfway across the world.

"I should explain to you what an angioplasty is. A small stent was placed inside his coronary artery, to expand the artery. This helped to prevent the artery from closing up again. The good news is, Louis didn't need to have heart bypass surgery, or what's known as open-heart surgery. Do you have any questions for me?"

"Will he wake up? Will he be okay?"

"Louis is stable and has woken up a few times. I'm very confident that he will make a full recovery. You just have to give him some time. He will need to be on proper medications: beta-blockers, anticoagulants, and be regularly monitored. He just needs time to recover, but I'm sure he'll live a long, happy life."

From his mouth to God's ears is all I can hope for. I want nothing more than to have my other half back. I thank the young doctor and start my journey toward the man I love.

It takes a good ten minutes before I will my limbs to take command. I walk slowly toward the love of my life. Every step feels like walking against a current. I haven't seen Louis with a three-day-old beard since our honeymoon at Turks and Caicos ten years ago. Back then, it was sexy and a declaration of our carnal need and love for one another. Louis had refused to shave until he accidentally chafed my inner thighs during one of his steamy, sexual onslaughts. I didn't complain. But seeing that stubble on his beautiful face now is tauntingly painful. It's a sign of his powerlessness.

I reach his bed. The sea of doctors part for me. One of the white coats is talking to me from somewhere in the room. I can't hear a single word he says. I'm gone. I can't be part of this world without this man sharing the same air as me. I don't remember taking his hand in mine. But when I look at our joined hands, I know he will always be my whole life. If he chooses to leave me either by adultery or death, I will never be whole again.

My useless legs refuse to hold me. I sink to my knees beside him, still holding on to his limp hand. I'm sobbing for myself and for my children who need this amazing man to wake up and continue being their father. I silently pray to my grandparents up in heaven for help. Louis is wearing my grandpa's wedding band. Maybe he can bring Louis back to me. I will never leave him again. I will move heaven and earth to keep my family together.

The doctors must've left. I open my eyes sometime later to find the room quiet and empty. All I can hear is the sound of my ragged, erratic breathing. I stand up, never letting go of Louis' hand. I bring my other hand to touch his beautiful face. I kiss his closed eyelids and take the first full breath since I got home. I inhale his scent into me. This is home. Louis will always be my home.

I remove my flats and climb in next to him, arranging myself to mold to his still body. I need to be close to him, I need to hear his heartbeat. I'm still holding on to his left hand while being careful not to move or touch any tubes. I notice he doesn't have on the necklace I'd given him for his thirtieth birthday. He hasn't removed it in the last ten years. They must've taken it off him when he had the heart attack. I kiss his bare neck, my tears running down and soaking his hospital gown. I whisper to him, *"You are part of my existence, part of myself. You have been in every line I have ever read since I first came here[39]."* My breathing calms down, but my tears won't stop. I continue quoting to the love of my life from his favorite book. *"You know I love you, you know that I have loved you long and dearly[71]."*

I imagine us dancing at our kids' weddings. I imagine us growing old together. This can't be the end of our story. I bring his familiar hand to my mouth and kiss every inch of it. I put my face in his hand and say one of his favorite lines from the book, *"To the last hour of my life, you can not choose but remain part of my character[39.]"*

I refused to sleep all night, afraid of missing him waking up. I sang to him every love song that I could think of. The last thing I remember right before I lost the battle with my tired eyes, was singing to Louis the song that always plays in my head whenever I think of us: "The Rose[72]" by Bette Midler. I was singing each word of that song to him like a hymn. Hearing the lyrics out loud made them feel as if each stanza was composed just for us. Our love was like a river that we both drowned in all those years ago. Our love was intense, penetrating and all consuming and it made us bleed. But knowing all that, it is still nonetheless ours, and it is beautiful.

"Louis, please wake up…"

This man will always be my heart. I am Emily Bruel, his wife, his lover, the mother of his children, and his best friend. I am the luckiest *little girl* in the world for having known him and been loved by him. Louis has been my dream from the very first day I saw him, and I never want that dream to end.

"Please, baby, come back to me…"

I was still singing to Louis past my tears. When I got to the last line of that song. I understood my whole life at that moment. It all became crystal clear that our beautiful love story is that seed that became *The Rose…* I will never give up on us, again.

"Please, you promised you'd never leave me."

Don't leave me this way...

"**M**iss! Excuse me, Miss!"

I start to slightly open my eyes, trying to figure out my sur-roundings. So much has happened in the last twenty-four hours that I can't even figure out where I am. I look toward the voice still calling at me. *Oh no.* It was that same nurse from the night before; Nancy, I think her name is, the one that was trying to kick me out of Louis' room last night. Why is she always an-noyed with me?

"Miss, why are you still here? You should've vacated this room hours ago. The staff needs to sanitize and clean everything before they bring in the next patient."

"Okay, sure," I answer her, still groggy and disoriented as I start lifting my head off the pillow. *Next patient? Did she just say next patient? Where is Louis?* I look down at the bed under me to see nothing but white rumpled hospital sheets. Where did Louis go? Cold sweat starts to cover my body and dread and fear are choking at my heart. Surely everything is fine. They must've taken him for some tests.

"Where is my husband? I fell asleep next to him last night. Where did they take him?" I manage to blurt out in a shaky, al-most inaudible voice.

"Let me get one of the doctors. I was sure you knew what

happened last night," she says as she storms out of the room.

I look at the door nurse Nancy just slammed shut. I then look all around and feel what I can only describe as an out of body experience. My head is heavy and I can't make the room stop moving. Why can't I remember them taking Louis from under me during the night? The last thing I recall was crying and singing to him, begging him to wake up. I pull myself off the squeaky bed and walk outside the room to find someone who could give me some much needed answers. The corridor, that only hours ago was full of our friends and family, is now completely empty; no Jenna, no Mike, no Eddie ... nobody! *What happened while I was sleeping?* I start walking toward the nurses' station. It's disconcertingly quiet. The only sound is coming from my shoes clanking on the floor and sending an echo down the hallway. Suddenly, as though out of thin air, I see one of Louis' doctors coming at me.

"Hi, Emily, I mean Ms. Marcus. Sorry, I meant to say Mrs. Bruel. I always think of you as Adele Marcus' daughter."

"Doctor Monroe, please, can you tell me where my husband is? When was he taken? I woke up and he was gone."

He gives a heavy sigh and looks anywhere but at me. Why isn't anybody telling me where Louis is? How could I have slept through him being removed from under me? Nothing is making sense today.

"You do remember what happened during the night, right?"

I shake my head from side to side, no, no. "What happened?"

Doctor Monroe gives another sigh before continuing. "Mr. Bruel had a heart attack."

"I know he had a heart attack, that's why he's here. But where is he now?"

The young doctor shakes his head before lowering it. In a defensive stance, he wraps his arms around himself and finally looks me in the eyes. When I see his eyes, I know. In a split second moment, like the one right before a train hits you, I know my life is about to end with his next words.

"Mr. Bruel suffered another heart attack during the night. We tried, but we couldn't save him this time. Emily, I'm sorry, he passed away at 7:21am..."

7:21 ... 7:21 ... 7:21...

I look up to see Louis standing in front of me with his signature smile. The smile that always stops the world and my heart. The smile that I know was meant just for me. He looks like he did at that party eleven years ago.

"It would appear that we share a birth date, my lovely Emily. You see; you were made for me. You're my *Bashert* as my dad would've said."

"Louis did you leave me?"

"Little girl, I had to go."

"Please, no..."

"Don't cry, baby."

"So, I lost you anyway?"

"You never lost me, Em. I was yours from that first day I laid eyes on you. You own every cell in my body. You are the only woman I have ever loved. Don't you know that? I lived for you, and to the last hour of my life you can not choose but remain part of my—"

Beep...
Beep...
Beep...
Beep...

I jump up in my sleep as if free falling. I snap my eyes open and it's still dark. I'm disoriented, gasping for air and crying uncontrollably. Machines all around me are buzzing and beeping.

The screens are the only things illuminating the blackness. I wipe my tears and rub my eyes open to adjust to the darkness. I feel a hard, unrelenting body under me. I can see Louis under me, motionless, but very much alive. *Oh, thank you, God ... thank God.* He hadn't moved since I fell asleep singing to him earlier. His chest is rising and falling. The heart monitors display his heartbeat. I put my head on his chest, listening to his body. I take a big gulp of air in, still trying to catch my breath and stop shaking from the horrible nightmare I'd just come back from. Thank God, it was only a bad, horrendous dream. I wrapped every inch of myself around my husband. I want to be connected to him in any humanly way possible. I am NOT going to let myself go back to sleep. I am not going to let anything happen to him ever again. This man is my whole world. I needed to listen and watch his heart beat until the sun comes up.

"Louis, wherever you are, you need to come home ... NOW!"

Stop rewinding and press play...

Louis

I open my heavy eyes. I try to move but I feel cramped. I'm in so much pain. *Fuck,* everything hurts. I can't even take a deep breath. I look down to see the most beautiful girl in the world tucked under my arm. She is wrapped around me like a present. Please, don't let this be an apparition. If I wake up and Emily is not with me, I'll know I'm dead. I move my hand a little, glad to be in slight control of my limbs. I bring my other hand over to try and touch my wife.

"Eeemmm" I say with a soft, choked up voice.

Why can't I talk, for fuck's sake? She doesn't move. I am too weak to try and speak again. I can feel her warm body pressed against me. She is here. She came back to me. I have to tell her that I love her. She needs to know what she saw is not what she thought. I only want my wife. I've only ever wanted her. Since I first looked into those eyes, I haven't wanted or needed anyone else. She needs to know our love will never be over.

If I am given the chance to live, I will never have secrets from her again.

Emily

I open my eyes, hoping against reason that I'm home with Louis in our bed. I pray it was all a bad, horrid hallucination. But hearing the beeping of the machines and looking all around me, I know my nightmare hasn't ended. I am still in hell.

I disentangle myself from Louis and stand up. I kiss his head and as I'm about to go call his doctors, he opens his eyes. Seeing his eyes looking back at me almost makes me faint. My heart jumps out of my chest and I follow it right to the owner of my heart, body, and soul. I smile and kiss his eyes.

"Louis, baby, you're up. Should I go get someone?"

He shakes his head slightly and lifts his hand, trying to touch my cheek. I lean down to let him touch my face. I remove his oxygen mask to kiss his lips.

"Em ... Are ... You ... Real?" he asks.

My heart breaks into a million pieces.

"Yes, Louis, I'm real and I'm here. I will never leave you again. I'm sorry I wasn't with you when this happened." I cry and kiss his warm, beautiful lips.

"I ... am ... sorry, too ... I neeeeed—"

I kiss and touch every part of his face.

"I know everything. It's okay; once we're out of here, we'll figure everything out. Right now, I need you to get better so we can go home." I can't stop touching him. I need to make sure I'm not hallucinating this. He's awake, talking to me.

"Em, I neeeed to say this ... 'Heaven[73]' by Warrant."

Oh. My. God. Louis Bruel speaks my language! I need to give him something back.

"'After All[74]' by Peter Cetera and Cher ... once we get out of here you can look up the lyrics."

He kisses me back softly when two doctors and a nurse

walk in. I am ecstatic I got to be here when the love of my life woke up. I kiss him and try to move over to let the doctors check on him. He won't let go of my hand and pulls me back down to him. Now that's more like the Louis Bruel I met at that party eleven years ago. I look at him and get rewarded with a dimple-bearing smile. My heart most definitely skipped a beat.

"I ... Love ... You ... Emily Bruel, only you. Did I miss our birthdays?"

"No, Louis, you're just in time. Happy Birthday, my love..."

A *Epilogue*
60

I'm fighting with myself. To call or not to call, that is the question. It's been two weeks since Louis came back home after being discharged from the hospital. He is up and about. We even made love for the first time last night. I was extremely worried about his heart; I couldn't even beg him to be his usual rough self with me. It was still amazing to finally have that contact back between us.

The last two weeks we spent endlessly talking, which was exactly what we needed after drifting apart for many months. He told me everything, including how close we came to losing our homes. I assured him that the only thing I wouldn't be able to deal with was losing him. I love our homes but they're replaceable. I wouldn't ever be able to replace him or us. He promised never to keep anything from me again, and I promised never to assume things. Our new motto is *"If you see something, say something."*

I told Louis about St. Lucia but I didn't go into details about William Knight, yet. I'm not about to break our new promise to each other about not keeping secrets by lying to him. I still haven't called Will back as promised. I feel I owe Louis an explanation first.

I need to get this out of the way now and deal with my husband's reaction. I walk into his office to find him hard at work and sit down across from him.

"Louis, I want to talk to you more about St. Lucia. I only told you part of the story."

"Should I be sitting or lying down for this?" he asks in a mocking tone, while still answering emails at his desk.

"Just sitting. I want to start by telling you that nothing happened. I have always been faithful to you."

He sits up in his chair, giving me one hundred percent of his attention now.

I continue, "I met someone in St. Lucia."

"Em, are you trying to give me another heart attack? Who the fuck did you meet?"

He gets up from his desk and starts pacing the room like a caged lion.

"Louis, if you want me to be honest with you then you better sit down and relax. I just told you nothing happened."

"If nothing happened why are you telling me about it just now?"

"Because something almost happened. I met a man as soon as I got to Le Spa"

"Did you say Le Spa? You didn't tell me that's the hotel you stayed at."

"What difference does it make where I stayed? It was the first place that a baggage porter recommended to me at the airport. I had no idea where I was going that day. St. Lucia was the first flight to leave New York and I just went."

"Okay, go on … you met a man."

"Yes, the resort was sold out when I got there so one of the managers came by to help me."

"I'm sure he did." Louis is seething. Steam is coming out of his nostrils. Maybe I should've kept my big mouth shut. In hindsight, maybe ignorance is bliss?

"Louis, he was very nice. He gave me his room so I had somewhere to sleep."

"You're fucking kidding, right, Em? Let me guess—he very gallantly gave you half of his bed?"

"Louis, it wasn't like that. I was a mess. I was crying. He was just offering a shoulder to cry on."

He is now sitting back behind his desk with his hands wrapped around his midsection. Brooding is one way to describe his facial contortion. Louis is ready to fight. Who? I don't know, but he looks as if he's about to ricochet off that executive chair.

"Em, get to the part where something almost happens."

"We got drunk. I wanted to forget about you. I wanted to dull the pain. I woke up in the morning and we were in bed together. Just sleeping! Louis, don't give me that look. I didn't have sex with him. I didn't even kiss him." My husband can't possibly think I slept with Will! But here he is, getting all worked up for no good reason. I add, "He assured me nothing happened."

"Were you naked?"

"I had my panties on. He didn't touch me."

"Was he naked?"

"Yes, he was naked. But, Louis, we didn't do anything. I told him that I was still married and that I love you and only you. I told him I wasn't interested in him, sexually. I didn't do anything for you to be upset with me. Will was the one who flew me home on his private jet."

"What did you just say?"

"I said, I didn't do anything for you to be upset with me about."

"Did you say Will? Was it William fucking Knight who came to your rescue?"

"How do you know his full name? Do you guys know each other?"

Louis is running both hands in his hair, talking to himself with hand gestures and facial expressions. I've seen my husband mad and angry before but this is a Louis Bruel I have never witnessed.

"Louis, calm down. You need to tell me what's going on. How do you know Will?"

"Emily, in the whole wide world why did you have to go and find William Knight? Am I ever going to rid myself of that treacherous woman?"

"Louis, can you please explain to me what's going on? I don't know what you're babbling about. What woman?"

"William Knight is the late Isabella Knight's younger brother. You walked into her parent's hotel in St. Lucia."

Fuck. My. Life...

Tali Alexander's latest book, *Lies In Rewind*,
book II in the Audio Fools series is coming Summer 2015...
Read on for the first chapter of LIES IN REWIND.

T A L I
ALEXANDER
LIES IN
REWIND

St. Lucia

William

"**Y**ou're a great singer Emily, that was wicked. I've never had anybody sing naked for me before. From now on I will always think of you when I hear this song."

She's jumping around on my bed with her beautiful hair and knockers swinging up and down, and I don't think I've ever smiled for this long in my whole entire miserable life. This woman, this beautiful woman, is a bloody godsend.

She finally gets tired and flops down next to me on the bed. I've had a hard tool for hours and I would give anything to have some relief. How sweet a revenge it would be if I banged his wife? He ruined my sister and I will ruin his wife, an eye for an eye, arsehole. I'm still floored by how I could've possibly hated this beautiful, innocent woman. She's a bloody saint, it's him that's the devil; she only knew him, fucked him, loved him. She had no experience, no idea what kind of life she could have without him. I could give her everything and I could love her in ways that bastard doesn't even know how. He's not capable of loving one woman, just cheating, lying, and eventually, destroying anything beautiful that he gets his dirty paws on.

I know she's currently smashed, but the way she smiles at me—she wants me, she *need*s me to make her forget that arse. *Liam, you can do this, make the first move,* I try to motivate myself. If she says *no* I'll back away and go wank off in the loo. This is it; I've waited to touch her all day. I start by taking her small hand in mine and turning it so I can kiss the inside part. *Touching her is heaven.* I watch her eyes as they slowly close in pleasure. I didn't think it was possible, but my dick just got harder; next level will surely be rapture. I continue kissing the inside of her arm, and her skin feels like pure silk. She smells of beach and pineapple juice. Emily had at least ten Malibu Bay Breeze cocktails while telling me everything there was to tell about her love life on the beach today. I lower my head to her stomach and give it a nibble. She starts giggling as my hair falls and grazes her skin. I look up to see her smiling with her eyes shut, and the sound of her laughter is the best sound in the world. *Does she make him feel this good?* I'm delirious just being alone with her.

I look at her sprawled before me and I want to suck and squeeze her tits, but I'm worried it'll be too much, too soon for her...I don't want to scare her. I know she's bloody naked in my bed with only her knickers on and everything she does is turning me on. I'm nuzzling her stomach dangerously close to her pussy, but she's most definitely intoxicated. *I should just tuck her in and perhaps give her a friendly goodnight kiss,* I think as I get a whiff of her arousal. My mouth actually waters and I may ejaculate prematurely just imagining how wet she is. I've been dying to kiss her perfect lips from the moment she told me her husband was cheating on her. How could that bastard ever want or need anything but her? All I want is to stop her from crying and kiss her so hard she forgets Louis fucking Bruel ever existed and that she happens to be his wife.

I can't help myself now, my hands have a mind of their own, and they're touching her beautiful tits and squeezing those hard nipples that I'm salivating to suck...as she moans, "Oh, Louis, please don't stop."

New York

Sara

I'm at my usual table eating my usual Nutella-filled chocolate croissant and sipping English breakfast tea with milk and two sugars. I look down at my favorite navy Prada suit paired with my nude colored Jimmy Choos. I smooth over my hair that, thanks to my useless alarm clock, I didn't have time to deal with this morning; therefore, it's pulled back. But I made it, I'm here and I wait. I wait almost every single day. I've only missed seeing them while I moved to London for a few years, but other than that—rain, snow, or shine—I'm always here.

The staff at Joanna's restaurant are incredible; I have been coming here almost every day for seven years and they just leave me to my business. They don't ask me what I want, they already know, they just nod their hello and bring me my usual. I sit in my customary tiny table by the window as I wait to see him leave his house. I have the perfect view of his brownstone from this angle. He sometimes looks up toward the corner restaurant before getting into his car, almost as if he senses me watching him.

I look down at my watch; it's almost half-past seven and he still hasn't left his house. I finish my flaky brioche and wonder for the millionth time how they fucking get all that velvety smooth chocolate inside without marring the pastry, *must be a syringe*, I conclude as I devour the last bite and look out the window just in time to see his black car pull up. A minute later, he finally emerges, clean-shaven and hair still slightly damp. I inhale as if I'm standing right next to him. The three of them get into the back of his chauffeured SUV and drive off.

Time's up! I think sadly to myself and whisper *"See you tomorrow, JJ,"* to no one in particular.

I finish my tea, collect my things, and leave. *I love the suit he had on today*, I think stupidly and smile to myself. Another day in the delusional make-believe world I live in, where I see off my beautiful love every morning as he heads to work. In my mind, I sometimes even fix his tie.

New York

45 Days Later

Sara

"Here Comes The Rain Again" by The Eurythmics

It's official; this is the worst week of my life. How can an educated, self-sufficient woman be this dumb? My stupid ex-husband, Gavin, has just evicted me and announced that he sold our Gramercy Park penthouse. *Fuck!* After all the things I've done for him, after everything we've been through, he has the gall to sell my place. I let him keep our flat in London because he promised me I could keep his place in the city. This marriage seemed perfect when he proposed it and is now slowly turning into a nightmare. We were supposed to fool everybody, not mislead each other. As usual, a good deal came along and his promises went out the goddamn window. I know the penthouse was legally his, but since I asked him for nothing from our worthless, bogus marriage or divorce, the prick could've at least let me keep the place I've been living and calling home for the past year. I'm on the verge of tears as I try to pack up all my shit.

I still haven't spoken to Jeffery today. I should probably start figuring out a place to crash for tonight. It's nice to come back home in the morning from breakfast to find a stranger standing in your house, telling you to pack your crap and go. I'm not moving back with my parents—that's for sure! If I move in with my brother, Eddie's wife, Michelle, will somehow inform the whole Upper East Side that her loser sister-in-law has been evicted by her loser ex-husband, and is now officially homeless. *Fuck, fuck, fuck!* Why am I crying? *Sara, stop fucking crying. Everything will be all right.* But I know that's just bullshit. There is no freaking way anything will ever be all right for me. Look at my pathetic life; people with half my problems require tons of drugs to survive…I'm beyond drugs. I should go straight into Bellevue and reserve a private suite in the psych ward.

I'm in a dark nook at my favorite corner bar. This place is not just a bar, it's my little secret portal to escape reality and feel the past exuding and mingling with my sad reality, and I feel at home as soon as I sit at my beloved booth. Most of the college students who frequent this place don't appreciate the fact that William Sydney Porter—AKA O' Henry—once wrote *The Gift of the Magi* in this very booth over a hundred years ago. That story of comic irony about foolish lovers and their foolish gifts to one another mirror my own idiotic existence. Thank God I have this little place to come to, a safe refuge to feel sorry for myself and get drunk at least once a week. Bruce, the owner, treats me like his own flesh and blood; truthfully, he treats me better than my own flesh and blood treat me. He would never let me walk home alone to my building around the corner on Irving

Place—*well, it's no longer my building,* I think dismally to myself as my dire situation becomes abundantly clear.

Here I am, crying into my Irish cream-spiked coffee, plotting the murders of Gavin—my ex-husband, and Jeffery—the person who's ruined me and my life forever, while ultimately, trying to understand my own worthless existence. *I should text Emily.* I pick up my phone, which I've set to vibrate just in case Jeffery decides to call, which is my way of ensuring I don't get any of his calls until I have a plan. But I've checked my phone three thousand times since I told him we're over for the umpteenth time last night, and I can't believe he hasn't called or texted me back yet. My phone starts vibrating in my hands—it's Emily. Emily always has the sixth sense to reach out to me just when I need her most. I really don't have anybody but her. I've lied to her about so many things that sometimes it's almost impossible for us to stay friends. When I moved to London and married Gavin, I tried to cut all ties with her and we've only really started talking again a month ago. Thank God for her; if I didn't have her to talk to, surely I'd need drugs and much more booze to continue living.

"Emily!" I say with my fake everything-is-perfect-in-my-world voice.

"Sara, I've been calling your house for hours. I need you pronto! I'll meet you at your place in a half hour." She sounds like she's already on the move. *Shit, I don't have a place anymore. Fuck, what do I tell her?* I'm hands-down the shittiest divorce attorney on the planet. I can negotiate properties for my clients that they have no knowledge of, and yet I can't even negotiate to keep the place I've called home for the past year.

"Emily, wait! Let's meet somewhere else. Maybe at your house." I feel like shit! I look like shit! But hey, what choice do I have? I don't have a home anymore.

"We can't meet here! I don't want Louis or anybody else hearing our conversation." She whispers into the phone, ensuring nobody overhears her.

"Are we throwing Louis a surprise party? You know he's recovering from a heart attack. I don't think he'll appreciate a surprise party." I try to be funny in the hopes of maybe eluding Emily and avoiding her seeing me until I get my shit together.

"Don't be stupid, no parties. I have a problem. I need your help," she answers back, still in a hushed tone.

We should all have Emily Bruel's problems. Thirty years old, looks like she's twenty-one, more money than she could ever spend in one lifetime, two stunning children, the love of a gorgeous husband who had a freaking heart attack because he thought she left him, a supportive family, and drum roll please...the best set of boobs I've ever seen. As much as I should hate her, I can't, I don't. I've always wanted Emily's life but not in a catty bitchy way, more like in a looking up to your sister kind of way. I always imagined my life would somehow unravel and fall into place the way her life has. She is the kindest best friend any girl could ask for. I wish her the world, and I know she wishes me the same. I love her, plain and simple. I would do anything for that girl. People like Emily get a happily ever after. Liars like me deserve pain-in-full, and I have plenty of that.

"I was actually about to text you," I tell Emily as I marvel to myself at her uncanny ability to always know to check up on me at my lowest point.

"A song I hope?" she says and I can hear the smile in her voice.

"Yep," I answer, smiling back.

When Emily and I grew apart, it was hard not being able to just say the name of a song to someone and know beyond the shadow of a doubt that they got me. Emily and I created our own language. The song lyrics would do the talking for us. We are so completely in sync with each other that we don't have to elaborate on our feelings or experiences further than just mentioning the title of a song and who sang it and *boom*—the other person knows exactly what's happening.

"Okay, now you can tell me instead of texting me. Is everything okay, are you still in bed? You sound a little off," she questions as she senses my state of devastation over the phone. If she only knew how off I really was. I don't think there's a song out there that could depict how fucked up my life currently is.

"Here Comes The Rain" by Annie Lenox was the best I could give her.

"Are you drunk? Why did you just say that? Oh my God, Sara, did you just say that 'Here Comes the Rain Again' is by Annie Lenox? You know that the song is by The Eurythmics!" I could almost hear the alarm bells sounding off in her head. That's how well I know my friend.

"Well, Annie Lenox sang it, so technically it's by Annie Lenox." Who was I kidding; my subconscious just sold me out.

"Where are you?" she asks in her no-nonsense voice.

Physically and emotionally I'm in Hell, but I tell her, "Pete's Tavern…it's this little—" she doesn't let me finish.

"I know where it is, I'll be right there." And she hangs up.

Great! I should've told her I wouldn't be staying here for long. This place is not Emily's style. Okay, I guess we'll need to address my problems first before I get to hear about hers. Here we go, when she sees me, she'll go into her Dr. Oz, Dr. Phil, and Judge Judy mode on me. *Fuck!* She will zero in on all my issues and see right through me. My life just keeps getting worse.

Half an hour later, Emily Bruel walks into Pete's as if she's a regular. Even in leggings and a T-shirt, she's stunning. I can see her eyes widen and her mouth form a "what the fuck" expression when she starts walking my way and spots my luggage scattered on the floor all around the O' Henry Booth I'm occupying. I try to smile as brightly as I can so that maybe she won't notice the bags, the weight loss, the red eyes, and my colored hair.

"Sara, did you forget to tell me something? Are you in the witness protection program, or are you bailing on me, again?" she asks with wide, worried eyes, staring at me in shock and awe.

"No, Gavin had me evicted this morning after I wouldn't give him the keys to the apartment a few weeks back. He sold it, and well…legally it still has his name on it, and since we're no longer married, I don't have any rights to be there. And to answer your question, I never had that officially changed because he promised me I could stay in New York and live in his apartment as long as we get our divorce settled quickly." I know what she's thinking. I know I fucked up because I didn't want to deal with reality. I trust people and believe their empty promises, letting them take advantage of me. While my job is to protect everybody else, I always somehow fail to protect myself.

"Okay, so what's the plan? Where are you planning on staying? You know you can always stay with us if you'd like." She finally slides inside the booth to sit down. She reaches out her hand and we lace our fingers together. It feels soothing to have another human comfort me, and yet an overwhelming amount of guilt blooms in my gut when I look at our joined hands.

"No, you and Louis are still working out your own shit, you don't need me there. I was thinking I'd crash at the Pla—" *Oh shit,* I was about to say the Plaza. That's the place where Emily caught Louis with some ho. That was the place where the shit hit the fan and started a massive shit storm for the Bruels. "I mean, The Pierre. You know The Pierre is my favorite hotel in New York." Emily's eyes close for a second as I see pain etched in her pursed lips, and I knew my big, stupid mouth fucked me up once again.

"Was the song for Jeff? Are you guys still, you know. . . together?" She manages to flip a switch and change the subject back to me.

"Yeah, I guess every song is about Jeffery. My heart wants any part of him that he is willing to give me. Apparently, the only part he wanted to share with me is his penis," I say with a wicked grin as we both finally crack a smile. Conversations about Jeff and myself never end well. I should therefore try to avoid them at all cost like I always do. The truth is, I sometimes don't even know what's true and what's a lie when it comes to Jeffery Rossi.

"Sara, he'll never leave her. They've been married for years and they have kids, and you know who her parents are. He isn't going anywhere." She sounds sincere and I know she means well, but if she only knew the truth. When it comes to my heart, there are only two people who are in the know. It has always been that way and that is how it needs to always stay.

"Emily, I know. I've had a front row seat to his life. I know what's important to him... Anyway, can we drop this shit? What did you want to talk to me about?" I need this Jeff conversation to stop. Talking about him won't change anything. I see the pity pass in Em's narrowed eyes, and I don't need her pity. I did this to myself.

"I know I keep telling you this, but something great is waiting for you. 'Don't Stop Believin'' by Journey. You will find happiness even if it's not with Jeffery Rossi." Happiness without JJ is not happiness, it's purgatory, and I know it all too well.

"Okay, my optimistic BFF. It's Friday, I have the day off today, so spill the beans." I need to hear someone else's problems. I'm sure I'm about to hear an *I-need-to-find-a-new-nanny* story that in Emily's world is the equivalent to mayday.

Emily looks around the empty bar as if making sure the drunks don't hear us, and whispers almost inaudibly, "I met a man while I was in St. Lucia running away from my overactive imagination." I'm not sure I heard her right.

"*What*?!" Okay, so maybe I keep misjudging my best friend. Clearly she's not as innocent as I think she is. This should be interesting; drama that, surprisingly, doesn't belong to me.

There are truly many people I need to thank for helping me make my dream of writing a novel a reality. First, I need to confess that I'm slightly in lust with my husband. Well, more than slightly. So, to the man who makes my heart beat, thank you for inspiring me to be the best Tali that I can be. Thank you for loving *me,* and understanding all the crazy little things that make me happy. I started writing this fantasy for you and will continue writing many more fantasies because of you. Know that *Everything I do, I do it for you* (I'm going with the story that Bryan Adams stole my line). It has always been us against the world and I wouldn't want it any other way. Me, you, our babies and Chewbic, you are all my little slice of heaven. I LOVE YOU.

Next let's talk about all my bitches. Yea, I said bitches! You know who you are, but I will list you anyway: Irene, Maya, Vicky, Rita, Karina, Angela, Ella and Alla. Thank you for being my sounding board, my crash test dummies, my beta readers or whatever you call it. Some of you had to endure this manuscript before it would be considered appropriate for human eyes or ears. I appreciate every single one of you ladies for supporting me, encouraging me and being proud of me. You spent hours on the phone with me listening and dissecting Emily and Louis ad nauseam. Without your valuable input this story wouldn't be what it is today. Writing this book was that much more fun because we got to do it together. I think it's been agreed that Louis

Bruel is our new sexy book boyfriend and Emily is: you, me, and every other woman who reads this book.

I would also like to thank my best friend and the woman who gave me life. I am very fortunate to have such a cool mom who doesn't judge her daughter for using the word "fuck" in her book like three thousand times. Mom, I love that you are always here for me and that you are part of every one of my life's endeavors. When I told you out of the blue one day that I was writing a novel you were excited and impressed and you didn't laugh in my face. You read *Love in Rewind* and loved it. You were one of my first supporters who urged me to finish writing this story and try and get it published. I hope that I make you proud. If I can be half the mother to my kids that you are to me, then I've succeeded.

I also want to give thanks for my little sister. Michelle, life is just not worth living without you making me laugh every step of the way. You are the first person I speak to each day and the last person I text at night. I know how nervous you are for me, and how you want everything that I touch to be a success. I love you for that and for many other reasons and I appreciate you always. I hope you will continue to inspire me and hopefully give me some good material to keep writing. I live vicariously through you. So, don't let me down!

To Stephanie Lott from Bibliophile. Thank you for doing all the dirty work. I know it wasn't easy navigating the spelling/grammar minefield I put down on paper. But, you did it and you lived to tell about it, punctuations and all. All kidding aside, you really made sense of my rambling mess of a book. I bet you're reading my acknowledgment right now cringing and hitting your head against the wall … LOL

Also, many thanks to my last line of defense Marie Piquette and Kristen Clark Switze. You both helped me *so* much, *so* very much. You are both *so* smart, and *so* meticulous. I am *so* thankful … and I promise to never use *so* again, *so* help me God :)

If you love the cassette tape and other graphics within this book as much as I do then the person we all need to thank for that is: Julie from JT Formatting ... great job!!! Sarah Hansen of Okay Creations designed the beautiful cover.

To my A-team, Koa Beck and Rob Alicea. Thank you for being my sunshine when all I felt was rain.

To my Facebook *Street Team*: *The Love In Rewind Bitches*. This is a group of wonderful women from all over the world who took me in and made me feel welcomed and loved. These ladies raved, sang and pimped about LOVE IN REWIND to all. Tanya Gaunt, JennyLee Ching, Lovmyfictional Boyfriends, Amenda Herrera, Merelyn Reads, Rebeka Christine Perales, Mariann J. Gandy, Eva Poole, Melanee Smith, Patricia Maia, Tara Ann and Layla Stevens ... Always know that you are the original members of *The Love In Rewind Bitches*. Thank you for everything and I love you all dearly.

Lastly, thank you to each and every person who took the time out to read my book. I hope you all fell in love with Emily & Louis Bruel and enjoyed their love story as much as I enjoyed bringing it to life.

Wow, it really takes a village to write a book...

♥ ♥ TA

1. http://en.wikipedia.org/wiki/John_F._Kennedy,_Jr.
2. http://en.wikipedia.org/wiki/Wall_Street_(1987_film)
3. http://en.wikipedia.org/wiki/Michael_Douglas
4. http://en.wikipedia.org/wiki/Johnny_Depp
5. http://talialexander.com/aha-take/
6. http://en.wikipedia.org/wiki/Love_Story_(1970_film)
7. http://en.wikipedia.org/wiki/Wild_Things
8. http://talialexander.com/berlin-take-breath-away/
9. http://en.wikipedia.org/wiki/Tom_Cruise
10. http://talialexander.com/police-every-breath-take/
11. http://talialexander.com/rolling-stones-start/
12. http://en.wikipedia.org/wiki/Alice's_Adventures_in_Wonderland
13. http://talialexander.com/billy-ocean-get-outta-dreams-get-car/
14. http://en.wikipedia.org/wiki/Great_Expectations
15. http://en.wikipedia.org/wiki/%22Crocodile%22_Dundee
16. http://en.wikipedia.org/wiki/Indiana_Jones
17. http://en.wikipedia.org/wiki/Lord_of_the_Flies
18. http://talialexander.com/belinda-carlisle-heaven-place-earth/
19. http://talialexander.com/chris-isaak-baby-bad-bad-thing/
20. http://talialexander.com/simple-minds-dont-forget/
21. http://en.wikipedia.org/wiki/Guns_N'_Roses
22. http://en.wikipedia.org/wiki/Flashdance
23. http://talialexander.com/queen-another-one-bites-dust/
24. http://en.wikipedia.org/wiki/The_Blue_Lagoon_(1980_film)
25. http://en.wikipedia.org/wiki/Pride_and_Prejudice
26. http://talialexander.com/roxette-listen-heart/
27. http://talialexander.com/christopher-cross-arthurs-theme-best-can/

28. http://talialexander.com/wham-careless-whispers/
29. http://talialexander.com/starship-nothings-gonna-stop-us-now/
30. http://talialexander.com/kim-wilde-keep-hanging/
31. http://talialexander.com/acdc-shook-night-long/
32. http://talialexander.com/foreigner-want-know-love/
33. http://talialexander.com/police-wrapped-around-finger/
34. http://en.wikipedia.org/wiki/Dirty_Dancing
35. http://talialexander.com/rome-promise/
36. http://talialexander.com/def-leppard-love-bites/
37. http://en.wikipedia.org/wiki/Emma_(novel)
38. http://www.goodreads.com/quotes/400854-i-loved-her-against-reason-against-promise-against-peace-against
39. http://www.goodreads.com/quotes/182796-out-of-my-thoughts-you-are-part-of-my-existence
40. http://talialexander.com/madonna-like-virgin/
41. http://talialexander.com/salt-n-pepa-push/
42. http://talialexander.com/john-cougar-hurts-good/
43. http://talialexander.com/billy-idol-white-wedding/
44. http://talialexander.com/modern-english-melt/
45. http://talialexander.com/elton-john-one/
46. http://talialexander.com/barbra-streisand-rest-life/
47. http://talialexander.com/tina-turner-simply-best/
48. http://talialexander.com/guns-n-roses-paradise-city/
49. http://talialexander.com/frankie-goes-hollywood-relax/
50. http://talialexander.com/soft-cell-tainted-love/
51. http://talialexander.com/journey-dont-stop-believing/
52. http://talialexander.com/bonnie-tyler-holding-hero/
53. http://talialexander.com/proclaimers-500-miles/
54. http://talialexander.com/joe-cocker-belong/
55. http://talialexander.com/flock-seagulls-ran-far-away/
56. http://talialexander.com/richard-marx-right-waiting/
57. http://talialexander.com/stevie-wonder-just-called-say-love/
58. http://talialexander.com/pat-benatar-belong/
59. http://talialexander.com/simply-red-holding-back-years/
60. http://talialexander.com/cher-turn-back-time/
61. http://talialexander.com/roxette-must-love/
62. http://talialexander.com/asia-time-will-tell/
63. http://en.wikipedia.org/wiki/Josh_Holloway

64. http://en.wikipedia.org/wiki/Lost_(TV_series)
65. http://en.wikipedia.org/wiki/Brooke_Shields
66. http://en.wikipedia.org/wiki/The_Blue_Lagoon_(1980_film)
67. http://talialexander.com/queen-show-must-go/
68. http://talialexander.com/journey-faithfully/
69. http://talialexander.com/rome-promise/
70. http://talialexander.com/bryan-adams-please-forgive/
71. http://www.goodreads.com/work/quotes/2612809-great-expectations
72. http://talialexander.com/bette-midler-rose/
73. http://talialexander.com/warrant-heaven/
74. http://talialexander.com/peter-cetera-cher/

"Nothing really to tell, what you see is what you get."

I am every woman out there that has fantasies in her head. I am a daughter, a granddaughter, a sister, a wife, a lover, a mother, and a friend. I happen to also be a Doctor of Pharmacy and a business owner by day, and now a writer by night. Writing and reading help me escape the scary world we live in. I hope my stories help readers experience many different emotions and ultimately, I hope I make them smile...
Writing keeps me sane. I hope reading does the same for you.
Many Thanks,
Tali Alexander

Goodreads
https://www.goodreads.com/book/show/20804287-love-in-rewind

Twitter
https://twitter.com/Tali_Alexander

Pinterest
http://www.pinterest.com/talialexanderbo/

Facebook
https://www.facebook.com/TaliAlexanderAuthor

Instagram
http://instagram.com/talialexander

e-Mail
TaliAlexanderBooks@aol.com

Made in the USA
Charleston, SC
22 September 2015